# GAMES
# OF
# CHANCE

# GAMES OF CHANCE

## by
## Peter Delacorte

SEAVIEW BOOKS   NEW YORK

Library of Congress Cataloging in Publication Data

Delacorte, Peter.
    Games of chance.

    I.  Title.
PZ4.D3327Gam  [PS3554.E433]     813'.54      80-5192
ISBN 0-87223-622-6

The author wishes to inform the reader that all the characters in this book, save several jai-alai players, are fictional, and that all the places in this book, save Madera Beach and Odriozola, are real.

Grateful acknowledgment is made to reprint lyrics from "Madame George" by Van Morrison, copyright © 1969, Web IV Music, Inc. International copyright secured. Used by permission only.

*To Bonnie*

Thanks to Jim and Stephanie Markham,
and to Gorka Landaburu.

*When you fall into a trance*
*Sitting on the sofa, playing games of chance,*
*With your folded arms in history books you glance*
*Into the eyes of Madame George.*

—Van Morrison

# GAMES
## OF
# CHANCE

At dusk, shivering, Esteban departed the deserted barn. It had been his best shelter in five days—not exactly a roof over his head, for it had none, but a wall to sleep against. He had been traveling by night from Figueras toward the French border, covering at best five kilometers per night. Fifteen years ago, when he was eighteen, he had hiked from San Sebastián to Dax, to visit cousins on the French side. That was much rougher country than this and it had taken, what, a week? How far could that have been: close to a hundred kilometers? But of course it was summer, he was walking by daylight, he was familiar with the terrain, and he was eighteen. And he didn't have a sixty-pound knapsack on his back.

He hoped to make it across tonight, hoped to make it by four or five in the morning, hoped to have a couple of hours of darkness to get far enough into France. If he were stopped and found out, he would be sent back, and everything would have been wasted.

If the sky remained clear, or even partially clear, he could do it. The second night he had almost given up. The full moon was enshrouded in clouds; he was stumbling, blind, up a hill when the rain began. Within half an hour he was on hands and knees, crawling to the summit. The descent proved worse, a series of stumbles and falls, a final fifteen-foot drop to mercifully soft ground. He had lain in the fetal position beneath an overhang for five hours, until dawn, soaked to the skin. Early in the morning he heard gunfire to the south, probably Nationalist soldiers shooting at rabbits, perhaps Nationalist soldiers shooting at

someone like himself. Freezing and miserable, he reasoned that
if he headed toward the gunshots he might find shelter. He might
be taken for a bedraggled peasant. He had no gun, he was out
of uniform, he could leave the knapsack. He had no papers,
though, nothing to identify him as anything but a Republican
deserter or a spy. They'd probably shoot him. Nature had provided the resolution: the sun came out. Esteban rolled out onto
the grass, was warmed and dried, and slept.

Esteban had never seen his son. Fernanda had stayed with
him in Barcelona until the obvious became the inevitable: the
Republic was going to lose the war, and Barcelona would fall
whenever Franco chose it to. Pregnant, from a wealthy Basque
family, possessing papers which identified her as an established
French immigrant, she had no trouble crossing the border.
Esteban, assuming the end was weeks away, assured her that
he'd join her in Perpignan before summer. Of 1938. It was now
the winter of 1939. Barcelona had been taken by the Nationalists
a week earlier. The Republican government had moved hastily
to Figueras. Esteban knew it was only a matter of time before
Figueras, too, would fall. His immeasurable hatred for Franco
and the Nationalists was approached by his anger at the chaos
he'd experienced in the last several months: the divisiveness and
pettiness that had threatened the Republic from its inception had
been brought to a head by crisis. Until finally the elite, this collection of idealists, Marxists, separationists, a noble group of men
with vastly different interests, found its common cause on the
brink of ruin. The elite in Figueras, sequestered in this little
Catalonian town, squabbling bitterly over what went wrong, and
making unrealistic plans for an impossible future.

Esteban, a colonel, a lackey in this company, a man without a
voice, decided to leave. He hardly considered it an act of desertion. Rather, it was an act of independence, of pragmatism, of
strength. He would find Fernanda and their son in Perpignan,
travel with them to Dax or to Pau, where they would be welcome.

He packed a week's worth of canned food, a change of
clothes, and all the family valuables that had followed him
throughout the war: several photographs, four gold plates, two
gold candlesticks, and a small, five-hundred-year-old gold chest.

These were heavy items, and worth a great deal of money. But their importance to Esteban lay not in their monetary value. They had been in his family for a score of generations. Other than his wife, his son, and scattered distant relatives, they were all that was left of his past.

He reached the final summit at twenty minutes to four. From where he stood he could see the lights of the frontier at Le Perthus, perhaps two kilometers to the northeast. He would be traveling northwest and downhill.

He moved with customary caution at first, respecting the treachery of the rocky slope, edging his way downhill. But as the angle of descent diminished he found himself in a fast walk and then, under the bright moon in a clear field, be began, despite the weight on his back, to run.

He ran until he was out of breath, five or six minutes at a good clip, then collapsed, exhausted and exhilarated. He'd rest a minute or two now. He could afford to. He was probably already in France, at worst a few hundred yards away.

He sat up, straightened his pack, and heard a noise: a crunching sound, to his left. He stood up, heard nothing, remained motionless for ten seconds, and took a tentative step northward. A voice to his left shouted something like "Ho!" He looked to the left and saw nothing.

Esteban began again to run, now in earnest, toward a grove of trees perhaps two hundred feet ahead. There was an explosion, a shot; he ran now in a zigzag pattern as a second and a third shot were fired. The fourth hit him in the left hand. The pain took half a second to reach his brain. He ran, he lumbered, his cumbersome heirlooms on his back, straight ahead now toward the trees. A fifth shot, a sixth, and shouting voices, two of them. His right foot caught a large rock on the upswing and Esteban fell and sprawled.

He heard them running toward him, ripped the pack off, stood up, fell again. His toes were broken. He turned on his side and watched them approach. No uniforms. Thank God. They were Catalan partisans, or French; in either case he was safe.

One man picked up the knapsack, the other stood over Esteban, grinning at him, pointing his rifle at Esteban's eyes.

"*Soy republicano,*" Esteban said. "*Soy su amigo.*"

The man continued to grin and said nothing. The other man approached, carrying Esteban's knapsack, displaying the gold chest. The two men chattered to each other in a Catalan dialect completely unknown to Esteban.

He tried French: "*Je suis votre ami. Je suis un soldat républicain. Je veux seulement aller en France.*"

The men had emptied the knapsack and were examining its contents, the grinning man looking occasionally at Esteban, who said, "Do you *understand* Spanish? You can keep all that. Just let me go. I am your friend."

The grinning man stood above him, pointing the rifle down at Esteban's head, talking to him.

"No!" Esteban said. "No, wait!"

The grinning man pulled the trigger. His final words to Esteban had been: "I don't care who you are. This is my land."

# 1

# Some Unusual
# Weather

As if searching for an emotion, Murphy wandered through his huge, dark apartment. What was he looking for? He stopped in the hallway between the living room and dining room and tried to remember. He had been sitting on the couch, watching television, and suddenly felt moved to walk down the long hallway to the bedroom. When he got there he realized he didn't remember the purpose for this brief trip; he turned around and headed back.

Now he switched on the overhead light in the hallway. Was it an object he'd meant to find? An address? A telephone number? He stood motionless and perplexed for several seconds, then walked to the kitchen. He switched on this overhead light, and several hundred cockroaches headed for the exits. Murphy had a profound distaste for cockroaches. He kept his kitchen clean. In fact, he kept no food in it. But the roaches had no respect for cleanliness or reason, and stayed.

Murphy opened the refrigerator and removed a can of Schaefer beer. He opened the beer, and remembered he was about to go play poker. No beer before poker. No way to keep the beer from going flat. There was a small, milling crowd of roaches on the counter by the sink, performing a pantomime called "Busy Roaches Devour Tidbits in Decadent Urban Kitchen." Murphy poured the can of Schaefer on them. They struggled and swam.

He sponged them into the sink and down the drain. Then he remembered why he'd been heading for the bedroom, and he headed back and opened the bedroom window. It was the only window that didn't look out on another building, the only way Murphy could get a clear view of what was happening outside, and Murphy had simply wanted to find out whether the rain had stopped. It was something of a disappointment, something of an anticlimax. It was an unseasonably warm and humid night, a New York meteorological grotesque—a hazy purple sky and sixty degrees Fahrenheit on a Saturday night in late February, 1973.

Murphy takes the West Side IRT from 86th Street to Sheridan Square and walks to Bloom's brownstone on Jane Street. The night air in Greenwich Village is almost as suffocating as it was in the subway, but people are out on the streets in shorts and T-shirts, oblivious to the low, toxic mist above them. Murphy knocks at Bloom's door.

"We just started," Bloom says.

"A few more days like this and we're all gonna be dead," Murphy says.

"Ah, fuck it," Bloom says. "It's nice not to freeze your ass off for a couple of days."

"Who's playing?" Murphy asks.

"The usual group, and a friend of mine . . ."

The usual group comprises Eliot Bloom (*Newsweek* associate editor), Bill Lundgren (*Newsweek* associate editor), Morris Wolfman (*Wall Street Journal* reporter), Ralph Mankowski (*New York Times* rewrite), Jack McMullin (ABC News writer), with a supporting cast of other people in this business, and Prosper Murphy (free-lance writer who met all these guys when he worked for the *Village Voice*). The youngest person here (McMullin) is twenty-five; the oldest (Bloom) is thirty-five, and Murphy falls exactly in the middle.

Bloom introduces Murphy to the newcomer. "Murph," he says, "this is Ray."

Ray stands and shakes Murphy's hand. He is a tall, muscular man, and well dressed. He doesn't fit in here. "Ramon Echaverria," he says in perfect American to Murphy. "Ray," Bloom announces to Murphy, "can get you the best coke in town." Bloom seems at once quite proud and fairly embarrassed that he's said this. Echaverria shows no expression at all. Murphy says, "I never drink the stuff, myself." Bloom explodes in laughter; Echaverria smiles ever so faintly.

The game goes as it's been going for years. Murphy knows these guys inside out by now—he reads their expressions, their actions, their voices with the same sort of second-nature facility one applies to a highway billboard. He always wins, and the extent of his winning is generally determined only by his mood. If he happens to be particularly happy or angry, or simply preoccupied, he might not win too much. Over the past several months, Murphy has been devastating. He has been neither happy nor angry, and never preoccupied, because he hasn't been doing anything. He emerges from his apartment to eat, to see an occasional friend, to go to the movies. He sees four or five movies a week. And on Saturday nights he plays poker with a keen, ruthless detachment.

"It's up to you, Murph . . ." Bloom's tone has assumed an aggressive lilt, which means he has a good hand. The game is seven-card stud, high-low, and only Bloom, Murphy, and Echaverria remain in the hand as the seventh card is dealt. Echaverria, with three kings showing, will be going high; Bloom will be going low with an 8-7-5-3 up. Echaverria has bet the maximum, five dollars, and Bloom has called his bet and raised another five dollars. Murphy examines his seventh card: it is a deuce, which gives him 2-3-5 in the hole to go with a four and a six and a pair of jacks showing. He has a low straight and an excellent low hand as well, but both could be losers. Echaverria has been betting heavily since the fourth card, and didn't get his third king until the fifth card, which probably means a full house. Bloom might have a 6-5-3-2-A or even a perfect 5-4-3-2-A, either of which would beat Murphy's 6-5-4-3-2. But Murphy figures that Bloom figures that Murphy has been going high all along, that he's chasing Echaverria. Murphy raises another five dollars. Echaverria takes the final raise. "Okay, declare!" Bloom announces, all aquiver, anticipating half of a large pot.

Echaverria drops a single chip on the table, Bloom and Murphy show empty hands. Bloom's expression shifts to apprehension. "You're going *low?*" he says to Murphy.

"Have been all along," Murphy smiles.

"Not with those two jacks you haven't. Jesus!" Bloom shuffles in his seat.

Echaverria tosses a five-dollar chip into the pot. Bloom looks at Murphy. "If you've got it, you got it on the last card," he says.

"This is seven-card stud," Murphy says, "not six-card stud."

"I don't think you've got it," Bloom says. "You wouldn't have said that if you had it." Bloom tosses two five-dollar chips into the pot and says, "Raise." Murphy throws in three five-dollar chips and Bloom says, "Oh, Jesus, he's got it." Echaverria takes the last raise, and Bloom is stumped. He speaks to no one in particular: "It's gonna cost me *ten dollars* to find out if the bastard has me beat! Well, what the hell, I've gotta have fifty in there already, what's another ten?" Bloom pushes two chips into the pot, Murphy adds the last five dollars and turns over his hole cards.

"Murphy, you lucky son of a bitch!" Murphy has heard this from Bloom at least once a week for three years. "You had a goddamn *straight!* Why didn't you go both ways?"

"Because he," Murphy says, looking at Echaverria, "had a full house."


The game breaks up at midnight, as always, and as always there are no hard feelings. Murphy lingers in the kitchen with Bloom, drinking a postgame beer. Bloom offers postgame cocaine and conversation, but Murphy declines. Bloom wonders what Murphy has to run off to, and Murphy explains that he just feels like going home.

Out on the street Murphy is surprised to find Echaverria leaning against a BMW Bavaria.

"How'd you do?" Murphy has nothing better to say.

"I won a little. Fifty or sixty. Not as much as you."

They stand silently for a moment on a now absolutely still street. The sky is no longer purple, just dark, but the supernal warmth lingers.

"You need a ride anyplace?" Echaverria asks.

"Where're you going?" Murphy replies.

"What difference does it make? You want a ride?"

"I don't want to take you out of your way."

Echaverria smiles broadly. "Hey, man, for Christ's sake, I like the way you play poker. I don't have shit to do for the next few hours, so I'll drive you someplace. You want to get a drink?"

"Sure," Murphy says, and they get into the car.


Donoghue's is a dingy little bar a few blocks from Murphy's apartment, in the heart of an old Irish neighborhood turned Puerto Rican. The bartender is Frank, himself a caricature of an old Irishman—tall and heavyset, florid of face. Why he remains is an anomaly. He doesn't own the place. He often wonders why the owners haven't replaced him with a Spanish-speaking barman. He suspects that one day they will. Murphy shares that suspicion, but advises Frank that if they haven't fired him already they probably never will.

"You're all right," Frank then shouts to Murphy over the Hispanic din, "for an Irishman."

"Only half-Irish," Murphy always shouts back.

"Then you're half all right," Frank always replies.

Murphy is at home here, especially at two in the morning, the place almost empty, the bowling machine easily available. Echaverria has ordered a Chivas Regal straight up. Frank has said, "I been behind this bar sixteen years, and that's the first fuckin' time anybody ever asked me for a Chivas." Echaverria has settled for Dewar's White Label, on the rocks.

Echaverria can't beat Murphy on the bowling machine. Murphy has been sliding the little steel puck down this miniature alley several nights a week for the last year. He knows the machine. He beats Echaverria at Regulation, at Strikes 90, at Flash, at Dual Flash.

"Regulation, one more time," Echaverria says.

"Your dime," Murphy says.

"I know it's my fuckin' dime," Echaverria says. He slides the puck through the sawdust, into the pocket. The pins spring up, a bell rings; Echaverria has struck.

Frank appears with a bottle of Miller's and a glass of scotch, places them on the table next to the machine. "On me," he says.

"Thanks a lot," Echaverria says. "I gotta come here more often."

Murphy throws a strike. Echaverria throws a strike.

"You don't think you're gonna beat this guy, do ya?" Frank says to Echaverria.

"Sure I do," Echaverria says. He throws a strike. Murphy throws a strike.

"You ain't gonna beat him," Frank says. "I been playin' this machine since 1967, and I can't beat him."

There is a call from the bar; Frank is off. Echaverria throws a strike. So does Murphy. "You like to win, don't you?" Echaverria says.

"I'm good at games," Murphy says.

"Unlucky at love?" Echaverria says, and throws a strike.

Murphy swallows a third of his Miller's, and throws a strike. "I don't think," he says, "that luck has a hell of a lot do with games or with love."

Echaverria throws a strike and says, "You didn't answer the question."

"The question was irrelevant," Murphy says, and throws a strike.

"Maybe it was," Echaverria says, "but you're all fucked up about something." The puck slides toward the make-believe bowling pins; this time the seven pin doesn't spring.

"You just lost," Murphy says.

"We'll see," Echaverria says.

Echaverria strikes out for a 279. Murphy strikes out for a 300. A perfect game.

"You *really* like to win, don't you?" Echaverria says.

Frank reappears. "Jesus! Do I see what I'm seein'? Is that a fuckin' three hundred up there?"

"That's what it is," Echaverria says.

"And you," Frank says to Echaverria, "*you* bowled a fuckin' two seventy-*nine?* Jesus fuckin' Christ! This ain't an easy machine, you know that?"

Murphy slurps down the last of his beer, basking in glory. What does it mean, though, to bowl 300 on a machine?

The three of them are momentarily alone at the bar, Frank having donated a round of celebratory booze, having told Echaverria that since the machine's installation only nine or ten perfect games have ever been bowled, that Echaverria's 279 could have won him a lot of money or drinks under other circumstances. Echaverria doesn't seem to give much of a shit.

For his part, Murphy is getting drunker than he'd wished to be, with all these free beers.

"What are *you?*" Frank says to Echaverria.

"I'm a bad motherfucker," Echaverria says.

"No, I mean, you ain't Irish, are you?"

"I ain't Irish. Right."

"What's his last name?" Frank says to Murphy.

"Echaverria," Murphy says.

"You ain't Puerto Rican?" Frank says.

"I ain't," Echaverria says.

"But that's a Spanish name, ain't it?"

"Not exactly," Echaverria says.

"Because," Frank says, "you don't look Spanish to me. You don't *act* Spanish."

Several mulatto patrons enter Donoghue's and sit at the opposite end of the bar. "Excuse me," Frank says.

"You think he might be a little bit prejudiced?" Echaverria says to Murphy.

Murphy says: "What do you mean I'm all fucked up about something?"

"Just an impression I had."

*Just an impression I had?* Who is this guy? "Look," Murphy says, "I just won three hundred dollars at a poker game, I just won a million beers from you on the bowling machine, I just bowled a *perfect game*, so how the hell am I all fucked up?"

"You're sittin' here with some asshole you've known for a few hours at three-thirty in the morning. Don't you have to get up in the morning?"

"Don't you?"

"No, I don't. In my line of work not a hell of a lot happens before three o'clock in the afternoon, so it's all right for me to be sitting here and bullshitting with you. But I figure you've gotta get up at eight and get down to your newspaper or your magazine or wherever the hell you work, right?"

"No," Murphy says, "I'm free-lance."

"What does that mean? Unemployed?"

"Self-employed. I work when I want to."

"So when do you work?"

"I'm on vacation."

"How long you been on vacation?"

"I don't know . . . a few months."

"How long you gonna stay on vacation?"

"As long as it lasts."

"As long as what lasts?"

"The vacation."

"You independently wealthy?"

"Nope."

"But you don't need to work for a living."

"I've still got a little stashed away, and no expenses."

"No rent?"

"Not much."

"You married?"

"I was."

"Before the vacation, right?"

Murphy shrugs, then nods.

"You're all fucked up," Echaverria says. He grins at Murphy.

"Listen to me," he says. "You were takin' those guys to the cleaners tonight, you know that? You can *think*, Murphy, and you can concentrate. Every time I dropped out of a hand tonight I watched you. There's the third queen, you're thinkin', and that's the last of the eights, right? Shit like that. When I play cards I just intimidate people, and I do all right, but I could never play the way you do because I just don't think that way. I don't concentrate that way."

"So what?"

"You're wasting your time with those assholes."

"Look, it's just a . . . recreation," Murphy says. "It's something I do for enjoyment."

"You ever play in a high-stakes game?"

"How high?"

"Minimum bet is ten bucks, maximum is a hundred. No limit on raises."

"That's a little bit out of my league," Murphy says.

"What if I told you that the guys in this game make your friends look like Amarillo Slim?"

Murphy feels the vaguest hint of adrenaline. "Who are they?"

"Dope dealers. It's just like your game—a bunch of guys in the same business gettin' together to play some cards. Except these guys have a little more money to throw away."

"Okay," Murphy says, "but let's be realistic. One run of bad luck and I'm out of that game in half an hour."

Echaverria grins. "I thought you said luck didn't have a hell of a lot to do with it."

"Luck or no luck," Murphy says, "if I get into a big hand right at the start I'm not gonna have enough cash to play it through. And if I'm playing scared, I can't play."

"I'll stake you, then."

Frank reappears. "You guys ready for another?"

This would be Murphy's seventh beer, or maybe his eighth. "No, Frank, I've had it," he says. Echaverria orders a double.

"What's in it for you?" Murphy says. "You're gonna be in the game too, right?"

"It's a hedge. I'll back you all the way, and the first thousand you win is mine. If you lose . . . what the hell. But I don't think you're gonna lose."

The adrenaline flickers and flames. Murphy hasn't felt like this in a long, long time: invaded by a sense of risk, of fear, of purpose. "When is it?" he asks.

"Tomorrow night," Echaverria replies.


Sunday morning, energized, Murphy waived his customary two hours in bed with the *Times*. Instead, he took the *Times* with him to the Cuban-Chinese restaurant at Broadway and 83rd for a gourmet breakfast. Then to the Red Apple on 87th, where he bought the most expensive can of roach spray on the shelf.

He began the short walk home under a threatening sky. It was still exceptionally warm, but now the wind began to pick up, blowing perversely toward the Hudson, blowing Murphy toward his destination. As he reached West End and 83rd the rain started, and he sprinted the remaining block to his apartment.

He stood in mid-kitchen, knotting an oversized handkerchief behind his head. The handkerchief covered his mouth and his nose. The roaches might not recognize him. The small space of air between his kitchen window and the adjoining building became darker than usual. A giant roach walked nonchalantly down the side of the refrigerator. Murphy switched on the light. The roach paused. There was a very loud noise, a Valkyrian clap of thunder. Murphy ripped the plastic top from the can of roach spray and sprayed the giant roach, which fell writhing to the floor. Lightning! With some considerable passion Murphy sprayed every baseboard, every crack and crevice, every drawer and cabinet, every millimeter of space between wall and appliance, every spot in the kitchen that might harbor a cockroach.

# 2

# A Conversation in French

"There's gonna be five guys," Echaverria says, "and they all think they know how to play poker." The Bavaria's sunroof is open as they cross Central Park. It's a few minutes past nine, a few degrees warmer than last night despite the morning storm.

"But poker means gettin' all coked up and boozed up and fucked up and sittin' around with the money goin' back and forth . . ."

"Okay," Murphy says, "but how're they gonna react to me? I don't know what's gonna happen, but say I win . . . say I win a lot. How're these guys gonna feel about an outsider taking their money?"

They leave the park and head down 84th Street. "Don't worry about it," Echaverria says. "Two things: first, you're with me, and that makes you okay; second, no matter what happens, these guys ain't gonna admit you're better than them. You win a few thou off them, you might not get asked back, but these guys gotta be cool, you know? You were just some lucky dude, some buddy of Ray's that got hot at the game one night."

Echaverria turns right on Second Avenue. "You want the *dramatis personae?*"

Murphy is astonished. "Where'd you pick up your Latin?"

Echaverria smiles. "Coke dealers gotta keep up on the dead languages. You wanta know who's playin', or not?"

Murphy nods. "Tell me."

"Three guys you don't have to worry about at all: Danny and Ernie, white guys, and Jimmy, who's black. They lose all the time and they don't give a shit . . . it's expensive entertainment. The guys you gotta watch for are Ramon, dude from the right side of the tracks in San Juan, 'cause he never gets too far gone, and he plays pretty good, and the guy you *really* gotta watch for is Curtis, the other black dude. Curtis is gonna play some tough poker till about midnight, and he's gonna win some money, and then he's gonna get wasted, and sometimes when he loses he tends to get a little mean . . ."

Echaverria pulls the BMW up in front of a garish and immense new apartment building on 71st Street. He hands the keys and a ten-dollar bill to the doorman without a word being exchanged.

Waiting for the elevator, Murphy says, "What happens when Curtis gets a little mean?"

"Don't worry about it," Echaverria says. "I know how to handle him."


Ramon's place is a new world for Murphy. Ramon greets them at the door in white suede from shoulders to toes, greets Echaverria effusively—soul shake, hug, soul shake repeated. Echaverria introduces Murphy: "This is the guy I told you about. He's a writer. Good dude. He's cool." Ramon looks Murphy over, and offers his hand; Murphy self-consciously executes the soul shake. Ramon sounds like Ricardo Montalban: "What do you write?"

"For magazines . . . rock and roll, movies . . ."

"You write reviews?"

"No, not really, more like . . . observations."

"About people?"

"Sometimes."

"You gonna write about what you see tonight?"

"No, I just came here to play some cards."

"Good." Ramon puts an arm around Murphy and ushers him into the apartment. Murphy feels like an intruder, an infidel derelict profaning this cocaine Taj Mahal. Thick white carpeting, suggesting the pelts of many white animals sewn together, white suede chairs and couches, chrome and glass tables, adjoining corner picture windows showing roofs and streets and a tiny piece of the East River. And on a white suede chair a woman so pale and blond that naked she might be invisible, and on the couch across from her a black man in elegant black leather. Looking back and forth between the two of them is almost painful to the eye. "This is Inge, my old lady," Ramon says, and Inge nods politely. "And this is Curtis, who's gonna be playing tonight." Curtis gets up: he is a man of moderate height, like Murphy, but the intensity in his eyes is intimidating. Another soul shake is effected, and Curtis mutters, "Good t'know ya, man, good t'know ya."

Ernie and Danny and Jimmy arrive presently—all well dressed, all radiating the same sort of cocky yet understated presence Murphy has already seen in Ramon and Curtis. But Murphy senses that Echaverria is absolutely right: that Ernie and Danny and Jimmy will be bit players tonight, that Ramon is someone not to be taken lightly, that Curtis must be played with a great deal of care.

The game is played at a long walnut table in Ramon's bar. Murphy sits between Danny and Ernie, Echaverria directly across from him, Jimmy next to Echaverria, Curtis at the end of the table to Murphy's left, Ramon at the other end. There are sufficient drugs on the table to see a professional football team through an entire season. As Ramon gives Murphy the ground rules, Curtis occupies himself by making a series of lines of cocaine on a large pocket mirror, then inhaling a couple of the lines by means of tightly rolled bill in nostril. Danny lights a joint, inhales, and croaks, "Anybody want some of this?"

"Whatcha got?" Curtis says.

"Panama," Danny exhales. "Good shit."

"Yeah," Curtis says. "Gimme some. Gotta get my head in the right place."

Murphy abstains. So does Echaverria. So does Ramon.

"First jack deals," Ramon announces. The fifth card, Murphy's card, is the first jack. Ramon hands him the deck. Murphy says, "Seven stud, high-low," and begins dealing. He gives himself a nine up, then checks his hole cards—a four and a jack. Not an

auspicious beginning. Jimmy, with an ace up, opens with two
white chips, twenty dollars. Echaverria calls. Ramon calls, Ernie
calls, Murphy drops. He turns his up card down and says, "I'm
out." Curtis says, "What was that? Nine of what?"

"Clubs," Murphy says. Danny calls the twenty dollars, and
Curtis tosses a red chip into the pot, silently raising the bet to
fifty dollars. Everybody calls. After one round of betting there is
almost as much money in the pot as Murphy won in five hours
last night.

Murphy deals and watches. The pace is fast and there is no
nonsense, no banter, hardly any conversation, except from Curtis,
who talks to himself and the cards: "Low, now. Stay low. Right
on. We in the game. We gonna be all right."

On the sixth card, the last up card, Murphy deals Curtis a three,
giving him 8-7-5-3 showing. Danny, with a pair of kings up,
checks to Curtis, who bets a hundred dollars. Jimmy has had the
dominant low hand, a five-two-ace, but has just been dealt a ten.
He peeks at his hole cards, deliberates, puts his hand on a blue
hundred-dollar chip, pauses . . .

"You in or you out, Jimmy," Curtis snaps. "Simple as that."
Jimmy flips over his cards and says, "Fold." Murphy is disappointed. He wants to know what that opening fifty-dollar bet
meant, whether it was a show of strength or a boast of strength.
As the cards fell, Jimmy became Curtis's only adversary on the
low side of the hand, and Jimmy dropped in the face of Curtis's
better four-card situation. Murphy isn't going to see Curtis's cards
now, so he can only speculate: that Jimmy's hole cards were bad,
and that Jimmy is intimidated by Curtis under any circumstances.

Ramon wins the high half of the pot with a well-disguised
straight over Danny's kings and nines. Curtis turns his cards over
and shoves them toward Murphy; Murphy divides the chips into
two equal shares, calculating . . . nine hundred dollars for Curtis,
nine hundred dollars for Ramon. Jesus. He pushes one stack of
chips toward Ramon, the other toward Curtis. He hears Curtis
talking softly to Jimmy: "Could you beat a king-eight?" and
Jimmy answering: "Shee-it," and Curtis, "I ain't jivin', blood, best
I had was a king-eight."

This means, Murphy, thinks, assuming Curtis isn't lying, and
he senses that he's not, that Curtis had either two pairs or three of
a kind to go with his 8-7-5-3. And one of his hole cards was a

king. And Danny had a pair of kings. Was the fourth king out?
Murphy does something unethical: while the second deck is
being passed to Danny for the new deal, Murphy riffles through
the several undealt cards from this hand: no king. The fourth
king might have been in Ernie's down cards, or in Echaverria's;
the odds against its having been Curtis's are four to one, but
Murphy is positive: Curtis bet fifty dollars on the first round because he had a pair of kings in the hole, then went with his low
cards and eased Jimmy out of the hand. It may not mean much,
but Murphy feels he knows Curtis a little better.

At midnight Murphy is six hundred dollars ahead, at one-thirty
he's three hundred dollars behind. It's been a frustrating game,
but Murphy has no cause to be worried. His cards have been
running cold—he has yet to win two hands in a row, or yet to hit
a hot streak that turns bad cards into good, when he can force
better hands out with a look, a gesture, or a big bet at the right
moment. But he's been learning the players: Danny will always
stay to the limit the hand after he's won a big pot, apparently be-
lieving that he's hot, no matter what cards he holds; Jimmy will
almost always yield to Curtis, almost never yield to anyone else,
and tends to lose both ways; Ernie plays close to the vest, folding
at the drop of a hat, losing slowly; Echaverria, true to his self-
evaluation, has great poker sense but makes simple mathematical
blunders; Ramon plays steadily and well, rarely bluffs, has probably won better than three thousand dollars so far; Curtis is
shrewd and flamboyant, more the latter and less the former as
the night wears on and his brain becomes increasingly permeated
by cocaine and cannabis.

It's a little after three and Murphy feels the streak entering his
veins like a strong and exotic stimulant. He's won three in a row,
two smallish five-card draw pots outright, one large split with
Echaverria. He's finally a thousand dollars up as Ramon deals
high-low seven stud.
Murphy checks his cards: a five and an eight in the hole, an
ace up, all hearts. The hand has possibilities.
"First ace," Ramon says. This is Murphy. He bets ten dollars;

Danny calls; Curtis, also with an ace up, tosses a red chip out. "Second ace ain't no chickenshit like the first ace," he grins at Murphy. "Second ace gonna bet fifty." Jimmy immediately drops, and everybody else calls Curtis's bold fifty.

Murphy's fourth card is the ten of hearts—four to the flush now, and still pretty good possibilities for low. Ramon deals Curtis a deuce, and Curtis croons, "Am I low or am I *low?*" Echaverria gets a second jack, and bets twenty dollars. Ramon calls, Ernie calls. Murphy looks at Curtis, smiles, and says, "First ace gonna raise that fifty." Curtis's grin is unchanged. Danny folds.

Curtis slides a blue chip into the pot, still grinning, and says nothing. Echaverria calls, Ramon calls, and Murphy considers raising. His flush chances are excellent, there being only two other hearts showing on the table; his low still has good potential—Curtis could have two huge cards in the hole, Echaverria seems high for sure, and Ramon seems as well to be heading for a flush. All the more reason not to raise, Murphy decides. Better to keep Echaverria and Ramon in the game, and sweeten the pot.

Murphy's fifth card is the six of clubs, Curtis's the eight of spades, Echaverria's a nine, Ramon's a low club to go with two high diamonds. Echaverria checks to Ramon, Ramon checks to Murphy, and Murphy bets a hundred. Curtis speaks to the pot as he adds a blue chip: "Motherfucker think he got me beat, but he don't." At this moment Murphy realizes Curtis is not going low at all—he has at least one ace in the hole, perhaps two, more probably a deuce or an eight for two pairs. To Murphy's surprise, Echaverria raises another hundred, suggesting the nine has given him a pair to go with his jacks, and he hasn't figured Curtis out. Ramon calls, which probably means another four to a flush. Murphy calls, wondering what Curtis will do. Curtis, perhaps using Murphy's reasoning of the previous round, or perhaps scared of Echaverria, silently pushes a blue chip into the pot.

Ramon announces, "Last up card," and deals Murphy the nine of hearts. He has his flush. Curtis gets the seven of diamonds, and chortles. Echaverria a queen, and Ramon the three of dia- monds. If Murphy is right, Ramon has a diamond flush, king high, because Curtis has the ace of diamonds. Murphy's heart flush is ace-high.

Echaverria bets fifty, and Murphy realizes he has a straight.

Ramon raises a hundred. He has the flush. Murphy raises a
hundred. Curtis raises a hundred; he's going low now, unless he
pulls a full house on the seventh card. Echaverria looks right and
left and across. He isn't quite sure what's going on, but he figures
his straight isn't good enough, and he folds. Ramon raises another
hundred, and Murphy does the same. Curtis pauses. "Gentlemen,"
he says, "at least one of us got to lose, and it ain't gonna be me."
And he raises a hundred. It dawns, apparently, on Ramon that
Curtis might be going high, that he might have a full house in
the making, and Ramon merely calls. It's Murphy's prerogative to
raise yet again, but at this point he doesn't want to add to Ramon's puzzlement and force him out, so he calls, and it's . . .

"Down and dirty," Ramon proclaims, dealing the final hole
card. Murphy's is the three of spades. He has a heart flush and an
8-6-5-3-A for low. He knows that his flush beats Ramon's. He
knows that if Curtis has two aces in the hole he can't beat Murphy low, but might have a full house and beat him high. He
knows that if Curtis *doesn't* have two aces in the hole, Curtis
could beat him low. He's positive Curtis has two aces in the hole.

Murphy bets a hundred, Curtis raises a hundred, Ramon raises
a hundred, Murphy raises a hundred, Curtis raises a hundred,
Ramon raises a hundred. . . . The raising proceeds through
seven rounds, the needle is stuck on the record, the pot approaches the gross national product of Senegal. It's Curtis's turn,
and he grasps a blue chip, sets to throw it in, and stops. "Gentlemen," he says, looking first at Murphy, then at Ramon, "you
wanna split this three ways?"

Murphy knows then and there he doesn't have the full house.
He shakes his head.

"I'll call the bet," Curtis says.

"Okay," Ramon says, tossing in a blue chip. "Declare."

There is minimal deliberation. Ramon shows one chip for high,
Curtis an empty palm for low. Murphy drops two chips on the
table. Ramon's face drops. It hasn't occurred to him until now
that Murphy has a better flush than his.

Murphy bets a hundred. Curtis's pupils are contracted as he
fixes on Murphy. "You ain't gonna scare me out now." Ramon
turns his up cards down, stands, and walks to the kitchen without
saying a word. Murphy raises a hundred. Curtis, a feral, noctur-

nal scavenger whose territory may be in question, slams down a blue chip.

"Show me what you got." Murphy does so. Curtis gives an angry jackal's snarl, then catches himself and grins.

"Pullin' it on the last card ain't nothin' but luck," he says.

There is a great deal of truth in that, but Murphy has no misgivings as he gathers in five thousand dollars' worth of chips.

Murphy folds the next hand early, not so much because of his cards, rather because he has a slight case of the shakes. The table has taken an odd cartographic turn—the chips in front of everyone else range from flatlands to gently rolling hills, but before Murphy stand the majestic Himalayas, topped by an Everest of blue chips.

Inge sits at a small table in the kitchen, watching a small television, and sipping from a large bottle of Perrier. "Hi," she says pleasantly. "How is it going in there?"

"Okay," Murphy says. "Is there a beer anywhere?"

"In the refrigerator. In the little brown one."

There is indeed a little brown refrigerator across from the big white one. Murphy stoops to open it and discovers a cache of Carlsberg and Heineken. He turns to Inge. "There wouldn't be a Schaefer anywhere, or a Miller's?"

"I'm afraid not. You don't like foreign beer?"

"Oh, sure, I love it. It just gets me drunk a little faster, and I don't want that to happen right now." He takes a Carlsberg out anyway, notices an old, hotel-style Coca-Cola bottle opener on the wall above the refrigerator, and uses it. He stands in the middle of the kitchen, drinks some beer, and looks at Inge. He can see her left breast in profile through her blouse; she is either entranced by whatever is on the small television, or staring blankly at it. "What's on?" Murphy asks.

Inge looks at him. "I don't know, some old movie. I think it has Clark Gable."

"Are you Swedish?"

"No, Danish."

"From Copenhagen?"

"No, Aarhus."

"I was there once, in 1953."

Inge brightens. "Really? Do you know it?"

Murphy wishes he could foray into the memory bank and come up with a snapshot of Aarhus, but all he remembers is the name. "No . . . I was ten years old . . . I was with my parents. We were there for a couple of days, I guess."

"It's a nice place," Inge says.

Echaverria appears in the kitchen doorway. He nods to Inge, speaks to Murphy. "You in or out?"

"I'm taking a little break."

"But you'll be back?"

"Yeah, sure. Next hand."

Echaverria stands in the doorway making staccato hand movements and looking at the ceiling. "You speak French?" he asks Murphy.

Do I speak French? "Yeah, I speak French."

Echaverria speaks French deliberately, and with an accent unfamiliar to Murphy: *"Deux choses—c'est parfait pour démolir le type noir, et notre hôte est un homme très jaloux et possessif."* Echaverria nods to Murphy, nods again to Inge, and departs. Murphy, still in the middle of the kitchen, has comprehended what Echaverria told him, and is trying to figure out why Echaverria speaks French.

"He told you," Inge says, "that a black person is perfect to be demolished, and that Ramon is a very jealous and possessive man."

"You speak French," Murphy says, ever observant.

"Evidently," Inge says, "he didn't know I do."

"I didn't know *he* did," Murphy says.

"Echaverria is a very intelligent man," Inge says. "He plays like he is not, but when he needs to be, he is."

"You know him pretty well?"

"Only through Ramon."

"You two have . . . been together for a while?"

"A year, I think."

Murphy decides to abandon his position in the middle of the kitchen and move in the direction of Inge and the doorway, not sure yet which is his objective. It occurs to him in transit that (1) he's asking a lot of questions, which he doesn't often do; (2) he is not simply making polite conversation with Inge; he would much prefer slipping off somewhere quiet with her to playing

more poker; (3) this has little to do with Inge per se; it is more a
reawakening of a part of him long dormant—the desire to get
laid.

Murphy has made up his mind to sit down across from Inge
when he comes face to face with Curtis instead. Curtis glides
into the kitchen looking crazed. "Hey," he says to no one in particular, "Where the beer at? You got Heineken's?" Inge points to
the little refrigerator, Curtis glides there, stoops, says, "Shee-it,
what is this shit?" comes up with a San Miguel, looks left and
right, says, "How'm I gonna open this sucker?" Murphy points to
the Coca-Cola opener. Curtis slams the bottle into the opener; it's
a miracle that only the cap comes off. He glides back toward
the doorway, stops in front of Murphy, looks at him sideways.
"You playin' or ain't you playin'? I got some gettin' back to do
with you, man . . ." And he glides back to the poker table.

Murphy changes his mind. Inge looks up at him and says,
"Well, it's been nice talking to you."

The streak is still on. Murphy bets more aggressively now, taking the losers' money in the early rounds, often guaranteeing
himself half of a high-low pot by the fourth or fifth card.

At four o'clock Jimmy quits. He pulls a roll of bills out of a
pants pocket, confers with Ramon, and counts out twenty-two
hundreds. A few hands later, Danny follows, goes through the
same routine with Ramon, but this time Murphy can't keep track
of the money transferred. He suspects that unless there is a disaster before dawn it's all going to be his.

At four-thirty Curtis wants to raise the stakes.

"We always play the same stakes," Ramon says.

"Only five of us left," Curtis says. "I'm down some an' I wanna
get it back. You dudes ain't a-scared of me, ain't no reason we
can't up it a bit."

"How much?" Echaverria says.

"Double the maximum. Two hundred."

"That's okay with me," Echaverria says.

"Yeah, well you ain't in the hole," Ernie says. "You guys raise
it to two hundred and I can't afford it no more."

"That's cool," Curtis says.

Ernie looks angrily at Curtis. "Well, fuck you, you nigger son

of a bitch," he says. "If you don't want me in the fuckin' game,
I'm gettin' the fuck outa the fuckin' game."

Curtis looks straight ahead and says, "That's cool."

Ernie stands up and slams his hands on the table. He speaks to
Ramon: "How much?"

Ramon looks at the tally sheet on the table next to him. "Sixty-
three," he says.

Ernie goes through his roll of bills. "There's fifty-five," he snarls,
dropping the whole wad on the table, "and I'm good for the
rest." He heads for the door.

Curtis shouts after him: "Hey, man, wait a minute!" Ernie
stops and turns around. Curtis fixes Ernie with the same crazed
look Murphy saw in the kitchen. He speaks now in a level conver-
sational voice: "You ever talk to me like that again, you a *dead*
motherfucker." Ernie stands totally still for a moment, in search
of a means to restore some dignity, then turns and departs.

Each of the four survivors now has a side of the table to himself, which makes Curtis Murphy's neighbor. Curtis snorts another substantial line of cocaine, then looks over toward Murphy.
"You want some of this shit?" he asks, and Murphy shakes his
head. "I didn't figure you did," Curtis says pleasantly enough,
"but I believe in bein' polite, ya know." Curtis does another line.
"That motherfucker called me a nigger son of a bitch," Curtis
tells Murphy. "Did you hear him? A nigger son of a bitch! Now
what the *hell* kinda thing is that to call somebody?"


Murphy rides his streak. Seven players, four players, hundred-
dollar limit, two hundred-dollar limit, it makes no difference. At
six in the morning he's eight thousand dollars to the good and he
feels invincible. With Ernie, Jimmy, and Danny gone there's less
easy money to be made, but Curtis has become an increasingly
vulnerable target. It seems a matter of honor that he at least
break even, and with every suggestion of a good hand he plays
boldly, too boldly, with only four players left. On several occasions Ramon and Echaverria fold after Curtis bets two hundred
dollars in the first round; Murphy sticks around and wins the pot.
Curtis becomes increasingly silent and intense, and between
hands he consumes cocaine or beer or tequila.

At a quarter to seven, Murphy folds a hand early and returns to the kitchen. Inge is gone. The sky is getting light. Murphy takes his second Carlsberg from the little refrigerator. He stands in his former middle-of-the-kitchen location and surveys the place. Not a roach in sight. Clean. And good-looking. An excellent kitchen. He sits in Inge's chair and drinks some beer. He flips on the little Japanese television, turns the volume knob off, and watches some well-dressed people having a civil conversation at this hour of the morning. How would Barbara Walters react if he told her he'd won almost nine thousand dollars tonight, playing poker with a bunch of cocaine dealers? How would Barbara respond if he explained that this nine thousand dollars was just short of being more money than he'd ever made in a year?

Echaverria shouts, "Hey, *Murphy*, your *deal!*"

She wouldn't give much of a shit, Murphy decides, and goes back to the game.

"Last round, okay? I have to do some business today," Ramon says. Murphy is surprised that Curtis accedes so quickly, then notices the change in his neighbor's chip stack. Curtis has won a big pot. Murphy deals seven stud, high only, gives himself a nine-six-three, and drops immediately when Curtis bets a hundred and Echaverria and Ramon call. Curtis wins another big one. Curtis deals the same game and wins again.

"The Big C is *back!*" he announces.

Echaverria deals five-card draw. Murphy opens with a pair of kings, betting a hundred, calls all around. Curtis takes three cards, as does Murphy, who emerges with kings and threes. He bets two hundred. Curtis raises two hundred. Echaverria and Ramon drop. Murphy raises two hundred, and Curtis raises two hundred. Murphy calls. Curtis displays three eights, and Murphy flips his cards over in defeat. In context, not a particularly painful defeat. Curtis emits a piercing guffaw and proclaims: "*Knew* I was gonna get even, an' I did. . . . *Knew* I was gonna get back on this lucky motherfucker, an' I *did!*"

Whatever shred of compassion Murphy may have felt for Curtis is obliterated.

"Last hand," Ramon says wearily. "Seven stud, both ways."

Curtis grimaces. "High-low, man? Shit . . . ain't but four of us left!"

"That's the game," Ramon says.

And Murphy is glad it is, looking at an ace and a five in the hole to go with a three showing. He has an inside track for the low, especially since Curtis, Echaverria, and Ramon all show face cards. Curtis, with a king up, opens for a hundred. To Murphy's relief, Echaverria and Ramon both call. Murphy tests the water and raises a hundred; Curtis raises another hundred, and Murphy is pleasantly surprised when Echaverria and Ramon call again. It looks like three good high hands going for half the night's last pot, and Murphy comfortably settling into the other half. And running the show.

The next two rounds of betting are almost identical to the first. Murphy now shows 3-4-5, Curtis K-8-8, Echaverria K-10-9 (all clubs), and Ramon Q-J-9 (all diamonds). With his ace and five in the hole, Murphy actually has a lousy low hand, but in this company nobody's going to notice. There are two potential straight flushes on the table, and one full house, but obviously no one has made it yet.

Murphy's sixth card is an ace.

"Motherfucker got a low, don't he?" Curtis sighs, then inhales sharply as Ramon deals him the seven of spades. "No help," he says. "But then I didn't need no help." Echaverria gets the eight of clubs . . . four to his straight. As before, Curtis opens for a hundred, but now Echaverria raises two hundred. He's got the flush. Ramon ponders, checking his hole cards, looking at Echaverria's cards, fingering his chips. After an uncharacteristically long wait he turns his up cards down. "I hate to fold a straight," he says, looking at Echaverria, "but I think it's a loser."

At this moment, Murphy thinks, that would be the best low hand on the table, since I've got two pairs and a three and a four. Murphy raises two hundred. Curtis throws four blue chips into the pot, calling both raises. Echaverria calls.

Murphy is taken aback. Why didn't Echaverria raise? Does he not have the flush? Is he simply trying to keep Curtis in for another round? Curtis would probably have sat through several more raises just to finish the hand, and Echaverria must know that. Or does Echaverria know, or sense, something that Murphy doesn't?

There is forty-nine hundred dollars in the pot.

It's still possible, of course, that Curtis will come up with a full house—all the more reason for Echaverria to have raised—or for that matter that Murphy himself will be dealt an ace or a five, either of which would give *him* a full house, or that Echaverria could hit the straight flush. . . .

"Last card, down and dirty," Ramon says, sounding like a man who has labored ten hours to lose a couple of thousand dollars.

Murphy doesn't look at his card. He doesn't need to. He knows he's going to raise two hundred dollars no matter what the card may be. Instead, he looks at Curtis and Echaverria. Curtis picks his three hole cards up and spreads them apart in slow motion; there is a perceptible flicker of eyebrow. Echaverria picks up the seventh card by itself and looks at it; no reaction.

Curtis bets two hundred, and Echaverria calls. Murphy raises two hundred, and Curtis raises two hundred. Echaverria folds without saying a word. Very softly, Curtis says: "Good move, brother. Good move."

Again, Murphy has no idea what Echaverria is doing. Curtis probably sits with kings and eights or three eights, Echaverria almost certainly has the flush.

Whatever, it's time for Murphy to look at the last card. He uses the Curtis method, sliding it atop the first two hold cards, picking up the trio, easing the familiar ace past the familiar five, then budging the five ever so slowly to reveal . . . a black card . . . a spade . . . an ace. A full house. Murphy raises two hundred. Curtis calls. Unless Curtis is prescient, unless Curtis has only the two eights he shows and has in addition X-ray vision, Murphy is going to win all of this pot.

Just to be sure, he declares high only, coming up with one chip in his hand.

Curtis's mouth drops. "You make a mistake?" he says, and Murphy shakes his head. Curtis looks hard at Murphy. "You ain't gonna jive me, motherfucker. Not now." He slams two blue chips on the table. Murphy counters with four. Curtis begins falling apart. He stares at Murphy's ace-three-four-five and says, "What the fuck you got? You got a straight? You ain't got no *flush*, an' flush wouldn't beat me noways, you *gotta* know that! I got a boat! Ray knew that, for Christ's sake! Shit!" Curtis throws another four blue chips in, and Murphy retaliates. Curtis looks hard again at Murphy's cards and finally realizes what might be underneath. He groans. "Awww . . . shit! Aww . . . Jesus fuckin' Christ almighty! I gotta see it." Curtis pushes the ultimate two blues into the pot. Murphy turns over his five and his two aces, and Curtis stands up and walks away.

The pot contains seven thousand, three hundred dollars. Murphy has won, for the night, in excess of sixteen thousand dollars. Curtis has disappeared. Echaverria and Ramon sit together at the end of the table and quietly discuss numbers. Murphy gathers the cards spread around the table and pats them into a neat deck, puts them down next to his chips, then leans back in his chair and closes his eyes for a while.

# 3

# The Polar Roaches

Ramon sits in front of a tremendous pile of cash. "I hope you don't mind a lot of hundreds," he says.

Murphy doesn't mind.

"It's gonna be bulky," Ramon says, beginning to count.

"Look, as long as it's not in pennies, it's okay," Murphy says. "Shit . . . even if it were in pennies I could afford to rent a truck. . . ."

Ramon can talk while counting. "You play well," he says.

Echaverria turns away from "Sesame Street" on the little television and says, "He was lucky as shit."

"But he played well."

"Sure, he played well, But if he hadn't pulled that ace on the last hand, Curtis'd be a rich man. . . ."

"Ay," Ramon says, still counting. "Curtis going to make somebody pay for that hand. I wouldn't want to be around him the next few days."

"He'll get over it," Echaverria says. "Kick the shit out of his old lady, burn a few suckers. He'll be playin' poker again next month."

"Will you?" Ramon speaks to Murphy. "I'd like to play you again."

Murphy feels like someone who does a few laps in the neighborhood pool every day, swims the English Channel on a dare, and as he's lying there gasping for breath somebody asks him if he'd like to make the return trip. "Sure," he says.

Ramon hands Murphy a tremendous mass of bills, and Murphy doesn't know where to put it. "You need an envelope for that," Ramon says. He disappears for a few seconds and returns with a parchment envelope, on which are embossed the initials RM. Murphy stuffs the envelope in the breast pocket of his jacket.

Echaverria and Murphy head for the West Side in the Bavaria. It's nine o'clock on Monday morning and the temperature must be close to sixty; traffic is miserable and the sky is a melange of pink, gray, and blue. Echaverria has the sunroof open and the radio full blast; Murphy is oblivious to everything, leaning back in his bucket seat, eyes closed.

Stopped in the middle of the 86th Street transverse, three or four light-changes from Central Park West, Echaverria turns the radio off and pokes Murphy on the shoulder. "You know why I dropped on the last hand?"

"Because Curtis had a full house and you only had a flush."

"Fuck Curtis, for Christ's sake, I wasn't even *thinkin'* about Curtis. I was pickin' up vibes from *you*, man . . ."

"I was going low all the way . . . I hadn't even looked at the last card. . . ."

They lurch forward in the traffic, then stop. Echaverria looks at Murphy. "Look, motherfucker, you're talkin' about *reason* and I'm talkin' about what *happened*. Maybe Curtis had the boat and maybe he didn't, but I would've stayed against him. I looked at you, man, and I saw magic written around your head . . . from the left ear to the right ear, reading clockwise, M-A-G-I-C."

"You're full of shit," Murphy says.

"Yeah, well maybe I am, but I know magic when I see it." And they lurch forward again.

Blocks away from Murphy's apartment, Echaverria pulls to the curb on Broadway. "We gotta celebrate," he says. "You got anything to drink?"

Murphy mulls this over. "Yeah. Two cans of Schaefer."

"That's not gonna do it." Echaverria points to a liquor store on the corner. "What'll it be?"

Murphy can't think of a thing he'd like to drink. "Jesus, I dunno . . ." He remembers Inge and Aarhus. "How about some Carlsberg?"

"You gotta make it tough, huh?" Echaverria scans the block. "Okay—you get your Carlsberg at the deli across the street. I'm gonna get myself a little Wild Turkey in here."

"It's my treat," Murphy says.

"The hell it is," Echaverria says. "It's gonna come out of my commission, which I ain't seen yet."

"Oh, shit . . . that's right . . ." Murphy takes Ramon's envelope from his pocket, counts out ten hundred-dollar bills, and hands them to Echaverria. He puts the envelope back in the pocket.

"You gonna walk across the street with fifteen grand in your pocket?" Echaverria asks, grinning.

"As opposed to what? Leaving it in the car?"

"Giving it to me."

Murphy feels a quick rush of apprehension. "Giving it to *you?*"

"You don't trust your old buddy?"

"I don't see the point."

"Murphy, look, it's just that I'm a little more experienced in carrying around large amounts of cash than I'd imagine you are, right?"

"Sure, but . . ."

Echaverria flips Murphy the car keys. "Just to make sure I come back," he says. "Yeah, I know the car isn't worth fifteen grand, but it has sentimental value."

Murphy hands over the envelope.

"You got enough for the beer?" Echaverria asks. Murphy nods. "Okay, I'll see you back here in a minute."

Murphy jaywalks across Broadway. A young black man jaywalks across Broadway behind him. When Murphy emerges from the delicatessen with a six-pack of Carlsberg, the black man is leaning against a parking meter. He stares hard at Murphy, then looks quickly away. Murphy jaywalks back to the BMW; as he crosses to the passenger side of the car he sees, or thinks he sees, the young black man running full tilt up 82nd Street. He wonders if he should mention this to Echaverria, decides that whatever concern he feels stems from the brief envelope melodrama, is entirely of Echaverria's making, and thus should be ignored.

They pull out onto Broadway. "I'm gonna hold on to the money until we're inside, if it's okay with you."

Again Murphy feels a shiver of disquietude. He shrugs and says, "Yeah, all right."

There is a parking place on Riverside Drive, around the corner from Murphy's building. Echaverria backs into it and gives Murphy a very serious look. "Did you notice a black kid following you across the street?"

Murphy nods.

"Do you understand why I wanted the money?"

Murphy nods again.

"Would it be all right with you if I keep it while you get out of the car and walk into the building?"

Murphy decides it's time to voice his apprehension. "Look," he says. "I don't want to sound ungrateful, but there's a chance this is all an elaborate setup. You figured I'd do well in that game, so you asked me to play. I won a lot of money, and now you've got me thinking somebody's gonna rip me off, so I hand the money over to you, I get out of the car, I walk home, and I never see you again."

Echaverria smiles broadly. "Murphy, you're a fuckin' genius," he says. "The only problem is that three or four members of Curtis's burn squad are gonna deprive you of fifteen grand if you get out of this car with that envelope."

"What if we get out of the car together?"

"We lose the element of surprise."

"What the fuck are you talking about?"

"There are more of them than there are of us."

"So . . . what difference does it make if I go first?"

Echaverria reaches under the seat and pulls out a large pistol. "If you go first," he says, smiling, "I can follow with this."

Murphy is 90 percent convinced. "Okay," he says, and he gets out of the car.

Murphy walks some sixty feet to the corner. This is the sort of thing that happens in nightmares—approaching the corner, sens-

ing that something loathsome is about to happen, blundering
ahead because it's only a dream.

It happens quickly. The young black man appears from behind
a parked car. He wraps his right arm around Murphy's throat and
grunts: "Be loose, motherfucker!" He eases Murphy against the
car. Murphy has trouble breathing. Another young black man appears from nowhere and begins going through Murphy's pockets.
He removes Murphy's wallet from his right rear pants pocket,
strews its contents across the sidewalk, then throws the wallet
down. "Ain't here," he says. A third black man now materializes,
and places a knife against Murphy's throat. He speaks in a stage
whisper: "Where's it at, motherfucker?"

Knife and arm are suddenly removed, and the man with the
knife is sprawled on the sidewalk. Murphy relaxes involuntarily
against the car. Echaverria is standing in front of everyone with
his pistol. Another black figure is heading down the street like
an Olympic sprinter. Echaverria kicks the knife into the gutter.
The man on the sidewalk starts to get up, and Echaverria kicks
him in the face. He goes down again. Echaverria speaks to the
young man Murphy had first noticed. "How you doin', Archie,"
he says, with only a touch of malice in his voice.

"Okay," Archie says, "You know, not too bad. . . ."

"That's great," Echaverria says. "I want you to pick up my
friend's wallet, and pick up everything you took out of it, and
put it all back together, and give it back to him."

Archie gets down on the sidewalk fast and begins picking
things up. The pocket searcher and the knife man are frozen in
their former positions. Archie hands Murphy his wallet and its
contents, and Murphy stuffs the mess into the pocket where the
envelope used to be.

"You tell Curtis," Echaverria says to Archie, "if he ever tries
anything like this again, I'm not gonna be his friend anymore."
Archie nods in staccato. "And if *you* ever try anything like this
again, I'm gonna shoot you in the balls." Archie finishes nodding.

Echaverria turns to Murphy. "I believe you're leaning against
Archie's car," he says. Murphy notices a pronounced tremor in
his knees as he steps away from the car; he doesn't know quite
what to do now finding himself suddenly the only moving part
of a weird tableau. Echaverria, the pistol, and the three contrite

young blacks are all briefly motionless, as if posing for a portrait. Murphy moves away toward his building.

Echaverria says, "You assholes get the fuck out of here," and the three men are inside the car and speeding toward Broadway within ten seconds.

Murphy squats against the wall, feeling wasted. Echaverria squats next to him. "Basically a nice bunch of kids," he says.

"But you wouldn't want them to marry your sister." Murphy is surprised he can talk.

"You okay?"

"Yeah . . . I'm fine."

"You don't look too good."

Murphy descends to full sitting position. "Look," he says, "my idea of a really good time is to spend all night playing poker with a bunch of guys on the most-wanted list, win all their money, come home, and get used as a fucking guinea pig. You didn't tell me about the knife. . . . That guy could've cut my fucking throat."

"Hey," Echaverria says, "if we didn't hit those guys now, they would've been back. They would've popped you when you least expected it, and maybe you *would've* got your throat cut."

This makes sense, and Murphy nods. He knows full well that what's pissing him off is nothing more than an abrupt change of roles: from Murphy the Conqueror at the poker table to Murphy the Protected on the street; and all this orchestrated by Echaverria. He cannot escape the feeling that Echaverria is in some way making use of him.

"You okay?" Echaverria asks again.

Murphy stands up. "Yeah. Let's go inside."

Not until they've entered Murphy's apartment does Echaverria hand over the envelope.

"I am to be trusted," he says.

Just to be sure, Murphy takes the envelope with him to the bathroom. He sits fully clothed on the toilet and counts with great care every bill, finding a total of $15,125. It's all there.

To his best recollection, Murphy has never drunk alcohol at 10 A.M. in his life. The very concept conveys to him a sense of weakness or decadence. But he can rationalize this Carlsberg as a nightcap, despite the obvious fact that it has been broad daylight for several hours now. He takes a hearty slurp and sets a precedent.

Echaverria calls from the kitchen: "Hey, you know what you got in your freezer? You got ice and cockroaches."

"They were on sale at the supermarket last week," Murphy shouts back. "Freeze-dried cockroaches. I couldn't resist."

Echaverria appears in the living room, holding an ice tray. He shows it to Murphy. "Would you look at that, for Christ's sake?" There is a roach frozen in an ice cube.

"What you don't realize," Murphy says, "what hardly *anybody* realizes, is that after countless centuries of living in close contact with the human race, roaches have become anthropomorphized, and that particular roach wanted to be Admiral Byrd."

"Yeah, well, you've got Roald Amundsen and a few others up there too," Echaverria says. "I don't know about this fuckin' ice."

"It's ice," Murphy says.

"I think I'm gonna settle for warm bourbon," Echaverria says, and pours himself a glassful.

"How'd you know about Roald Amundsen?" Murphy asks.

"I watch a lot of television."

"They doing situation comedies about Scandinavian explorers now?"

"Shit, Murphy, his name pops up all the time—Amundsen this, Amundsen that, you know . . ."

"Where'd you go to school, Ray?"

"Same place as everybody else, man . . . on the street."

"You really are full of shit, aren't you? Did you know Inge speaks French?"

"No shit! Does she?"

"Yeah. And she said an interesting thing about you. She said you're a very intelligent man and you pretend not to be."

"She turned you on, didn't she?" Echaverria says immediately.

Murphy is well aware that Echaverria's trying to change the subject. "That's beside the point," he says.

"Why the hell is it beside the point?" Echaverria is animated. "I walked in there and I could see what was goin' on with you. She's a good-lookin' lady, Murphy, and you talk about intelligent, Jesus, she's it . . ."

Murphy is trapped. "What the hell is she doing with Ramon, then?"

"Hey, man," Echaverria says, "Ramon's a dealer, just like me. Ain't an ounce of difference between us."

"Except that Ramon's French probably isn't too good."

Echaverria maneuvers: "You wanna know why Inge's with Ramon? Because he can afford her, man. Because Inge does about two bills of good nose a day, man, and Ramon gets it wholesale."

So the first woman to stir Murphy's loins since 1970 turns out to be a dope fiend. He is silent for half a minute, after which Echaverria says, "Jesus Christ, Murphy! You just won fifteen fuckin' grand in a fuckin' poker game! What're you all fucked up about?"

Murphy ponders a few seconds more. "What are you up to, Echaverria?" he eventually says.

The direct approach catches Echaverria off guard: "What am *I* up to?"

"What are you up to?"

"You still fucked up about that bullshit on the street?"

"That's part of it."

"What else?"

"You're evasive."

"How am I evasive?"

"You maneuver conversations."

"It seems to me you're maneuvering this one."

Murphy chuckles. "You're doing it right now."

"What the hell am I doing?"

"Setting up defenses, setting up diversions, going off on tangents. . . . You're like a really good used-car salesman: I ask you if the engine's in good shape, and you tell me how good the tires are . . . I ask you about the engine again, and you tell me it'll be fine if *I* take good care of it."

"I don't know what the hell you're talking about," Echaverria says.

"I don't know anything about you," Murphy answers.

"You know as much about me as I know about you."

"Okay," Murphy makes a dramatic offensive, "but I didn't invite you to a big-stakes poker game, and I didn't send you out to get mugged, and then come out and rescue your ass."

Echaverria swallows at least an ounce of Wild Turkey with no

visible reaction. He looks wide-eyed at the ceiling, as if asking it
for guidance. "Murphy," he says, "maybe it's boring, but I've
gotta play the same record one more time—I asked you to play because I was sure you were gonna win, and no matter what happened to me, I'd get the first thousand you won." He pauses for
a few seconds. "And maybe because I wanted to see what you'd
do to Curtis, 'cause there is a dude that needed to get his face
pushed in, and you did it. You did it better than I thought it
could've been done . . . You did it *so* good that Curtis put his
burn squad out on you, and that's somethin' I didn't think about
when I asked you to play, but it's somethin' I thought about when
I saw Archie's car."

"How did Archie know where to go?" Murphy asks.

"You in the phone book?"

"Sure."

"You remember when Curtis took off, after the last hand?"

Murphy nods.

"He was callin' his boys. They had a car behind us, all the way
over here, just to make sure this was where we were goin' to.
That was Archie's car. That's why I stopped on Broadway. I
figured they wouldn't hit you there, with all the people around,
but I watched that son of a bitch follow you across the street, and
then when he took off I knew they had this place staked out. The
only way to get those motherfuckers off your back was to send
you out. . . . They weren't gonna cut you, for Christ's sake, and
I figured you could handle bein' slammed up against the car and
gettin' cursed at for a while . . ."

There is a brief period of silence during which Echaverria
looks at Murphy, expecting approval, and Murphy looks at Echaverria with mixed feelings. Again he knows what Echaverria's
about: Echaverria has made him extremely guilty with his recap
of the play-by-play; any suspicion Murphy may have had that
Echaverria set *every*thing up is now severely lessened; but still he
feels there's more to this than Echaverria wishes to reveal; yet he
knows he must yield to the really good used car salesman if only
because he's trying so hard . . . and, of course, because he's
provided Murphy with fifteen thousand dollars. Which puts him
back at the beginning of this line of reasoning.

"Okay?" Echaverria asks.

"Okay," Murphy nods, giving in.

Echaverria rummages through Murphy's record collection. "Jesus Christ," he says, "You got a shitload of records . . . How many you figure there are here?"

"I dunno," Murphy says, "eight hundred, nine hundred . . . Most of them were free."

"You stole 'em?"

Murphy suspects Echaverria is kidding, but he isn't sure. "They came in the mail."

"Now that's a scam," Echaverria says. "You write about rock and roll, so they send you the records, right?"

"Right. And I get free tickets to concerts, and I get to see movies for free before they open, and I get invited to press conferences and cocktail parties, and when the Rolling Stones come to town somebody calls me up and asks me if I'd like an interview with Mick Jagger."

Echaverria gapes in ersatz veneration. "You mind if I play something?" he asks.

"Feel free," Murphy says.

Echaverria switches on the ten-year-old amplifier and puts a record on the six-year-old turntable. "For an important guy, you got a shitty stereo," he says.

Murphy hears the opening notes of *Astral Weeks*, by Van Morrison, the first song on an album which, in Murphy's opinion, is among the three best ever recorded.

"You like this guy?" Echaverria swallows some warm Wild Turkey.

"Yeah, he's good," Murphy says.

"I think he's fuckin' *great*," Echaverria says.

Murphy shrugs.

"You were saying," Echaverria persists, "that they call you up and they want you to interview Mick Jagger, so whattaya say?"

"I'm busy," Murphy says.

"So you don't care to interview Mick, right?"

Murphy finds himself descending into a dismal mood, and he can identify its ingredients: extreme fatigue, a burgeoning hangover from the poker game not to mention the subsequent skirmish, and frustration at his inability to figure out Echaverria.

"I've had it. I think I'd better get some sleep." Murphy stands up, and sways a bit.

"Is it okay with you," Echaverria asks, "if I crash here for a while? I don't feel much like drivin' back down to the Village."

"Sure," Murphy says. "There's a pillow and some blankets in the linen closet."

"Forget it, man," Echaverria says. "I'm just gonna lay down on the couch here."

"Okay," Murphy says. "Thanks for the game, and thanks for saving my life."

"No problem," Echaverria says. "See you later."

Murphy trudges down the long hallway and into the bedroom. The window with the view lets in bright sunlight, and he pulls down the shade. He undresses, gets into bed, and notices the envelope sitting on the floor just outside the bathroom some ten feet away. He considers getting up and stuffing it under the pillow, decides that would be nothing more than a gesture, and hears Van Morrison closing "Cyprus Avenue" as he falls asleep.

# 4

# A Major Purchase

Murphy is awakened by Robert and Johnny singing "I Believe in You" at the top of their lungs. He looks at the digital clock radio next to his head and discovers that the time is 2:37. A.M. or P.M.? In either case, why is somebody playing an old Robert & Johnny record in his living room? And why is he freezing? He sits up and grabs the blanket and comforter from the foot of the bed, pulls them over him. Robert & Johnny fade out in a chorus of oh-oo-oh-oos, and Major Lance commences "Monkey Time." Whatever's happening here, Murphy decides, someone has good taste in music.

He looks around the room, spots the envelope on the floor, between bed and bathroom, and everything comes back to him. He wonders briefly if it was all a dream. If so, who's that out there playing records? Draped in the comforter, Murphy stumbles out of bed and closes the window, not before a gust of wind comes close to freezing his teeth. There's been a change in the weather. He heads for the bathroom, picking up the envelope en route. He plants himself on the toilet seat, which feels like a miniature hockey rink, and counts his money again: still $15,125.

Echaverria sits on the living-room couch reading the *Daily News;* Darrell Banks sings "Open the Door to Your Heart." Murphy turns the stereo down a bit, and Echaverria looks up.

"Hey, good to see ya, Murphy! Did I wake you up?"

Murphy nods, and shrugs, and sits down on the chair directly across from Echaverria's couch.

"Hey, about an hour ago, man, I'm lyin' here and I wake up, and I'm freezin' my *ass* . . . the fuckin' temperature must've gone down about thirty degrees, right? So I get up, I'm lookin' for the linen closet, I don't know where the fuck the linen closet is, so I open the first closet I come to . . ."—Echaverria points toward the hallway—". . . and there's about a million forty-fives! So I start goin' through 'em, and there's every fuckin' record I ever loved in my *life*, man, and I forgot about the fuckin' blanket. . . ."

Murphy nods again.

". . . So, I'm goin' through 'em, and playin' 'em, and I get to fuckin' Robert & Johnny. . . . Jesus! I haven't heard that since nineteen-fuckin'-fifty-six! So I turned it up."

Murphy nods once more.

"I wanted to wake you up," Echaverria says, more sedately. "Let's go get something to eat."


Murphy and Echaverria share beef lo mein and *ropa vieja* at the Cuban-Chinese restaurant.

"You realize it's been a goddamn *day* since I ate anything?" Echaverria says between immense mouthfuls.

"Me too," Murphy says.

"Yeah, well from the looks of your refrigerator I'd say that's not unusual for you. Unless you eat roaches."

"You should try them pan-fried."

"You don't have a fuckin' pan to fry 'em in."

"Caught again," Murphy says.

"Hey," Echaverria says, "what're you gonna do with the money?"

Murphy thinks for a while. "I don't know," he says. "I guess I'll just put it in the bank."

Echaverria gives him a look of disgust. "Shit . . . don't put it in the fuckin' *bank*—then you've gotta pay taxes on it, for Christ's sake!"

"I was planning to pay taxes on it," Murphy says.

Echaverria shakes his head. "I didn't figure you were a flag-waver."

Murphy is insulted. "A *flag*-waver?"

"Yeah," Echaverria says indignantly. "I don't know what the hell else to call somebody who scores fifteen grand nobody has to know about, and then he wants to pay taxes on it."

"Look," Murphy says, "politics has nothing to do with it. It's just a question of honesty—if I make some money, I pay the tax. That's all there is to it." Echaverria displays what Murphy interprets to be a patronizing smile.

"You're a deep thinker, Murphy," he says.

There ensues some silent eating. Murphy cleans his plate, considers some more lo mein, and finds that Echaverria has just taken the last of it. He stares at the empty plate.

"What do you mean, I'm a deep thinker?"

"That was what we guys in the drug business refer to as irony," Echaverria says, smile intact.

Murphy is addled. Echaverria has again lulled him into a position of feeling at least moral, if not intellectual, superiority, then pulled the switch and left him wondering. "You guys in the drug business don't pay taxes," Murphy says, trying to be aggressive, feeling tentative.

"Sure, we don't," Echaverria says. "Here I am, fillin' out my 1040. Let's see . . . here it says 'Occupation,' so I fill in 'Cocaine Dealer, self-employed.' Now, let's see . . . I gotta do Schedule C, and Schedule SE for Social Security . . . I can deduct my rent, and my transportation, but can I deduct the fact that these guys who just came in from Colombia gave me some low-grade shit and I've gotta lower my prices? I better call my accountant on that one."

"Don't fuck around with me," Murphy says. "I'm not one of your East Side clients."

"Who said I had East Side clients?"

"It's obvious," Murphy says, with some anger. "You put all your street bullshit on the shelf, and you put on a business suit and you have lunch with Mr. Lawyer or Mr. Stockbroker and you sell him some cocaine, right?"

"Okay," Echaverria shrugs, "what if I do. . . . So what?"

"I'm just trying . . ." Murphy pauses, trying to figure out why he's so pissed off. ". . . I'm just trying to tell you that you can't bullshit me. You can't *manipulate* me."

Echaverria breaks into a broad, self-assured grin. "Now why

the hell," he says with what Murphy interprets to be a preposterous mixture of sincerity and sarcasm, "would I want to do that?"

"I don't know," Murphy replies. "But I get the feeling you're doing it."

"I'm just tellin' you if you put the money in a bank, you're an asshole."

"To you, I'm an asshole," Murphy says, "but to me, I'm not. Just because I ventured into your game and made some easy money doesn't mean I have to start playing by your rules, does it?"

"Nope," Echaverria says.

"Okay, then if I'm not gonna put it in the bank, what am I gonna do with it?"

"Spend it."

"On what? I don't *need* anything that costs fifteen thousand dollars."

"Take a trip. Get your head together."

"My head's as together as it's ever going to be."

"You look to me," Echaverria says, "like somebody who's bored out of his fuckin' mind."

There are several moments of silence, after which Murphy smiles and submits: "I wouldn't say I'm bored. I'd say I'm numb."

"Yeah," Echaverria agrees, "that's more like it."

They arise, pay the check, and leave the restaurant. Then, underdressed, they walk back to Murphy's apartment, against the cold wind off the Hudson River.


Back in Murphy's living room, Echaverria plays, "I Fought the Law" by the Bobby Fuller Four. "Great record," he tells Murphy. "Fantastic." Echaverria is drinking one of Murphy's Carlsbergs. "Did you know," he shouts over the record, "this was the only hit the dude ever had, and he killed himself right afterwards." Murphy nods. There is a list in his head of at least twelve people who died right after their only hits. The gist of Bobby Fuller's song is that when you fight the law, the law wins.

"I'm not keepin' you from anything, am I?" Echaverria asks. Murphy shakes his head. Echaverria returns to the closet with the forty-fives and rummages. "How come this place is so fuckin' big?" he says.

"That's the way it was built," Murphy answers.

Echaverria returns with a new stack of treasures. He plays "This Can't Be True" by Eddie Holman. "So whaddayou do with yourself on an average day?" he asks Murphy.

"I don't do anything," Murphy says flatly. "I go out to eat. I go out to the movies. I go out to Donoghue's once in a while. And I play poker once a week."

"You're not gonna go back and play with those assholes again, are you?"

"Sure I am."

"Jesus." Echaverria plays "Things Get Better" by Eddie Floyd. "You gotta get your ass outa here," he says to Murphy.

"To where?" Murphy says.

Echaverria turns down the volume. "You ever gamble on anything but poker?"

"I have."

"You ever seen jai alai?"

"No."

"You know what it is?"

"Yeah . . . there's a big court, and guys with things on their arms . . . it's like handball . . ."

"You a sports fan?"

"Yeah . . . sure."

"Jai alai's gonna blow you out, Murphy. In addition to being the greatest fuckin' game ever invented, you can *bet* on it . . ."

"I don't think I'm ready for a trip to Spain," Murphy says.

"*Spain?*" Echaverria guffaws. "I'm not tryin' to send you to Spain, for Christ's sake . . ."

"Where, then—Havana?"

"How about Florida?"

Florida. Of course. Murphy recalls *Variety* headlines to the effect of jai alai being boffo in Miami. Murphy also has pleasant memories of driving to Florida in his 1963 Valiant convertible, spending a languorous week by the beach in Boca Raton. "I don't want to go to Miami," he says.

"How about West Palm Beach?" Echaverria says.

West Palm Beach. Right up the road from Boca Raton. "I might be interested," Murphy says.

"You mind if I make a long-distance call?"

Murphy shrugs, and Echaverria proceeds to the wall phone in the kitchen. Murphy watches him dial a number he evidently

knows by heart. Echaverria says, "Angie? It's me. How ya doin'?"
Echaverria listens for a while, then says, "Okay . . . you know,
the usual. . . . Listen, there's this friend of mine, really good
dude, I wonder if you could put him up for a few days?" Echaverria listens again. "No, nothing like that, Angie . . . he's a
writer. Plays a good game of poker. You're gonna get along great."
Echaverria listens some more. "Yeah . . . no problem . . . okay,
look, he'll call you, all right?" Some more. "Okay, Angie, talk to
ya soon . . . bye." Echaverria hangs up.

"This is a great lady," he tells Murphy. "She's an old friend of
mine and she's got a nice place near West Palm Beach. She's crazy
about jai alai, too—she can tell you everything you'd wanta
know . . ."

Murphy has been bristling. "And she owes you something," he
says.

"She doesn't owe me shit," Echaverria says. "She's a friend."

"Look," Murphy says, "I appreciate the gesture, but I don't
want to spend a few days with some old girl friend of yours,
okay?"

Echaverria's tone remains neutral and calm. "She's not that
kind of old friend," he says. Murphy doesn't reply. "You fly down
to West Palm Beach, she'll pick you up, you can stay at her
place, that's all there is to it. You'll like her."

"You want me to like her," Murphy says.

"Sure, I want you to like her. I think you'd get along."

Murphy decides to change the subject. "I'm not going to fly
down," he says, "I'm going to drive."

Echaverria is surprised: "You got a car?"

Murphy is pleased. "I'm going to buy one."

"What kind?"

"I haven't given it much thought."

"If you don't object to dealing with one of my East Side clients,"
Echaverria says, "I could probably get you a pretty good deal
on a BMW."

"I'm not proud," Murphy says.


The salesman is a young, bearded man in a very stylish suit.
He and Echaverria perform an involved handshake, and Echa-

verria says, "Mr. Trammell, this is Mr. Murphy. Mr. Murphy wishes to purchase an automobile. He's a personal friend, so don't fuck around with him."

The salesman and Murphy extend hands, and after an awkward moment of mutual indecision they shake in the traditional manner. The salesman says, "I'm Bob."

"Nice to meet you," Murphy replies.

"What did you have in mind?" Trammell asks.

"A used 2002," Murphy says.

"Aah, okay," Trammell says, perhaps a bit disappointed. "I've got a couple over here. . . ." He leads Murphy and Echaverria through a rear door of the showroom and into the service area. "I want to assure you," he says, "that there's nothing wrong with these cars. We've got them back here just because we don't have room in front . . ."

"We're not a couple of fuckin' idiots, Trammell," Echaverria says.

The service area is noisy. Parked side-to-side are two small, box-shaped German cars—one deep red and battered, the other a hideous light green, but intact. "This," Trammell says, pointing to the red car, "is a sixty-nine. It needs some body work, it's got some miles on it, but it's in good mechanical shape, and I could let you have it for twenty-five hundred dollars."

Murphy looks the car over: he feels compassion for it, but nothing more.

Sensing a lack of interest, Trammell moves on to the green car. Echaverria says to Murphy, *sotto voce*, "They always show you the bad one first."

Trammell says, "This is a really nice little car. It's a seventy-one, low miles, great condition . . ."

Murphy opens the driver's side door and checks the odometer: 29,781. He looks around: sunroof, AM-FM radio, no visible signs of deterioration; he doesn't know what else to look for. He emerges to find Echaverria grilling Trammell.

"Water pump gone yet?" Trammell shakes his head. "No rusting?" Trammell shakes his head. "Anything wrong with it?"

"There is nothing wrong with this car," Trammell says.

"Why'd it get traded in?"

"The customer bought a new Bavaria . . ."

Murphy interrupts: "How much?"

"For the Bavaria?"

"For this," Murphy says.

"Four thousand dollars," Trammell says, with a look of strained sincerity that suggests all the vicissitudes of this section of the free-enterprise system.

"Shit," Echaverria says, "the car didn't cost that much when it was new."

"The mark has gone up against the dollar," Trammell says.

"Kiss my ass, Trammell, you didn't get this car from Munich, you got it from some dude on a trade-in."

"I have been *instructed*," Trammell says, "to ask four thousand dollars for this particular car."

"Well," Echaverria says, "I will instruct Mr. Murphy to offer you *three* thousand dollars for this particular car."

Trammell laughs nervously. "I couldn't consider that."

"Thirty-five hundred," Murphy says. Echaverria gives him a look connoting something between disgust and astonishment.

"I don't know . . ." Trammell says.

"That's our final offer," Echaverria says.

"Well, uh . . . Mr. Murphy," Bob says, "You've just made yourself a pretty good deal."


Forms are filled out. Trammell wants to know how Murphy plans to finance the car. Murphy says he plans to pay the full amount today. Trammell points to the clock on the wall, which reads five after five. "There's no way we could get an okay on your check today."

"Cash," Murphy says.

"Oh," Trammell says, "Well, that's different."

He punches a few keys on his adding machine. "With tax, it comes to $3780."

"Forget the tax," Echaverria says. "He's gonna register the car in Florida."

Trammell attempts a smile. "Okay, but he's still got to pay sales tax here, state and city . . ."

"No he doesn't," Echaverria says flatly.

"Look, Ray," Trammell becomes earnest, "if this were a *new* car, sure, he could go down to DMV and get in-transit stickers and he wouldn't have to pay the sales tax, but his is a *used* car. It's already got New York plates, he's buying it in New York, and it doesn't make any difference *where* he's going to register it."

"So tell the fuckin' state and the fuckin' city it's a fuckin' new car . . ."

"You know I can't do that."

Echaverria sits on the desk. "Trammell," he says, "I know, and if you don't know you *should* know, that if Mr. Murphy hadn't offered you thirty-five hundred, I could've got you down to thirty-two fifty . . ."

Trammell shakes his head and tries to interrupt. "Ray, look, that's beside the . . ."

Echaverria continues: "And you know goddamned well you're still gonna make a profit, 'cause you sure as hell didn't give no three grand on the trade-in."

"Ray, I don't run the place, for Christ's sake, and this is going to come out of my pocket!"

"I think you better stop thinkin' about your pocket and start thinkin' about your nose," Echaverria says, pleasantly.

Trammell bristles. "What the hell do you mean by that?"

Echaverria raises his voice, overacting: "I mean that if you'd like to keep scoring excellent cocaine . . ."

"Hey, Ray, *Jesus* . . . keep it down, will ya?" Trammell looks left and right at neighboring cubicles. None of his fellow salesman have called in the narcs so far.

"Mr. Murphy's thirty-five will cover the tax," Echaverria says. "Am I correct?"

"I've gotta redo this fuckin' bill of sale," Trammell says.

Murphy removes the envelope from his jacket and counts out thirty-five hundred-dollar bills.


The green BMW sits against the curb, on Park Avenue outside the showroom, ready to go. Murphy keeps thinking, Jesus, that's my *car*. Echaverria says, "The money's starting to mean something now, isn't it?"

"You didn't have to pull that last number," Murphy says.

"Look," Echaverria says, "I know that asshole, and if you

hadn't opened your mouth I could've had him down to thirty-two fifty in five minutes."

Murphy computes. "I saved myself ten dollars," he says.

"How do you figure that?"

"The tax on thirty-two fifty would've been two hundred and sixty dollars."

Echaverria computes, and nods. "Murphy, the problem with you is that you can think, but you don't know what the hell to do with it."

Murphy shrugs. "You want a lift to your car?"

"I can walk a fuckin' block and a half," Echaverria says. "When are you gonna take off?"

"Tonight," Murphy says. "As soon as I can. I'm just gonna pack some stuff and go."

"You gonna call Angie?"

"Sure," Murphy says.

Echaverria's face assumes extremely sincere configurations. "There is," he says, "no jive involved in this. I think you'd like each other."

"I'm gonna call her," Murphy says.

"Okay." Echaverria takes a tiny notebook from one pocket and a pen from another. He writes, and pulls a page from the notebook, hands it to Murphy.

> Angela Wilson
> Waterway Cove
> Madera Beach, Fla.
> 799-5255

"Just south of West Palm Beach," Echaverria says. "You take the last West Palm Beach exit off the turnpike, you go to Route One, and you turn right. It's about twenty minutes from jai alai, and Angie can tell you a hell of a lot about jai alai."

"Okay," Murphy says, putting the little piece of paper in his jacket, next to the envelope. "Thanks."

"Send me a postcard," Echaverria says. He waves, and walks away down Park Avenue.

The parting is somewhat abrupt. Murphy feels there is something he should have said to Echaverria, but he doesn't know what it is. He stands on the sidewalk for several seconds, mulling.

Then he realizes he's freezing. He gets into the green BMW and heads back to the West Side.

It's been a long time since Murphy last packed a suitcase. Packing a suitcase, he conjectures, is one of those arts never forgotten once learned, the problem being that he has never learned. It occurs to him at this moment that Mary was an excellent packer of suitcases, versed in all the tricks of the trade—shirts folded correctly, socks stuffed inside shoes, every inch of space used, and everything came out neat, unwrinkled, and just so. It occurs to him that Mary's efficacy at suitcase-packing is one of the very few fond memories he has of her, the several others being of a more carnal nature. This is, he stops and calculates, his first packing job since . . . 1968. That was the year he married; late 1971 was when he became unmarried, and in the year and a half since he has ventured no farther than a few miles outside Manhattan Island.

One of the big problems of packing is figuring out what to take, and fortunately Murphy doesn't have much to choose from. He pulls his six wash-and-wear shirts off their hangers and tosses them on the bed, takes his three shirts that go to the laundry out of the drawer and throws them on the bed, takes two decorated T-shirts out of the drawer and puts them on the bed. Eleven pairs of socks, eight pairs of boxer shorts. He removes his new boots and puts on his old boots, better for driving. He stuffs socks into the new boots, a packing trick that presents no conceptual difficulties. What else? He rummages through closets and drawers, finds a bathing suit, a tennis racket, a bottle of suntan lotion, three Dexedrine capsules, a road atlas (1966 edition), a portable radio, and a pair of sunglasses. What about the suit? It is his only concession to fashion, a three-hundred-dollar item bought at Bloomingdale's, light gray and nifty. What the hell; he throws it on the bed. He stuffs most of this into the old vinyl suitcase, puts the radio, the road atlas, the sunglasses, and the Dexedrine in a paper bag.

He carries all this to the front door, then goes to the living room and spends several minutes putting Echaverria's recorded selections back in their proper places. He turns off the overhead light, heads back to the hallway, and notices the ice tray sitting atop the speaker, the explorer roach now thawed, still dead, floating placidly in its little cubicle. Murphy carries the ice tray into the kitchen and turns on the light, and there is no roach to be seen. "Do you fuckers know I'm going?" Murphy asks the empty kitchen. There is no reply.

# 5

# Murphy Goes South

Sitting in his new and stationary car, stopped dead in traffic, surrounded by the deceptively exotic twinkling of several thousand oil refineries lining the New Jersey Turnpike, Murphy makes an alarming discovery: the radio in this car has no pushbuttons. He has driven this nice little automobile from Park Avenue to the Upper West Side, then down West End Avenue and Eleventh Avenue to the Lincoln Tunnel, all the while getting used to things—the tension of the clutch, the precision of the steering, the effectiveness of the brakes, the sensation of being very close to the road.

Then for no apparent reason all the traffic slows, crawls, and stops. Murphy is dissatisfied with the pimple ointment commercial on WABC (button number three), and moves in conditioned reflex for WINS (button number four). In mid-reflex he realizes that when he hits the button he's not going to get Murray the K, he's going to get all news, twenty-four hours a day. At the conclusion of reflex, when his right index finger hits flat plastic, he recognizes that he's the victim of a Teutonic plot. This radio, this sleek, elegant Blaupunkt, has AM and FM. It has crystal-clear sound. It has a cassette deck. It has bass and treble and balance controls . . . but no buttons! It is one thing to be without buttons in a traffic jam on the New Jersey Turnpike, when one has all the time in the world to turn the tuning knob. It is another thing to be in North Carolina at four in the morning, craving sleep, pushing on, without buttons. Shit.

Traffic begins to lurch forward. Murphy tunes in WWRL, which plays "Be Thankful (For What You Got)."

The pace picks up to thirty, to fifty, to sixty. Murphy spots an opening in the right lane, cuts across two lanes without signaling and accelerates to eighty-five.

Midnight finds him midway between Baltimore and Washington, ever more pissed off at the radio, and tired. He has slept three hours of the last thirty-eight. He is about to run out of gas. He is debating whether to continue or stop for the night, or perhaps just to turn around and go home.

There is a neon Shell sign ahead on the right. Murphy pulls off Interstate 95 with no great hope for the Shell station's being open. It is. Super Shell costs 45.9 cents per gallon, which is an outrage, but better than nothing.

He tells the pimply teen-age attendant to fill it up, asks if there is a motel in the vicinity. The kid thinks about it for a long time, and shakes his head.

"No motel?" Murphy says.

"Which way you headed?" the kid says.

"South."

"Well, there's all kinds of motels and hotels in Washington."

"How about north?" Murphy asks, hoping against hope.

"Baltimore," the kid says. "They got lots of 'em."

Murphy pays five dollars and seventeen cents for the tank of gas, a king's ransom. He lumbers over to the soft drink machine and obtains a bottle of root beer, has a sip, and returns to the BMW. He is not about to search the Maryland countryside for lodging, nor to enter either Baltimore or Washington. The choice has thus been narrowed to going south or going home. Either, Murphy decides, would be impossible in his current state. He opens the trunk, removes the paper bag, finds the Dexedrine, and washes one capsule down with a slug of root beer. The amphetamine enters his bloodstream in no time at all, and it becomes clear that to proceed south is the answer.

Murphy catches himself humming tunelessly as the BMW hurtles toward Richmond. He turns on the radio, twists through the AM dial, finds nothing, and switches to FM. A station in the middle of the band plays "Jumpin' Jack Flash." In stereo. Murphy accelerates to eighty-five. "Jumpin' Jack Flash" segues into Creedence Clearwater's "I Heard It Through the Grapevine," all three hours of it, followed by Van Morrison's "Domino," by which time Murphy has hit ninety-five. "Ninety-five, officer?" he says aloud, "well, ain't that the speed limit? I keep seein' all them little blue and red signs *tellin'* me to go ninety-five."

There will be no police, Murphy knows. He is at least for the moment charmed and chosen. Invulnerable, untouchable, and uncatchable.

I-95 evaporates about a hundred miles short of Georgia and a few minutes before dawn. Murphy wends cautiously down Alternate 17, crawling through Waterboro and Alkehatchie and Cooswhatchie at twenty-five, zooming back up to eighty for long, solitary stretches of two-lane highway. The sun comes up, the faraway 50,000-watt clear-channel voices fade away, the amphetamine ebbs and disappears, and Murphy enters Georgia. He stops for breakfast just south of Savannah. It's not exactly tropical here in northern Georgia in the fourth week of February, but it sure as hell isn't cold. The Nehi thermometer hanging outside LeRoy's Diner reads exactly fifty degrees. Murphy gets back in the car and back onto U.S. 17.

The interstate reappears, disappears, reappears, and goes away for good. He drives mechanically now, trying simply to stay at precisely ten miles an hour above the speed limit, to make good time and have no encounters with the law. Murphy has come down several notches from omnipotence, but for an exhausted son of a bitch who has no idea what he's going to do when he gets where he's headed, he feels pretty good.

Florida. Murphy must remind himself several times that he's really not almost there, that crossing the imaginary line between Georgia and Florida still leaves him five or six hours north of his destination.

It gets warmer, and still warmer. Murphy rolls down the window and turns the Blaupunkt up close to full blast.

Near Vero Beach there is the first of a series of warning signs: INTERSTATE ENDS 3 MILES. He coasts down the exit ramp, turns left onto a two-lane road, speed limit thirty. He's been here before: a twenty-minute crawl into Vero Beach on this highway, followed by an endless stretch of traffic lights down U.S. 1, then a sluggish trek west to the Florida Turnpike. He curses the state of Florida, the Interstate Highway Commission, local merchants, and whichever other forces of corruption and stagnation have slowed his flight.

But what's this? A discreet blue sign advertising an imminent TRUCK ROUTE. Truck route to where? What the hell—Murphy turns right into two-lane blacktop, not another vehicle in sight, speed limit sixty. He goes ninety down State Route 505, hopes he isn't heading for Tampa or Seattle, follows the little blue signs at the speed of sound for half an hour, hits a four-lane highway, turns right, and find himself fifty yards from the turnpike entrance. Ah, Murphy—are you *hot?*

He reaches the West Palm Beach toll gate at 3:55, a shade less than twenty hours from the Lincoln Tunnel, which figures to an average speed of 66.2 miles per hour. What's next?

Murphy stops at an Arco station midway between the turnpike and U.S. 1. He orders a dollar's worth of premium, heads for the men's room with his Gillette Techmatic, in order to transform himself from someone who has just driven a car 1,321 miles to someone who's going to decide what he wants to do now that he's here. Walking is something that requires concentration; the reflection in the mirror proffers the same mixture of fascination and repugnance he might hold for a run-over cat—and yet he turns out not to look half as strange as he feels. The eyes are red, the pupils a bit dilated, the hair askew, the face as a whole made to look a bit sinister by two and a half days' growth of beard. But after a shave and a general wetting down he strikes himself as approaching respectability.

In the car, he removes Echaverria's notebook page from the pocket he'd put it in a day or a decade or a few minutes ago. In the phone booth, he deposits a dime and stares at Angela Wilson's number. He stands there, holding the receiver in his left hand, for several minutes. He is reluctant to dial . . .

Because he doesn't know what to say.

Because he feels uncomfortable inviting himself to stay, even though, indirectly, he's already been invited.

Because he doesn't quite feel in control of himself.

Because for one night at least he should stay in a motel, get his head clear, and make this decision tomorrow.

Because of Echaverria.


The news at the Holiday Inn isn't good: height of the season, conventions, we (Holiday Inns from here to the Azores) are booked solid, but you could try some of the little places. Murphy tries the little places from West Palm Beach down to Boca Raton. It is inconceivable that in the whole of southern Florida there is no vacant motel room, but as he proceeds now to the really seedy cabin joints, it appears he's been preceded by several hundred other voyagers. The consensus at this point is that he might find a motel bed in Vero Beach to the north, or a hotel bed in Miami to the south.

He pulls into a 7-Eleven in Boca Raton and buys a six-pack of Genesee beer, opens a can in the BMW, sips, and ponders. His options would now appear to be. . . . He can think of no options except falling asleep in the car. Murphy cannot remember ever having been this tired, and this isn't a good time to be tired. He yields finally to the lure of another Dexedrine, washes the capsule down with a slurp of Genesee, anticipates a flash of clarity and inspiration, and falls asleep while doing so.

The drug, as if offended that it should be wasted on a sleeping person, plays havoc with Murphy's unconscious. He has a series of violent and chaotic dreams that manage to incorporate virtually every threatening agent or being to have entered his life to date. In each instance Murphy escapes, but only to the next dream, out of the frying pan, perilously closer to the fire. The final dream opens with Murphy at the wheel of his BMW, driving cautiously through unfamiliar and precipitous terrain. The sky is a menacing gray, suggesting not twilight but an impending storm. Murphy doesn't know where he's going; he knows only that he wants to get away from where he is as fast as possible, but his fatigue and the sheer, dangerous road keep him at a snail's pace. He decides to stop and rest, and climbs into the back seat, where he falls asleep. He dreams that the car begins to move, downhill, faster and faster on the winding road, with him still in the back seat. He awakens from the dream to find that the car *is* moving frighteningly fast down a mountain road, surrounded by deep green trees, and that Echaverria is driving it.

"It looked like you needed some help," Echaverria says.

"I did, but I think you're going too fast," Murphy says, frightened.

"You want to get out of here, don't you?" Echaverria says.

"I want to stay alive," Murphy says.

The car is going much too fast. "Don't worry about it," Echaverria says. "I know what I'm doing." He drives the car through hairpin curves as a car can be driven only in a dream—it snaps through the curves like a whip. Murphy wants to get out, but he's held in the back seat by force and lassitude. He can't reach the door handle. He can see the drop—hundreds, maybe thousands of feet down—each time the car slides to the edge of the road.

"It's my car," Murphy says, "and I want you to slow down." At this point the car leaves the road and soars off the mountain, hovering above the chasm for a moment, as if it were the same weight as the atmosphere, before beginning to drop.

Murphy awakens from the dream to find that the car is sitting still in a 7-Eleven parking lot, surrounded by other cars, and that he is in the driver's seat. This comes as considerable relief, but it takes him a while to ascertain just where this 7-Eleven parking lot is, and what he's doing here. The instrument of revelation proves to be a can of Genesee, which sits laterally on the passenger seat. "Shit!" Murphy says, looking in disgust at the puddle of beer which has doubtless dribbled onto the carpet behind the seat. He knows precisely where he is.

During the next ten minutes, Murphy returns to the 7-Eleven and buys a roll of paper towels; asks the counterman for the time and is told it's seven thirty; wipes up and sops up spilled beer; undergoes a pronounced personality change as the same amphetamine which has tortured the unconscious now massages the conscious into a state of great well-being; decides that this is the perfect time to call Angela Wilson; dials her number from the pay phone and lets it ring thirty times before hanging up; decides to try her again, later; approaches the 7-Eleven counterman for the third time in the last two hours and asks him where Jai-Alai is.

"Which one?" the counterman replies.

"The nearest one," Murphy says.

The counterman contemplates. "Well," he says after a good while, "Dania could maybe be a little closer, but West Palm's a hell of a lot easier to get to."

"Okay," Murphy says. "Tell me how to get there."


For the past seven years Murphy has been in the business of telling people what to like. He has been loath to consider his job as such, preferring to believe that he simply informs people of his own predilections and hopes that they'll agree. But he's been uncomfortable in this line of work almost from the start—primarily because he feels there is a fundamental hypocrisy involved. If he has a dark mistrust of anyone who tells him to see or hear or buy anything, what right does he have to impose his own tastes, in print, on anyone else? Disenchantment with his profession has grown as he's found those tastes becoming progressively narrow, his nature becoming progressively suspicious, his heart and mind progressively detached from the music that once gripped and enthralled them.

So the reluctant tastemaker finds himself a long way from home—and what the hell is he doing here? He's been lured into a poker game whose stakes were light-years over his head, come out of it with a tremendous, ludicrous pile of money. A suggestion has been made that he take this pile and go to Florida. Why Florida? Because there's a game he should see and a woman he should meet. Murphy will allow that the lurer/suggester has enabled him to come here, but he's convinced that ultimately the decision was his alone. He expects nothing from jai alai, he expects nothing from Angela Wilson. He is, meanwhile, in his properly circumspect manner, out of his mind.

# 6

# Love at
# First Sight

Murphy spends two dollars and fifty cents for a reserved seat and
steps for the first time inside a jai-alai fronton. He spends an
additional thirty-five cents on a program. Murphy and the young
woman selling programs are alone in the fronton's expansive
lobby. "Big night?" Murphy asks, gesturing to the empty lobby.

"There's a game on," she says. "There's plenty of people in
there."

"How many games are there?"

"Twelve."

"How many have I missed?"

"This is the fifth game."

"But I don't get a discount on the program, right?"

"Right," she says, with a little smile.

Murphy begins a brief tour of inspection. The lobby is parti-
tioned from whatever is beyond it by a row of cashiers' windows;
catty-corner from there, to the left of the entrance, is a large
scoreboard. Here Murphy finds lineups for games yet to be
played, results of games already played. He examines the results,
trying to force his frayed brain into its gambler's mode.

There appear to be eight teams per game, each team consisting
of two players with Spanish names (some seem to be first names,
some last names, some nicknames). Games one, three, eight, and
ten, however, are played not by teams of two, but by individuals.

So Murphy will be watching two games of singles, five games of doubles. The payoffs for games already completed are in familiar pari-mutuel language—win, place, show, daily double—but for a couple of terms not in Murphy's betting vocabulary: quiniela and perfecta.

Their significance is deduced without difficulty: the fourth game was won by Team 6, Team 1 placing; the scoreboard reads:

QUINIELA (1–6) $58.20

PERFECTA (6–1) $174.90

Obviously a perfecta involves picking win and place teams *in order,* a quiniela merely picking win and place teams, the smaller number coming first.

He moves on. Here is the entrance to the Sala del Toro, a restaurant. Here is a noise, from far away, an intermittent *thock,* probably the sound of a jai-alai ball hitting a jai-alai wall. He checks the Sala del Toro's menu. The Bull's Room offers a banal bill of fare, heavy on the beef, which makes sense. There are two notations at menu's bottom: Not Responsible For Steaks Well Done, and NO CREDIT CARDS ACCEPTED. Murphy recognizes a class joint when he sees one.

As he moves gradually, almost cautiously toward the game, the arrhythmic *thock* sounds become louder, as does the crowd noise, itself intermittent, coming in brief bursts and consisting largely of shrieks and yelps. There is very little applause. Murphy has been following a pattern of small, rectangular swatches of paper since passing the cashiers' windows a minute earlier: discarded pari-mutuel tickets, each representing somebody's two dollars down the drain, lead him around the partition into the betting area, where tickets virtually carpet the floor.

The lobby and the betting area actually form one huge room, perhaps a fifth of which is filled by the partition, the other side of which houses a long row of betting windows. At the far end of the betting area are a refreshment stand, a men's room, a ladies' room. At the near end, Murphy stands between a reciprocal refreshment booth and a display of famous people who have been photographed at West Palm Beach Jai Alai. He recognizes James Franciscus, the actor, Dick Williams, the baseball manager, Curt

Gowdy, the sports announcer. It would seem that Pinky Lee, Henry Kissinger, and Annette Funicello have requested that their pictures not be displayed.

He passes the refreshment stand and approaches the first of six entrances to the $2.50 reserved seats. The *thock* sounds are now close by.

It's a clear case of love at first sight. What Murphy sees is a playing court of majestic expanse: close to two hundred feet long, he'd guess, and perhaps forty feet high; it would be an immense rectangular solid but for the absence of a front, where there is instead a thick mesh screen which at once permits the spectator to view the action, and keeps him from being killed. There are four men on the floor, all wearing white pants and sneakers and helmets, two wearing white shirts, two wearing red shirts, all bearing curved, yard-long appendages on their right arms. With these devices the men catch and throw a small white missile, about the size of a baseball. But no baseball could ever travel this fast unless propelled from a cannon. The four men dart about the court this way and that, catching the ball off the front wall, the side wall, the back wall, falling down, getting up, hurling the ball at various angles whence it caroms, soars, gyrates. . . . Murphy thinks of tennis, of squash, of handball, all of which must be blood relatives to this game. But, Jesus, this is Cinemascope to their home movies.

The problem is that it's a foreign movie to which no one has thought to affix subtitles. Between games, Murphy leafs furiously through the program, looking for the rules, or a little bit of background. But the program isn't geared to the beginner: it is a morass of statistics and arcana. No doubt when Murphy has figured out what's happening it will be useful to know how many times Olabarri has won the sixth game this season, or how many times the fifth position has won the fifth game. The program does have its moments. "No person," Murphy reads, "who is a fugitive from justice, or whose conduct at a race track in Florida, or elsewhere, now or heretofore, has been improper, obnoxious, unbecoming, or detrimental to the best interests of racing, shall enter or remain upon the premises, and all such persons shall upon discovery or recognition be forthwith ejected." There is evidently a gang of escaped convicts roaming the state of Florida, ordering Steaks Well Done at race tracks, and West Palm Beach Jai-Alai wants no part of them.

Drug-crazed and addled, Murphy most properly and unobnoxiously watches Game Six, and the learning process begins. He is at first bewildered by the order in which teams play, but quickly understands that it's a round-robin process in which the losing team goes to the back of the line. So unless the teams lose in sequence, the logical succession of their numbers loses its meaning after Team 8 has played its first point.

He is also surprised by the fact that some points seem to be worth one point while others are worth two points. But on the obnoxious-and-improper page of the program he discovers a short story called "The Spectacular Seven": "This exciting system of scoring has become very popular. The game has eight teams and seven points are required to win. The first time each team appears on the court, the value of a point scored is *one*. Thereafter, each point is scored *two*. The result, of course, is that a team which is seemingly beaten in the later stages of the game has a better chance for a 'comeback' win. So never give up on your team."

Murphy may be severely lacking in sleep, may be in unfamiliar territory, may be subject to amphetamine strangeness, but he wasn't born yesterday. The real result, of course, is that West Palm Beach Jai-Alai can squeeze in a few extra games every night and greatly increase the number of losing two-dollar tickets on the floor. Murphy would like to beat this game. But the guys about to play Game Seven are not the same guys who played Game Six. This is not a little disturbing to Murphy because he's been toying with the notion of placing a small wager on Del Rio or Olabarri. He flips forward through the program. The new guys will be playing from now on.

He watches: These guys are better than the others. The points last longer; the shots seem more adventurous; the crowd becomes more involved, and much noisier.

Team 6—a Mutt-and-Jeff combination of Lasarte, very tall and strong in the backcourt, and Zaguirre, quite short and quick in the front court—demolishes Teams 5 and 7 in the space of a minute. Team 8 trots onto the court. Lasarte and Zaguirre change their tactics, throwing a series of high, arching shots that rebound off the back wall, there to be caught and returned by 8's sluggish backcourt man. 8's frontcourt man doesn't touch the ball once during what seems to Murphy to be several hundred exchanges. Finally the backcourt slug makes a weak return; Zaguirre rushes in, takes the ball on the fly off the front wall, and throws a monstrous shot whose flight off the rear wall is far beyond the slug's reach. 8's frontcourt man fields it on the bounce, makes a marvelous head fake that draws Zaguirre toward the screen, then throws a low line drive off the front wall. Lasarte is some twenty feet away when the ball takes its second bounce.

Team 1 uses the same strategy against 8, and this time it works. The slug drops the ball on the third exchange, and Team 8 goes to the back of the line possessing one point, just when each point starts to be worth two. Never give up on your team.

Murphy checks the program: Team 8's frontcourt man is named Elu; he is five feet, seven inches tall and Basque, but then practically everyone in the program is five feet, seven inches tall and Basque.

The game progresses. Several teams seem on the verge of the magical seventh point, only to throw the ball out of bounds or overserve at a crucial moment. Elu and the slug are resurrected.

Never give up on your team. Elu goes berserk, plucking a serve off the wall here, running backwards to cover the slug there, doing things that Murphy is quite unprepared for, beating the hell out of 7 and 2 and 4, and winning the game. There appears to be one Basque here who plays the game better than the other Basques, yet Team 8 pays a respectable $11.40 to win. Is it possible that they handicap Elu with a slug every time out? Could there be that many slugs?

Murphy will have to wait a while to find out, because Elu isn't scheduled to appear in the eighth game—which, to Murphy's considerable frustration, is a singles game. The bastards keep switching things around on him, bending over backwards to confuse him. But he's determined to bet, and to make a smart bet. The reasoning faculties are put into gear.

It comes down to Lejarcegui and Zaguirre, both of whom played well in Game Seven. Murphy guesses that a quick, sly frontcourt player should have the advantage in singles, and Zaguirre is a quick, sly frontcourt player. On the other hand, a quick, sly frontcourt player could be overpowered by a bigger stronger man, which Lejarcegui is. Murphy realizes that he's following an almost irrelevant line of thought, since Lejarcegui in post position two and Zaguirre in post position seven might not even play each other.

The public-address system tells him he has just five minutes before Game Eight. Murphy searches for the telling statistic that will make up his mind, and finds it. In 34 Game Eight appearances, Lejarcegui has won twice; in 44 Game Eight appearances, Zaguirre has won seven times.

He hurries up the aisle to the betting area with three minutes to go. The lines stretch to infinity. Is he going to get to a window in three minutes? If so, is he going to bet Zaguirre to win? To show? Perhaps to win, place, and show, across the board? To hell with it. He wanders over to the refreshment stand next to the Sala del Toro and orders a beer. Sipping, he notices an electronic scoreboard at the far end of the room. With two minutes to go, Zaguirre is at 8 to 5 and Lejarcegui is at 20 to 1. Nice odds on Lejarcegui, but he'll never win, and he'll probably pay $2.80 to show.

Murphy leans against the counter and has a conversation with himself. I don't need to bet, he says. Look at all those pathetic bastards lining up to lose their money. Never in their cumulative lives will they do what I did last night. No, it wasn't last night, was it? He rubs his eyes. The night before last? On some recent night I won a tremendous amount of money. Well into five figures. I don't need this penny-ante jai-alai bullshit. What I need is a place to spend the night, but if worse comes to worst I can . . .

The most beautiful woman Murphy has ever seen appears from stage left. She stops in front of him, four feet away. He sips his beer and stares at her as she studies her jai-alai program. What about her has smitten him? Is it her high cheekbones? Is it the suggestion of her breasts under a light sweater? Is it the utter perfection of her composition—a small person, a lithe young woman in blue jeans and sandals, dark brown hair to her shoulders? Is it because all the other women here are Doris Days gone to seed in pink pantsuits? Is it because he's been away from the hunt so long?

She proceeds. She has excellent buttocks. She stops at a line

Murphy hasn't noticed: one of three win-place-show windows at
the far right of the partition. All those fools are betting quinielas
and perfectas. He follows.

The man behind the window says, "Next," and Murphy says,
"Two."

"Two how?"

The number is Lejarcegui's the logic is nonexistent. "Two" is
simply what he felt compelled to say, and he feels foolish when
the closing odds drop to 7 to 1—especially foolish when Lejarcegui
looks oafish in losing the game's first point to Azpiri.

But no one takes command of the game. Lejarcegui's turn
draws nigh with no winner in sight. Never give up on your team.
Baranda overserves: Lejarcegui has won two points without
touching the ball. And so it goes.

Lejarcegui serves to Del Rio, who misjudges the ball and makes
a weak return that barely hits the front wall. Lejarcegui easily
puts him away.

Lejarcegui beats Egurbide, the 2–1 favorite, when Egurbide misses an easy put-away shot. This is his third double-point,
his fourth coming when Azpiri muffs the serve on game point.
Lejarcegui has seemed blessed by something—perhaps by Murphy, or perhaps they have some mutual blesser. In any case, they
have won, and Lejarcegui pays $27.80 across the board.

Murphy heads up the aisle to collect his winnings. As he hits the
discarded-pari-mutuel-ticket carpet he stops for a moment, having realized that his pulse rate is about to exceed the red line.
Are fatigue and amphetamines getting to him? Their participa-
tion cannot be denied, but he supposes that for the most part it's
jai alai getting to him, and he decides that it's funny. He's on
the verge of cardiac arrest over a six-dollar bet. Not forty hours
ago he put down a hundred times as much on a single card, without so much as a palpitation.

He collects his winnings and proceeds to the men's room,
where he relieves himself profusely. On the way out he is trans-
fixed by a pay telephone. He stands for the better part of a minute
staring at the phone, buffeted by men's-room traffic, trying to
remember why the presence of a telephone is important. Angela
Wilson. He finds her number in his pocket and dials it. The operator tells him to deposit sixty cents; he does so, and Angela

Wilson's number rings twenty times before he hangs up. He takes three steps toward the men's room exit, remembers, and retreats for his sixty cents.

Five minutes before post time for Game Nine, Murphy is back at the refreshment stand. He has bought another beer, he is studying the program, and he is hoping for the reappearance of the Beautiful Woman. The first event of what will prove to be a fortuitous chain is his discovery of Team 6: Elu and Lejarcegui. The sensation of Game Seven paired with the charmed winner of Game Eight—this can only be a message from the gods. And undoubtedly a message received by everyone in the house. Murphy checks the scoreboard: with four minutes to go, the odds on Team 6 are 7 to 1. It can't be true. Maybe everybody else knows something he doesn't know. Maybe Elu and Lejarcegui despise each other.

He sips his beer and waits. The odds flash again; Team 6 has gone to 8 to 1. Three minutes to go, no sign of the Beautiful Woman. But what's Murphy going to do if she does show up? Probably stand behind her in line and watch her walk away again.

She walks directly under the scoreboard and toward him. He is dazzled. When she is a few feet away their eyes meet. Hers are a light green. She stops at the same window as last time. Murphy stalks.

"You did okay on that one," the ticket seller says to her. He is a middle-aged man with a pleasant, florid face, and with the vestige of a foreign accent.

"It went pretty well," she says. "Give me six this time—across the board."

The seller punches out her tickets; she picks them up and hands him six dollars. He says "Good luck, Angie," she nods and departs.

Angie? Murphy watches her walk away again.

"Next," the seller says again. Murphy steps to the window. "Look," the seller says, "you want to watch the girls, that's okay, but there's people waiting to bet. . . ."

"Sorry," Murphy says. "Six to win, ten times," and he does something clever. He hands the seller a fifty-dollar bill. As the man makes change, Murphy says, "Her name wouldn't be Angela Wilson, would it?"

The seller slaps a ten and a twenty on the counter. "Tickets here, nothing else," he says, with a bit of a smile.

Murphy picks up his tickets and the twenty. "That's a tip," he says, nodding at the ten-dollar bill.

"Thanks," the seller says. Murphy stands there. "People waiting to bet," the seller says.

Murphy moves on, minus a fifty-percent surcharge on a twenty-dollar bet. By game time, the odds on Team 6 have dropped to 7 to 2.


He wanders back to his seat, the game already in progress. At this stage of consciousness, and at this stage in what seems to be a sustained winning streak, Murphy is prepared to be surprised by nothing. Were the Beautiful Woman in fact Angela Wilson, it would make perfect sense. He has nothing more than a moderately common name as hard evidence, and even that might have been misheard. Or wishfully heard. But the guy at the betting window didn't say she *wasn't* Angela Wilson. Murphy is convinced that his ten dollars weren't spent in folly.

He makes it to his seat in time to see Team 3 beat Team 2, after which 4 beats 3, and 5 beats 4. Enter Elu and Lejarcegui.

This might well be a sequel to the script of Game Seven but that Lejarcegui is no slug and there is little suspense. Again Elu doesn't get to touch the ball very often, but now Lejarcegui functions as more than a ball-return machine in the backcourt, enabling Elu to play less desperately. When Elu does see the ball he is magnificent, either luring his frontcourt opponent into a mistake or throwing a dazzling outright winner. Team 6 runs through the field without a loss, winning three single-points and two double-points. At 7 to 2, they'll pay at least nine dollars to win, which means a seventy-dollar profit for Murphy, tip excluded.

He endures a lengthy playoff for place and show, this one involving Teams 2 through 5 and taking longer than the game proper. He is pleasantly immune to the croaks and exhortations of the quiniela and perfecta addicts, looking forward to his payoff and an imminent meeting with the Beautiful Woman at the WPS cashier window.

Team 2 beats Team 5 for show after a brief but boring exchange, and at last the numbers flash on the tote board. 6 pays $9.80 to win, multiplied by ten tickets: ninety-eight dollars for Murphy.

He hustles up the aisle, hustles past the refreshment stand and the Sala del Toro. He doesn't want to miss her. The blue-haired lady behind the cashier window smiles and hands Murphy four twenties, a ten, a five, and three ones. He hands her back the three ones. "Well, *thank* you," she says in a raspy, chain-smoker's voice. Murphy flashes a beatific, winner's smile.

He waits. Game Ten is eight minutes away. Singles, with Elu again in position 6. He'd like to duck around the partition and check the odds, but he dares not leave. Six minutes away. He needs to go back to the bathroom, but he dares not leave. Five minutes. Maybe the Beautiful Woman collects her winnings only every other game, maybe she's left and will pick up her winnings tomorrow. Maybe she's not Angela Wilson.

With a shade under three minutes to go, she appears, again from the far side. Murphy's heart jumps. She walks to the blue-haired woman's window. Murphy moves slowly toward her. He watches her chat with the blue-haired woman; he expects she'll turn in the direction of the WPS windows and him, but she doesn't. She heads back toward the far side, which puts Murphy in the embarrassing role of chaser. He catches up with her and says, "Excuse me. . . ."

She stops and faces him. "My name is Murphy . . ." he says.

She appears mildly surprised, and says nothing.

"Are you Angela Wilson?" he says.

She makes a barely perceptible nod.

"I'm Ray Echaverria's friend. From New York."

Her eyebrows rise in recognition.

"He called you, yesterday afternoon, said I was coming down . . ."

"Oh yes," she says, "you're the poker player . . . the writer."

These are among the sweetest words Murphy has ever heard. "I tried to call you," he says.

"I didn't expect you so soon," Angela Wilson says. "You must have driven straight through . . ."

"I did," Murphy says.

"You must be exhausted. You look exhausted."

"I'm fine."

"If you'd like to go, I could give you my key and tell you how to get there . . ."

"No, really," Murphy says, "I'm okay. I'm fine." The public address system announces one minute to go. "I have to make a bet," Murphy says. "Will you sit with me?"

"Sure," Angela Wilson says, and they walk quickly around the partition.

The odds on Elu are 3 to 1 as Murphy addresses the man behind the window: "Six to win, five times." The man nods to Angela as he punches out Murphy's tickets.

"He's a friend of Ray's," Angela says. "His name is Murphy. This is Andy," she says, turning to Murphy.

Murphy nods at Andy. Andy says to Angela, "He's a nice guy. A big tipper."

They head for the game. "You realize you just brought the odds on Elu way down," Angela says.

"With a ten-dollar bet?"

"Nobody bets win, place, and show here."

"I've noticed that, but I didn't think ten dollars would mean much."

"You'll be lucky if Elu goes off at two to one."

They sit down just as the game begins. As in the last game, Murphy has no interest in the first four points, but it is evident that Angela does. She roots quietly for Orbe (position 2) against Roberto (position 1), and applauds briefly when Orbe wins the point. "You bet on Orbe?" Murphy asks.

"In the quiniela," Angela says.

Orbe loses to Aretio in position 3 on the following point, and again Angela claps briefly. "Your man lost," Murphy says.

"I have Aretio, too," Angela replies.

Aretio loses to Nuarbe in position 4. Angela sits in silence.

"You don't have Nuarbe," Murphy says.

"No."

Nuarbe faces Lopetegui in position 5, and Angela, almost to herself, says, "Come on, Lopey."

There seem to be an awful lot of people in her quiniela. Lopetegui dispenses of Nuarbe with one shot. Enter Elu. Murphy remembers that he's forgotten to check the final odds, looks up at the scoreboard: Elu has dropped to 9 to 5. The beautiful woman with the populous quiniela knows what she's talking about.

Lopetegui and Elu play an artful game of cat and mouse, Elu the cat, ever on the attack, Lopetegui the mouse, ever anticipating. Murphy is supremely confident that Elu will win, especially when Elu scoops up Lopetegui's bold line drive off the front wall on the short hop and throws a line drive of his own, with Lopetegui hopelessly out of position. But Elu's drive hits the front wall with a clank, having struck the topmost inch of out-of-bounds metal. Angela claps briefly.

"How could you bet against Elu?" Murphy asks.

"I didn't," Angela replies. During breaks between the three subsequent points she proceeds to explain that while Elu is by far and away the best player here, he is no more than an even bet to beat Lopetegui at singles. Thus, convinced that either 5 or 6 would score a lot of points and probably win the game, and that Orbe would beat Roberto, she has bet a 2-5 and a 2-6 quiniela. Not sure about what would happen between Orbe and Aretio, she has also bet a 3-5 and a 3-6 quiniela. As Lopetegui easily handles Lasarte in position 8, it appears that Angela's analysis is foolproof, and that Murphy has a lot to learn.

He is astonished to find himself abandoning the never-give-up-on-your-team philosophy as Lopetegui has a tough struggle with Roberto. If Roberto wins the first two-point point, Elu will almost undoubtedly come up again. But Murphy wants Lopetegui, and Angela, to win.

Roberto goes for Lopetegui's drive on the short hop, and drops it, and Lopetegui is one point away from victory. He puts Orbe away quickly with a two-wall shot, and Murphy applauds vigorously.

Angela says, "It's not over yet."

Indeed, while Lopetegui has won the game, Orbe and Aretio and Nuarbe have one point apiece, and Nuarbe has no place in Angela's quiniela.

Aretio makes quick work of Nuarbe, eliminating him and guaranteeing either a 2-5 or a 3-5 quiniela. Murphy grins at Angela and says, "You've won it!"

Angela displays only the hint of a smile. "Now we're for Aretio," she says.

"Why?" Murphy asks.

"Because a three-five's going to pay a lot more than a two-five."

Aretio, the tall, skinny backcourt man, overpowers Orbe in no time at all. Without premeditation, Murphy puts his arm around Angela's shoulder, hugs her, and gives her a kiss on the cheek. He becomes aware, as the excitement passes, that he's touching her for the first time, and touching her quite intimately. The sensation of his hand against her skin, his lips against her skin, is so intense as to imply a much further intimacy. Beyond that, he fears he may have overstepped his bounds, he may have done something dangerous. Angela neither responds nor withdraws; it is Murphy who moves away.

She beams as the scoreboard flashes QUINIELA: $48.00. She has won forty dollars; Murphy has lost ten.


"I'm sorry you didn't win," Angela says. They're on the way to the quiniela cashiers.

"No problem," Murphy says. "I'm still ahead."

"You've been betting all along?"

"Just the last three games . . ."

"How do you like it?"

"How do I like betting?"

"How do you like jai alai?"

"Oh, Jesus . . . It's great. I don't know what's going on, but I love it."

"That's good," she says.

Standing beside her, Murphy estimates that Angela is the three hundred and tenth person on line. "It goes quickly," she says.

Murphy feels a touch of claustrophobia. "I think I'm gonna go over there and try to figure out the next game," he says, nodding toward the nearly deserted WPS cashier windows.

"Okay," she says, "I'll see you there in a minute."

He walks dizzily around the quiniela lines to his former surveillance position. He opens the program to Game Eleven, has difficulty focusing, but spots Elu in position 7, with Baranda. That's too bad. He looks for Lopetegui and Zaguirre and Lejarcegui, but the large, bold letters begin to blur. He moves up against the wall, can't quite maintain equilibrium, and slowly slides into a squatting position. He closes his eyes for a moment, opens them to a sea of legs and pari-mutuel tickets.

His vision clears after a vigorous shake of the head. Lopetegui in position 8 with Lasarte . . . Zaguirre in 3 with Aretio . . . Lejarcegui in 2 with Azpiri. A quiniela seems in order here, in Angela's style: 2-7, 2-8, 3-7, and 3-8. But Baranda might be too much of a liability for Elu—another slug—and this is faster company than Game Seven.

Out of nowhere, Angela kneels next to him. "Are you all right?" she says.

"I'm fine," Murphy says. "I just thought I'd sit down for a while."

"You don't *look* fine," Angela says. "Your eyes look like strawberry sundaes."

"What's the matter with strawberry sundaes?" Murphy says, and to prove that he's fine he stands up, no hands. It's almost a virtuoso performance. He remains upright, but has to lean against the wall to do so.

"Do you have a first name?" Angela asks.

"Prosper," Murphy replies.

"Prosper," Angela says, "I think you could use some sleep."

"I probably could," Murphy agrees. "But I'm all right."

"Stay here for a minute," Angela says. "I'll be right back."

Murphy stays. No one has called him by his first name in months. He wonders how he's drifted into a state of one-namedness. He attempts a comprehensive catalogue of one-named people, comes up with Savonarola, Charlemagne, Charo, Liberace, Houdini. There must be more. Pele. Murphy walks a step, and another. Hannibal. He really *is* fine. He is, after all, the same person who several years ago drove from New York to Chicago, went to a concert and a party, drove back to New York, wrote an article about the concert and the party, delivered the article to a magazine, went to another concert, wrote an article about it, watched a movie on television, and went to bed. This little skein of sleep deprivation is a drop in the bucket. Would Ann-Margret count?

"Where's your car?" Angela asks, gently. She has reappeared, as beautiful as ever.

"Outside, in the lot," Murphy says, "but look, if this is any trouble, I'm really . . ."

"Prosper," Angela says, "it's no trouble. Andy's going to drive my car and drop it off. I don't want you to run into a palm tree and kill yourself. Okay?"

"Okay." Murphy has great regard for this woman.

It's a beautiful night. Angela drives Murphy's car down Military Trail, a deserted two-lane road several miles west of U.S. 1. She drives quite fast. There are long stretches of road with nothing to look at but stars, which is fine with Murphy.

"This is a nice car," Angela says.

"It is a nice car," Murphy replies.

"Does it cost a lot to take care of?"

"I don't know . . . I got it day before yesterday."

A brief silence.

"Ray has a BMW, doesn't he?"

"Yeah. . . . As a matter of fact, Ray's the reason I have a BMW. He took me over to the showroom, he introduced me to the salesman, I made a deal I thought was pretty good, and then Ray conned the poor son of a bitch out of most of his commission, or maybe all of it."

Angela smiles. "That sounds like Ray."

Another brief silence.

"How long have you known Ray?" Angela says.

"Since Saturday night," Murphy replies.

"This Saturday night?" Angela seems surprised.

"This Saturday night," Murphy says. "I met him at a poker game."

Yet another brief silence.

"How could you have driven all the way down here," Angela says, "with a radio that doesn't have any buttons?"

Murphy grins. "Angela," he says, "I love you."

Angela takes this with a grain of salt. "Why do you love me?"

"Because," Murphy says, "you know how important it is for a radio to have buttons." What might have been still another brief silence is extended when Murphy falls asleep.

He awakens to the sound of Angela's voice. She is not speaking to him. "This is Mr. Murphy's car," she says. "Mr. Murphy will be

staying in my apartment for a while . . ." Murphy opens his eyes
and sees that Angela is talking to a man wearing a khaki uniform
with a badge on its chest. The man is standing in what appears
to be a little guardhouse. ". . . A friend of mine is going to be
driving my car here. He should be getting here in an hour, and I
want you to let him in so he can park my car in my spot, and let
his wife in—she'll be driving their car—so he won't have to spend
the night in the garage. Okay?"

"Sure thing," says the man with the badge. "No problem at all,
Mrs. Wilson."

*Mrs.* Wilson? The way she talked to the guard, she must be
married to the warden. But would Echaverria steer Murphy to a
married woman? He might at that. On the other hand, it's con-
ceivable that Angela is the beneficiary of an affirmative-action
program and runs the place herself.

The BMW moves slowly down a long driveway and turns left.
Three tall, horseshoe-shaped buildings come into view. This is not
the Madera Beach Correctional Institution. On the contrary, Angela lives someplace opulent enough to have its own security force.

These immense buildings seem strikingly misplaced in a colony
of gas stations, low-slung shopping centers, and ranch-style
houses. In the dead of night they're eerily beautiful. Looking
around, Murphy can make out a swimming pool and what appears to be a tennis complex. He has evidently fallen directly
upon the lap of luxury.

"Nice place," he says.

"You're awake," Angela replies.

"Yeah," Murphy says, "I woke up when you were talking to the
receptionist back there. I wondered if you were taking me up to
the big house."

"I hate that nonsense," Angela says. "Every time I drive in or
out I feel obliged to smile and wave. Whenever people come over
I have to warn them that they're going to be stopped and inter-
rogated . . . It's really more trouble than it's worth."

"How, uh . . . does it happen that you live here?" Murphy
ventures.

"It was convenient for my husband." Angela's tone is brusque.

Murphy lurches on. "You're not still married?"

"No," she says in the same tone, "divorced."

"Me too," Murphy says, for what it's worth.

Angela pulls the car in between a Lincoln Continental and a huge Mercedes. "This is where you have to park," she says, indicating the general area. "They have your license number at the gatehouse. If you park anywhere else, they'll start leaving notes under your windshield wiper, and after they do that they'll start calling me at seven in the morning."

"I'll be good," Murphy says, imagining that Echaverria must have parked on the tennis court.

He gathers his suitcase, his paper bag, and his five-pack of Genesee. On the way he asks, "Why do you stay here?"

He is surprised by the extent of Angela's reply: "Because I'm used to it . . . because once you get used to knowing that you're under surveillance all the time, and that your neighbors all voted for Nixon, it's not a bad place. And because it's convenient for me, too."

The explanation seems a bit practiced, a bit glib, but Murphy considers the last two years of his stretch in the Upper West Side mausoleum and decides to pursue this line of questioning no further.


Angela's apartment is 914-C, at the southeastern tip of the horseshoe, on the top floor. She must hold the record for Fewest Items of Furniture, Luxury Condominum Living Room. The room, which is actually a combination living room–dining room, contains a small Danish modern table with two Danish modern chairs, a brown leather couch and Danish modern coffee table, a Danish modern leather armchair, and a modest mahogany bookcase which supports several books and a tiny Sony television. The room, perhaps a third the size of the mausoleum's living room, appears to have twice as much open space. At the far end of the room, glass doors lead to a deck; just to the right of the front door there is a semi-enclosed kitchen, as cluttered with appliances as the living/dining room is empty of furniture. Murphy guesses that the appliances came with the apartment.

He puts his beer in the freezer, where its only company is an icemaker.

"Are you in the habit of freezing your beer?" Angela asks.

"I thought we might drink a couple," Murphy says.

"I have to get up at seven o'clock," Angela says, "and you need to sleep for about two days."

"What the hell," Murphy reasons, "if we'd stayed for the last two games we wouldn't even be here yet."

Angela smiles slightly. "We didn't stay for the last two games, though."

"But you would have if you'd been alone, right?"

"That's beside the point. Prosper, look, you need some *sleep* . . ."

"I just had some. I'm ready to go."

Angela shrugs and says, "I have to go to the bathroom. Let's get your stuff put away."

She picks up the paper bag, he the suitcase, and he follows her down a short hallway. There are three doors: two across from each other halfway down, one at the end. Angela opens the door on the right. "This is your room," she says, and points to the door on the left. "That's your bathroom." She waves and heads for the door at the end of the hall, shutting it behind her. She hasn't said good night, which might be a good sign or a bad sign.

Murphy puts his toothbrush, toothpaste, razor, deodorant, and his last Dexedrine capsule in the medicine cabinet. He crosses the hall to his bedroom and begins hanging articles of clothing in the closet. This is efficiency born purely of anxiety. Five minutes later, he's run out of things to hang up. He sits on his small bed and notes that his small bedroom is as sparsely furnished as the living room: the bed, a little chest next to it upon which sit a lamp and a small electric clock. Nothing more. He pulls the drape open, finds another glass door to the deck, and is in the process of walking outside when Angela appears, in robe and slippers.

"I'd like to have a beer with you," she says, "but we should both get some sleep."

"I have plenty of time to sleep," Murphy says. He stands in his doorway, Angela stands in hers. From the deck comes a flicker of warm breeze.

"How did you know me?" Angela asks.

"What?" Murphy says, ingenuous.

"At jai alai . . . how did you know who I was?"

Oh . . . *Jesus*, Murphy says to himself. He sets about searching for a quick, clever explanation and quickly decides that if
there's ever been a time for the truth, this is it.

"I was leaning against the hot dog stand before the eighth
game," Murphy says, "and I saw one of the most beautiful
women I'd ever seen walk up to Andy's window. I was tremendously attracted to you. After the game, I tried to telephone
you. I didn't have a place to stay, and I didn't really have a
chance for a place to stay if I couldn't get you, but I almost
hoped you wouldn't answer because I was so turned on by the
woman I'd seen at Andy's window. I waited for you to come
back, and you did, and I heard Andy call you Angie, and I
gave him a ten-dollar tip to find out if you were you, and he
wouldn't say yes, but he wouldn't say no. So I figured you *were*
you, and you were."

After a while, Angela says, "You're not making that up, are
you?"

"No," Murphy says. "I cross my heart."

"Well . . ." she says.

"I'm glad I came," he says.

"I'm glad you like jai alai," she says.

He takes a step toward her. "I have to go to sleep," she says.
He stands before her. She says, "Good night" and reaches up to
give him a little kiss on the cheek. She is out of the room and
down the hall when Murphy replies, "Good night."


Murphy stands by the railing on the deck. At a few minutes
before one, it's still pleasantly warm. And preposterously quiet.
The deck overlooks a narrow body of water, probably the Inland Waterway. Over the last half hour, Murphy has been
aware of only two sounds. One is constant and subtle—it being
the Atlantic Ocean, at most a mile away. The other is erratic
and weird. At irregular intervals there is a loud and startling
*plop* from the water directly below. Moonlight makes the water
vaguely visible, but Murphy so far has been unsuccessful at
spotting what must be a very large aquatic creature.

He finishes his Genesee and starts toward the kitchen for
another, but decides to wait a while for the creature's next leap.

He waits an eternity, perhaps three minutes, before his beer craving overcomes his curiosity. Two steps along, not even into the living room, he hears the *plop*. He curses and continues to the kitchen, where he removes four nicely chilled cans from the freezer, puts three in the refrigerator, and keeps one for himself.

Back on the deck, he renews the vigil in earnest, waiting the creature out. He doesn't have to wait long. His eyes happen to be focused directly upon the spot from which the immense beast emerges—on first viewing it is huge and dark and shaped like a gigantic bird.

A few seconds later it surfaces again a few feet away, then again and again, as if doing a little Inland Waterway ballet for Murphy's benefit, as if telling him, "All right, asshole, you wanted to see me? Here I am!" The creature is nothing more or less than a manta ray—a gigantic fish, but quite a benign one, except to fishes of inferior stature, which it eats.

The waterway reverts to stillness. Murphy sits cross-legged on the chairless deck.

He has spent some nine hundred consecutive nights in the company of several thousand strangers—a revolving cast of unknowns whose yells, screams, and bursts of piercing laughter, whose horns, sirens, and screeching brakes have awakened him from sound sleep, have deadened his conversations, have taken him from his typewriter and, at their or his extremes, made him want to hide under something. Now, for no apparent reason, he has been transported to a place of encompassing quietness and warmth, and is a right and left turn away from someone who has completely beguiled him.

Murphy concentrates on the sound of the Atlantic. This is where he'll swim tomorrow, this is his late-night motif. He is startled anew by a gargantuan offering from the manta ray. Whether the ray serves as leitmotif or as an intruder in Murphy's opera is unclear, but Murphy proceeds to his private room and sleeps blissfully.

# 7

# Pale Fire

Ramon Echaverria considers himself basically a pragmatist, and something of a conservative. The fact that he deals regularly in a substance which is illicit, and which is associated in this era with much of the romantic bravado bullshit applied to alcoholic beverages in a previous era, does not alter his self-image. If anything, his affiliation with cocaine and all the people he encounters day to day, all the desperado dealers, all the would-be mafiosi or actual mafiosi, all the death-wish hustlers, not to mention all the pretentious assholes who actually *buy* the stuff, has probably caused him to become more the way he is. He believes in certain things. For instance, he has a profound sense of honor: he will not cheat anyone, and he will kick the shit out of anyone who cheats him. The latter quality is common in his trade; the former is unusual, and has rewarded Echaverria with a regular and well-heeled clientele, most of which he despises. He avoids socializing with the upwardly mobile poltroons who buy his merchandise, but has on occasion slept with their wives.

He lives for the most part on his own island, tolerating the rest of the world and sometimes enjoying the designs of his tolerance, more often retreating into the certain things he believes in.

He lives on the top floor of a brownstone on Jane Street, in Greenwich Village. By normal standards, his apartment is expensive, almost luxurious, at five hundred dollars a month, but for someone as successful as Echaverria in the cocaine trade it is spartan. The apartment has four rooms, three of which are hardly furnished. His bedroom contains a bed and a radio and a clock, his living room a table and chairs and a couch, a ten-year-old television and a record player, his kitchen a stove, sink, and thirty-year-old refrigerator. The fourth room is cluttered. Its furniture is limited: an old rolltop desk and chair, a decrepit sofa, a cast-iron floor lamp. But the room is stuffed with *things*—piles of old magazines and newspapers, stacks of record albums. And the walls are covered with memorabilia—a diploma, several framed jai-alai posters, and many aged photographs of men in berets, men in military uniforms. One particular photograph, larger than the others, encased in a gilt frame, hangs above the desk. It shows a beaming couple: the man bears a goodly resemblance to Echaverria and a wide smile; the woman is quite beautiful, but seems frightened.

Echaverria is never awake at two A.M. without a reason, and tonight he's expecting company. He sits on the living room couch reading Vladimir Nabokov's *Pale Fire* for the sixth or seventh time. Echaverria has read everything Nabokov has written, most of it at least twice, and claims to despise him. He has no doubt that Nabokov is the best American writer of the twentieth century, but believes that Nabokov has spent the better part of the twentieth century jerking off, with *Pale Fire* the supreme jerk-off. An old acquaintance and occasional client of Echaverria's teaches English at Columbia; the two of them have spent several hundred hours over the years discussing Nabokov, to whom Echaverria will refer in the acquaintance's presence only as Vladimir Dzherkov. "If you hate him so much," the acquaintance will ask, "why do you spend so much time reading his goddamned books?" To which Echaverria will reply, "Look, it'd be one thing if he was fuckin' around with me and I didn't know it, like you. But I know it, and that old cocksucker *knows* I know it."

The buzzer sounds. Echaverria puts *Pale Fire* aside and presses the button that opens the front door four stories below. He then vaults down the stairs in time to meet his visitor before she's finished hauling her two large suitcases in the door. He speaks to her in Spanish: "Sofia, you don't know how good it is to see you." He embraces her before she has a chance to say anything. Her body seems colder than a ten-second trip from taxi to door would merit. "Did it go all right?" he asks.

"Yes, Ramon," she says, "but please don't ask me to do it again. Not so much. It frightens me."

He hugs her again. "This time was special. You won't have to do it again."

Echaverria carries her bags upstairs, Sofia follows. Despite his being the one carrying the load, he must stop for her at each landing.

Inside the apartment, Echaverria removes Sofia's coat, revealing a stewardess's uniform. He urges her to have a seat on the couch, and she complies. Sofia is a youngish woman with olive skin, broad, Indian features, and light brown hair. Echaverria brings her a glass of brandy and says, "Tell me how it went."

"It was perfect," Sofia says. "I told Maria and Dolores I was waiting for someone. I waited until they left, I rented the car, I drove to where you told me, the man gave me the suitcase, I gave him the money, and I drove away. But then I was always afraid someone was following me, or that I would have an accident and . . ."

"But no one followed you?"

"No. I left the car where you said, and I called for the taxi, and I told the driver to go around the block, and no one followed. So I picked up the suitcase and we came here."

"And you gave him a big tip?"

"Twenty dollars."

"Sofia, I love you," Echaverria says.

"For what I do," Sofia replies.

Echaverria smiles and shakes his head. He sits down beside her, kisses her, and begins undressing her.

"Ramon," Sofia whispers, implying both resignation and anticipation.

Echaverria removes her upper garments and spends a minute kissing her breasts, as Sofia leans against the sofa back. He unhooks her skirt, pulls its top to the sofa cushion, and lifts her body with his left hand as he draws the skirt off with his right. Now he kneels in front of her and peels off her pantyhose and panties.

"Ramon," Sofia whispers again.

Echaverria kisses and licks her inner thighs, moving progressively upward until he reaches the central point of her body, whence he begins licking her clitoris, at first quite slowly, accelerating gradually to a furious pace, Sofia breathing all the more heavily and repeating his first name with increasing frequency, until finally she arches, clasps his shoulders between her legs, squeezes him thus for fifteen seconds, and collapses. Echaverria picks her up and carries her into the bedroom, places her gently on the bed. He removes his own clothing and joins Sofia on the bed, straddling her upper torso so his buttocks are over her chest, his penis rigid above her mouth. She grasps it in both hands, murmuring, as if on the brink of a lullaby, and draws it down to her lips. "That's perfect," he whispers. "Perfect. My little angel." He closes his eyes, his body tensed, head pointed toward the ceiling, as she engorges him, and he feels the first throbbing signal of conclusion. He pulls away, waits half a minute, slides his body down, enters her, and maneuvers within her until she comes again. Then, at last, he allows himself that luxury.

"This is why I do it," Sofia says, several minutes later, "not for the money."

Echaverria kisses her between the breasts. "How long will you stay this time?" he says softly.

"Only tonight," she says. "I go back to Bogotá in the afternoon."

"You should spend more time with me, Sofia."

"You know I can't, Ramon . . . and I think you like it this way . . ."

"Sofia, if you weren't already married, I'd come to Bogotá and live with you."

"You're a wonderful liar," Sofia says, smiling.

They are both aware of that. This is going to be a busy day, and Echaverria knows full well the precise hour of Sofia's return flight. He can recite the rather limited schedule between Bogotá and New York backwards. He caresses Sofia's thighs.

"I'm exhausted, Ramon," she says.

"Once more?" he whispers.

"In the morning," she says.

He waits until she's in a deep sleep, a courtesy, before getting out of bed and opening the smaller but considerably heavier of the suitcases. Inside it are twenty plastic bags, each containing a kilo of white powder. Echaverria selects three bags at random and takes a tiny taste from each. He is pleased that it seems to be uncut. These forty-four pounds of cocaine have cost him a lot of money: close to fifty thousand dollars, more than half of which has gone to persuade various Colombians and Americans to take part in a very complicated series of events. This is by far the largest shipment Echaverria has ever received, by far the largest amount of money he's ever risked, but the scheme had only two possible flaws: could he count on Sofia to use the twenty thousand dollars he'd given her for the wholesale purchase, or would she and Umberto buy a house in the suburbs? Could he count on the baggage supervisor at Kennedy, whose take was a mere thousand dollars, to set the suitcase aside, circumvent customs, and be waiting for Sofia by the Air France freight area at the appointed time? He had little doubt concerning Sofia, and not much more about the baggage man, who'd been enticed with promises of future deals of the same magnitude, and who certainly didn't have the guts or the connections to move the stuff himself.

Echaverria sits on the floor of his living room surrounded by enough cocaine to keep every member of, and everyone connected with, every rock and roll group in the world high for a week. Sold by the ounce in its current state, his twenty kilos would net over eight hundred thousand dollars. Were it sold by the gram in its current state, that figure would more than double. Had Echaverria the time, the employees, or the desire to cut it and sell it in dribs and drabs, the contents of Sofia's suitcase would eventually be worth over five million dollars.

Echaverria has none of the above. He is in fact about to get out of the cocaine business, and will be content with a profit of between 400 and 800 percent.


He sleeps in fits and starts, awakening to every street noise and to Sofia's every unconscious movement. When awake, he runs through his timetable over and over. There is a great deal to be done during the next few days.

Sofia stirs just after dawn, and they make love the better part of an hour. Sofia goes back to sleep; Echaverria gets up and takes a shower, then makes eleven telephone calls. His first meeting will be at four o'clock this afternoon.

He takes Sofia to lunch at a French restaurant on East 54th Street. The headwaiter greets him as an old friend. They sit at the best table in the house. They have a sumptuous five-course meal. The check comes to a hundred and ten dollars, and Echaverria leaves a fifty-dollar tip.

He drives Sofia back to the airport, parks in front of the terminal, takes her two featherweight cases from the trunk.

"I could see you next week," she says.

"I won't be in town."

"The week after that, then."

"Sofia," Echaverria says, "I have to go away for a while. I don't know when I'll be back, but I'll be in touch with you. I promise."

"I don't believe you."

"It's the truth." He hugs her and kisses her neck. "Look, somebody would have to be very crazy if he told the most beautiful woman in Colombia he didn't want to see her again."

"You don't say it," Sofia says, "but I'm afraid you mean it."

"I swear to you on my life," Echaverria says. He summons a porter and hands him a five-dollar bill, directs him to take Sofia's luggage to the Avianca counter. He embraces her again, and hands her a thousand-dollar bill.

"Ramon," she says, "you've already paid me."

"Not enough, Sofia," he says.

Echaverria heads for the Queens-Midtown Tunnel well above the speed limit. He's got a lot to do, and not much time to do it.

# 8

# Françoise Dorléac

At his moment of waking, Murphy sits up abruptly in bed and looks around, as if to prevent the sudden metamorphosis of this small, sunny room to his vast, somber bedroom in New York. It stays the same. He really is in Florida, with close to twelve thousand dollars in his pocket and a green BMW properly parked outside.

He pays a quick visit to the bathroom, puts on his pants, and returns to the deck. It's a beautiful day, warm and cloudless, and Murphy is enthralled by the tableau before him. The waterway below, a dark blue, is flanked on this side by palm trees, on the opposite side by a small pine forest. To the southeast, above the pines, the blue-green Atlantic merges with the pure blue sky. More reason for Angela to have stayed here.

The kitchen clock reads 11:20; Murphy hasn't slept more than nine hours in years. On the counter between kitchen and living room he finds a note and a pair of keys. He reads: "Little key is for door to bldg. Big key is for door to apt. Sorry there isn't much in refrig., but help yourself to what's there. I'll be back late aft. Angela."

The refrigerator contains three eggs, two chicken breasts, three cans of Genesee, a half-gallon jug of orange juice, and a half-gallon jug of grapefruit juice. This is fine with Murphy, who is repelled by the concept of a well-balanced breakfast. He removes some grapefruit juice and makes a brief, unsuccessful search for drinking implements among the kitchen's several hundred cupboards. Holding the jug with both hands, he slurps down a pint of grapefruit juice.

Someone has mistaken his car for an oven and set it at two hundred and fifty degrees. Murphy rolls down all the windows and rolls back the sunroof. He drives to the guardhouse, where he is given a decal to stick on his windshield. The decal says: WATERWAY COVE GUEST No. 13854. The decal is shaped like a manta ray.

Murphy has intended to turn right on Waterway Boulevard and take it west to U.S. 1, to buy a newspaper and a sandwich and go to the beach. But he can smell the ocean, the car is still oppressively hot, and what the hell. He turns left, and a minute later he's in the parking lot of the Madera Beach public beach. He changes clothes in the car and walks to the beach, towel in hand.

Upon sighting the placid surf he begins to run, then to sprint, dropping the towel a few feet from the ocean, then sprawling into the water. His timing is such that an almost imperceptible wave meets him headlong, ceasing his momentum and giving him a nose full of seawater. He stands up, shakes his head, blows his nose, dives back into the ocean, and begins swimming in the general direction of Europe. He swims vigorously and compulsively, straight ahead, for a good while. Then he stops; out of breath, he treads water and looks back at the shore, five or six hundred yards away. He experiences a moment of panic. It's been three years since he's swum more than the length of a backyard pool, and here he finds himself a third of a mile from shore. He closes his eyes and floats for a couple of minutes, waiting for his lungs to restore themselves. When they do, he swims laterally south for another hundred yards until he is painfully breathless. At that point he begins moving slowly back toward the beach, letting the ocean carry him naturally, inevitably back to earth.

After ten minutes on the beach, Murphy's lungs have stopped burning, his heart has resumed its mundane rhythm, and he longs for a newspaper. He sets about imagining what Angela looks like with her clothes off. This proves to be briefly erotic, but frustrating. He concentrates instead on jai alai: first on the sounds . . . the ball cracking off the front wall, thocking off the

floor, popping into the wicker appendage. He recalls his exhila-
ration after Elu's final shot in Game Nine; he sees Elu advancing
on the ball in the frontcourt, making a head fake, throwing the
two-wall carom shot. He wonders what Angela's breasts are like.
The ocean ebbs and flows, the sun shines, Murphy reclines
amidst tropical paradise, hungry and horny and bored stiff. He
gets up and heads for the car.

West of the beach, west of Waterway Cove, the heart of
Madera Beach is indistinguishable from the hearts of Vero
Beach, Riviera Beach, Boynton Beach, or any of the other little
nontowns which together form a gargantuan megasuburb running from the northern limits of Miami up to Fort Pierce. The
heart of Madera Beach is a three-mile strip of U.S. 1 that seems
to contain every franchised business known to the United States,
or at least those involving gasoline, hamburgers, fried chicken,
tacos, groceries, and beds for the night.

As hungry as he is, Murphy doesn't want to settle for junk
food. He drives Madera Beach's length southward, searching for
something at least a little out of the ordinary, but comes up
empty, makes a U-turn, and almost gives up. Half a mile from
his starting point, perilously close to the local McDonald's, he
turns into an immense shopping center whose headliners are
J. C. Penney, Montgomery Ward, and Firestone. Murphy drives
up this aisle and down the next, past pet stores and shoe stores
and bookstores and drugstores and record stores, and everything
a resident of Florida in 1973 could possibly want or need, except a good place to eat.

He's talking himself into a quarter-pounder with cheese when
he sees Fat Lou's Philly Subs tucked in between Pets Galore
and Shoes Unlimited. There is nothing in the world that would
please Murphy more right now than a pepper steak submarine
sandwich.

Indeed, it's right up there on the board: #19 Steak with
Green Peppers & Cheese. Murphy orders a Lg. #19 and asks
the quite attractive blond teenager behind the counter where he
might find a newspaper. She directs him to a vending machine
five doors down, in front of First American Savings & Loan,
where he buys a copy of the *Fort Lauderdale News*.

Murphy retreats to an empty booth with his pepper steak, his
small root beer, and his *News*. The sandwich is good, the Knicks

have won handily, Walt Frazier scoring thirty-seven points, the Rangers have won narrowly, Gilbert with a goal and an assist. Such pleasure.

Now to the Baskin-Robbins four doors away, whence he emerges presently with a Jamoca almond fudge sugar cone, takes a hard look at First American Savings & Loan, and thinks about his money. It's in the car, still in his inside jacket pocket. Since his conversation with Echaverria, Murphy hasn't given much thought to the money, and it occurs to him now that it might be considered irresponsible to leave twelve thousand dollars in one's unlocked car. Murphy considers Echaverria's advice. Who knows but that in the next few days or weeks he may in fact find something he wants to buy? If so, what *is* the point of letting the United States know he's won a bundle in a poker game? On the other hand, there's bound to be an unnecessary quantity of anxiety if he stuffs the money in a shoe or under his mattress.

Finishing off his Jamoca almond fudge, Murphy finds himself in the sort of stalemate that's plagued him over the years. He has twelve thousand dollars, which itself is undeniably a good thing. His strong urge tells him to walk a hundred feet to First American Savings & Loan, hand over the money, and be done with it. Nothing to worry about, the money's safe, it's earning interest, and he can withdraw it any time he wants. But Echaverria's disgust sits on Murphy's mind—it's *free money*, so why the hell should be give a quarter or a third of it to the government? Had this twelve thousand dollars remained in the pockets it came from, the IRS would certainly never see a penny of it.

If his brief acquaintance with Echaverria has taught Murphy anything, it's to avoid the stalemate by acting decisively, to treat the rest of the world the way he handles his opponents in a poker game.

As he swallows the last morsels of cone, Murphy hits on the solution. It is so simple he's surprised it hasn't occurred to him earlier.

First American Savings & Loan has been created either by a Young Republican whose whiskey sour was spiked with a malignant hallucinogenic, or by someone with a vicious dislike of savings and loan establishments. The floor is covered by a pink shag carpet; the walls are in slightly different shades of blue pastel; the desks and counters are made of white molded plastic; the tellers, all young women, wear pink uniform dresses with white racing stripes, and cleavage. This must be where the Chamber of Commerce holds its bimonthly orgy.

"Can I help you, sir?" The voice belongs to LuAnne, according to the plastic nameplate on her chest. LuAnne is not in uniform, but has huge breasts and cleavage nonetheless.

"I'm thinking about opening an account," Murphy says.

"Why don't you come with me?" LuAnne suggests, and Murphy follows her several feet to her white plastic desk.

"Passbook, or certificate of deposit?" LuAnne asks after they've sat down across from each other.

"The kind where you can withdraw the money any time you want," Murphy says.

"Passbook," LuAnne says with unctuous certainty. "All right, then. I'm going to ask you some questions." She rolls a piece of paper into her white plastic typewriter. "Full name?"

"Walter Frazier," Murphy says.

"No middle name?" LuAnne asks.

"Two, actually," Murphy says, "but I don't use them."

"I know what you mean," LuAnne says, grinning like a lunatic. "Address?"

Murphy gives LuAnne Angela's address, which seems practical and undangerous. Everything else he tells her is fictional, right on down to the final question.

"Mother's maiden name?"

Murphy is intrigued by this. "Why do you need to know my mother's maiden name?" he asks.

"Well," LuAnne responds brightly, "Like if you lose your passbook and somebody picks it up they can come in and withdraw off your account, you know, and we ask them for their ID, and like if they stole your wallet too, then we would ask them for their mother's maiden name, and they wouldn't possibly know your mother's maiden name, right?"

"What if I had my mother's maiden name written in my wallet?"

"Well, they wouldn't know it was your mother's maiden name, would they?"

"I have it written on a card," Murphy says in all earnestness, "in case I forget it. On one side it says, 'Mom's maiden name,' and if you turn the card over, there's her name."

"You're puttin' me on," LuAnne says.

"Cross my heart," Murphy replies.

"Why do you need to remember your mom's maiden name, anyway?" LuAnne asks.

"Because there's always a chance somebody in a savings and loan might think I look suspicious," Murphy says.

"I don't believe you," LuAnne says. "Show me the card."

"I don't have my wallet with me," Murphy says.

Throughout their conversation, even during its latter stage, LuAnne's facial expression has never diminished beyond a mild smile, which Murphy has come to accept as permanent. But now it drops into something approaching a frown. "Then you don't have your driver's license," LuAnne says.

"Right," Murphy says.

"Then you can't open an account."

"Why not?"

"Well, if we're gonna clear your check, we have to know who you are . . ."

"I don't have a check," Murphy says. "I have cash."

"Well, Mr. Frazier," LuAnne says, and stands up, "I'll have to talk to Mr. Trough about this. Excuse me."

She returns in short order with a man just short of middle age. He has a pot belly, grotesquely styled collar-length orange hair, and wears a red-and-white checked leisure suit, with white belt and shoes. If this man had been seen on the streets of Madera Beach five years ago he'd have been drawn and quartered, but times have changed.

"Mr. Frazier," he says, "I'm John Trough." Trough extends his hand. They shake, and Trough leads Murphy back to a prominently placed white plastic desk.

"They call you Walt?" Trough asks.

"Sure," Murphy says.

Trough ruminates. "There's a basketball player by that name, isn't there? Plays for New York."

"I don't follow basketball," Murphy says.

"Well, no matter then," Trough says. "You can call me John, Walt." Murphy nods, and Trough scans the form LuAnne has filled out. "The girl told me you didn't have any identification with you, Walt."

"That's right," Murphy says.

"And you were hopin' to open an account with cash?"

"Right."

"Well, I'll tell ya, Walt . . . normally, even with cash, we like to see a little somethin', like a Florida driver's license . . ."

"I'm afraid I don't have one of those."

"Or an out-of-state license?"

"No, I never have gotten around to driving."

"You just walked up here from Waterway Cove?"

"I sure did. It's a nice walk over here."

Trough gives a little whistle. "Better part of four miles, I'd say."

"That sounds about right."

"Well, Walt, how you choose to get around's your own business, and if you plan to walk all over Madera Beach, I say more power to ya. But that still leaves us with a problem." He pauses, looks down at his desk, and then locks eyes with Murphy. "How much were you plannin' to deposit?"

"Ten thousand dollars," Murphy says.

"Ten thousand dollars, cash," Trough says.

"Cash," Murphy says.

Trough looks at his desk again. "I guess," he says, "that we could forget about the identification for now. But I sure would appreciate it if you could bring some by. You have a major credit card?"

"All of them," Murphy says.

"Well, that would do fine," Trough says. He scans the form again. "We're still gonna need your mother's maiden name."

"Ah, right," Murphy says. "Françoise Dorléac."

"French, huh?" Trough says. "Could you spell that?"

Murphy spells Françoise Dorléac while counting out hundred-dollar bills. He hands Trough ten thousand dollars.

"Just to satisfy my curiosity," Trough says, "how do you happen to be walkin' around with ten thousand in cash?"

"You probably won't believe this," Murphy says, "but I won it in a poker game."

# 9

# Going Out
# of Business

Echaverria leaves the elevator on the thirty-fifth floor of a building on Sixth Avenue, several blocks south of Central Park. He
carries a suede attache case that nicely matches his suede jacket
and pants. He enters the anteroom to an office and waves to an
attractive young blond woman behind a desk. She wears a
diaphanous silk blouse, a great deal of makeup, a great deal of
jewelry.

Echaverria says, "How ya doin', Chris?"

"Pretty good," she replies with a shrug.

Echaverria tosses a tiny envelope on her steel and walnut desk.
Chris picks it up and rubs it between her fingers. "What's this
for?" she asks, surprised.

"It's a free sample."

"How come?"

"Because I can see your tits."

"You've seen them before . . ."

"Yeah, but it was dark."

Chris slips her finger into the envelope and rummages inside
it. "Jesus, there's about three grams in here."

Echaverria smiles.

Chris removes her finger, wets it, puts it back in the envelope,
and licks off the white powder. She sits in consideration for a

few seconds, as if tasting wine, and says, "Ray, this is fantastic stuff . . . this would cost me about five hundred bucks . . ."

"It's a bribe," Echaverria says.

"You don't need to bribe *me*," Chris replies.

"It's a present," Echaverria says.

"Ray, you're one crazy bastard," Chris says. She picks up her phone and presses a button. "Barry," she says into the phone, "Ray's here, and if I were you I wouldn't give a shit who's on the other line." She listens for a second or two and replaces the phone. "You can go right in, sir," she says to Echaverria. Echaverria nods and starts toward the inner office. "Wait a minute, Ray," Chris says. Echaverria stops; she comes out from behind the desk and gives him a hug. "Thanks," she whispers in his ear.

"My pleasure," Echaverria says.

"Let's see each other more often," Chris says.

"I've got a meeting," Echaverria says. "I'll see you in a few minutes."


The inner office is furnished with a carpet so deep and thick that a rabbit couldn't cross it without a machete, with an opulent, eight-foot tan leather sofa, and several matching chairs. The walls are lined with replicas of 33⅓ r.p.m. records in gold and platinum. Behind a much larger version of Chris's desk sits a man of about forty. He is small and somewhat pudgy, wears what appears to be a very expensive French suit, and has on his head what appears to be a salt-and-pepper permanent-wave Afro.

"Good to see ya, Ray, baby," he says exuberantly, shaking Echaverria's hand. "Watcha got?" He hands a tiny spoon to Echaverria, who dips it into another tiny envelope and hands it back. Barry places the spoon under his right nostril, his left index finger against his left nostril, and snorts mightily. He sits down. Thirty seconds later he says, "Not bad."

"Not bad," Echaverria repeats, nodding. "Look, Lipschitz, that's the best shit you've ever tasted, and it's the best shit you'll ever taste, and you know it."

Lipschitz smiles cunningly at Echaverria. "This is your way of telling me prices have gone up."

"You know I don't fuck around," Echaverria says.

"Okay," Lipschitz says, "so tell me what's happening."

"It's a sale," Echaverria says, "to certain preferred customers, but only if they buy in quantity."

"Like what kind of quantity?"

"By the pound."

Lipschitz jerks his head. "What the fuck am I gonna do with a pound of cocaine?"

"The same thing you do with an ounce, only it'll last sixteen times as long, and it'll be a hell of a lot cheaper."

"How much cheaper?"

"We'll talk about that."

"Ray," Lipschitz says after a while, "I'm not big on ready cash, you know . . ."

"Make me an offer."

"You in some kinda trouble?"

"No, I'm not in any kind of fuckin' trouble. I'm offerin' you a one-time-only deal, and you'd be an asshole to turn it down."

"A pound, huh?" Lipschitz says, and engages in some quick multiplication. "I could come up with five grand . . ."

"Be serious, Barry," Echaverria says.

Lipschitz throws his hands in the air. "I *wanna* be serious, Ray, but this is a hell of a lot of bread we're talkin' about."

"You just put the word out, Barry. You tell your friends. You know you couldn't get this quality for fifteen hundred an ounce, right?"

"Yeah, I guess . . ."

"Fuck that, you *know* it. You multiply fifteen hundred by sixteen, you get twenty-four thousand, and I'm prepared to sell you a pound of this for twelve thousand, two pounds for twenty, three pounds for twenty-eight. Okay?"

"Sure. Okay."

"Does that seem like a good deal?"

"Yeah, sure. It sounds like a great deal."

"All right. Get back to me tonight or tomorrow night. If I'm not in, keep calling, 'cause if you don't get it, somebody else is gonna get it. Okay?"

"Okay."

# 10

# Murphy Grows Up

At a point perhaps midway through the first grade it occurred to Murphy, who was a bright, perceptive child, that in an area very important to six-year-olds he was quite different from his peers. His name was Prosper. He was called that at home and by his teachers, but to his classmates he quickly became "Murph." At six, Murphy's concern was not with the irony of a situation in which all his friends were diminuted by the addition of a "y" to their first names while he was by the subtraction of the same letter from his last. His question, as first presented to his father, was, "Daddy, why don't I have a name like all the other kids?"

Walter Murphy, a fifty-two-year-old lawyer who'd married late in life, didn't understand his son's imprecise question. "You do, Prosper," he said. "Your name is Prosper."

There were a few moments of silence as young Murphy tried to rephrase the question for the benefit of old Murphy. They were driving from a basketball game in Princeton, New Jersey, to their house in New Hope, Pennsylvania. The car was a new 1949 Buick, of which young Murphy was intensely proud. "I mean," Murphy said, "it's a funny name."

"Why do you think it's a funny name?" Walter Murphy asked.

"Because it isn't like the other kids' names," Prosper Murphy replied.

"That doesn't make it funny, does it, Prosper?"

"They don't call me Prosper. They call me Murph."

"What's the matter with that?" Murphy's father said in the gentlest of tones. "That's your name, too."

Whether the elder Murphy was trying to bolster his son's sense of identity, or whether he simply didn't comprehend his son's quandary (the latter being more probable) was far too difficult a concept for the younger Murphy to deal with. They rode on in silence for a minute or two before Murphy asked his father where his first name had come from.

"Do you know what prosperity is?" Father asked Son.

"Being rich?" Son offered.

"Not just being rich, but being happy and successful. Now, you take the last three letters off that word . . . take away the 'ity,' and what have you got?"

"Prosper," Murphy said.

"That's your name," his father said. And so much for that conversation.


A day or two later Murphy posed the same question to his mother, with whom he could be more direct. The former Anne-Marie Chotineaux was at the time thirty-four years old. She had met Walter Murphy twenty years earlier in Montreal, had been most attracted to this young lawyer who stayed with her parents, had run into him at a party in New York just before the war, when she was twenty-four, and spent the night with him at the Waldorf-Astoria. She was his fourth lover, he her second.

Murphy's mother was in the kitchen, ironing a shirt, listening to Martin Block's "Make-Believe Ballroom" emit from an old and cumbersome Philco on the counter. Murphy sat at the kitchen table and watched her, appreciated her. "Did you have a good day at school?" she asked him, still looking at the shirt. There was an elision between "you" and "have," a failure to aspirate the "h." Murphy nodded. His mother, who wasn't looking at him, did not perceive his nod. "Did you hear me, Prosper?" Another elision: did you 'ear me? Prosper nodded again, was again unperceived.

His mother continued to iron. "Are you all right, Prosper?"

"Mommy," Prosper said, "why did you name me that?"

She looked at him. "Why did we name you Prosper?" She was quite taken aback.

Murphy nodded again.

"Well, it's a very famous name, my darling."

"Why is it famous?"

"Well, there was a writer, you see, a French writer, who lived a long time ago, who had your name, and also someone in your family who lived a long time ago."

"Who?"

"My father's father's brother, who was a general in the army."

"In the Canadian army?"

"No, my darling, in the French army. He was a very brave man, who fought with the Germans."

"If he was French, why did he fight with the Germans?" Prosper asked, knowing full well what his mother meant.

"*Against* the Germans," she said.

Two parents; two explanations. Could Walter Murphy possibly have been unaware of Anne-Marie's great-uncle and the great writer as well? Did they slip his mind? Or did he for one reason or another choose his own ellipsis that day—perhaps out of Irish-American chauvinism, or because he felt that all essays on his wife's side of his son's heritage should be left to her?

For his part, Prosper accepted the differing exegeses as two parts of a whole. They were, after all, not contradictory, and within the context of his relationships with his respective parents, they were most rational.

A decade later, in the dead center of a four-year stretch at an asylum in New Hampshire, reputed at the time to be the best secondary school in the United States, Murphy found himself reading *Carmen* and *Mateo Falcone* in French 3. His teacher, who had been General DeGaulle's aide-de-camp in the latter stages of World War II, and now spent his weekdays fondling schoolboys, his weeknights in drunken solitude, and his weekends in Boston steambaths (altogether not a bad life), asked Murphy if he happened to have been named after the great French writer.

"*Non,*" said Murphy, "*mon père voulait que je suis content.*"

"*Que je sois,*" replied the teacher, stressing the subjunctive.

After four years of coats and ties, chapel every morning, church every Sunday, and petty bullshit as far as the eye could see, Murphy set his sights on the West Coast and freedom. He applied to virtually every accredited university in California. And, in deference to his father, to Princeton, where he figured his chances of acceptance weren't too good anyway. But such, apparently, was the asylum's prestige that Murphy got in everywhere, and spent the early spring of 1961 comparing the catalogues of several acronymal institutions between San Francisco and San Diego, none of which was more than twenty miles from the beach.

Ostensibly on her way to Montreal, Anne-Marie showed up in New Hampshire in early May. Murphy knew something was afoot when he was given permission to accompany her to Boston on Thursday night, when the rest of the inmates would be under lock and key. She took him to a French restaurant, plied him with wine, told him that his father would be very happy if he chose Princeton. Murphy said he knew that, but his mind was set on California. Anne-Marie told him that Walter at this moment was in the Mayo Clinic in Minnesota, where he'd been told he was dying.

Murphy went to Princeton, and Walter died on schedule, in November, 1963, less than a week after someone shot the President in Dallas. Murphy had been prepared for the latter death, was shocked by the former, but shed no tears over either. Two important people had died, but neither had been very close to him.

He took his exams in January, passed everything, and left. Leaves of absence were hard to come by at Princeton in 1964, but the death of one's father can melt even a dean's cold heart, especially when one's father was a relatively wealthy alumnus.

He went to France, having assured Anne-Marie that Walter's death hadn't canceled his commitment to Princeton. He went with a couple of thousand dollars in traveler's checks and a notebook full of distant cousins' addresses, with fantasies of sitting in sidewalk cafes, chatting fluently with lithe and pliant Parisiennes.

But after two weeks of unabated xenophobia, of reading the
Paris edition of the *Herald-Tribune* cover to cover every day
and spending his evenings at any American movie he could find,
he'd had it with France, and one miserably lonely Sunday night
he took a cab back to Orly, there to discover that the next flight
to New York was eight hours away. He needed, at the very least,
to talk to someone, and considered a transatlantic phone call to
Anne-Marie. An admission of defeat. He turned to the notebook:
a profusion of relatives in the south. Many Chotineaux in Marseille, in Cannes, in Nice. Perhaps he'd only had it with Paris.

The Hertz counter was still open; Murphy rented a tiny Renault and stumbled onto the Autoroute du Sud after much confusion and despair. Driving south through the Gallic night, he
once again imagined himself edging toward his fantasies.


Instead, he found Mary. It was ten o'clock in the morning and
she was engaged in a furious argument with the desk clerk at
the Hotel des Amériques in Nice. The argument seemed rather
pointless to Murphy, standing there with his two suitcases. Here
was an American girl screaming English obscenities at an obviously very officious and surly French person who was quite able
to equal her decibel level, the problem being that neither spoke,
or would speak, the other's language.

What a grand opportunity for the bilingual happener-upon-
the-scene, especially so because the American girl was very
pretty, the French person a wormy little amalgam of everything
Murphy had come to despise in Paris.

He intervened, and was received graciously by both parties.

"You speak English? Oh, thank God. This bastard won't give
me back my passport. He says I stole some fucking *glasses!*
Listen, I've been here three days, and let me tell you nothing in
this place is *worth* stealing . . ."

It was true, said the clerk, the glasses were missing from this
girl's room, and this girl is crazy, she is *vachement folle*, she is
behaving like a maniac, all she has to do is return the glasses
and her passport will be returned.

The American girl requested a conference, took Murphy aside,
removed two Hotel des Amériques water glasses from her purse,

and stuffed them into his overcoat pockets. "It's a matter of principle," she said.

Murphy reported to the clerk that the American girl had agreed to let him search her luggage. "And her purse?" That, too. The clerk went through everything, found nothing, looked at Murphy in utter shame. "Tell her I regret this from my heart, I feel a profound sorrow. It must have been the maid."

He was driving her to the railroad station. She was an "army brat," taking a year off from Mount Holyoke; she was supposed to be taking courses in Heidelberg, but she'd decided to take some time off from there, too. "Listen," she said, "let's go someplace together. Let's go someplace we've never been before."

"I've never been anywhere," Murphy said.

"Oh, God, do you know I've *lived* in practically every country in Europe? Look, let's go to Morocco. Or Turkey."

Murphy said that he didn't want to be a wet blanket, but he'd been up all night, needed some sleep, and planned to look up some relatives nearby. Mary told him he'd be a fool to go back to the Hotel des Amériques, told him she knew a really nice *pension* in Monte Carlo.

She granted him five hours' sleep, then dragged him off to the casino. Bleary-eyed, he watched her play baccarat, heard her groan when she lost, yip when she won. The groans were more frequent than the yips. She was certainly good-looking. What was he doing here? He excused himself, took a walk around the casino, feeling disoriented but not nearly so desperate as he'd been twenty hours earlier. The din of the casino was almost pleasant: all these wheels turning, all these people murmuring in exotic tongues; and Murphy was suddenly drawn to a roulette table.

He thought better of it, moved away, and was drawn back as if by magnetic force. It was an inexpensive table, with a ten-franc minimum; he bought fifty francs worth of chips, played odd and even, red and black for ten minutes or so, was twenty francs ahead when the number twenty-six for no reason at all began turning somersaults in his head. Twenty-six wasn't his age or his birthday; it didn't appear on his draft card or his

Social Security card or his driver's license. He put ten francs on
twenty-six, and the wheel came up fourteen. His brain continued
to pound. The wheel came up eighteen. Getting closer, anyway. He was now even with the house, figured he'd give it
one more try—the little ball veered and skipped and stumbled,
slipped and bounced, and dropped solidly, inexorably into the
slot under twenty-six.

His brain said, "More!" Murphy left twenty francs on twenty-
six and lost, then thirty, then forty, then fifty. This was hardly
sensible betting, but Murphy knew, or felt awfully sure, that
something magical was happening. Twenty-six screamed at him,
and he placed a hundred francs in its little felt box.

"*Vingt-six,*" the croupier said, in an absolutely normal tone of
voice. There was considerable oohing and aahing from Murphy's
neighbors, nickel and dime players who'd just seen someone win
thirty-five hundred francs on a single roll of the wheel. Murphy
handed the croupier a hundred-franc chip. The croupier nodded
politely.

He found Mary at the baccarat table, distraught. "Prosper,"
she said, "I can't believe it! I've lost a hundred *dollars*. . . . I'm
gonna have to go home!"

"Let's go," Murphy said.

"No, listen, can you lend me some money?"

"Come on," he said, and he lifted her out of her chair.

They walked back to the *pension*. She was in trouble, she said.
She didn't have enough money to get back to Germany. She'd
have to wire her family back in Massachusetts, and that would
be all right if her father were there, but her father was in Vietnam. Did Murphy know where Vietnam was, somewhere near
China? Murphy did. Anyway, if her mother found out she was
in Monte Carlo instead of Heidelberg, there'd be hell to
pay. . . .

In their little room, one tiny bed for him, one tiny bed for
her, Murphy grinned and emptied his pockets of francs. Thousands of francs. "You *won* that?" Mary was all over him. Things
certainly had turned around for Murphy. Not a lithe Parisienne,
but a lithe Américaine, a welcome substitute, and under the
watchful stare of Prince Rainier these new friends made love
extravagantly.

They traveled. They went by train across northern Italy: up to Turin, down to Genoa, up to Milan, over to Venice and Trieste. Why the ups and downs? Because Mary had never been to any of those places. Why not Rome, Murphy wanted to know. Mary'd been there. She'd *lived* there, and it was boring. Murphy spoke no Italian; neither, despite her status as a former resident (she had been very young) did Mary. But it was she, in a bizarre mixture of sign language, English, and American-accented German, who got directions from policemen, who bought their tickets, who got them spacious rooms in not quite elegant hotels. "We can afford it," she'd say to Murphy, whose bankroll was still impressive, and in the inevitable over-stuffed bed with the inevitable huge pillows she'd say, "Have you ever done *this?*"

Down the Yugoslavian coast. In a picturesque town called Split, they almost did. The map showed Sarajevo couple of inches to the north. "Where World War One started," he told Mary.

She'd have none of it. Mountains. Too cold. A long bus ride with a lot of smelly peasants. Murphy pointed out that these were all conditions they'd endured before, that he was tired of just beginning to get his bearings someplace and having to leave, that he knew full well Mary's only real objection was that Sarajevo wasn't on a straight line down the coast.

She said maybe the time had come to go their separate ways. He said if that was what she wanted it was all right with him. He had the money. They went to Sarajevo, Mary sulking and snorting as Murphy, filled with a grand sense of history, stood in Gavrilo Princip's approximate footsteps. She ignored his every attempt at conversation on the miserable bus ride back to the coast at Mostar. But once at Dubrovnik, back on course, in a room with a terrace overlooking the stormy Mediterranean, and with one of the seven television sets in Yugoslavia, she put a voracious end to their three-day departure from sexuality.

By train to Athens, by boat to Izmir, to Rhodes, Cyprus, and Beirut.

They had covered, in fast reverse, the route of some fabulous infidel conqueror, and Beirut seemed to be the logical place to stop—or at least to rest. Especially because it was a beautiful city, the weather suggested July instead of late March, everybody spoke French, their room cost about two dollars per day, lavish and endless meals were available for less than that, and side trips to Baalbek, to Byblos, to Damascus, to countless relics of the Crusades, the Romans, even the Hittites, were there for the asking.

But after four days, Mary was ready to move on—there were still so many places to see. Where? Murphy asked: what could possibly be better than Beirut? It wasn't a question of better, she explained, it was a question of *different,* and different right now might mean Afghanistan, or it might mean Egypt.

"Okay," he said. "You go to Afghanistan. I'm going to the movies." He put on his jacket.

"Thanks for inviting me."

"Come on then. I'd love you to come. I didn't think you'd be interested."

"What's the movie?"

"It's a French movie, called *Jules et Jim.*"

"You know I don't understand French."

"There'll be subtitles."

"I don't understand Arabic, either."

"Subtitles in Arabic and English. You can read English, can't you?"

"Oh, fuck you, Prosper. Go to your fucking movie."


Back at their room in the early evening, there was no sign of Mary, no indication of where she might have gone. Murphy waited half an hour, grew painfully hungry, and headed out the door for something to eat. At the staircase he remembered he was almost out of Lebanese money.

His traveler's checks weren't where he'd left them; the little blue folder was instead on the chest of drawers by the window. Five, perhaps six twenties were missing. To Afghanistan with a hundred dollars? No, her clothes were still in the closet.

He knew where she was.

At the Casino du Liban, playing baccarat, her right shoulder under the arm of a swarthy, middle-aged man in a tuxedo, a large pile of chips in front of her. Murphy stood behind them, examining the remarkable forest of hair on the man's hand. "Mary?" he said.

She turned. "Oh, *hi*, Prosper . . ."

"What's going on?"

"Prosper," not the least perturbed, "I'd like you to meet Ahmed."

Ahmed nodded pleasantly at Murphy, his arm remaining upon Mary.

"I think we should get out of here," Murphy said.

"No. I'm staying right here. I'm winning."

"You can win somewhere else, without that bastard's hand on you." Ahmed either spoke no English or was very tolerant.

"Prosper, I ran out of money and Ahmed lent me a hundred pounds. Now I'm winning, and I'm not going to insult him."

"A hundred *pounds?*" Murphy was becoming enraged. The Lebanese pound was worth considerably less than the American dollar. "You just borrowed a hell of a lot more than that from me . . ."

"I know that, Prosper. Look, everything's going to be fine. I'll just be a while . . ."

The croupier placed a fresh pile of chips in front of Mary. Ahmed spoke to her in German, gave her a little hug, she squealed and kissed him on the cheek.

How preposterous this was, how profane. "Mary," he said, "I'm getting the hell out of here."

She winked at him. "I'll see you back at the hotel."


He took a taxi there. She'd *winked* at him. You and me against the foreigners. He waited an hour, left word at the desk that he'd gone out to eat, returned, waited another hour, left word at the desk that he'd gone out for a beer, returned, fell asleep, woke up, paced the floor, packed his bags, roused the desk clerk before dawn and paid their bill, waited half an hour for a taxi, hoping for and dreading Mary's besmirched arrival, not to be. And flew home to New York.

# 11

# A Day at
# the Beach

Friday. Murphy's fourth day in Florida, like the previous three, is blissfully sunny and warm. He follows what has become a pleasant routine: getting out of bed at ten, drinking some juice, stopping on the way to the beach for a *New York Times* and a *Fort Lauderdale News,* reading and basking on the near-empty beach for an hour, then taking his marathon swim, reading and basking for another hour, driving to Fat Lou's for lunch, then back to Angela's apartment. Waiting for her, he studies jai alai. He has three programs from West Palm Beach now, plus three days' results from Dania, printed in the *News.*

He remains equally fascinated by jai alai and Angela; the former he seems to be figuring out, the latter he cannot penetrate. From their meeting until this midafternoon, they have spent some thirty hours together (not including time passed in adjoining bedrooms), and Murphy has learned as much about Angela as he might normally discover during the course of a fifteen-minute conversation with a stranger at a cocktail party. At jai alai, she is animated and expansive, full of information regarding players or shots or strategy. But should Murphy pose a personal question, her mien shifts immediately.

This was discovered during his first day and second night in Madera Beach. Fresh from his conquest of John Trough at First American Savings & Loan, Murphy returned to the apartment, read the Dania Jai-Alai results in the *News,* compared them to the West Palm Beach results, considered his own observations of the previous night, and concluded with some elation that he'd found an edge: it might be just a little edge, or it might be a tremendous edge.

Angela appeared at five, looking harried and weary. Would she like to go to Jai-Alai? Yes, she'd like to go to Jai-Alai, but dinner wasn't necessary, as she needed a nap, and they'd miss the first two or three games were dinner to intrude. He insisted anew, she acceded, napped, and they went, at Angela's insistence, to a franchise steak house on U.S. 1 in West Palm Beach, because it would consume neither too much time nor too much money.

In the car, Murphy laid out his edge: the first three post positions, Teams 1, 2, and 3, are almost always in the money, not because they're the best teams, just because they get to play more points; most bettors are so concerned with quiniela and perfectas they don't deign to bet win, place, show. Those who do bet WPS generally don't know what they're doing, or so it seems, because the odds on Teams 1-2-3 generally represent their comparative lack of talent instead of their advantageous post positions. Thus, Murphy concluded, were the sagacious bettor to eschew the big payoffs and to concentrate instead on the best of Teams 1-2-3, or even to bet on *all three teams* across the board in each game, there was money to be won. He cited figures: at West Palm Beach last night, betting 1-2-3 to win all twelve games would have netted $30.20, betting them all across the board $67 even; at Dania, the same methods would have won $55.80 and $94.60.

Angela listened in the manner of someone who's heard this sort of thing before, but her skepticism seemed mixed with at least a scintilla of interest.

Minutes from the fronton, she explained to Murphy one thing he knew and several he hadn't considered. "If you bet all three teams across the board," she began, "you could lose eighteen dollars a game." Murphy knew that. Angela proceeded to explain with great care that: WPS payoffs were often spectacular because only one or two people had made a particular bet, and Murphy's bet would thus decrease them substantially; his research consisted of one night's results from two frontons, and was hardly definitive; last night's games at West Palm Beach were all short games, finished in the second round, and in such games Teams 1-2-3 are always in the money; but there are nights, many nights, when the games are long and Teams 1-2-3 might not win at all.

Murphy was impressed by Angela's knowledge, even more by her presentation. What a wonderful teacher she'd make, he thought. He bet eighteen dollars a game that night, 1-2-3 across the board (despite the fact that the evening's first three games, which they'd missed, had gone 6-4-7, 5-1-3, 8-5-2, and his strategy would have cost him $34.60), and won a small fortune: $82.80.

Driving back to Madera Beach, he said, "What do you do?"

"What do I do?" Angela replied. "You mean for a living?"

"For a living," Murphy affirmed.

"Ray didn't tell you very much about me, did he?"

"No, he didn't. He didn't tell me very much at all."

Angela nodded, as if to herself. "I'm a teacher."

Murphy smiled inwardly. "What do you teach?"

"Spanish."

That wouldn't have been his guess. "How do you happen to teach Spanish?"

"Because I don't speak Persian."

"No, really . . ."

"Because I speak Spanish."

"How do you happen to speak Spanish?"

"I majored in Spanish, at school."

"Which school?"

"What difference does that make?"

"It doesn't make any difference at all. I'd just like to know more about you."

"What school did you go to?"

"To college?"

"To college."

"Princeton."

Angela smiled, and nodded again. "What club were you in?" she asked.

"What difference does that make?" Murphy said.

"We're even," Angela said.

By Murphy's count, they were hardly even. But he'd gotten the message, and spoke of nothing but jai alai the rest of the way home.

Thursday morning there was a note on the kitchen counter: "I didn't mean to be hostile. I teach at Madera Beach High School. I went to Barnard. Angela."

That night Murphy's winnings plummeted to $17.20. He had been ahead $74 midway through the program before Elu, playing exclusively in positions 6 through 8, won four games and put another crimp in the system. Still, Murphy had won.

"How did you happen to go to Barnard?" he ventured.

"I grew up in New York. They gave me a scholarship, and I wanted to stay in New York."

Murphy hesitated long and hard before asking the next question: "Why did you come down here, then?"

"For the same reason I live at Waterway Cove."

"Because your husband wanted to?"

"Right."

"You don't strike me," Murphy said with great trepidation, "as someone who'd do something because her husband wanted to."

There was a long silence before Angela said, "There were other reasons."

And Murphy decided to quit while he was ahead.


He hears her key in the door at three-thirty; she enters smiling, and says, "Hi." Murphy responds in kind. Angela nods at his collection of jai-alai data. "Are you trying to find a better system?"

"No, just working on the old one," Murphy says. "I would have lost eighteen dollars at Dania last night."

"You would have won a lot more than you did at West Palm if you'd started betting on Elu when we realized he was hot."

Murphy shrugs. "It would have been against the rules."

"Common sense should never be against the rules," Angela says. She walks into the kitchen and pours herself a glass of grapefruit juice, then sits across from Murphy on the couch. "Did you have a good day?" she says.

"Sure," he says. "I've had nothing but good days since I've been here."

"You went to the beach?"

"Right."

"You wouldn't feel like another swim, would you?"

A precedent is set. He assumes she's asking him if he'd like to swim with *her*, and thus to do something other than going to jai alai with her. Had she asked if he'd like to go wrestle a few alligators with her, he'd have responded as he does. "I'd love to."

"You don't object to the pool?"

"The pool is fine."

Murphy stands in the living room wearing bathing suit, T-shirt, and sneakers. He is suddenly conscious of his body, of the fact that his knees are red. Angela emerges from the hallway in a robe.

At poolside, she tosses the terry-cloth robe on a settee and immediately dives into the water. By any standard, Murphy's glimpse could not be deemed particularly erotic: Angela's bikini isn't immodest, he's seen her from behind and for an instant; but his erection is direct and potentially embarrassing, as the pool area is well populated, so he follows her in, much less gracefully.

They lie side by side half an hour later on juxtaposed metal and vinyl settees under the late-afternoon sun.

"I have to do something tomorrow, Prosper," Angela says.

The suggestion is that tomorrow, Saturday, Angela has some obligation which will keep them apart, perhaps even a date. Murphy cringes in silence.

"I have to get together with some old friends . . ."

Murphy's sigh of relief.

". . . they're not really my old friends, they're friends of my husband's." She pauses, supine and beautiful. Murphy's eyes are fixed on the beads of water and sweat running, traipsing down her upper thigh. "I see them every couple of weeks. They have a barbecue at the beach . . ."

Murphy sits up to disguise at least partially his burgeoning tumescence.

"I wonder if you'd come with me?"

"I have no other plans," Murphy says.

That night the system gets killed. After six games, Murphy has cashed two place tickets, three show tickets, for a return of $19.20 on an investment of $108. In other words, he's lost $86.80 and the evening's only half over.

Angela points to the program. Elu is about to make his debut for the night, playing in the eighth position with Nuarbe. Elu and Nuarbe won last night's twelfth game in a walk. "You're crazy if you bet one-two-three this game, Prosper," Angela says.

"I've got to stick to it," Murphy replies.

"Okay, but split a perfecta with me, too."

"That's money down the drain, Angela. It's a sucker bet."

"No, it's not. Elu's going to win this game."

"Okay, I'd say Elu has a good chance to win this game, but there're seven teams that can come in second . . ."

Angela runs her finger down the program; she is as intense as Murphy has seen her. "All right, look, Eguia has a bad back, and he doesn't play well with Del Rio. We can forget one. Two's good—Olabarri and Lejarcegui—they should beat one and three, because Azpiri's been lousy, and then they'll probably lose to four, but Roberto and Churruca should beat four and six, and maybe seven, if they throw the ball to Baranda enough . . ."

"So it's between two and five?"

"No, we box them, two-five-eight. Both ways."

"Angela, that's eighteen dollars, for Christ's sake."

"Nine for you and nine for me."

"Look, if you're so sure Elu's going to win, why don't we just bet it eight-two and eight-five, and we'll save twelve dollars?"

"Because I'm not so sure Elu's going to win. I just know he's going to win a lot of points."

It seems at first that Angela has handicapped the game to perfection. At the conclusion of the first round the teams in their perfecta have scored seven of the eight points. But Elu and Nuarbe lose the first double-point to Team 1, which proceeds to beat 3 and 4 and attain six points, and an almost certain spot in the perfecta. "It's not over yet," Angela says. Never give up on your team.

Indeed it is not over. It is not over for a long time. One of the nice things about Murphy's system is its simplicity—its compactness—as opposed to the confounding complexity of this perfecta business. Team 1, loses to Team 2, part of our "team." But 2 now has five points. Should it win its encounter with 6 the game will be over, Murphy will have a 2-1-5 finish and plenty of WPS money, but no perfecta. He roots, perversely, for 6, and the long shot 6 wins handily.

"We've got a chance," Angela says.

"I know we do," Murphy replies. "But not a very good one."

It goes on forever. Disaster, in the form of a fatal game point, is averted five times, and each time Angela responds by giving Murphy a pat on the knee, an arm, on the shoulder. "We're going to do it," she says.

They do it. It comes down to 2, still with five points, versus 1, with six points, yet again. Somebody's got to win the game here, and 2 does, quickly, anticlimactically. What now? There are three teams with six points: 1, 5, and 6. 1, it seems, is eliminated from the playoff because it has just been up. 5 serves to 6. Zaguirre fumbles the serve.

"We did it!" Murphy says. Angela kisses him on the cheek. He grabs her and kisses her on the lips. He feels her left breast pressing softly on his rib cage. He is aflame. The numbers flash. Angela pulls away. The 2-5 perfecta pays $138.80; Team 2 pays $18.40 across the board. Murphy's profit is $87.80, putting him a dollar ahead for the night.

He can't lose, it seems.


The BMW inches toward the parking lot exit. "How'd you end up?" Murphy asks.

"I won some," Angela says, her expression neutral.

"How much?"

"You tell me first," she says.

"Eleven dollars and forty cents," Murphy says.

"To the penny?"

"To the penny. How about you?"

"A lot," Angela says. She grins.

"Drinks are on you, then," Murphy says.

"Which drinks?"

"We're going to a classy night spot."

"No, we're not," Angela says.

"Why not? You don't have to get up in the morning . . ."

"Unless you want to drive into Palm Beach, there isn't a classy night spot within thirty miles of here."

"Okay. How about a sleazy night spot?"

"Just for a while?"

"Just for a while."

"Turn left," Angela says, "and go about half a mile down Forty-fifth Street. It's called La Pelota."

It's a cozy little bar, owned and operated by a former jai-alai player who greets Angela with a hug and gabbles with her in Spanish for several minutes before she can introduce him to Murphy. "He's a friend of Ray's," she says.

"Very delighted to meet you," the large man says in a moderately heavy Spanish accent. "How is Ray? You seen him recently?"

"A few days ago," Murphy says. "He's fine."

The place is decorated almost entirely by jai-alai accoutrements: baskets hanging on the walls, balls with inscriptions in little glass cases, fifteen or twenty photographs here and there, a red jersey on the wall behind the bar. Were it not for the jukebox and the pinball machine, Murphy might imagine himself in Spain.

His Budweiser and Angela's glass of red wine are on the house. Murphy heads instinctively for the jukebox as Angela continues to converse with their host. It's an old Seeburg, half of whose selections are in Spanish; the rest are along the lines of "Honey" by Bobby Goldsboro, "Happy Birthday" (anonymous), supplemented by great country music banalities. But G-7, unaccountably, is Otis Redding's "Dock of the Bay"; H-4 is "Hey Jude." Does Murphy have two dimes? Yes, of course. But what the hell: he deposits a quarter, plays "Dock of the Bay," "Hey Jude," and "Happy Birthday."

Back to the bar. "Happy Birthday" comes on first. "Did you play that?" Angela says.

Murphy nods.

"Is it someone's birthday?"

"It must be," Murphy says. "The pinball machine is available."

Angela, who claims to have never before touched a pinball machine, misses a few important flips but nevertheless kicks Murphy's ass in the first game, 37,650 to 28,190. To score a replay, however, one must hit 80,000. It takes a few games to learn a new machine. Murphy deposits two more dimes. The second time is the charm. He scores 35,000 on the first ball alone, then slumps to 7,800 on the second, soars to 21,000 on the third. Loses the fourth almost immediately. He keeps the fifth ball in play, looks up at the scoreboard whenever he can: 72,000, 76,000 . . . he's going to do it. The little silver ball bumps around, bounces into target number seven; one more and he'll get an extra ball and two, maybe three replays. The ball now takes a dipsy little roll, pauses, and drops straight down, between the two flippers. Unreachable. Murphy looks up: 79,970. Jesus Christ! The machine must be rigged.

"Did you see that?" he asks Angela. But she isn't there. Where is she? She's at the bar, talking to a middle-aged man. To Andy, the ticket seller.

"I forget your name," Andy says.

"Prosper Murphy."

"Andrés Mendizabal." They shake hands.

"You're Spanish?"

"No, I am from Spain, but I'm Basque."

"He used to be a player," Angela says. "In Miami."

"Many years ago," Andy says.

"Not *that* many years ago," Angela says.

Murphy buys a rum and Coke for Andy, another Budweiser for himself. They sit at a booth.

"Most of the players are Basque," Murphy says, "according to the program."

"Well, that's where the game comes from, the Basque country."

"I'm afraid I don't even know where the Basque country is," Murphy says.

"In the north. The northeast of Spain, and across the border in France. But they don't play too much jai alai in France. Mainly in Spain." Andy looks at Angela. "How come you didn't tell him this already?"

"He didn't ask me," she says.

"Is the pay better over here?" Murphy asks. "Is that why the players come here?"

"Well, it's better, yeah, but not that much better. From the profits they make over here, they can afford to pay the players more than they do . . ."

Murphy considers the 17 percent of every dollar bet that's taken from the pool. Some of that goes to the state of Florida, some for operating expenses. But let's see, if two thousand people bet two dollars per game, and there are twelve games, that's $48,000. More realistically, those two thousand people are probably averaging at least five dollars per game, and that's $120,000. Jai alai is played eight times a week; that's just under a million dollars gross every week, of which perhaps $130,000 goes to the house, not counting the concessions, the Sala del Toro. . . . It's like printing money.

"What do the players make?" Murphy asks.

"Here?" Andy mulls. "The good ones, the late-games players, maybe they make twelve, maybe fifteen thousand dollars a season. The other ones, the young ones, the ones who play the early games, some of them maybe five thousand, six thousand, maybe less."

"That's incredible," Murphy says.

Andy shrugs. "It's not so good."

"Is it the same everywhere? In the other frontons?"

"Well, in Miami they make more money, but it's a much bigger fronton. The people bet a lot more money."

Murphy computes again, comes up with a seasonal profit of about two and a half million dollars for this fronton, of which maybe four hundred thousand dollars goes to the players.

"Tell Prosper about the strike," Angela says.

Andy shakes his head. "No, let's have a good time."

"I'd like to hear about it," Murphy says.

"It didn't work," Andy says.

"It was in 1968, Prosper," Angela says. "The players struck, and the frontons managed to drag up enough players to open the season . . ."

"Where the hell do you find scab jai-alai players?"

"They asked *me*," Andy says. "I was forty-five years old. I spat in their face."

"They got them from Mexico," Angela says, "they got Cubans from Miami, they found people who'd play."

"Basques, too," Andy says. "Kids sixteen years old, who didn't know how to play yet, and old men like me."

"People went to see that?" Murphy says, the slightest tremor of anger in his voice.

"Americans," Andy says, "just like to bet. They don't care too much what they bet on."


Murphy sits on the beach early Saturday afternoon, munching an overdone hot dog and sipping a Michelob, and sizing up Hugh Whitaker. Whitaker appears about forty years old: he is close to bald, his remaining blond hair worn curiously long in back; he is fairly tall, and conceivably at some point in the past was quite sturdy, but now his stomach and pectoral muscles have gone to flab; his face is anomalously unlined but excessively florid, and not, it would seem, from the sun, because the rest of his body is alabaster. I hope, Murphy keeps thinking, that I won't look like him when I'm his age.

A few minutes later, Whitaker says, "Angie tells us you went to Princeton."

"Right," Murphy says.

"What year?"

"Sixty-six. Sixty-seven, technically . . . I took a year off."

"Well, we might have run into each other at a couple of ball games, then. I'm Yale, sixty-four."

Jesus, Murphy thinks, either this man started college at an advanced age or he's only two years older than I am.

Whitaker asks Murphy what club he was in, then runs through ten or twelve did-you-knows, and is completely shut out. Murphy can think of only one acquaintance who went to

Yale—a homosexual Jewish socialist—and doesn't bother to reciprocate.

It's another beautiful day: nary a cloud in the sky, the beach somewhat more populated on Saturday but still uncrowded, resplendent Angela in a purple bikini juxtaposed with frumpy Elsie Whitaker, mother of two, pregnant again, both of them on beach chairs. Mark, age six, and Jason, age three, well-mannered boys, alternately attend their immense and growing sand castle and race into the sea.

"You ready for another?" Whitaker asks, heading for the cooler.

"No, I'm fine," Murphy says.

Whitaker returns and pops open his Michelob. On the way back from jai alai last night, Angela told Murphy that Whitaker had been her husband's law partner in Boca Raton, that he was somewhat fatuous, but basically a nice guy, that Elsie was a pleasant woman, something of a fussbudget, that the Whitakers were the only local people she kept in touch with. Her implication, perhaps, was that Murphy not queer the deal.

Angela and Elsie are a good fifteen feet away, the surf is plangent, there is a healthy breeze, but Whitaker plops down next to Murphy and speaks in an absurdly low voice. The man obviously doesn't want to be overheard. "Prosper, look, I feel like a damn fool asking you a question like this, but are you and Angie . . .?" He shrugs enormously. "You know . . ."

"No, we're not," Murphy says.

Whitaker consumes close to half a can of beer on one gulp. "Look, Prosper, I feel like an ass because it's none of my business, you know, but she's a hell of a girl, and I guess I feel, you know, *protective* . . ."

Murphy imagines that Whitaker might just want to do more to Angela than protect her. He nods several times.

"If you don't mind my asking, how do you know her?"

"She's a friend of a friend of mine, in New York."

"You didn't know Dave, then?"

The name Dave, in the context of Angela, is unknown to Murphy.

"Dave and I were partners here, and Elsie and I thought that Dave and Angie were a hell of a couple, Prosper. They had their problems, you know, we've all got our problems, but it surprised the hell out of me when they split up."

"I can imagine," Murphy says.

"You don't know her family, I guess?"

"No, I don't."

"Well, I always figured it was her family more than anything Dave might have done that broke them up."

There is a pause. "What did Dave do?" Murphy asks.

Whitaker finishes his beer, crushes the can, and places it carefully in a plastic waste bag. "He probably fooled around a little."

"You don't know for sure?"

"Oh, hell, pretty much for sure. Dave never told me. You ready for another?" Whitaker is back by the cooler.

"Not yet," Murphy says.

Whitaker drinks another large amount of beer and resumes his place next to Murphy. "Dave was a really jealous type. I think he always figured Angie had something going on the side, you know? Maybe that's why he did whatever he did. But I'll tell you, Prosper, it's been over a year since the divorce, and as far as I know Angie's been all by herself all that time."

Murphy, having nothing to say, nods repeatedly.

"She's a hell of a girl, Prosper, and for whatever it's worth, for whatever she means to you, I'd appreciate it if you take good care of her."

"Sure, Hugh, of course," Murphy says. He's taken an odd kind of liking to Whitaker, who seems a frustrated but generous person. He senses that Whitaker, old before his time, envies him, suspects or is positive that he and Angela have been cavorting erotically these last several days, that Murphy shares his Ivy League sensibility of courtesy and restraint, and so will not let on. Alas, only the latter of Whitaker's suspicions approaches reality. Murphy swallows the last of his first Michelob as Whitaker finishes his fourth. Murphy's eyes are fixed on Angela, who cozes idly with Elsie as the sun pours and the waves break.

Whitaker is at the cooler. "You ready now?"

"Sure," Murphy says.

# 12

# Echaverria
# Furioso

It's a dismal, icy Sunday morning in New York. At seven o'clock the traffic is negligible, but Echaverria drives cautiously, up First Avenue to the Queens-Midtown Tunnel. In the tunnel there is only one car behind him, several hundred feet back. Just to be sure, Echaverria slows from fifty to forty; the car behind him comes closer, then drops back. He speeds up again, and after a similar delay the car behind him does the same. Leaving the tunnel, he downshifts rapidly from fourth to third, third to second, decelerating quickly, showing no brake lights. The car behind approaches to within a hundred feet or so, to a point where Echaverria can identify it as a late-model blue "compact," probably a Chevrolet, a Pontiac, or a Buick. He continues at thirty miles an hour; the car gets to fifty feet behind, pulls from the extreme right lane to the extreme left lane, and roars by. It is a blue Camaro with three occupants, all black men. Echaverria takes the first exit and spends ten minutes reading the Sunday *Times* Week in Review, then proceeds.

On the Van Wyck, he spends as much time looking in the rearview mirror as he does looking at the road. Traffic is still sparse, but there are now some thirty vehicles within his eastbound field of vision, and one that causes some concern. He fluctuates now between forty and fifty-five, still in the extreme right lane; there is a van several hundred yards back which

gains when he slows, falls back when he speeds. He assumes
the van is regulating its speed to his as a matter of safety, as the
blue Camaro was probably also doing. The Van Wyck is as
badly kept up as every other major artery in New York; water
collects in depressions and freezes, the ice patches are irregular,
sporadic, but for the most part dangerous only when braked
upon. So it makes sense to leave a few hundred yards between
yourself and the vehicle ahead of you. What doesn't make sense
is the car behind the van—following the same pattern of acceleration and deceleration, but consistently only thirty or
forty feet behind the van. At this distance it's impossible for
Echaverria to identify the car.

He takes the Kennedy turnoff and pulls onto the shoulder.
He gets out of the car and stands next to it for several minutes,
during which twenty-seven cars pass by, none of them a blue
Camaro. He gets back in the car wishing he could afford a
few more minutes' wait, but he has an appointment at 7:45 and
doesn't want to be late. At the Cargo Area exit there is a brown
Chevrolet van parked on the grass, its parking and taillights
flashing. This may well be the van that was behind him, but there
are thousands of vans on the road, the odds are against it, and
Echaverria doesn't have time to wait. It's already 7:43.

He parks amidst a vast area of warehouses and walks up a
concrete strip surrounded by dead grass. At the end of the strip
is a short staircase, which Echaverria ascends, then a door, upon
which he knocks discreetly. The door is opened by a small,
bearded man.

"*Comment ça va*, Pierre?" Echaverria says.

"*Ça marche*," Pierre accompanies his reply with a little Gallic
grimace. Echaverria hands him a rather fat manila envelope;
Pierre takes it with no change of expression, turns and disappears for a few seconds. He comes back with a heavy cardboard box, about two feet in each dimension.

"*Je m'emmerde de ça*," he says, glaring first at the box and
then at Echaverria.

"Yeah, well you got paid for it, didn't you?"

Pierre shrugs his shoulders and spits on the floor.

"I'll see you in Marseille sometime, you little froggy bastard,"
Echaverria says. He claps Pierre on the back and departs; Pierre
shuts the door after him.

The box weighs, or should weigh, just about ninety pounds. It feels about right. Echaverria balances it on his right shoulder as he navigates the icy path back to the car. He puts it in the trunk, takes a good look around before getting back in the car, and drives off.

Two hundred yards down the narrow roadway, coming out of curve, he sees the brown van stopped lengthwise in the middle of the road, all but blocking it. A young black man in a bright red ski parka and black gloves frantically points to the van with his right hand and gestures with his left for Echaverria to stop.

Echaverria doesn't know precisely what's coming down here, but it's a foregone conclusion that the van isn't disabled and the black man doesn't need help. His first instinct is to slam on the brakes and swing into a 180-degree turn. This is a gamble because there's a good chance slamming on the brakes will send the car careening either forward or sideways into the van, and perhaps the black man as well. But it seems a better tactic than trying to go around the van: the road will be iciest at its edges; should he try to pass on the left he'll skid, possibly losing control, possibly being rammed by the van; should he try to pass on the right, he has a five-inch-high curb to deal with, and the probability that his car would deflect off the curb rather than climbing it, and smash into the van. Were he to succeed in getting around the van on either side, he has a strong suspicion the blue Camaro would be waiting just down the road.

So he slams on the brakes and pulls the steering wheel hard left: the brakes grab, the car begins to slow and turn, then hits some ice and slides at about thirty degrees. The black man, curiously, begins to move in the same direction as the car, to his right rather than to his left. His left hand is still in the air, imploring Echaverria to stop. His expression has evolved from bogus anguish to genuine anguish. The Bavaria's tires fix anew on a patch of uniced roadway; they screech, and the car slows and turns a bit more, approaching ninety degrees. The black man slips, almost falls. The car crosses another patch of ice followed by another patch of asphalt—sliding, catching, turning. The car's hind end misses the van by three feet, but its rear fender hits the black man's left leg and swats him onto the frozen grass. The car proceeds to about 140 degrees and enters a berserk, fishtailing slide that culminates on the grass twenty feet beyond the wounded black man. Three other black men come running from the van. The Bavaria's engine has quit; Echaverria attempts to restart it. Two of the men approach their fallen colleague, a third approaches the Bavaria, carrying a gun. The engine won't catch. The man with the gun looks a lot like Archie. He hits an ice patch and goes sprawling, the gun skittering several yards away. The engine still won't catch. One of the other two black men now approaches from the other side, apparently weaponless. The blue Camaro is nowhere in sight. Archie, or Archie's look-alike, crawls for the pistol, seizes it, and resumes the hunt. The engine starts. The other black man is hanging on the passenger-side door handle and pounding on the window; Archie, and to be sure, it *is* Archie, is within five feet. Echaverria puts the Bavaria in first gear and lets the clutch out ever so slowly, finds traction, and starts moving forward on the grass, pulling the passengerside black man with him. The car makes it to the asphalt, slides and grabs, the black man lets go and falls down; there is an explosion, and the car veers and stops because Archie has murdered its left rear tire.

Archie places the pistol against the driver's side window, which Echaverria rolls down. Archie's chin is bleeding. Echaverria yells: "What the fuck are you crazy bastards up to?"

The gun barrel is now two inches from his face, and Archie's hands are none too steady. "You shut the fuck up, motherfucker," Archie says.

"You blew it, Archie."

"I said shut the fuck up, asshole!"

"You tell Curtis he picked the wrong time . . ."

Archie screams: "I said *shut up!* Curtis don't have nothin' to do with this!"

And shit don't stink. The pistol looks like a .357 Magnum. Echaverria shuts up.

Archie has been joined by the hanger-on, who seems in pain and rubs his right elbow with his left hand. "Willie," Archie commands, "tell Joe and Otis they get they ass over here."

"Don't you move," Archie says to Echaverria, "and don't you talk one fuckin' word to me." The pistol oscillates. Echaverria wonders why the Camaro hasn't appeared. Perhaps its occupants, Curtis and friends, or just Curtis's friends, are trying to charm their way into Pierre's place of business. They'd have an easier time getting an audience with the Pope.

Willie reappears, with Joe in tow. "Motherfucker busted Otis leg," Joe tells Archie.

"Otis done busted Otis leg," Archie tells Joe. "Done run the wrong fuckin' way. Wasn't this motherfucker's doin'."

Faint praise for Echaverria. Droplets of blood fall from Archie's chin. "Get in the other side," he says to Joe. "Open that door for him, and do it nice," Archie says to Echaverria.

Echaverria opens the passenger-side door and Joe hops in. He thoroughly desecrates the glove compartment: maps and official documents and papers of various age or importance are sent flying. "Nothin'," Joe announces to Archie. Echaverria's gun is in the trunk, underneath the spare tire in its well.

"Okay, take the keys out," Archie says to Echaverria, who does so. "Get out the car, slow." The gun remains intimate with Echaverria's head. He opens the door slowly; Archie backs off, still pointing the pistol. Echaverria emerges, followed by Joe.

"Open the trunk up."

Echaverria walks slowly around the car, conscious of the ice, confident that Archie doesn't intend to kill him, aware that a slip or slide on either of their parts might result in the trigger's being pulled.

He opens the trunk, which would seem to contain nothing but a large box.

"Open that up," Archie says to Joe. Joe leans in and rips open the box. "What is it?" Archie asks.

"I dunno," Joe replies.

"Take it out," Archie says.

"Motherfucker be heavy," Joe says, heaving the bag out of the trunk and placing it before Archie on the pavement.

"What is it?" Archie says to Echaverria, looking at the contents of the box.

"Nothing you'd want," Echaverria replies. "Nothing Curtis wants."

"I *told* you this ain't got nothin' to do with Curtis," Archie says. The four of them stand around the box for twenty seconds in silence. Snow begins to fall. Otis of the busted leg still lies sixty feet yonder. "Gimme your wallet," Archie says.

Echaverria hands over his wallet, which contains some twelve dollars and no credit cards. Archie riffles through it and drops it on the asphalt. "Gimme the keys," he says. Echaverria hands over the keys, and Archie throws them far away; Echaverria watches their flight carefully.

"Joe," Archie says, "you take this box here to the van. Willie, you go get Otis." Joe and Willie depart for their respective tasks.

"I ain't to be fucked with," Archie tells Echaverria, "and you one lucky son of a bitch I didn't kill your ass, you hear me?"

"I hear you, Archie."

"You fuckin' *better* hear me."

Archie turns and heads for the van, Echaverria heads for his keys.


Two hours later, Echaverria paces from room to room of his apartment, angrily and without direction. He is furious, not so much at the ignominy of being ripped off by a bunch of apprentice assholes as by its absurdity. Everything has been running perfectly on schedule, better than he could possibly have expected—and now because of something he couldn't possibly have expected, everything is fucked.

Did Curtis actually think that after moving as much merchandise as he has in the last several days he'd be going back for more? Or has Curtis been oblivious to his recent movements, was this nothing more than random retaliation? In either case, the hit logically should have been made before the exchange, which is perhaps what Archie and the boys had in mind, what Echaverria ironically prevented by pulling over after leaving the tunnel. If they had hit him before he'd reached Pierre, somehow, he'd now be out fifty thousand dollars, which in the present context would be a minor problem. He'd have thirty-one hours to get his money back, and considering the predictability of Curtis's movements that wouldn't be extremely difficult. But Curtis didn't get the money, he got the goods. And the question is: what the hell is Curtis going to do with the goods? If he hangs onto the box, looking to make a deal, there's every chance of getting it back because Curtis doesn't have connections in this realm. But if he figures out what it is, decides he wants nothing to do with it, straps it around Archie's ankles and drops them both off the Triborough Bridge . . .

Echaverria has $371,000 in his safe deposit box and nine pounds of the best cocaine in the world sealed in the wall behind the refrigerator. He had intended to leave it there as a bit of an insurance policy.

He dials a Connecticut number. "Sarah? Hey, how you doin'? This is Ray. . . . Listen, I got somethin' here you could really be interested in . . ."

Twenty minutes later he's back in the Bavaria. At ten-thirty, after paying $83.50 for a new spare tire and explaining to the man at Dino's Sunoco that he doesn't care about the warranty on his deceased Michelin radial ("Jesus," the man said, "I don't know what the hell made this one blow—you could probably get a new one free from a dealer . . ."), he's on the New England Thruway.


"Ray," Sarah says, leaning back, "this stuff is incredible. But look, man, it's Sunday, so I'd have to write you a check . . ."

Echaverria stands by a picture window, looking at the Long Island Sound. "You think you could round up some people who might be interested in this?"

"Sure."

"I'm talkin' about a lot of it."

"What, like a pound?"

"Nine pounds."

Sarah sits up, speechless.

"Do you trust me, Sarah?"

"Of course I do."

"Would I rip you off?"

"No, you wouldn't."

"Would you rip me off?"

"No, of course I wouldn't."

"Okay, here's the deal . . ."

Echaverria explains that he's going away for a while, that he isn't quite sure when he'll be back. He'll leave all nine pounds with Sarah on the condition that she can raise fifty thousand dollars and have it sent to a certain address within a week. The next twenty-five thousand dollars will go to Echaverria upon his return, and anything above that amount will be Sarah's, free and clear.

"I could make a hell of a lot of money." Sarah says.

"You'd be half-assed if you didn't."

She mulls. "Sarah," Echaverria says, "I don't give a shit how much money you make. The only thing that makes any difference to me is whether you can raise fifty grand and get it there in a week."

"I can do that," she says.

"Okay," Echaverria says. He removes nine pounds of cocaine from his briefcase and puts it on Sarah's bed.

"You're gonna stick around for a while, aren't you?" Sarah says.

Echaverria regrets that he has things to do.


Back in the city, Echaverria sets out on a peculiar sort of Cook's Tour. He leaves the West Side Highway at 125th Street and drives to Lenox Avenue, parks the car in a bus stop and walks into a bar. He has a brief conversation with the bartender, a large, middle-aged black man; he hands the bartender a fifty-dollar bill, they engage in a soul shake, and Echaverria departs. He repeats the process in several other bars and clubs, and on a few street corners. The amount of money exchanged varies between twenty dollars and fifty dollars.

He drives down Broadway, starting at 125th, stopping at a few spots on the Upper West Side before his next major operation, around Times Square. He takes 42nd Street across town and hits a few seedy singles bars, then drives down Second Avenue to the East Village, up Eighth Street to the West Village. By five-thirty, when he gets back to his apartment, he's handed out approximately twelve hundred dollars to thirty-seven assorted bartenders, bouncers, junkies, prostitutes, and hangers-out. His payments have been without regard to race, color, or creed.

He begins making telephone calls to hospitals: "Hello, I wonder if you could help me. I was witness to an accident this morning . . . a hit-and-run accident. There was a young black man hit by a car. I think his leg was broken. I didn't get his last name, but his first name was Otis. I've reported it to the

police, but they say they can't investigate unless they have a
last name . . ." Fourteen likely hospitals have no young broken-
legged black male patient named Otis. Otis has evidently been
ditched somewhere under an assumed name, or maybe Curtis
has been going to medical school in his spare time.

Like cockroaches, Curtis and Archie are going to come out
at night. Somewhere. At six-thirty Echaverria hangs up the
telephone, abandoning the hospital tactic.

He begins to pack. Between six-thirty and eight, he packs four
suitcases. At eight, he cooks his second meal of the day and
first in fourteen hours. At nine, as he's finishing dinner, the
phone rings.

"Hey, Ray, this is Mario." Mario is a Chinese/Portuguese
vagabond/hustler who exists around Sheridan Square. "Listen,
man, I just seen one of those dudes . . ."

"Which one?"

"Archie."

"You sure?"

"Yeah. I wouldn't call if I wasn't sure."

"Where'd you see him?"

"Him and a couple of chicks just went into Caesar's . . ."

"On Washington Place?"

"Yeah."

"Where are you?"

"At the Riviera."

"Okay, get your ass back to Caesar's, okay? Stand outside,
and I'll be there in ten minutes."

Echaverria is there in eight minutes, on foot. Mario stands, as
ordered, in front of the discothèque.

"He still in there?"

"Yeah. At least he didn't come out."

"Okay, thanks a lot." Echaverria hands Mario two twenties,
doubling his earlier payment.

"Anytime, Ray," Mario says.

Echaverria spots Archie almost immediately—at center stage
on the dance floor, gyrating implausibly on platform shoes with
heels that must be a foot high. Above the shoes, Archie wears
a purple suit with a fur collar. His partner is a beautiful black

woman in a slinky purple dress and equally tall shoes. They
dance to "Reach Out, I'll Be There" by the Four Tops. What
a waste, Echaverria thinks. On Sunday night the place is not
too crowded, but the hundred or so people at Caesar's are in
constant animation—on the dance floor or otherwise. Echaverria
stands apart, against a wall, watching and waiting for Archie
to take a break. There is a group of tables directly in front of
him, occupied primarily by energized couples. Perhaps twenty
feet away sits a lone white woman, who looks vaguely familiar
to Echaverria. She's probably a local hooker, and she's probably the other "chick" who came in with Archie. A white
adolescent sidles up to Echaverria.

"You want some ludes, man?"

"Get lost."

"You want some reds? Some coke?"

"Get *lost*, asshole."

The kid wanders away, unoffended. "Soul Makossa" segues
into "Swing Your Daddy," and Echaverria waits.

Twenty minutes later Archie gives the black woman a final
twirl and swaggers off the dance floor; she follows at a respectful distance. Archie walks straight to the table occupied by the
white hooker. Evidently the black woman is his dancing date,
the white woman his companion for later doings. Or perhaps it's
to be a threesome. For the moment, it will be a quartet. Echaverria sits down between the two women, making it boy-girl-
boy-girl. Archie, his face beaded with sweat, is deep in conversation with the hooker. He might be aware that someone has just
sat down across from him, but he hasn't looked up. The black
woman looks at Echaverria, who leans to speak into her ear, to
be heard over the music.

"Would you tell Archie I'd like to talk to him?" he says.

The black woman leans in similar fashion to relay the message,
and as Archie turns to listen he sees Echaverria. His eyes open
wide.


Were Echaverria prone to clichés, he might say something to
Archie about his not being such a tough guy without that gun in
his hand.

They stroll down Seventh Avenue and Echaverria strokes Archie's fur collar. "You kill that squirrel yourself?" he asks Archie.

Who replies: "What you want from me, man?"

"Hey, Archie, why the fuck would I want somethin' from you? It ain't like you pulled a gun on me this morning and ripped me off . . ."

Archie raises his voice: "What you *want* from me, man?"

"You know fuckin' well what I want from you."

Archie, not so predictable as Echaverria might have thought, swings a backhand right fist that glances off Echaverria's cheek; he takes a backward half-step as Archie lights out. For a moment Echaverria regrets not having brought his gun along, but Archie, sprinting absurdly on his platforms, sprawls to the pavement on his seventh step.

Echaverria stands over him; the scab on Archie's chin has opened, and blood dribbles onto the fur collar. "You don't wanna mess with me, motherfucker, you know that . . ."

The implication this time is that it's someone else who should be messed with. "Where is he?" Echaverria asks.

"I dunno, man," Archie says, still on the sidewalk.

Echaverria gives him a gentle kick on the chin wound. A small, hesitant crowd of people has gathered to watch the unscheduled street drama. Archie has assumed the fetal position. Echaverria kneels and repeats the question.

"Over at the Puerto Rican dude," Archie whispers. "The rich dude, on the East Side."


Echaverria walks casually away, reaches the corner, and starts to run. He's back in his apartment within five minutes.

He dials Ramon's number. If Curtis answers, he will of course hang up immediately. If Ramon answers, Echaverria will have a few questions to ask. If Inge answers, he's in business.

She does. "Inge? Hey, this is Ray. My old friend Curtis wouldn't be there, would he?"

"You don't want to talk to me, Ray?"

"I love talking to you, Inge. If there's anybody I don't want to talk to it's Curtis."

"You just want to know if he's here."

"Right."

"I have a feeling I shouldn't answer the question."

"It's important to me, Inge."

"It's a matter of honor, isn't it, Ray?"

"Hey, Inge, fuck honor . . . that bastard stole something from me this morning and I need to get it back."

"There won't be any trouble?"

"Look, if I have to kick his ass I'll do it outside. In the elevator."

"Okay . . . he's here."

"You figure he's gonna be there for a while?"

"I should think for a long while."

"How about Ramon?"

"Ramon's not here."

"Is he likely to show up?"

"I don't think so. He went to San Juan this afternoon."

"When did Curtis show up?"

"I couldn't tell you that. He was here when I woke up."

"When did you wake up?"

"Oh, one-thirty, I think, or two . . ."

"When did Ramon leave for San Juan?"

"His plane was at four."

"Why didn't you go with him?"

"I never go with him. I don't like it there."

"Okay, Inge, look, I'm gonna be over there in about fifteen or twenty minutes. Is that all right with you?"

"As long as you don't kill him on my white couch."

"If it has to happen on your white couch, I'll poison him."

"Okay, Ray. I'll tell the doorman to let you in . . ."


Echaverria takes Eighth Avenue uptown to Central Park, zips through the park to the East Side and gets to Second and 71st in eleven minutes. He double-parks in front of the building. The doorman is unfamiliar. "Ray Echaverria, I'm expected in 19-D."

"Yeah, she called down. But you can't leave your car there . . ."

Echaverria reaches for his wallet and extracts a ten-dollar bill.

"I can't take that," the doorman says.

"How about a twenty?"

"Listen, buddy, no offense, but you could wave a fifty in my face and I couldn't take it. I just got this job, and I don't wanta lose it, okay?"

"It's gonna be about ten minutes," Echaverria says. "How about a hundred?"

"The last guy had this job, he let everybody double-park, they probably gave him a lotta money, and he got fired. The heat comes down from the cops, they give it to the management, and I'd like to keep the job. You understand?"

Echaverria not only understands, he admires this little son of a bitch.

The odds against finding a legal parking space at 10:20 on Sunday night are unspeakable. Echaverria intends to leave the car in the first available illegal spot, figuring it won't be towed and he can afford the ticket. But 71st between Second and Third is not to be parked upon, even the several fire-hydrant spaces having been taken. He is about to turn right on Third when, just as the light changes to green, he notices the car parked on 71st across the intersection. He proceeds slowly across Third Avenue and pulls up next to a blue Camaro. There are undoubtedly several hundred blue Camaros parked in Manhattan at any given time. Echaverria maneuvers the Bavaria adjacent to the Camaro, about two inches away from it. He turns on the Bavaria's flashers and walks back to Second Avenue.


Inge stands by the open door. Her feet are bare, the rest of her body semi-evident under a light silk robe. "You didn't have to get dressed up for me," Echaverria says. Inge smiles.

"He still here?" Echaverria asks.

"He's still here," Inge replies. "In the guest room, with a friend. Do you want to socialize with me for a while, or do you want to take care of your business right away?"

With his quarry a few yards away, Echaverria sees no reason not to relax for a few minutes. "I would be honored to socialize with you," he says.

"You just told me to fuck honor," Inge says wryly.

"There's honor and there's honor," Echaverria replies.

She leads him into the white living room. *Columbo* flickers silently on the television screen. "Would you like a drink?"

"Yeah, I would . . . a little bit of Wild Turkey, with some ice."

Inge sets the drink on the glass table in front of the white couch; as she does so she reveals her torso from navel to neck. She sits down next to him.

"Are you trying to seduce me, Inge?" Echaverria says.

"I'm always trying to seduce you, Ray."

"Ramon would probably kill us both."

"Ramon is like a little boy."

"I don't think that would prevent him from killing us."

"I would prevent him from killing us," Inge says with great conviction, and Echaverria imagines she knows what she's talking about.

"Well, I think the seduction's gonna have to wait till next time, anyway," he says.

Inge shrugs, "What did Curtis steal from you this morning?" she asks, her tone of voice unchanged.

"Something that's important to me, something that couldn't mean shit to him."

"Is that why he stole it?"

"No," Echaverria says.

"Because he thought it was cocaine," Inge says.

There is a brief silence. Echaverria drinks half his Wild Turkey. "Inge," he says, "did Ramon plan this trip, or did he just decide to go all of a sudden?"

She shrugs again. "He was planning to go. Maybe it wasn't going to be today. I couldn't say."

Were Echaverria not well acquainted with Inge's strange amalgam of forthrightness and insouciance, he might at this point be extremely suspicious: that she knows precisely what's going on here, that she's attempted to lure him to bed for some ulterior design. He trusts her, at least partially by instinct. He has no particular affection for Ramon, but Ramon has always treated him as a friend, so he has always treated Ramon as a friend. But at this moment Curtis, whose morning activities have violated all sorts of articles and sections in Echaverria's private book of regulations, occupies Ramon's guest room for his pleasure. It's possible, even likely, that Ramon has no idea what happened this morning. It's also possible that Ramon has departed for San Juan entirely because of what happened this morning. And finally, it's possible that both the above are true.

Echaverria glances at the television screen: *Columbo* has ended, the eleven o'clock news has begun. He finishes the bourbon with a second swallow, and stands up. "I won't break anything," he says to Inge.


Padding silently down the hallway, Echaverria removes the gun from his leather jacket and stops by the door to the guest room. It's dark in there. He turns the knob slowly and soundlessly, pushes the door open. Light from the hallway reveals a blissful, innocent scene: Curtis and an unidentified Caucasian female sprawled on a king-size bed, covers askew. Echaverria moves toward Curtis's clothing, scattered on the floor. As he picks up Curtis's pants the girl stirs. She's sleeping on her back, the dim light is getting through to her, and her unconscious is trying to decide whether to stay that way or to see what's happening. Echaverria finds Curtis's wallet. The girl blinks her eyes open. She looks about sixteen. She sits up and sees Echaverria, who puts down Curtis's pants, waves the gun at her with his right hand, and moves his left index finger to his lips. She obeys to the extreme, turning over and hiding her head under the pillow. Curtis stirs and snorts, but stays asleep. Echaverria removes the wallet from the pants: it contains $2,352. Not enough, but a start. He puts the money in his right pants pocket, then goes through Curtis's overcoat, shirt, shoes, and socks. No more money, but in the overcoat he discovers a ring from which are suspended two General Motors keys.

He shakes Curtis by the shoulder. Curtis says: "Not yet, sugar." He grabs Curtis by the shoulder and flips him over on his back.

Curtis is not without aplomb. He wipes his eyes and says, "Hey, Ray, what's happenin'?"

"Get dressed." Echaverria stands over him, pointing the gun at his teeth.

"Aw, *man* . . . what the fuck you pullin'?"

"Curtis, there ain't time for jivin'. You get dressed or I'm gonna drag your naked ass on the street, okay?"

"Whatever you say, Ray . . ."

Echaverria moves to the side, picks up Curtis's clothes and throws them to him. As he dresses, Curtis speaks to the girl, who remains invisible. "Sorry about this, honey. You don't never know when some dude gonna get some crazy idea. I make it up to you. I be back. Just gotta straighten the dude out, you understand . . ."

Echaverria follows Curtis down the hallway, through the living room. They both look at Inge, still sitting on the white couch; her eyes remain on the television.

In the elevator, Curtis says, "What's it about?"

"This morning."

"What about this mornin'?"

"Talk to me, Curtis, or shut the fuck up."

"Where we goin'?"

"Three guesses."

"Don't you go tryin' nothin', Ray, or I'm gonna scream bloody murder, an' you ain't got no permit for that . . ."

"You're a pathetic son of a bitch, Curtis, you know that?"

They walk single file past the doorman. Echaverria smiles and waves, the doorman smiles back. Outside, Curtis turns left. "The other way," Echaverria says, and Curtis obediently turns right.

"If I knew what this was about, Ray," Curtis says.

Echaverria sees the Bavaria's taillights flashing. "What?"

"Maybe we could cut a deal?"

"What kind of deal?"

"I dunno what it's about yet . . ."

"Then just shut up, Curtis."

They cross Third Avenue. The Bavaria and the Camaro are exactly as before. Echaverria sits on the Bavaria's trunk and tosses Curtis his keys. "Open the trunk," he says.

"How the fuck'm I gonna open the trunk?" Curtis replies.

If this is somebody else's Camaro, that's a good question. "You take that key, the one with the round top that says GM on it, and you put it in the lock," Echaverria says.

Curtis puts the key in the lock and the trunk pops open. For several seconds neither man moves, then Curtis takes a half step backward and says, "What now?"

"Where is it, Curtis?"

"Where is *what*, man?"

"Curtis, you got about fifteen seconds to get your shit together, 'cause if you don't I'm gonna shoot you in the balls."

Curtis emotes a guttural laugh. "You ain't about to shoot me here, Ray. This the East Side. They got *cops* here."

"For what you did to me this morning, motherfucker, I'd shoot you in front of City Hall. I'd shoot you in the fuckin' mayor's office with fifty cops takin' pictures."

"What *I* did?"

"Don't try to tell me this ain't your car, Curtis."

Curtis's eyeballs dart about frantically for a second or two. His voice becomes softer, more reasonable: "Listen, man, I didn't do nothin' to you you didn't do to me. You bring a goddamn professional player to the game . . . I seen you and him out in the kitchen together . . . man, that's cheatin'. Far as I'm concern now, we even."

"Where the fuck is it, Curtis?"

"What you gonna do with me if you get it back?"

"I'll take you to Disneyland."

"Look, I still got it. You ain't gonna mess with me, okay?"

"Where is it?"

"Right here, man," Curtis points to the trunk. "I took it out the box, you know, I put it down with the spare."

Echaverria has little reason to believe him. Curtis's delaying tactics point to the likelihood of the box's contents being long gone; he's been buying time, in all probability, and has decided that his best chance lies with whatever really is in the trunk well—a gun, perhaps, probably the .357 Magnum encountered this morning. Still, it's possible that the stuff really is down there.

"Get it out," Echaverria says. He slides off the Bavaria and stations himself in the crosswalk, three feet behind Curtis. Traffic on Third is light; traffic on 71st Street is none; not a pedestrian is in sight. Ecchaverria trains the gun on Curtis's back.

Curtis looks over his shoulder and says, "I gotta lift this thing out a here, but I'm gettin' it . . ." Echaverria hears the trunk partition scraping against sheet metal.

In the next instant Curtis moves like lightning, wheeling

from his bent position to face Echaverria, his right arm extended.

Echaverria responds in kind, going into a crouch at the first sign of violent movement.

The difference lies ultimately in their respective weapons. Curtis's tire iron sails at most three inches over Echaverria's left shoulder and clanks harmlessly across Third Avenue. Echaverria's bullet hits Curtis in the upper right thigh, driving him back against the Camaro. Curtis sits on the pavement. "Oh, *shit!*" he screams.

Echaverria unlocks the Bavaria and pushes it several feet forward. He takes the keys from the Camaro's trunk lock and tells Curtis to get up. "I can't fuckin' get up," Curtis says. He drags Curtis to the sidewalk and leans him against a mailbox. Cars go by on Third Avenue. Echaverria unlocks the Camaro, starts its engine, and drives it to a point directly in front of the Bavaria. Then he gets back in the Bavaria and parks it in the Camaro's former spot. He removes a tool kit and a crowbar from the Bavaria's trunk and tosses them in the Camaro's back seat. He picks Curtis up by the arms and says, "Walk."

"I can't walk," Curtis says. "You done shot me in the fuckin' leg!"

Echaverria propels Curtis to the passenger side of the Camaro, unlocks that door, and shoves Curtis in. He walks around to the other side and they drive off.

"Where you goin'?" Curtis asks through gritted teeth.

"Shut up," Echaverria replies.

"Man, I'm bleedin' . . . you take me to a hospital or I'm gonna *die*. . . ."

"You shut up, or you're gonna die."

Echaverria drives south on Lexington Avenue. Curtis sits massaging his leg below the wound, as if trying to keep the blood from getting to it. Echaverria doesn't imagine Curtis is losing too much blood, the upper thigh being a pretty good place to be shot if you have to get shot. They cross Houston Street, Canal Street, descending to the bowels of Manhattan on Broadway.

In the Bowery, Curtis breaks the silence. "You ain't gonna kill me, are you, Ray?"

"Probably."

"Aw, *Jesus*, man . . . what the fuck you mean by *that?*"

"Just what I said."

"What I gotta do so you don't kill me?"

"Shut up."

Echaverria stops the car in an alley off Wall Street. There could be no more appropriate location for the sort of transaction about to take place. He faces Curtis, who is scrunched in the passenger seat, staring at the pistol in Echaverria's left hand. "Curtis," he says, "if you don't level with me, if you ain't completely fuckin' honest with me, I'm gonna blow your fuckin' brains out. Then I'm gonna set fire to the car. Then I'm gonna take the subway back uptown, get my car, and drive home. And in the morning I'm gonna pick up the *Daily News* and read about how they found an overdone nigger on Wall Street. You hear me?"

"What you wanna know, man?"

"Where's the box?"

"Hey, Ray, look, if I'd a knew what it meant . . ."

"Where is it?"

"Ramon."

"You're a clever son of a bitch, aren't you, takin' it to Ramon?"

"Archie brung me the shit. I didn't expect nothin' like that. I figured you was just gonna pass it on an' make somethin' off it. I didn't know what the fuck to do with it, so I call Ramon to see if he's interested. He say yeah, sure, bring it on down . . ."

"What'd he give you for it?"

"Wasn't nothin' . . ."

"How much?"

"Ten grand."

"You're fuckin' around with me, Curtis . . ."

Curtis's voice goes up an octave: "It's the goddamn truth, man, you think I'm gonna lie to you now?"

"Where's the ten grand?"

"You sittin' right next to it—in the door."

Echaverria reaches into the back seat for the tool kit and crowbar. He opens the door, steps outside, removes one screw, and pries open the paneling. A thin stack of bills encompassed by a rubber band falls to the street. Ten thousand-dollar bills. He puts the money in his pocket and crosses to the other side of the car. "Lie down," he tells Curtis, who obeys. He pries open the paneling and an identical packet of bills tumbles out. "More?" he asks Curtis, stretched out across both bucket seats, bleeding.

"Yeah, in the trunk. Pick up the tire."

Echaverria finds two more ten-grand clumps in the spare-tire well. "I got forty. Is that it?" he says to Curtis.

"I swear. I promise," Curtis says.

"Your word as a gentleman, right?"

"Yeah, Ray, it's the *truth* . . ."

"Cross your heart and hope to die, right?"

The word "die" weighs heavy upon Curtis. "I ain't never gonna mess with you again, Ray."

Echaverria stands by the open, mangled passenger door, next to Curtis's feet. "You're damn right you ain't," he says.

"Don't do it, Ray! For Christ's sake don't do it!" Curtis's plea is somewhat muted because his face is two inches deep in the driver's seat. Echaverria slams the passenger door and walks to the other side of the Camaro.

"Get the fuck off the seat," he says.

Curtis scrambles back into the passenger seat, Echaverria sits behind the wheel and starts the car. Curtis's eyes blink furiously, dual metronomes gone berserk.

As they cross Canal Street, Curtis says, "You ain't *gonna* kill me, are you?"

"Curtis, I'll tell you the truth," Echaverria says. "What I planned to do was shoot you about five more times—in the legs, in the arms—and then I was gonna run over you with your own fuckin' car. But when you gave me your word, when you told me you weren't gonna mess with me no more, it turned me around."

"That was no jive, Ray."

"I'm gonna trust you from here on, Curtis."

"Well, look, man, if you could take me to a hospital . . ."

"I'm on a tight schedule, Curtis."

"I'm bleedin' bad, man . . ."

"Just think good thoughts. It'll stop."

Ten minutes later, at 1:35, Echaverria pulls the Camaro up behind the Bavaria, in the crosswalk.

"I don't know if I can drive it, man," Curtis says.

"You ain't gonna drive it," Echaverria replies.

"What the fuck am I gonna do?"

Echaverria removes a ten-dollar bill from Curtis's wallet and tosses it on his lap. "Take a taxi," he says.

"I can't fuckin' *walk*, Ray . . ."

"Then crawl," Echaverria says, pulling the keys from the ignition, and leaving.

"I'm gonna freeze to death out here, motherfucker!" Curtis calls after him.

Wouldn't that be funny, Echaverria thinks as he pulls the Bavaria away from the curb.


He assumes that Curtis will survive. Even if the miserable bastard can't walk (which he doubts), the police will be along to ticket the Camaro within five or six hours, probably sooner, since the car is jutting out onto Third Avenue. Curtis will lose a lot of blood, spend a few days in the hospital, get out and come down on Echaverria with everything he can muster—there will be ten or twelve Archies lurking with their big guns, waiting to follow him, to catch him isolated, unguarded, and blow him away.

But as he drives back through the park, Echaverria feels immense satisfaction. He is a master gamesman who's been momentarily surprised, then embarrassed, by an illogical move. He has responded with the whole of his skills, and administered something close to total humiliation upon his opponent—the final move, of course, being yet to come—it will probably take Curtis and his mercenaries several weeks to figure out that he's not in hiding, but gone for good.


He parks at a meter on Seventh Avenue and drops Curtis's wallet and keys in the corner drain, whence they will shortly join other sewage.

Not until he's ascending the steps to his apartment does he remember that he's failed. And immediately afterward he recalls Inge's suggestion that he was involved in a matter of honor. He unlocks the door, turns on the light, and sits down next to the telephone. He's failed to recover what was stolen, what was so important. Why, then the satisfaction?

There's no time to worry about it now. He needs to move fast, and to sleep. He dials ten numbers, and a groggy voice answers on the fifth ring. "It's me," Echaverria says. "Listen carefully, because the situation has changed."

# 13

# A Visitor

There is no jai alai on Sunday.

Murphy stands by the kitchen counter, a can of Genesee in hand. Angela is three feet away, removing bones from pieces of chicken. He watches her fingers work, watches her face, so intent on the chicken, watches the slight movements of her right breast. They've spent a second consecutive full day in each other's company—the morning and early afternoon at Lion Country Safari, the late afternoon at *Save the Tiger*, for a singular feline doubleheader. Now in the early evening of the Lord's day, Murphy is nearing the end of his tether. He is decidedly in love, and fed up with this platonic bullshit. But what is he to do? Something explicit, physically or verbally: a discreet sidling followed by an obvious caress, perhaps; or a direct question (Angela, would you like to sleep with me?), or a not-so-direct question (Angela, do you think of me as a guest or . . .). Murphy cringes at the successive alternatives; he envisions her moving politely away from the caress, he hears her advising him not to confuse a pleasant relationship, or worse.

He is, in short, afraid to try.

Give Murphy a deck of cards, several people who want to take his money, and he'll be cool and logical and kick their asses. Give him a pari-mutuel situation where the odds are 17 percent against him and he'll figure a way to beat them. Give him an ocean which will drown him at a moment's notice and he'll get back to shore. Give him anything he can compete against, the

rules set down in black and white, and Murphy is a creature of
confidence approaching genteel arrogance. But in the absence of
rules he founders and spins, and often gives up.


They finish dinner at seven. The plan is to watch *Upstairs,
Downstairs* at nine. For the moment she is in the shower and he
rinsing dishes and placing them in the dishwasher. There is a
buzz from the security intercom. Murphy walks to the door and
pushes a button marked "Listen." "Yes?"

"Mr. Murphy?"

Murphy pushes "Talk" and says, "Right."

"We got a guy here that wants to see Mrs. Wilson. Name is
Gutierrez. Should I let him through?"

"Can you hold on a minute?"

"Sure thing."

Murphy heads down the hallway in fast march, knocks per-
emptorily on Angela's bedroom door despite hearing the shower.
In her bedroom he wonders what to do. The bathroom door is
open. He shouts her name. No response. He walks to the door
and shouts again. Still, apparently, she hasn't heard. He enters
the bathroom and sees the outline of her body through frosted
glass. The effect is curious: in the blur he perceives a dull tri-
angle of pubic hair and a corona of shampooed head hair. He
pirouettes away, groin stirring, and knocks backhanded on the
door. The shower is turned off. "Sorry!" Murphy shouts, un-
necessarily.

"What is it?" Angela asks.

Facing the bathroom door, Murphy speaks in a normal tone,
"There's a guy at the gate named Gutierrez. They want to know
if they should let him in . . ."

"Tell them to let him in."

"Okay."


Moments later the doorbell rings. Angela still hasn't appeared.
Murphy opens the door to a tall, handsome Cuban in a blue
suit. He carries a buckskin attaché case and says, "Angie here?"

"Yeah, she's just taken a shower," Murphy says. "Come in."

Gutierrez enters. "Have a seat," Murphy says. Gutierrez sits down on the couch. "Would you like a beer?"

"No, that's okay." Gutierrez's accent is slight.

They sit in silence for half a minute. Murphy is suddenly quite tense. He is tempted to return to Angela's bedroom to tell her Gutierrez has arrived, but imagines she's heard the bell.

"Nice day," Gutierrez says.

"Nice night, too," Murphy replies.

Another silence. "You her old man?" Gutierrez asks.

"No, just a friend," Murphy says.

"You know her a long time?"

"Just a few days."

"She's a tough lady."

Murphy doesn't have an easy response to that one, nor does he know exactly what Gutierrez means, so he nods.

"A very tough lady," Gutierrez adds.

Angela enters barefooted, wearing a robe. She has evidently been drying her hair, whose ends still dangle moistly. She glances and smiles at Murphy, thanking him for filling in.

Gutierrez rises and says, *"Hola."*

*"Como estás?"* Angela says, offering her hand. Gutierrez gives the hand a brief shake, then leans down to kiss Angela on the cheek. They sit next to each other on the couch and converse in rapid Spanish. Murphy has no idea what they're saying, but listens intently. Two words that pop up frequently are *dinero* and "Ramon." Could they possibly be talking about the poker game? Gutierrez has embarked on a lengthy narrative, or explanation; Angela's expression has become quite serious. Numbers are involved. Vast numbers. *Milles.* Thousands. Hundreds of thousands. Hundreds of thousands of something. Hundreds of thousands of *dinero*, perhaps, in which case they're not talking about the poker game. Some other Ramon, and some other *dinero*. They get up.

"We'll just be a minute," Angela says to Murphy.

"Excuse me," Gutierrez says to Murphy, picking up the attaché case and following Angela to her bedroom. He closes the door behind him.

Murphy waits. He finishes his beer and opens another. He switches on the miniature TV and flips through channels; the image in his mind is Angela's body, much of which he knows so well, the rest of which he sees as a blur through a frosted shower door. What lurid events might be taking place now in her bedroom? What might she, the chaste divorcée, be engaging in with this suave Cuban? Murphy watches Mike Wallace interrogate some poor bastard on 60 *Minutes*. He has no idea what they're saying, either, because the sound is turned off.

Twenty minutes later they emerge, still babbling in Spanish. They walk straight to the front door. Gutierrez gives Angela another kiss on the cheek, then looks at Murphy and says, "Nice to meet you." Murphy waves, and Gutierrez exits. Angela closes the door.

"I'm sorry about that," she says. "I didn't expect him tonight."

"Who is he?" Murphy asks.

"He's a friend of Ray's."

"What was all that about?"

"Nothing," Angela says. "Just some business."

"What kind of business?"

Angela walks past him, into the kitchen. She takes a can of Genesee from the refrigerator and opens it. This is the first time Murphy has seen her approach an alcoholic beverage without invitation. "Prosper," she says, "what's going on with you?"

"Nothing's going on with me," Murphy says. "I guess I just don't think it's very . . . *polite* of you to disappear into your bedroom for half an hour with some sleazy bastard . . ."

"You're angry at me, aren't you?"

"Yeah . . . okay, I guess I am . . ."

"Why are you angry at me? It's not as if we're lovers . . ."

Murphy chuckles.

"What are you laughing about?" Angela asks.

"You'd have to be there to appreciate it," Murphy says.

"Be where? What are you talking about?"

"Your friend Whitaker thinks we're lovers," Murphy says. "And I imagine your friend Gutierrez does, too."

"Well, I guess that's a fairly natural assumption," Angela says, "when two people past the age of consent are sharing an apartment . . ."

"What I'm laughing about, Angela, is that it's no fun to be the object of suspicion when you didn't do it."

"Is it any fun to be the object of suspicion when you *did* do it?"

Murphy can't help smiling, more at the game than the implication. "In this case, I can't help thinking it would be."

"What do you mean by that? That it would be fun to sleep together?" Angela's voice has risen nearly an octave.

Murphy frantically runs both his hands through his hair in a final gesture of frustration. There's only one direction left to follow. "No," he says, "I mean that I want to sleep with you more than I've ever wanted anything before. In my life."

Angela's face is transformed in a tenth of a second: her expression softens, her eyes moisten. She says, "Are you kidding me, Prosper?"

"No," Murphy says. "Of course not. How could I be kidding you?"

"You never said anything. You never did anything."

He takes the two steps that separate them (thinking, My God, it was there all along, My God, My God), and puts his arms around her waist. They kiss with an absurd passion, two characters from a Victorian novel, or two displaced, lonely, repressed American refugees. Murphy's fingers have suddenly been given magical license—they slide between the folds of Angela's robe and roam, touching and stroking all those parts of her previously only seen or imagined. This *is* magic. His knees tremble. Their lips are locked, their tongues entwined. He feels his belt unbuckled, feels his pants dropping to his ankles, feels her fingers around his penis. "Come," she says, "let's go."

"Wait," he says, and stumblingly pulls his pants past his shoes and off. She leads him into her bedroom, pulls back the covers, throws off her robe. God, she is magnificent. Murphy struggles with his shirt, gets it off, struggles with his shoes and socks, gets them off, slides his underpants down, eases into bed next to her, replaces his mouth on hers, slips his left index finger inside her. Angela emits a sudden profound sigh, as if experiencing a forgotten pleasure. Seconds later she pulls her mouth away and whispers, "Now, Prosper. Don't wait. Now."

She guides him home, and he enters ever so slowly, feeling every wondrous millimeter of her. This is a transcendent moment, one of the tiny few in Murphy's life. There is in this moment no flaw, no suggestion of imperfection. He wants, and is wanted. He loves, and is loved. His bliss creates an illusion (or results from the illusion, or both) that the moment might not be transitory, that this instance of mere sexual coupling is the answer, the vindication, the resolution, the solution.

The moment is short-lived, *sui generis*. Moving out as marvelously slowly as he'd moved in, he senses definite pre-orgasmic tremors, realizes there's absolutely nothing he can do. A price must be paid for ecstasy. He moves back in, the first spasm beginning. "Angela," he says, "I'm sorry, I can't . . ." and the erupting orgasm deprives him of the power of speech. It lasts well beyond the boundaries of measurement. Over a period of decades, or millennia, Murphy secretes several thousand, or hundred thousand cubic inches of semen into Angela, and still after the last drop has been discharged it continues.

He feels her fingers running up and down his back. He says, "It's . . ." and can't remember the rest of his line. He'd intended to say: "It's been a long time."

"Don't talk, Prosper," Angela says.

A minute or five minutes later, Murphy says, "Angela, I can't describe . . ."

She joins her hands on his back and says, "Don't try."

"I'm sorry it was so fast," he says, "I'm out of practice."

"You're not the only one," Angela says.


They do it again. This time Murphy is capable of more restraint, but not enough. Angela walks bareassed and glorious into the living room, returns with the little television. They watch *Upstairs, Downstairs* in bed. Murphy feels great fondness tonight for everyone upstairs and downstairs, and for Alistair Cooke. They watch *Nova*, which examines the lives of various people who function on just a few minutes' sleep per day, some with no sleep at all. Murphy is fascinated. Midway through the program, as the narrator explains that it seems to have something to do with genes, Murphy returns to speak to Angela and realizes that she's asleep.

He lowers the volume and spends the next half hour alternately watching the little television and looking at Angela. She lies on her back, one arm on Murphy's pillow the other across her stomach. Her shoulders are slightly sunburned, most of her torso lightly tanned; her breasts, in contrast and in this dim light, resemble two small mounds of porcelain delicately tipped in russet. Her lips are an eighth of an inch apart; she breathes in slow rhythm, serene and beautiful.

At *Nova's* end Murphy slides carefully out of bed and puts on his underpants. He unplugs the television, carries it back to its place in the living room, gets a can of Genesee from the refrigerator, sits cross-legged on the deck. Immersed in warm silence, he makes a quick state-of-the-self analysis. He is in love. The person he loves loves him in return, or close to it. He has ten thousand dollars in the bank, almost two thousand in his wallet, and neither a care nor an obligation in the world.

There comes a loud *plop* from below, followed by several more. "I hear you, brother," Murphy says to the giant fish, who continues nevertheless to flip and flop in his manner.

It occurs suddenly to Murphy that there might be something dangerous about his ten thousand dollars being in Walter Frazier's name. What? He doesn't know what, but considers a trip to First American tomorrow, perhaps to re-establish the account in his real name after some glib explanation of the deception, or better to withdraw the money and deposit it elsewhere in his real name. There is something about First American, in retrospect, something beyond its mere sleaziness, that doesn't sit right.

The manta ray does a bellyflop. In this Madera Beach silence the sound might be mistaken for distant thunder. Murphy returns to Angela's bedroom in darkness. He slides back in next to her. She stirs. He kisses her lips and says, "I love you." Still asleep, she says, "I fell asleep."


Murphy is awakened in the middle of the night by the telephone. He sits up on the first ring and remembers that he's in Angela's bed, Angela beside him, the phone on her bedside table next to the clock radio, which reads 2:15. She remains asleep as the phone rings a second and third time. He wonders what to do. A phone call at 2:15 in the morning must be either important or a wrong number. He kisses her and says her name.

She wakes up. He says, "The phone." She picks it up on the fifth ring. She says, "Hello," and proceeds to listen for a few seconds. When she speaks again it is in Spanish. For the most part, she listens. When she hangs up the clock radio says 2:21.

"Gutierrez?" Murphy asks.

"No," Angela says, no longer serene, "it was Ray."

"Echaverria?"

"Yes."

She eases back onto her pillow and closes her eyes. Murphy is tempted to let her fall back to sleep, but far more strongly tempted by a new wave of jealousy.

"Angela," he says gently, "what is he to you?"

"Oh, Prosper . . . don't ask me that now."

Murphy feels his guts constricting. "I have to know," he says.

"He's very important to me."

"In what way?"

Angela opens her eyes. "Oh, my God," she says, "you don't know, do you?"

"I don't know what?"

"Ray is my brother," Angela says.

Murphy struggles through a maze of relief and confusion, re-playing various conversations. It seems unlikely that Angela's lying to him now, and he realizes that nothing she's said to him regarding Echaverria has been intended to mislead. "He said you were an old friend of his," Murphy tells her.

Angela responds with a faint, resigned smile. "In a way, he was telling the truth."

"Why didn't he just tell me, for Christ's sake," Murphy asks himself as much as he asks Angela.

"Because he was playing one of his goddamned games with you. With us."

Murphy wonders as to the game's implications.

Angela presses against him. "But we won, Prosper," she says. At least for now, that will suffice.

# 14

# Echaverria in Charge

Early Monday morning Echaverria drives to a garage in eastern Queens, where he has contracted to leave the Bavaria in dry storage for a year, paid in advance, He brandishes an envelope and speaks to the garage man in charge. "You got a safe place for this?"

"You want me to put it in the safe?"

"Yeah, put it in the safe."

"If I don't show up in a year," Echaverria says, "you open that up and it'll tell you what to do with the car. You understand?"

"Yeah, sure I understand."

"I fuckin' hope you understand, 'cause my lawyer has a copy of everything in there."

Echaverria has no lawyer. The envelope contains the Bavaria's title certificate and a note in impressive legalese to the effect that should Raymond Echaverria not claim his vehicle by the end of February, 1974, title of said vehicle will revert to Mrs. Angela Wilson of Madera Beach, Florida.

His taxi arrives. He transfers three suitcases from the Bavaria's trunk to the taxi's trunk, elects to keep the smaller overnight bag with him in the back seat. He directs the driver to Air France at Kennedy.

Echaverria flies to Paris, where he is waved through customs. He flies to Bordeaux, where he rents a car, a sumptuous Citroën Pallas, and drives southwest, then due south, arriving in the coastal town of Hendaye a few minutes before ten. He leaves the highway, heads up a slight incline, and parks in front of a stately two-story house on Avenue Pellot.

He is greeted warmly by a group of old friends, who bestow upon him an extensive meal. Well after midnight, he drinks wine with three young men and one young woman. He tells them the story of Curtis and the Box, and they react with appropriate horror, admiration, disappointment. Then he displays for them the contents of his overnight bag. Hundreds of thousands of dollars. By this they are truly impressed. He takes one young man aside and asks if the documents are ready. Of course, the young man replies. You understand, Echaverria then says, that by accepting this money you're putting me in charge. Of course, the young man says again. I'll need some education, Echaverria tells him; I'll need a great deal of information, but I want it to be clear always that I'm in charge. Of course.

Echaverria now directs his attention to the young woman, with whom he goes upstairs at a quarter past two.


Tuesday morning he makes a transatlantic telephone call, then drives north, but only for half an hour, stopping at the Hertz agency in Bayonne. He explains that his American friend, M. Echaverria, has rented this Citroën in Bordeaux, intending to drive it to Spain on his vacation. But M. Echaverria has been called back to America on business. He would like to pay M. Echaverria's bill and then rent the car for himself. Is this possible?

"Yes, certainly, why not?" replies the girl behind the counter.

She works out the bill. Echaverria hands her 186 francs and a French driver's license which identifies him as Jean-Pierre Bordagaray, a resident of Hendaye. As she fills out his form, he explains pleasantly that M. Echaverria is an old friend, that his Spanish holiday is already paid for, that it would be a shame to waste it. The girl nods and murmurs through all this. She hands the completed form to Echaverria, who signs his new name. He hands it back to her and asks her name. Ginette, she says. He asks Ginette if she'd like to come to Spain with him. She regrets that she has to work. What a pity, he says.

He drives west to the winding coast road. To Biarritz, Bidart, back to Hendaye. The sky has been a murky gray all morning, and now a light mist has begun drifting. To Echaverria's right, the ocean is several different shades of blue, with distant patches approaching green as the sun breaks through the clouds. He remembers these warm, ominous winter days, when morning sun was no guarantee against afternoon rain or evening snow, and days like this especially—when a certain chosen spot of earth or sea might go unrained upon all day, another might be thoroughly saturated, the rest to be wetted and dried intermittently, unpredictably.

He remembers a fierce closeness to his mother, and a paradox of alienations. He spoke to her in Spanish, to his schoolmates in French. She was unable or unwilling to speak French, and as such her communicants might have been limited to her son and the various other refugees in Hendaye, but for the existence of Euskara—the language of her (and his) ancestors. It was still not as if she could chatter away with the neighbors, since her Euskara subsisted largely on words borrowed from Spanish, theirs on words borrowed from French. Every afternoon they were visited by Mme. Ithurbide, an elderly widow who lived across the street. The two women would converse carefully, haltingly, one or the other constantly nodding to indicate she understood, while Echaverria—childishly fluent in two languages but totally ignorant in the third—waited for an impasse. Then, with great pride, although without context, he would translate from French to Spanish, or vice versa, that the Euskaran exchange might resume.

His career as an interpreter began to end in the spring of 1946, when Mme. Ithurbide introduced his mother to her grandson, Antoine Bordagaray. Bordagaray was one of Hendaye's war heroes—a lieutenant in the French army at the age of twenty-two who was taken prisoner by the Nazis in 1940, escaped, joined the resistance, was taken prisoner again in 1943, tortured, but escaped once more; made his way to England, and spent the rest of the war teaching British commandos how best to kill Germans.

Fernanda Echaverria was charmed by Bordagaray, more so

when he requested a visit after their introduction, flattered when his visits became regular. He was twenty-nine, she twenty-seven.

Echaverria, now eight, listened in wonder as his mother spoke a few words of French to her first-time visitor. As her linguistic ability increased, so did his reputation among his contemporaries, who pressed him for every detail about their heroic Bordagaray.

For his part, Bordagaray introduced a fourth language to the household, teaching Echaverria a word of English here and there. He went away in September, to Paris.

In December, Fernanda Echaverria informed her son that Bordagaray was about to become his father. This came as no surprise to Echaverria; he'd been hoping for it. He would no longer be the son of the woman romanced by the hero, but the son of the hero as well. He was stunned by the rest of the news: his father-to-be had accepted a job; the job was in New York; New York was in America.

Antoine and Fernanda were married on Christmas Eve and sailed for New York the third week of January. In March, shortly before Echaverria's ninth birthday, he became a brother.

He doesn't stop at the house in Hendaye, but continues through town, past the string of gas stations and banks on the outskirts, to the frontier. The French guards wave him through to the Spanish side, where he stops behind a tiny Seat 600 whose license plate indicates it's from the province of Vizcaya. Spanish border guards, machine guns slung over their shoulders, are in the process of searching the Seat's every nook and cranny as the driver, an undernourished young man shabbily dressed, stands by and watches. They have begun to dismantle the innards of the little car's trunk when a guard motions to Echaverria: pull over here. Echaverria drives the Citroën alongside the Seat. "Documentos," the guard says, extending his hand. Echaverria gives him the French passport, the Citroën's registration, and the Green Card. The guard takes a quick look at the passport picture, a quicker look at Echaverria, hands him back the papers, and says, "Pase," waving him on.

As the rape of the Seat extends, the sleek Citroën glides effortlessly into Spain. This is nothing more than a trial run—he will spend the day wandering around San Sebastián, visiting points of interest in the best touristic manner, then return to Hendaye in time for dinner—but for the first time in his life, in grand and gracious style, Ramon Echaverria has come home.

# 15

# A Suspicious Vehicle

Sun pours through the bedroom window. In half-sleep Murphy watches Angela dress. Soon she crouches by the bed.

"Are you awake?"

"More or less."

"I have to go. I'll be back."

"Will you teach me Spanish?"

"I'm a little pressed for time right now."

"Okay. I can wait."

She kisses him on the lips, lingering a few seconds, and is off. He goes back to sleep.

At the beach a few hours later, he swims half again his usual distance, spends a couple of minutes gasping and drying. He gets up and runs half a mile south, passing a total of seven human beings, stops and runs back to his encampment: a towel, his clothes, and the Sunday *Times*. The following half hour is spent with The Week in Review: 20 More Freed POWs at Clark AFB; Vietnam Fighting Goes On Unabated; Body of Marshal Pétain stolen from tomb, discovered, reburied; Laos Peace Pact Signed (Nixon Says Paris Accord Can Bring Lasting Peace); B-52s Bomb Laos Less Than a Day After Truce; Israelis Down a Libyan Airliner in the Sinai, Killing at Least 74, Say It Ignored Warnings to Land (Nixon sends his condolences to Libya); Iran Will Buy $2 Billion in U.S. Arms Over Next Several Years; Dollar Recovers Abroad.

The *Times* has omitted the week's hottest story by far: Murphy Streak Continues—Extends to Passion.

Not everyone has been doing so well. At Fat Lou's, Murphy turns to the sports and is twice stricken. The Rangers have lost to the California Seals, 5-3, this being the Seals' first victory in their last sixteen games. The Knicks have blown a 26-point lead and lost to the Chicago Bulls, 84-83, with the real Mr. Frazier held to six points.

The bogus Frazier recalls his decision to set things straight at First American Savings & Loan. Since it's just down the mall, why doesn't he drop in on John Trough right away. A good idea, Murphy decides. But first he's going to buy some veal, some bread crumbs, some olive oil, and some lemons. Having spent the better part of his life being cooked for or eating at sundry equivalents of Fat Lou's, Murphy is incapable of baking a chicken or broiling a steak. But his favorite dish, just ahead of *enchiladas en salsa verde* and chicken-fried steak, is veal milanese. After a year and a half of living alone, eating hamburgers and Cuban-Chinese food, Murphy one day bought an Italian cookbook and a pound of veal scallopini, and spent the following week perfecting a singular art. His first effort very much resembled a chicken-fried steak, and as such wasn't bad; his final creation was the equal of any veal milanese he'd ever consumed. In a week's time, Murphy had become a culinary idiot savant. Tonight, Angela will be the first outsider to taste his secret masterpiece.

He pushes a cart down the vast aisles of the shopping center's boss supermarket, an immense Grand Union. Here on aisle six are bread crumbs, then on aisle twenty-two the lemons, way over there on aisle two the olive oil. In passing, he picks up two six-packs of Genesee and a six-pack of Carlsberg, quite reasonably priced at three dollars and thirty-five cents. Now to the meat section, approximately the length of two football fields. Beef. Pork. Chicken. Turkey. Lamb. Ham. Ground beef, turkey, pork. Sausages and frankfurters of every known variety of meat, and various other substances. Press bell for service. An acned

youth with a white butcher's hat appears. "Where's the veal?"
Murphy asks.

"You didn't see no veal?"

"I didn't see no veal."

"What kind of veal you want?"

"Veal scallopini."

No reaction.

"Cut really thin. It's pink, almost white."

"Oh, yeah, I know what you're talkin' about—that stuff's goin'
for about four dollars a pound!"

"Yeah, that's about right . . ."

"We don't carry that kinda stuff. People around here don't
wanna spend that much for meat, y'know . . ."

Indeed they don't. Murphy hits two more supermarkets and
even finds a butcher shop, if a picture-windowed meat store may
be described as a butcher shop. The latter possesses a shoulder
of veal which, its owner insists, may be cut in such a way as to
closely resemble veal scallopini. Murphy declines the shoulder
and heads back to the apartment with a paper bag full of beer
and olive oil and bread crumbs and lemons. First American and
John Trough are forgotten.

He puts the beer and the lemons in the refrigerator, removes a
Carlsberg, has a sip, considers calling various places where meat
is sold in West Palm Beach. Angela should be home within the
half hour. He wants to be here when she returns. The veal can
wait. Tonight, if she's willing, they'll go to Miami and eat someone else's veal.


Bedraggled, Angela insists upon a swim. In the pool, Murphy
embraces her and asks if she thinks a more extreme aquatic show
of affection might cause concern among the several sunbathers
present.

"How extreme did you have in mind?" Angela asks.

"Very extreme," Murphy says.

"Genital contact?" Angela asks.

"Decidedly," Murphy says.

"How about the sauna?" Angela asks.

"The men's sauna or the women's sauna?" Murphy asks.

"The men's is a bit more discreet," Angela suggests.

"Let's go, then," Murphy says.

They clamber out of the pool, hastily gather towels and keys, and walk briskly, dripping, past the exposed women's sauna, to the door of the men's sauna under the building's overhang. The coast is clear. Murphy opens the door and peeks inside: the sauna is vacant.

They scamper within, through the changing room, past the stall toilet, into the sauna proper. Murphy turns the dial to medium, turns to Angela and puts his arms around her; she reciprocates. Within seconds the temperature has risen fifty degrees. Murphy slides Angela's bikini bottom down her legs, she pulls down his bathing suit. He tries to enter her standing up; she bends her knees, he bends his; he can't get in. They walk awkwardly—he backward, she forward, still intertwined, to the narrow sauna bench. Murphy sits down, Angela eases on top of him. Her knees hit the wall. "This isn't going to work," she says. "Wait." She stands up, then sits down beside him. Murphy catches on quickly. He does a deep knee-bend without the return and enters her, finally. His position is difficult to maintain, even with Angela's hands laced behind his neck, keeping him from falling over. But the clumsiness of the position, the stress in his knees, serve as balance against the quite extraordinary sensation. In other words, unlike last night, Murphy can hold off. He is suspended in a near-ecstatic limbo for God knows how long—leaning back, plunging in—while Angela, eyes closed, moves her head up and down in slow rhythm. Murphy watches droplets of perspiration fall from her nipples to her thighs, watches the veins pulsate within her neck, feels his knees disappear, cease to exist. He feels her contract, whether voluntarily or not he doesn't know, but that does it. Near-ecstasy makes a neat transition to ecstasy. As he comes, he feels her hands tightly gripping the back of his neck and he wonders if she's coming, too. A final plunge, a final lean, the knees suddenly return to the body, and Murphy drops gently to the sauna floor.

"I was so close," Angela whispers, eyes still closed.

Murphy struggles to a kneeling position, places his head between her legs, feels her hands encircle his head, and hears the sound of key in lock.

"Jesus!" Angela says.

Murphy withdraws his head; Angela stands up, puts on her bikini in a flash. Sitting on the floor, Murphy struggles to pull the bathing suit up his legs.

An elderly man appears from the changing room, towel around waist. Sighting Angela, he is visibly disturbed. "Men only!" he says.

Murphy pushes himself to a kneel and falls back to the floor.

"He can't stand up," Angela says, pointing to Murphy.

"Just had an operation," Murphy says. "She has to come with me wherever I go."

The elderly man offers his hand, Angela offers hers, and together they get Murphy standing. Thanks are uttered.

"You should put up a sign or something," the elderly man says. "I could've come in here stark naked."

Murphy and Angela ascend to the apartment in good humor. She removes top and bottom, and heads for the shower. Murphy grabs her and says, "I owe you something."

"It can wait," Angela says.

He lifts her and puts her down on the bed, on her pillow, in fact so again her back is to the wall. Now he lies between her legs, and within several minutes the debt is paid. Her thighs compress around his ears, and relax.

"Prosper," Angela says, "I'm very happy."

Does she know a good Italian restaurant in Miami? She knows several Italian restaurants, none particularly good. Does she know *of* a good Italian restaurant in Miami? She knows of several, but they're awfully expensive. Does she know of a good, expensive Italian restaurant near Miami Jai-Alai? She knows of one not especially near Miami Jai-Alai, but on the way to Miami Jai-Alai.

"Let's go," Murphy says.

"Tonight?"

"Right now," Murphy says.

"Prosper, I can't . . ."

"Of course you can."

"I have tests to grade. If we go to jai alai we won't be back till one-thirty."

"How long will it take to grade the tests?"

"Oh . . . two hours, maybe three . . ."

"Grade the tests in the car."

"I get carsick when I read in moving cars."

"Okay, then you drive and I'll grade the tests."

"You don't speak Spanish."

"Okay, then take a Dramamine, I'll drive, and you grade the tests."

"I don't have any Dramamine."

"We'll buy some Dramamine."

"You're not going to give up, are you?"

He's not. They go, stopping for Dramamine. Angela dutifully grades tests under the BMW's dim overhead light all the way down the Florida Turnpike. She experiences not a scintilla of car sickness.

At the expensive Italian restaurant they are hovered over by a bona fide Italian waiter who snorts when Murphy refuses ground pepper on his tortellini and cringes when Murphy orders beer with his milanese, even if the beer is Kronenbourg at a dollar seventy-five a bottle. Angela has saltimbocca and a half-bottle of Verdicchio. The milanese surpasses Murphy's—far surpasses it, in fact, but then this is the first time he's ever spent fifteen dollars for it. With dessert and tip, the check comes to fifty-seven dollars, well more than double what Murphy has ever spent previously on dinner for two. He can afford it.

On I-95 Angela resumes grading tests, pauses to tell Murphy where to leave the highway, alternately directs and grades for the next five minutes, and finishes as they arrive at the parking lot.

Miami Jai-Alai is to West Palm Beach Jai-Alai as Madison Square Garden is to a respectable small-college gymnasium. While the playing courts are about the same size, everything else here is gargantuan by comparison. Having become used to the small-town mill and flow of West Palm Beach, Murphy is awed by so much higher a level of chaos. Their five-dollar seats, while on the service line, are a good hundred feet from the action. Angela has been here only twice before; she knows the players more by reputation than anything else. There could be no better time for Murphy to use his system, which relishes anonymity.

They have arrived during the interval between the third and fourth games. Murphy struggles to find a WPS window, makes his 1-2-3 across-the-board bet just before the buzzer sounds. He clears $38.80 on his first bet, and so it goes. There is no game in which all three of his teams are out of the money—they win six of nine, place in four of nine, show in four of nine. Angela makes no bets, applauds every well-played point, puts her heart into it only when one of Murphy's teams is involved. He wins $128 even for the night.

In the car, Murphy says, "Well, it worked here . . ."

"It wouldn't over the long run," Angela replies.

"Why wouldn't it?"

"Because there are more good players in Miami. At West Palm Elu's the only one who can win consistently from the bottom post positions. At Miami there are three or four frontcourt players who do it, and a few backcourt players too. There aren't any good backcourt players at West Palm."

"These guys didn't look any better to me . . ."

"Prosper, I don't want to sound obnoxious, but you have a lot to learn."

"Okay, teach me."

"The court is longer in Miami, and the walls are rougher so there are a lot more bad bounces. Most of the players at West Palm Beach would look terrible in Miami."

"So what we saw tonight was better jai alai."

"Much better."

"The best?"

"No, not the best."

"Where's the best?"

"In Spain."

"I had the impression that all these guys came over here because there was more money to be made."

"The strike, Prosper. . . . Remember?"

"Yeah, but that was five years ago, wasn't it?"

"They were banned. . . . Practically all the players who struck. The Florida Racing Commission decided they'd breached their contracts. They're not allowed to play here."

"Forever?"

"Forever."

"Jesus Christ!" Murphy says. "That can't be legal. That's restraint of trade or something, isn't it?"

"Maybe it is, but no one's done anything about it."

Murphy imagines himself writing a lengthy exposé of the great jai-alai labor scandal. For whom? The *Voice*? *Sports Illustrated*? Forget it. A book, perhaps. A waste of time, probably. The BMW rolls north at eighty miles per hour. "Let's go to Spain," he says.

"Fine," Angela says, her voice a bit tart, "turn right at the next exit. The road stops a few thousand miles short, though."

"I'm serious," Murphy says.

"I'm falling asleep, Prosper. . . ."

Within seconds, she has.


Forty-five minutes later, Murphy takes the Madera Beach exit and drives the several two-lane miles to U.S. 1. Half a mile from Waterway Boulevard he realizes there is a police car perhaps a hundred feet behind. He checks his speed. He's going forty-six in a forty-five zone. He slows to forty. The lights are green all the way, and Murphy signals his right turn well in advance. The police car fails to signal, continues to follow. Murphy signals a move into the left lane, preparatory to the left turn into Waterway Cove. His rearview mirror is suddenly awash in flashing blue light. He wonders if they want him to stop here, in the left lane of a major artery, or if they want him to make the turn and then stop. He assumes that if they'd desired the latter they would have waited until then to switch on their flashing blue light. He stops and is momentarily blinded as a powerful white light replaces the blue in the mirror.

Angela wakes up and says, "What's going on?"

"I don't know," Murphy says. "Cops."

"Were you speeding?"

"I wasn't doing anything," Murphy says.

"What the hell is that light for?"

"I don't know."

A policeman appears at the window. He is a tall, slender young man, about twenty-five by Murphy's estimate. He wears a tan uniform, is hatless, has styled blond hair and a neat blond mustache. The plastic nameplate on his chest says WILSON. He says: "Could I see your license and registration please, sir?"

"Could you please turn that light off?" Murphy replies.

"I'm afraid I can't do that, sir," the cop says, not unpleasantly.

"It's a very bright light," Murphy says.

"Yes sir, it's supposed to be."

"Could you tell me why you're shining that light into my car?"

"Yes sir, that's ess oh pee."

"What does ess oh pee mean?"

"Standard operating procedure, sir."

"Why is it standard operating procedure to shine a bright light into my car?"

"Because, sir, I can have a clear view of what's happening in your vehicle, and my partner, back there in the car, he can too."

There is a moment of silence. Murphy says, "Would you imagine by now that there's nothing going on in my vehicle?"

"Yes sir, I sure would."

"Then would you turn off the light?"

"Could I see your license and registration, sir?"

Officer Wilson speaks with deliberate courtesy, and with the quasi-Southern inflection seemingly common to all policemen south of New Jersey. He's giving Murphy a big pain in the ass. "What if I said," Murphy says, "that I wouldn't show you my license and registration until you turn that goddamn light off?"

"I'd have to arrest you, sir."

"For what?"

"For disobeying an officer."

"I don't believe you could do that," Murphy says.

Angela says, "Prosper, I think you should do what he says."

Murphy says to Angela, "This is ridiculous. They can't just pull us over and shine a goddamned searchlight into the car. They need probable cause, or something."

"I know, Prosper. Let's get it over with. I have to get up in a few hours."

Murphy emits an angry sigh. "There's an envelope in the glove compartment," he says to Angela. She hands it to him. He fumbles through his wallet, finds his driver's license, hands it to the cop, then pours the manila envelope's contents on his lap. The envelope was supplied by Trammell, the salesman; Murphy hasn't given it a thought. He finds a bill of sale, a certificate of title, an owner's manual, a directory of BMW service stations across the world, and no registration.

Officer Wilson examines Murphy's license by flashlight. "Excuse me," Murphy says. The cop looks at him. "I just bought the car. I have a bill of sale. I have the title. I can't find the registration."

Wilson nods, accepts Murphy's documents, and heads back to the police car without a word.

"You didn't go through a red light or anything?" Angela asks.

"Nothing," Murphy says.

"The car is registered?"

"I guess it is—I bought it from a friend of your brother's. A client of your brother's."

"Not a friend of Ray's who happened to have a BMW for sale, I hope . . ."

"No, it was legitimate. I don't know what these bastards are up to." It occurs to Murphy that he can minimize the searchlight by turning his rearview mirror upward.

A new policeman appears at the window—an older man, close to forty, nameplated RAYMOND. "Would you please step out of the car, sir?" His accent isn't quasi-Southern but deep redneck.

"Why?"

"Would you please get your ass the hell out of the car?"

Murphy gets out of the car, notices Officer Wilson in the police car, talking into a microphone. The blue light flashes.

"Open up the trunk," says Officer Raymond.

Opening the trunk, Murphy says, "Would you mind telling me what you're looking for?"

"Why don't you tell me?" replies Officer Raymond, who shines his flashlight into the empty trunk. "Where's the spare tire in this thing?" he asks Murphy.

"Underneath," Murphy says.

"Open it up for me."

Murphy lifts and moves aside the plywood panel. Officer Raymond shines his light at the spare tire and says, "Take it out."

"The tire?"

"What the hell you think I'm talkin' about?"

Murphy removes a nut and a plate and lifts the tire out of its well. The tire is airless. Murphy mouths a curse at Trammell, thirteen hundred miles away.

Officer Raymond inspects the well with great care, shines his light on the tire itself, instructs Murphy to put it back where it came from. "Close it up," he says, and moves to the right side of the car, shines his light into the back seat.

Officer Wilson approaches Murphy. "This is a citation," he says, offering Murphy a piece of paper, "for driving an un-registered vehicle."

"We both know damned well it's a registered vehicle," Murphy says, accepting the piece of paper.

"You've got ten days," Officer Wilson resumes, "to either pro-duce a valid registration at the courthouse or to get the vehicle registered in Florida. If you don't do either of them there's gonna be a warrant for your arrest issued."

"Why did you stop me?" Murphy asks.

"Suspicious vehicle," says Officer Wilson. Officer Raymond switches off his flashlight and returns to the police car.

"Suspicious in what way?" Murphy asks.

"I'd suggest," Officer Wilson says, pointing to the citation, "that you get that taken care of."

"Suspicious in what way," Murphy repeats.

"Have a good night, sir," Officer Wilson says, and with a lit-tle salute he returns to his vehicle.

Murphy sits anew behind the steering wheel, trembling slightly in rage and frustration. The bright light ceases as, a second later, does the flashing blue light; the police car backs up and roars around the BMW into a U-turn. Murphy readjusts the rearview mirror. "Two very personable gentlemen," he says to Angela.

"Did they say why they stopped you?"

"Suspicious vehicle."

"Suspicious in what way?"

"They didn't elaborate." He turns left into Waterway Cove.


Angela arranges her graded tests on the kitchen counter. Murphy takes a can of Genesee from the refrigerator. "You want one?" he asks her.

"I have to go to bed," Angela says.

"Jesus!" Murphy says, slamming the refrigerator door. "Things like that really piss me off!"

"Don't worry about it, Prosper."

"I mean . . . is this just a question of two cops sitting out there on Route One and one says to the other, 'Okay, we'll stop the next car,' or 'we'll stop the next foreign car,' or 'we'll stop the next German car with New York plates'? I mean, what the hell is a *suspicious vehicle?* Why does that son of a bitch take me back and search the fucking trunk?"

Angela isn't at all sure whether the preceding has been rhetorical or directed to her. She says, "Prosper, you haven't been involved . . ." She can't complete the question.

Murphy waits, drinks some beer, waits some more, finally says, "Involved in what?"

It's a struggle for Angela, an increasingly complex puzzle of unknowns and loyalties. She wishes that at this moment she might lock herself away in some quiet, private place, and presently realizes that that's where she's been for the last good while. She forces herself to speak: "You haven't been involved in something with Ray?"

"Like what?"

"Something . . ." she shrugs, ". . . against the law?"

"I was about to ask you the same question," Murphy says.

They stand two feet from each other, each waiting for the other to speak. Eventually Angela averts her eyes, and Murphy says, "I'll tell you everything if you tell me everything."

"Okay," she says.

They sit facing each other on the couch. He tells her about the poker game—about Ramon and Curtis, about his phenomenal winnings. She sits, impassive, apprehensive. He tells her about the setup, the ambush, the rescue; she gives nods of recognition, of resignation, as she has before, as if this is ground she's been down before, as if any story involving Echaverria must to her be a twice-told tale.

"He threw me out the window," Murphy says, "and then he ran downstairs and caught me."

"He enjoys that," Angela says.

"Then he suggested that I look up his old friend in Madera Beach."

His eyes are fixed on hers, looking for any trace of misgiving, any sign of conspiracy, of betrayal. He sees instead a moistening, a tear trickling to her chin. Murphy stares at this solitary little sphere—poised, waiting to drop, to be absorbed in the fabric of her clothing. He leans over and saves it, licks it from her chin, ingests it. She embraces him, leans back, pulls him down on top of her.

At 2:45 they lie naked on the floor. Murphy runs his hand across Angela's damp abdomen, watches the beads of sweat collected in the cavity at the base of her neck. "You were going to tell me something," he says.

She closes her eyes. "I might have to do something for Ray."

"Something to do with cocaine?"

"No."

"With Gutierrez?"

"No. Not really. Indirectly."

"You're not going to tell me any more, are you?"

"I can't."

"Why not?"

"Please trust me, Prosper."

She sleeps. He cannot. He stands naked at the kitchen counter, drinking beer and writing himself instructions: call Echaverria and find out what's going on; call Trammell and find out where the registration is; go to local motor vehicles place, get car registered and get Florida driver's license; go to First American and withdraw money, redeposit it elsewhere in actual name . . .

The phone rings at ten minutes after three. Thinking only of Angela, Murphy races to the living room extension. She'll have to be awake and alert in scarcely more than four hours; the caller will be either Echaverria or a bad dialer. He catches it in the middle of the second ring and speaks a brusque "Hello."

The voice on the other end is fuzzily distant: "Who the fuck is that? Murphy?"

"Yeah, it's Murphy all right," Murphy says. "Do you always call here between two and four in the morning?"

Echaverria's reply is drowned out by electronic clanking. Murphy says, "What? I didn't hear that."

"I said you're getting a little proprietary, aren't you?"

"I'm thinking about your sister," Murphy says. "She has to get up in the morning."

"Things happen, Murphy."

"Yeah, I know they do," Murphy says. "I have a couple of questions I'd like to ask you. I was going to call you tomorrow . . ."

Echaverria says something unintelligible.

"This is a shitty connection," Murphy says. "Do you want to get the operator, or should I just call you back?"

"I'm at a pay phone," Echaverria says.

"Give me the number," Murphy says.

"I'm in a hurry," Echaverria says. "Ask your goddamned questions."

"Why didn't you tell me she was your sister?"

"If some degenerate cocaine dealer told you to look up his sister, would you do it?"

"I'd say the chances are about the same as if some degenerate cocaine dealer asked me to look up an old friend."

"Then what difference does it make? I figured you'd enjoy each other. Was I right?"

"You were right."

"Okay, then don't give me any shit about it. What's the other question?"

"Who is Gutierrez?"

"What?"

"Rafael Gutierrez. Who is he?"

"He's an old friend of mine. A Cuban guy, from Miami."

"I know that."

"Then why did you ask?"

"Why did he come here on Sunday?"

"Murphy, for Christ's sake, you said you had a couple of questions and I answered a couple of questions. Now will you get Angie on the fuckin' phone? I don't have a lot of time."

"I'm not going to wake her up."

"You have to wake her up."

"Why did Gutierrez come here last night?"

"He owed me some money. Did he bring a briefcase or something? Did he give Angie something?"

"Yeah, he did, but she doesn't want to talk about it."

"It was money, Murphy,"

"Why didn't he bring it straight to you?"

"Because he's in fuckin' Miami and I'm in fuckin' New York and she's in fuckin' Madera Beach."

"It's still got to get to you, one way or another."

"Yeah, but I feel a lot safer when Angie has it than when Gutierrez has it."

"I don't," Murphy says, "and I don't think she does, either."

"Proprietary and presumptuous," Echaverria says.

"I think I might know her a little bit better than you do," Murphy says, "or at least I think I might care about her more than you do."

"I think we're talking about apples and oranges here, Murphy."

"We are and we aren't."

"Would you put her on the phone, please?"

"Why don't you call back at about seven-thirty?"

"Because I have to talk to her now. Right now."

"Okay," Murphy says. "Hold on."

He runs his hand through her hair and kisses her cheek. She stirs. "Ray's on the telephone," he says.

She sits up and says, "Now?"

"Now," Murphy says. "It's something important."

"Okay, thanks." Angela shakes her head, as if to circulate the blood or activate the brain, and picks up the phone. Murphy, still naked, hastens back to the living room to listen in.


"Does he speak Spanish?" Echaverria asks, in Spanish.

Groggy, disoriented, struggling with the connection, Angela says, "Who, Prosper?"

"I have a feeling he might be on the other phone."

"He doesn't speak Spanish, Ray. Look, I'm starting to feel really foolish about this. Compromised."

"You falling in love?"

"That's beside the point."

"He's falling in love. He told me he knows you better than I do."

"That's entirely possible."

"You're not going to let me down, are you?"

"If I've told you I'll do something, I'll do it. But he wants to know what's going on, and I'm sick and tired of this cloak-and-dagger business."

"It's not going to last much longer. I think I might have some good news, anyway . . ."

"Well, wait, I have to tell you—something very strange happened tonight. We went to Miami tonight, to jai alai, and on the way back we were stopped by the police. Not for anything in particular. They searched Prosper's car, and one of them gave him a sort of tough-guy treatment . . ."

"Cops being cops."

"You don't think it might have something to do with Gutierrez?"

"Were they local cops? Madera Beach cops?"

"Yes."

"How the hell would they know anything about Gutierrez?"

"I was led to believe that Gutierrez is fairly notorious."

"Angie, the cops see an out-of-state car early in the morning, they're bored . . . Did Murphy give them any trouble?"

"A little."

"Okay, so they gave him a little trouble back."

"I hope it's as simple as that."

"Of course it is. Look—the reason I called, the good news is that you might not have to come."

"I *might* not have to come?"

"I met with some people last night. They were disappointed I didn't bring the stuff, but they say they can get hold of it pretty easily. It's just a question of availability and of when it's needed. You understand what I'm saying?"

"I think so."

"Okay. It's probably not going to be needed for a while—for a few months—but if it is, and if we can't get it through their sources, you might still have to go, because Pierre is only going to deal with me or you. He doesn't know these people, and he doesn't trust anybody he doesn't know."

"He doesn't know me."

"He knows you almost as well as Murphy does. He knows where you lived when you were five years old, and who your best friend was, and he's going to ask you . . ."

"I don't think I look forward to that."

"Then don't worry about it. All you're probably going to have to do is bring over the rest of the money."

"And when am I going to have to do that?"

"When's your spring vacation?"

"Oh, God, I don't know . . . late March or early April. Should I check?"

"No, it doesn't matter now. I'll be calling again. But you can make it a honeymoon, you and Murphy. Drop the money off in Hendaye, we'll have dinner together, and then you two can do whatever you want to do."

"You can be very charming, Ray, can't you?"

"Angie, I know better than to pull anything on you."

"I'm afraid that sometimes you forget you're talking to me."

"Never."

"Okay. What should I do with the money for now?"

"Put it in a safe-deposit box. You should be getting the rest at the end of this week or the beginning of next week, and if I don't call you, put that in the safe-deposit box too."

"What if you do call me?"

"Okay—I'm going over today, just to test the water. I'll be back tonight, then I'll be over there until Friday. If I call you it'll be Saturday or Sunday, from here . . ."

"What's the earliest you'd call?"

"Saturday morning."

"Which would be Friday night here."

"Right. But I'm probably not going to call."

"But I should be here just the same."

"It would be a good idea."

"And where are you going to be in Spain?"

"You don't need to know that."

"Yes I do, Ray."

"Why?"

"In case I need to find you."

"You can find me in Hendaye."

"Tell me where you'll be in Spain."

"Zarauz."

"Where is Zarauz?"

"On the coast road, about an hour from San Sebastián."

"Okay. Can I go back to sleep?"

"Sure," Echaverria says in English, "sweet dreams, and sweet dreams to you too, Murphy."

Murphy switches off the kitchen light and pads back to the bedroom in darkness. Sweet dreams, indeed. He gets into bed; Angela stirs, and he says, "Are you asleep?"

"Not quite," she answers, barely audible.

"You're not going to tell me anything, are you?"

"I need to sleep, Prosper."

"Tomorrow, after you've slept, you're not going to tell me anything are you?"

"I don't think so. I'm confused, Prosper. I don't want to think about it."

"I'm not going to push you, Angela."

She kisses him. "Were you listening?"

"Of course."

"Did you understand anything?"

"Nothing."

"I'm sorry, Prosper. I don't want to . . ."

He waits for the sentence to be completed. He waits twenty, thirty, forty seconds before becoming aware of her slow, rhythmic breathing. The sentence is unfinished, indeterminate. Eyes now accustomed to the dark, he watches her sleep, feels a regular, gentle breeze on his left hand, which rests two inches below her face.

He closes his eyes and attempts to concentrate. That he understood nothing is not quite the truth. There was an exchange, for instance, concerning police—perhaps tonight's police—and toward the end of the conversation he made out "Friday," "Saturday," "Sunday," then Friday and Saturday again. And finally Angela wanted to know where something, or someone, was.

> A: ¿. . . *dónde . . . en España?*
> E: (Incomprehensible.)
> A: *Sí . . .* Ray . . .
> E: *¿Por qué?*

A: (Incomprehensible.)
E: (Incomprehensible.)
A: ¿. . . dónde . . . en España?
E: Tharahooth.
A: ¿Dónde está Tharahooth?
E: . . . San Sebastián.

Whether Tharahooth is a person, place, or thing, Murphy cannot say. He would, however, bet a dollar to win a penny that it's in Spain, a dollar to win a nickel that it's somewhere near San Sebastián, a dollar to win a quarter that Echaverria wasn't calling from New York, and a dollar even up that Echaverria, at this moment, isn't very far from Tharahooth.

Angela moans in her sleep, kicks the covers. Murphy strokes her head. "No!" she says. He stops, surprised, and watches her, practically feeling her nightmare. "Make them stop!" she says. He resumes stroking and after a few seconds she relaxes, and turns from supine to prone. All is quiet, all is still, here in the tropics, even the ray of the waterway having taken a few minutes' surcease. Murphy closes his eyes and begins slipping away toward a few nightmares of his own.

# 16

# Je Me Souviens

Upon his return to New Hope in 1964, Murphy had found himself about to be a displaced person. Anne-Marie had returned to Montreal during his absence, had visited her family and old friends for the first time in over twenty years. She had been introduced to a man named Jean-Claude Labossière, who was something of a tycoon. Within a week, Labossière had asked her to marry him. Anne-Marie had at first taken the proposal lightly, had returned to Pennsylvania and become lonely and bored, then flown back to Montreal, had a long and serious conversation with Labossière, and accepted.

"It is not because he's rich, Prosper. He is a very nice man. A fine man. He's very much like your father in some ways. And he can make a good home for us. Your father didn't leave us very much, you know."

This did not sit well with Murphy. After a three-month interlude in strange lands that had ended with a curious act of betrayal, he had come home for an infusion of stability and was dumbfounded by the imminence of losing the only home he'd ever had. He searched for an argument, groveled for a point of view that might sway his mother: for instance, how unthinkable was it even to consider marriage only five months after his father's death! How craven to rip up these roots and transport this family to a foreign country!

It was such nonsense that Murphy couldn't bring himself to speak it. He didn't particularly miss his father, and he imagined that if Walter Murphy had been permitted a word from the

Beyond it might have been, "Of course, darling. If that's what you'd like to do, go ahead and do it."

Anne-Marie and Labossière were married in May. Labossière was a cheerful, cherubic capitalist, aged fifty-two, worth several tens of millions of Canadian dollars. He had two children by his first marriage, both boys, both snotty upper-class French-Canadian adolescents who seemed to have no interests beyond les Canadiens and les Alouettes.

In June a Mayflower van trucked everything from the house in New Hope to the mansion in Outremont, and Murphy spent the first two weeks of his life in Quebec fiddling with his step-father's first present, an absurdly expensive multiband Grundig radio. Picking up Moscow or Hobart was a snap, but he had a hell of a time finding a good rock and roll station.


Labossière was indeed a very nice man, at least off the play-ing fields, at least to Murphy. His second present was a car: a 1963 Valiant convertible, a "demo" with 836 miles on its odometer. His third present was tuition at Murphy's choice of Canadian colleges.

"You know I'm going back to Princeton in February," Murphy said.

Labossière smiled, nodded. "Fine. You wish to go back to Princeton, you go back to Princeton. But for now, you go to school here."

So Murphy chose the French-speaking University of Montreal over the English-speaking McGill.

He took three French literature courses that summer, made some friends, fell in with a group of middle-class bohemians, let on to no one where or how he lived. At a party in July he heard a familiar voice: Otis Redding singing "Security." Murphy knew the record existed only because it was on *Billboard*'s rhythm and blues chart; he had scoured Montreal's record stores in vain in search of it.

He sought out his host. The record didn't belong to him, he said; it had been provided by Aurore. He pointed to a small, pretty girl perhaps a bit younger than Murphy. She wore blue jeans, boots, a work shirt, and had very long dark brown hair.

The record had been a gift from an American musician who'd just finished an engagement in Montreal. Would she, Murphy asked with some passion, like to hear some more Otis Redding? Certainly, she would.

He drove her straightaway to Outremont. "You live here?" she said. Murphy tried to explain that he lived here by accident, that he was really from a small town in Pennsylvania, but when he pulled into the mansion's driveway, when she saw the name on the mailbox and realized that this wasn't just *any* Outremont address, she was horrified. "I will not enter," she said.

"Will you wait here, then? I'll be right back."

"I have no choice."

Heading back whence they'd come, with a cache of obscure R & B gems in the back seat, he made further attempts to acquit himself. Aurore told him that his stepfather was one of the top ten Fascists in Quebec: a usurer, a slumlord, a lackey of the United States, and a pig who placed the interests of (English-speaking) Canada above those of (French-speaking) Quebec. Murphy might only protest that his guilt was by association alone. These were new politics to him.

He played "These Arms of Mine" and "Pain in My Heart" and "Come to Me" on her ancient phonograph, fearful that the grooves would never be the same. She emptied the tobacco from a filter cigarette and filled it with marijuana, a substance new to Murphy. He played Arthur Alexander's "You Better Move On," and she sighed, *"Ah, quelle musique."* He played Don Covay's "Mercy, Mercy," and recognized that Aurore was sprawled supine across his thighs. In a state of mild psychosis he unbuttoned her shirt, moved his left hand across her stomach, up toward her chest, found lovely, soft skin instead of fabric. No brassiere! He sat for some moments tremendously excited but fixated, stroking Aurore's nipple. How perfect everything was.

*"Tu aimes ça?"* she said.

What? *"Quoi?"*

"Do you like my breast very much?"

Ray & Bob sang "Air Travel." Do I like her breast very much?

Murphy wondered. "I love your breast," he said. "Both your breasts."

They made love endlessly on Aurore's ratty couch.


What an odd match it might have seemed at first glance—this well-dressed, well-groomed bilingual scholar daily departing the swankest part of town in his convertible, parking in front of a rundown building in a working-class neighborhood, spending a few hours or the night in a dingy apartment furnished by the Salvation Army, engaged in furious verbal or carnal intercourse with a *petite Marxiste* whose wardrobe comprised three denim shirts, three pairs of blue jeans, two pairs of sandals, and one pair of hiking boots. This was the stuff of Romance.

This was the stuff of illusion. Aurore's parents were both doctors in the city of Quebec, both Socialists and both fervent nationalists. Each drove a Mercedes-Benz automobile and made lots of money. Murphy had been temporarily thrust into the upper class, Aurore had chosen to spend some time in the lower-middle, but aside from petty geographical differences it might be said that their backgrounds were almost exactly the same.

There was, to be sure, one major area of divergence: Aurore had been raised with a cause, and Murphy with none. She was a *Québecoise,* whose ancestors had over the centuries been oppressed by the English imperialists and their allies, the French-speaking capitalists (Labossière) who conspired to deny Quebec its heritage, to deny French Canadians any power in their own land.

"That has nothing to do with me," Murphy said. "Just because my mother married one of your enemies, that doesn't make me part of him."

"But you must be part of something," Aurore said.

"Okay, but whatever I'm a part of, it isn't here. It has nothing to do with Quebec or Canada."

"With the United States, then?"

He sensed himself being backed into a corner. He admitted that he considered himself a person from the *États-Unis.*

"*Alors, qu'est-ce que vous faites au Viet-Nam?*"

"*Je ne fais rien au Viet-Nam, moi.*"

"*Mais, il faut que tu fasses partie d'un 'vous,' Prosper.*"

You (singular) must be part of a You (plural). If you disconnect yourself from Labossière and Quebec, then you must be part of the country that's doing bad things in Vietnam.

"That's ridiculous," Murphy said. "For one thing, I don't even know what's happening over there . . ."

Aurore smiled slyly. "For another?"

"I was going to say that you don't have any right to tell me."

"But you didn't say it."

"No. Because obviously you have the right to tell me."

"And you have the right to pay attention or not."

"*Oui*," Murphy said, "*d'accord.*"

This exchange took place on a pleasant summer night in midsummer of 1964, before either Lyndon Johnson or Barry Goldwater had been nominated by their respective parties.

As far as either Anne-Marie or Labossière knew, Murphy had no steady girlfriend. His late nights were condoned, his occasional two- and three-day absences accepted by his stepfather with winks and chuckles. "You are having a good time in Montreal, eh?" Labossière would ask. "Maybe you'll stay here."

No, Murphy was more determined than ever to go back to Princeton. No one, least of all Aurore, ever pressed him as to why—which was fortunate, because it was something Murphy himself didn't entirely comprehend.

From time to time it occurred to him that he was in love with Aurore, but he knew that she would never set foot in Labossière's mansion, and he suspected that her mission was more important to her than he was. The concept of a Free Quebec was almost as meaningless to him as was the phenomenon of Labossière's wealth. His double life here had been exciting in every sense of the word, but (and here he might make a rational observation) he saw it as having no resolution. What Murphy couldn't, or wouldn't, identify was something outside the purview of rationality: a blind, stubborn desire to go home.

He drove the Valiant to Princeton in February, 1965, moved into a single room in North Edwards Hall. Automobiles were illegal, but the Valiant sat undetected in a faculty parking lot.

Murphy drove it to New York every weekend, sucking in all the music he could: the Apollo in Harlem, the Village Gate and Vanguard, Gerde's Folk City. He did an all-night show twice a week on the surprisingly powerful campus FM radio station. He returned to Montreal for spring vacation, spent a passionate week with Aurore, told her he'd decided to spend the summer in New York. Would she come with him? She might.

He moved into a sleazy little sublet on Bleecker Street in June and immediately called her.

"No, Prosper, I couldn't possibly do it. I've gotten much more involved here. It's important that I stay."

"Just for a few weeks, then. The revolution can get along without you for a month, can't it?" Silence. "I miss you, Aurore."

"Then you come here."

"I can't go there. I've just rented this apartment for the summer. Aurore, listen, Otis Redding's going to be at the Apollo two weeks from now, with Carla Thomas and Sam and Dave. It's fabulous here, there's everything you could want . . ."

"Everything *you* could want," Aurore said.

It was a good summer anyway. It was full of music, and toward its end Murphy began to see the beginning of a career. Rock and roll in 1965 seemed to be going in several billion directions at once. The Beatles, a year and a half earlier, had sprung forth at exactly the right time, when American music was suffering from a bad case of Lesley Gore. Born of a marvelous mixture of influences, like the litter of a promiscuous cat, rock and roll had been homogenized into something horrible, had skipped both the baroque and the rococo stages of evolution and been steered straight into a state of banal decadence. But the British groups had resurrected the old vitality, and now things were going crazy. The Byrds had just had a number-one record with Bob Dylan's "Mr. Tambourine Man"; Dylan himself had recently gone electric, and "Like a Rolling Stone" was on the radio every half hour. It was obvious, meanwhile, that the Beatles, or at least John Lennon, had been influenced by Dylan.

And Otis, the great Otis, had made the top-forty stations for the first time with "Mr. Pitiful."

Murphy knew what was happening. He composed a brief analytical piece, dropped it off at the *Village Voice* on Sheridan Square. They printed it, and paid him a few dollars. He asked them if they wanted more. They did, and they gave him a press card. He began hearing music for free. He had a brief and pointless but very gratifying conversation with Bob Dylan.

Back to Montreal for a week in late August. Aurore's phone didn't answer, and she was nowhere to be found. He drove to Quebec, where her parents told him she'd been working with a separatist group and was probably somewhere in Montreal. He didn't find her.

In fact, he never saw her again.

He talked to her on the telephone perhaps fifteen times over the next two years. She never called him. She was always fine, always busy, always unable to come down to New Jersey, always elsewhere when Murphy was in Montreal.

Murphy went to college, did reasonably well, spent as much time in New York as in Princeton. He graduated.

June, 1967, Montreal. Anne-Marie: "Prosper, you have to make some decisions, you know that? You know that Jean-Claude thinks very much of you? He's going to offer you anything you want here, and I think that when you take all things into consideration, you should consider what he says very seriously."

All things?

"The draft, Prosper. You don't have to do anything illegal if you stay here."

Murphy sat with Labossière at poolside. This was no ordinary pool: it was huge, and heated, and had a retractable top, so one might swim when the temperature was forty degrees below zero.

Today was in the low eighties, not a cloud in the sky. Labossière reclined on a deck chair, his belly sprawling over his baggy trunks. "What do you think of all this, Prosper?" His right hand made a circle in the air.

"It's wonderful."

Labossière looked him straight in the eye: "*C'est à moi, et à toi.*"

"*Non c'est pas à moi.*"

"*Mais, si.*" Labossière became earnest. His natural sons were worthless, destroyed by their mother. Lounge lizards. Murphy should now go to business school in Quebec, or if he were tired of school, he might start at once in any of Labossière's holdings, and not on the ground floor.

Murphy became diplomatic. He *was* tired of school. He feared that among Labossière's holdings there was nothing he'd want to do. But he was most honored by the offer.

After a long silence, Labossière spoke in English: "What about the draft?"

"I'm working on that," Murphy said.

Labossière spoke in French: "Your attitude isn't very practical."

"*Mais, c'est à moi.*"


The invitation to report for a pre-induction physical in Montreal was forwarded to his loft on Varick Street in New York, Murphy dutifully replied by letter to the American authorities in Canada that he was back here in the States, please advise. This was in August of 1966.

He waited for the other shoe to drop.

He wrote weekly for the *Voice*, occasionally for monthly magazines with slick paper, but most of his income came from anonymous projects: one-shot magazines published to coincide with such events as the Rolling Stones' latest tour—tens of thousands of words poured out in a matter of days. By the middle of 1967 he was turning people down. Too busy, he'd explain, and they'd up the ante. No, really, I'm too busy. Okay, look, Murphy, we've never paid more than twenty-five hundred dollars for a job like this, but we'll go to three thousand this time if you can deliver the copy in two weeks. . . . Murphy had cornered the rock and roll market.

Up to Montreal for Anne-Marie's birthday in October. Aurore's number had been disconnected; now even her parents had no idea where she was, or perhaps they just weren't telling. Labossière was impressed by Murphy's success in New York, and suggested that Murphy might start a magazine of his own, in Canada. Murphy said he'd have to think about it. Anne-Marie sat with him at the kitchen table. "Prosper, you're not lying to me? There's been nothing since last August?"

"No, mother, I'm not lying to you. They've lost me. Or maybe they're just confused because I don't fit the pattern. Everybody else is coming up here to get away and I'm down there at the same address I gave them last year."

"You should stay here, Prosper, just to be safe. Jean-Claude wants to start a magazine with you."

"I'm safe, mother. I'm sure of it."

Just the same, as the Valiant skidded toward the border during an unseasonal blizzard, Murphy had visions of being apprehended on the U.S. side, being whisked off to Leavenworth. He was waved through.


His telephone rang at midnight in late December. He was sound asleep, having completed three hours earlier an eighty-thousand-word history of the Monkees. He waited for the caller to quit, decided on the fifteenth ring that something might be up, and danced thirty feet across a cold wooden floor.

"Prosper?" A French inflection. Could it be?

"Aurore? *C'est toi?*"

"*Oui, c'est moi . . .*"

"Oh, my God, where have you been? I've been trying to find you for the last year and a half . . ."

"Prosper, I've just heard."

"You've just heard what?"

"About Otis Redding."

"What about Otis Redding, Aurore?"

"You don't know, then?"

Otis Redding, *le chanteur noir des États-Unis, qui avait vingt-*

*six ans,* had been killed when his private plane crashed en route from Cleveland, Ohio, to Madison, Wisconsin. She'd heard it on the CBC.

This was unquestionably the worst news Murphy had ever heard. He wanted to know what the hell Otis Redding was doing in Wisconsin in the middle of winter, to know if this was definite information, if there might have been some mistake; but most of all he wanted to talk to Aurore.

*"On fait des choses ici,"* she said.

"So much has happened," Murphy said. "There's so much I'd like to tell you about. Look, I don't really have much to do for the next couple of weeks. I could come visit you, if that's all right."

"No, not now, not right now."

"Are you with someone else?"

"No, it's not that."

"What is it, then?"

"Prosper, I'll talk to you again." And she was gone.


Woodstock. Half a million people gathered for a gigantic fraternity party in upstate New York. Someone among the press corps suggested that this might be the second biggest city in the state. What about Buffalo? Did anybody know the population of Buffalo? No. Did anybody know how many people were here? Not for sure. What about Syracuse?

Murphy slogged through the mud with his tape recorder. He had a cold, or hay fever, or perhaps just a reaction to some bad cocaine (courtesy of one of the network news people). Whatever it was, his head ached and his nose was running and he wished he had an aspirin. He wished he were in a dry living room in Buffalo. But there were journalistic standards to be maintained.

You having a good time? Sure, man. How come? Well, you know . . . it's really far out! Why is it far out? Because everybody's *here,* man. Can you hear the music this far from the stage? Nah, not really. What's so great about everybody being here if you can't hear them? I didn't mean *them,* man, I meant all these fuckin' people; everybody in the whole fuckin' *world* is here!

Not quite everybody. Adolf Hitler and Martin Bormann, for instance, are in the midst of their afternoon meal somewhere in the dense Paraguayan jungle. Hitler's copy of the *Asunción Daily News* is dropped from a helicopter. Bormann retrieves it. "Bad news, *mein Führer*," he says. "They have broken another of your records—five hundred thousand at a youth rally in Amerika." Hitler sighs. These last few years have been difficult. The way Nixon's been handling Vietnam, how will anyone remember the Sudetenland? A secret plan for peace—what a masterstroke! Hitler peruses the article, turns to Bormann. "Martin, what does this mean: *far out?* Can an adjective modify a preposition?" Bormann considers. "Well, I don't think so, *mein Führer*, but *far* might be considered an adverb in this case . . ."

Murphy staggered back toward the stage, intent on finding the TV man and comparing symptoms. He sat on a cot in the press tent, sipping a beer, putting down a few misanthropic notes. A female voice said, "Prosper?" He looked up. He hardly recognized her: her blond hair was arranged in a maze of profuse curls; she wore a full-length, translucent Mexican dress, with what appeared to be a miniature bedspread over her shoulders. She squatted down to his level, the bedspread parting so he was staring at her breasts.

"Mary," she said.

"I know," Murphy replied.

"I've been looking for you. I've read practically everything you've written."

He asked her quite diplomatically what she was doing in the press tent. She explained that she had carte blanche: she was here with a member of a well-known band from San Francisco. She'd been his "old lady" for over a year. Murphy nodded, said that was nice. Mary said she was tired of running all over the country. Murphy agreed that it must be tiring. Mary said she'd decided to settle down, and New York seemed like a good place to do it. Well, there might certainly be worse places, Murphy said. Well, maybe we'll run into each other, Mary said.

His head cleared, Murphy lay on the grass next to the Valiant in the morning sun, waiting for the last vestiges of the Woodstock Nation to get the hell out of here so he could drive back to the city in a minimum of traffic. Mary lay down next to him and gave him a wet kiss on the lips, and within moments Murphy had a lengthy if belated taste of what the festival had meant to all those people.

Recovering from ecstasy, he saw her nascent black eye. "I told him to fuck off," she said. "Can you give me a lift?"

There was a marvelous coincidence: the arrival of Murphy's twenty-sixth birthday and the re-emergence of a rock and roll legend in Las Vegas, to which Murphy and his guest were flown for free.

He sat with Mary at a five-dollar blackjack table in Caesars Palace, eighty dollars ahead of the house. There are no clocks in Caesars Palace. "What time is it?" he asked Mary. "Five minutes after midnight," she said.

Murphy was undraftable; it was official. "I'm free," he said, hugging Mary. "Prosper," she said, "let's get married."

Why not? A taxi to an all-night wedding chapel, a ring provided by the house, and it was done.

It was not, as any rational person might have guessed, a match made in heaven.

Mary made her Montreal debut during Christmas week of 1969, and the reviews were mixed. "She has a way with men," Anne-Marie said, almost dispassionately. Murphy nodded. "She flirts with Jean-Claude, Prosper. Have you seen that?" He had. "She's a very nice girl, Prosper, but I think you have to be careful with her."

Labossière insisted on a major wedding present. Murphy insisted one wasn't necessary. With Anne-Marie abstaining, the vote was two to one in favor. Mary wanted to leave the loft, and Labossière would doubtless have bought them a town house on the East Side, but Murphy insisted on a ceiling of fifty thousand dollars.

That was precisely the price paid for the huge, tenebrous, roach-ridden co-op on Riverside Drive. The mausoleum.

Things went surprisingly well during the first several months of 1970. Murphy wrote a book, *The Politics of Rock and Roll,* whose gist was that politics and popular music, like church and state, should be kept as far apart as possible, that when musician is co-opted by politician it is inevitably the former who suffers.

Mary began a master's program in psychology at NYU; by spring she had developed what Murphy considered a rather shallow social conscience, which is to say that she had come to disagree with the premise of his book.

She, who once had told him that Vietnam (then Viet Nam) was somewhere near China, whose father (now dead) had personally overseen the deaths of tens of thousands of gooks, began to march, and to preach: "Prosper, it's incredible to me that you can just *sit* there. I mean, you've got a hell of a lot of *power,* do you know that? People *read* what you write, and you make *fun* of musicians who're trying to end the war. What the hell kind of an attitude is *that?*"

The note she left him in September, after she'd departed for Berkeley with the NYU professor who'd taught "The Psychology of Power": "Prosper: People *really can change.* People really can wake up, if they try to. I'm sorry you couldn't change with me. Maybe you'll learn to. Mary." An image flickered through Murphy's brain: Benito Mussolini hanging upside down in one Italian city or another. Mary was bound to make somebody's train run on time.

He slowed down, and stopped. He was perhaps more affected by her departure than he would admit. The apartment was darker and gloomier in her absence. During the first ten days of October there were two major political kidnappings in Quebec, and Pierre Trudeau invoked the War Measures Act, which placed the province under martial law. Murphy gave a call to his folks. Labossière was appalled by the kidnappings; Anne-Marie was appalled by the War Measures Act. They were both appalled by Mary's act of desertion.

At 5 A.M. of a sleepless night he got out of bed and threw some clothes into a suitcase. He walked toward West End

Avenue, where the battered and aged Valiant was parked. He wasn't sure where he was headed, but it was probably Montreal.

The Valiant's spot was occupied by a yellow Fiat. Was this perhaps not where he'd parked the Valiant the day before? He knelt on the corner of West End and Eighty-third Street, ran through the past few days' parkings in the cool darkness, in the deathly silence. No, this was the place. The Valiant had been stolen.

The *Times* was on his doorstep when he returned to the apartment. He sat down by the telephone and looked at the front page. One of the two men kidnapped by Quebec radicals, a French-Canadian member of the government, had been found dead in the trunk of a car. Murphy leaned back on the couch and closed his eyes. He saw himself next to Aurore, in her bed, then remembered her words spoken from hundreds of miles away: *on fait des choses ici.*

# 17

# A Basque Matinee

Tuesday morning. Murphy is awake and exhausted when Angela's alarm goes off at seven-thirty. "How do you feel?" he asks.
"Horrible."
"Why don't you call and say you're sick?"
"I'll be all right. I just have to wake up."
She heads for the bathroom. He closes his eyes, tries to avoid thinking about either the Madera Beach police or Echaverria, but cannot. He listens to Angela's shower, derives some pleasure from watching her dress; she moves with such fine grace even in near stupor. She tells him to go back to sleep and kisses him goodbye. He hears her briefly in the kitchen, falls asleep, hears the front door close, falls asleep, hears a conversation in the hallway twenty minutes later, falls asleep, and so it goes. Shortly after nine he decides that there's not much future in sleep this morning.
At nine-thirty he's on the phone to Bob Trammell in New York.
"Oh, hey, yeah, how ya doin'? How's the car?"
"The car's fine."
"Say, look I'm with a customer . . . can I call you back?"
"Trammell, do you think you can stop being a goddamned salesman for about two minutes and listen to me?"
"Sure thing."

"I got stopped by the police last night. I'm in Florida. I don't have a registration."

A pause. "Oh, yeah. We sent it to you."

"You *sent* it to me?"

"To your address. The one you gave me."

"Why the hell didn't you give it to me when I bought the car?"

"Can I call you back?"

"No, you fucking can't call me back. Why don't I have a registration for the car you sold me?"

"Mr. Murphy, you may recall that things were a little . . . confused when you bought the car."

"Trammell, this is your responsibility. I have ten days from last night to prove the car is registered. What am I going to do?"

"You're not having your mail forwarded?"

"I'm not having my mail forwarded."

"You could get it registered there . . ."

"How can I get it registered here if I can't prove it's registered there?"

"You have the title, right?"

"Right."

"Okay, go to the DMV there, show 'em the title, tell 'em the situation, just like it is, and if there's any trouble tell 'em to call me."

"Collect."

"Fine. No problem. Taken care of?"

"The spare tire was flat."

"Okay, nice talking to you, Mr. Murphy."

Murphy hears a beep as Trammell hangs up. He mutters, "Fucking asshole," and immediately calls Eliot Bloom at *Newsweek*.

"Eliot, this is Murphy."

"Hey, we missed you last week."

"I've been away."

"The wealth was redistributed, Murphy. I actually won some money."

"Was Echaverria there?"

"No, just the five of us."

"Have you seen Echaverria?"

"Talked to him, on the phone."

"What about?"

"The usual . . . his product."

"Was there anything unusual?"

A pause. "Yeah, I guess there was."

"Will you tell me about it?"

"Why do you want to know, Murphy? He didn't burn you, did he?"

"No, nothing like that."

"Where are you?"

"In Florida. Near West Palm Beach."

"What the hell are you doing there?"

"Eliot, look, it's a long story I don't have time to go into. It's important to me to know what Echaverria said to you."

"You're talking to a reporter, you know."

"So are you."

"But you're the one who's asking questions."

"Eliot, for Christ's sake let's cut out the bullshit. I'm talking to you as a friend. I'm asking you questions in relation to a matter of the heart. It's very important and some day I'll tell you all about it, okay?"

"You're not the teasing type, are you, Murphy?"

"You know goddamned well I'm not."

"Okay, what the hell. I talked to Ray last week . . . maybe on Wednesday, and he told me he wanted to move a great deal of his product at considerably reduced prices, in volume. There was an implication that it was some kind of going-out-of-business sale, but that could just have been my impression . . ."

"But you didn't see him."

"No, the whole thing was out of my league . . ."

"A lot of money?"

"Yeah, you know, he was talking about *pounds* . . ."

"Can you give me his phone number?"

"I don't know it. He's always called me."

"Do you know where he lives?"

"Half a block away, on Jane. That's how I met him."

Murphy is about to ask Bloom to check Echaverria's apartment, to see if he's there, or if he's been there during the last several days, but decides that this would be an unnecessary imposition. "Thanks, Eliot," he says. "I'll be in touch."

As if to prove that some cosmic force is still on Murphy's side, the morning sky begins to darken, a cool wind sweeps off the ocean. He won't be going to the beach today; the sky has catered to his every whim so far, has held back, and now seems prepared to let loose.

It began to sprinkle as he searches for the local branch of the DMV, located—like everything else here—in a shopping center. By the time he gets there, it's pouring rain. Clutching documents, he runs inside. It turns out to be absurdly easy.

"Naw, sure, happens all the time," the wizened man tells him. "Long as you got the title to the ve-hicle an' it's got some plates on it, you're all right." Murphy hands over all his papers; the old man goes through them, clears his throat a few times, and says, "I'll need them New York plates."

Murphy looks out at the torrent. "You wouldn't have an umbrella?"

"Sorry."

He races out to the car, opens the trunk, locates the tool kit, finds the screwdriver, detaches the rear plate fairly easily, semi-circles to the front of the car, encounters a screw that won't turn, and falls against the curb in a backward kneel. The rain is falling as fast and as copiously as it ever has anywhere in the world, and he's the only fool in the universe trying to unscrew a license plate under a faucet. He sits up, puts his weight against the screwdriver, feels the screw give, then turn easily. He returns to the office as wet as if he'd been swimming with his clothes on. A few minutes later the old man hands him a Florida plate—10D-17737—and tells him he now must have his car inspected. Murphy drives several miles west, nearly to the Turnpike, runs the BMW through its functions; everything works. An inspection sticker is stuck on the lower left corner of the windshield. He drives back to town, speaks to the clown face at Jack-in-the-Box, is issued a huge, tasteless cheeseburger, eats it, returns to Angela's apartment. He puts on dry clothing, finds a huge black umbrella in the hall closet, sets out for the Madera Beach public library.

SAN SEBASTIÁN, *a port and seaside resort of northern Spain, capital town of the Basque province of Guipúzcoa* . . .

*lies at the mouth of the Urumea River in the Bay of Biscay,
10½ mi. (17 km.) W of Irún on the French frontier by rail. . . .
The principal industries are fishing and the manufacture of cement, chemical and metallurgical products, beer, chocolate, and
phonograph records. . . . San Sebastián, first mentioned in a
document of 1014, was granted privileges by Sancho the Wise
of Navarre about 1160–90. . . . It was formerly the summer
residence of the Spanish court.*

So says the *Encyclopaedia Britannica.* Rand McNally concurs,
placing San Sebastián in the upper right corner of Spain, a
quarter-inch from France. Murphy focuses on the fine print in
search of Tharahooth, scans a two-inch semicircle, is on the
verge of giving up, does a lingui-geographic double take. There
it is—millimeters to the left of San Sebastián. Zarauz.

Back to the *Britannica,* to find that nothing lies between
ZARATHUSTRA (see ZOROASTRIANISM) and ZARIA.

Back to the apartment, doubting that Echaverria has involved himself in fishing, cement, metallurgical products, beer,
chocolate, or phonograph records. A connection with the late
Sancho the Wise seems equally improbable. Turning into Waterway Cove, Murphy recalls that he's forgotten to stop at First
American Savings & Loan. Forgotten again. He considers a
U-turn, but the prospect of a nap is far more inviting. Under
Angela's umbrella he strolls unwet from the visitors' parking
area, past the unattended pool to the elevator. Up to the apartment, into the bed. He feels he's accomplished a great deal.

He wakes up to find her sleeping beside him. He slides gently
out of bed. The refrigerator contains nothing but its usual com-
plement of juice. Murphy gets dressed and descends to the
parking lot; the rain has stopped, seems likely to resume. He
drives to Route 1, wonders which way to turn, decides to go
south. What would he like to eat? What would Angela like to
eat? He again considers his veal, imagines he'd require a week's
investigation just to find the raw materials. Burger King. Burger
Chef. Burger Town. Happy Burger. Super Burger. The rain
resumes. Maybe north would have been a better bet. Murphy
checks the rearview mirror before moving to the left-turn lane.

There is a Madera Beach police car thirty feet behind. He moves left; so does the police car. He waits for the green arrow, so does the police car. He makes a U-turn; so does the police car. Murphy drives the length of Madera Beach at twenty-five in the rightmost of three northbound lanes. Maybe they'll stop him for driving too slowly. They've had more than ample time to record his new license number. He crosses into Boca Raton, and the bastards remain on his tail. Here, certainly, they have no jurisdiction. He accelerates quickly to forty-five, seconds later sees a neon sign on the southbound side—Taco Socko—performs an ungraceful U-turn across a double yellow line, pressing his luck, and pulls into Taco Socko's parking lot. The entrance is off the sidewalk; Murphy glances to his left and sees the police car parked at the curb twenty feet behind. In the darkness he can see two figures inside, nothing more.

Four tacos, two enchiladas, two chiles rellenos, two orders of nachos, two orders of rice and beans. Dinner for four, at least, but he doesn't know what Angela likes. It comes to six dollars and eighty-seven cents. The police car has disappeared, but the instant he crosses back into Madera Beach it pulls out of a Sunoco station and tails him back to Waterway Cove, dropping off when he turns left. He's forgotten the beer. He turns left, heading for the beach. The dutiful police cruiser swings back into action half a mile down the road, executing a sudden U-turn into traffic, getting right back on him. Thought he could fool *us*, did he? Murphy pulls into the 7-Eleven at A1A; the police car stops at the curb. He buys two six-packs of Genesee and drives back to Waterway Cove, followed every inch of the way.

Angela loves Mexican food; the food isn't bad. Cardboard trays and wax paper are strewn across the kitchen counter and the dinner table. Murphy opens his third can of beer and paces the living room floor as Angela finishes an enchilada at the table.

"I don't know what they're up to," he says. "I'm sure they've got better things to do than just picking somebody out and deciding to follow him for a few days."

"You're sure . . . you're positive they were following you?"

"Yes, I'm sure. They followed me into Boca Raton. They al-

most ran into a station wagon so they could follow me into the
goddamn 7-Eleven. It's ridiculous."

Angela looks perplexed and perhaps a little sad.

"Will you tell me some things?" Murphy asks.

"Of course, Prosper."

"Has Gutierrez been here before?"

"Not recently."

"But he's been here before."

"Three years ago, when Ray was visiting."

"When you were still married?"

"It caused some friction."

"Between you and Dave?"

Angela looks away at the mention of her ex-husband's name.
"Dave," she speaks the name in embarrassment or distaste, "said
that he didn't mind Ray being here, because he was my brother,
but he wished that Ray's fucking spic buddies could get together
with him somewhere else."

"I don't imagine that sat too well with you. . . ."

"No." She smiles. "I hit him."

"What did he do?"

"He left. He spent the night with a friend."

Murphy sits down and faces her, two feet away. "Dave
seems to have been something of an asshole," he says.

"He was. He was a handsome, well-bred, fairly intelligent
asshole." She laughs slightly.

"Did he have good reason, a good non-racist reason, not to
want Gutierrez in his home?"

"Prosper, if he'd said to me 'I don't want that goddamn
sleazy drug dealer in my apartment,' there wouldn't have been
any argument, or at least I wouldn't have hit him."

"So Gutierrez is a drug dealer."

"Oh, sure he is, and he probably does plenty of other things
against the law. Ray collects people like him. He has a power
over them. He's so much smarter than they are . . ."

There is a long silence. Murphy picks at a chile relleno. "Do
you think it's possible," he asks, "that there's some connection
between the fact that Gutierrez came here and the fact that the
police have been on my ass?"

"Yes," Angela says. "I think it's possible."

"Can you think of any other reason?"

Angela hesitates, then shakes her head.

A longer silence. "I know where he is," Murphy says.

"Where who is?"

"Ray. He's in Spain. Near San Sebastián."

"You're very clever, Prosper," Angela says; she gets up and begins walking to the bedroom. Murphy follows. She lies down on the bed, her face in a pillow.

"Angela . . ."

Her voice is muffled; she seems to be sobbing. "Please, Prosper, don't try to be a detective."

He lies down next to her and says softly, "I'm sorry." He doesn't know exactly what he's sorry about.


Wednesday morning the rain is hard and unceasing. Murphy cleans up the Mexican debris, is chagrined to throw out two intact but greasily congealed tacos, wonders what to do. He wants, or more accurately he feels compelled, to continue being a detective. What he has in mind is another call to Bloom, a request for photocopies of every clipping in *Newsweek*'s Spain file for the last year, maybe the last two or three years. Bloom, after several minutes of bitching and snarling, would dispatch some lackey to do it, and Murphy would be picking up a fat manila envelope at Madera Beach general delivery on Friday, or Saturday at the latest.

But there is an equally powerful force holding him back. It is composed of various ingredients, not the least of which is confusion. Angela wants him to ease off. Not to do so would certainly jeopardize her current feelings for him. He assumes that whatever chore Echaverria has in mind for her is something she doesn't particularly look forward to; he further assumes that Echaverria has some "power" over Angela, some power of blood, heritage, or God knows what. Murphy imagines that he must figure a way to break the bond—and here confusion is rampant. Does he, having known Angela for nine days and a few hours, having been her lover a third of that time, stand the remotest chance of breaking through? If so, must it not be done carefully, gradually?

Standing by the kitchen counter with a glass of grapefruit juice, he has a moment of great clarity and resolve. He's got to *move,* to strike, to attack.

He walks toward the telephone in the bedroom, sits down on the bed, and thinks some more. Most of his anger and frustration is directed not at the fraternal relationship he's trying to destroy, but at the Madera Beach police. If he were to call Bloom, if he were to impose an hour's labor on some journalist of the future, if he were to get a bundle of Xeroxes in the mail secretly, to read them in the bathroom, what the hell would he find out? He would undoubtedly learn a great deal about Spain, but isn't it a bit fantastic to expect that *Newsweek's* clippings would tell him what Echaverria's doing in Spain?

He picks up the phone. And dials West Palm Beach Jai-Alai. They have a matinee today, starting at noon.

He leaves at ten-thirty, forgetting the umbrella, getting drenched on the way to the car. He stops at the 7-Eleven and buys the *Times* and the *Fort Lauderdale News,* then slops up Route 1 in the monsoon. Amongst all the stopping and starting, the weaving to avoid small ponds on the road, his mind jerks back and forth between Angela and Echaverria, between jai alai and the police.

Not far from the fronton, cruising at seventy down puddle-free I-95, he attains an uneasy sort of continuity. What if the rescue in front of his apartment building was a setup? What if those black kids had actually been hired by Echaverria? He remembers the wild look in Archie's eyes when Echaverria appeared, the general aura of terror that preceded their getaway, and the what if? seems very unlikely, as unlikely as the poker game itself having been, to some extent, fixed.

That first night at Bloom's house Murphy had been measured, evaluated. Possibly just as someone who played poker well and might pick up Echaverria an extra thousand dollars. Possibly as someone Angela might enjoy, someone handpicked by big brother to bring her back to life. If so, if Echaverria anticipated what's come to pass, what does he now have in store for Murphy? Murphy doubts that he's simply expected to take care of Angela's apartment while she's away.

It's strange to be in the fronton at midday, stranger still to be there without Angela. Murphy arrives half an hour early and tries to study the program, but names and numbers are meaningless despite their familiarity. He decides to stick with his system in the early, pre-Elu games, but to go it one better, to box teams 1-2-3 in quinielas, at six dollars per game. The players seem as distracted as he. There is a great deal of fumbling and misjudging, noisy derision from the several hundred bettors present. It works to his favor, as usual, the mathematics being on his side. He watches in hazy disinterest as he comes within three hairsbreadths of winning five quinielas in the first five games. He must settle for two, which pay $36.40 and $28.20. Ahead of the game, he raises his stakes and boxes 1-2-3 perfectas, doesn't come close in Game Six or Game Seven (which Elu wins from position 8), but hits big in Game Eight, the 2-3 paying $160 even. Game Nine is a bust. Game Ten is singles, and he isn't about to bet against Elu, so he drops in on Andy at the WPS window, bets $20 on Elu to win.

"That's going to bring the odds way down, you know. . . . There's hardly any money in the pool."

"Yeah, I know, but what the hell."

Andy punches out Murphy's tickets; with no other bettor in sight, Andy's in the mood to chat. "I didn't see you the past few nights."

"We've been busy . . . went to Miami on Monday."

"What did you think?"

"I couldn't tell the difference, but Angela tells me there is one."

"There is, believe it." Andy nods to emphasize the difference. "How is Angie?"

"She's fine. Working hard."

"You hear from Ray?"

"Yeah, he's called a couple of times."

"He's doing all right?"

"Yeah . . . fine."

A customer appears. "You take good care of Angie, okay?" Andy says, and Murphy nods, smiles, departs.

Elu wins easily, paying $3.20. Murphy collects his $32, stops for a hot dog, pages through the *Times*. Not much happened yesterday: more POWs have come home; Nixon; Kissinger; various crimes committed in and around New York City. From page eleven a dateline jumps out. Two days earlier, the headline might have been scanned, the story ignored.

### BASQUE MILITANTS
### KILL POLICEMAN

San Sebastián, Spain (March 2)—Credit for the ambush killing of a paramilitary policeman in the coastal town of Pasajes was claimed today by the Basque separatist organization, E.T.A.

Jose Marquez Trias, 34, a sergeant in the Spanish Civil Guard, was killed yesterday on a streetcorner by gunmen firing from a passing car.

A communique from E.T.A. (Basque Land and Liberty) described Trias as a "torturer" and a "murderer."

Murphy hurries back to Andy's window, taking a quick look at the program on his way: Elu and Lejarcegui playing in position 6.

"You see what you did?" Andy says. "Three-twenty to win!"

"Okay, I learned my lesson. Give me six to win, twice."

Andy punches out two tickets. Murphy hands him four dollars and says, "You have time for a drink after the last game?"

"Sure," Andy says. "I'll meet you at La Pelota."

Andy takes a sip from his rum and Coke. "You know what they call this drink? A cuba libre. You know what that means?"

Murphy's never thought about it before, but if "cuba" is Cuba and "libre" means the same thing in Spanish as in French, it's worth a guess. "Free Cuba," he says.

"Free Cuba, that's right. I used to play in Havana. Did Angie tell you that?"

"She didn't."

"When I was a kid, a boy. I had the best time in my life in Havana. It was a crazy city, you know. And they had the best jai alai there. The best fronton, and the best players. But no more. They don't have nothing there now."

"Since Castro," Murphy says.

"Since Castro," Andy agrees.

"You don't think too much of Castro?"

Andy grimaces, then chuckles, points to his glass. "He freed

Cuba, some people say, but they don't say that in Miami. Me, I don't care. I was there, I had a good time, and there was people starving. Now there's no jai alai, there's no people starving, so what the hell. Maybe it's good, maybe it's bad. I'm not a political man."

"But you're a Basque."

"Sure, I'm a Basque."

"I get the impression that Basques tend to be political."

Andy shrugs. "How do you get that impression? From Angie?"

Murphy's brain participates in a brief waltz. "No, of course not," he says.

"From Ray, then," Andy says.

Murphy tries to phrase his question as casually as he can: "Why would I have gotten that impression from Ray?"

"Well," Andy says, "because Ray is Basque. Angie is Basque. How many Basques do you know?"

Murphy tells himself to smile, realizes that he's smiling involuntarily. What a shrewd interviewer he is. How perceptive he's been all along. "Just the three of you," he says to Andy.

"Then tell me how you get that impression?"

"From the newspapers," Murphy says.

"Ah . . ." Andy grins. "ETA. You been reading about ETA." He speaks the acronym as a word, prounounced somewhere between "Etta" and "Aytah."

Murphy must concentrate to pick up his beer glass and bring it to his mouth, such is the suggestion of manual tremor. With all the nonchalance he can summon he asks: "How do you feel about ETA?"

"Two ways," Andy says. "First, I hate Franco. I was a boy in the Civil War, I lived in a little town near the ocean, my father, my two older brothers, they went to fight, and thank God none of them got killed, but a lot of men from my town was killed, and after the war it was terrible. We weren't allowed to speak our language, to leave our village, you know. So I hate Franco, and I hate the government in Spain. But second, I don't know about ETA. I don't know if it's a good idea to kill people . . ."

"Have they killed a lot of people?"

Andy shrugs. "Maybe. Not so many. I don't know."

"Do you still have relatives back there?"

"Sure. We all do."

"Ray and Angie do?"

"Sure, they must. We all do."

Murphy takes a large gulp of Budweiser. "I never talked to Ray about politics," he says. "What about him . . . is he political?"

"Ray?" Andy smiles. "Maybe he is. He's proud of being Basque, I know that. And he doesn't take nothing from nobody."

"But he never talked to you about ETA, or anything like that?"

"Oh, sure. We all talk about ETA. But Basques are like anyone else. When you get away from a place, maybe you stop caring about it so much. When you make some money, like my brothers in Spain, maybe you stop hating Franco so much. Maybe you forget. Me, if I was back in Spain, I don't think I'm on the side of ETA. I don't think no good can come from it, killing the police."

"How about Ray? How do you think he feels about ETA killing police?"

"Ray," Andy says, "is a tough guy. But he's a smart guy. So I don't know. Why don't you ask him?"

"Okay," Murphy says, "maybe I will."


At quarter to six traffic will be murder on Route 1, so Murphy takes I-95 to its terminus at Okeechobee Boulevard, zips west to the turnpike, south to the Madera Beach exit. As he hits Route 1 and turns right, the rearview mirror shows a Madera Beach police car several lengths behind him. He drives with utmost caution to Waterway Boulevard, makes his right turn; the police car follows. He turns into Waterway Cove; the police car proceeds down the boulevard, heading for A1A.


Angela is supine on the bed, watching the news. She smiles as he enters.

"Hi," she says. "I missed you. I thought you might have had some trouble . . ."

Some trouble? Murphy sits on the bed. "I went to the matinee."

"How'd you do?"

"Okay. I won a few dollars. I had a drink with Andy after the last game."

"How's Andy?"

"He's fine. He sends you his love." Murphy nods toward the little television. "What's happening in the world?"

"Nothing," Angela says.

Murphy wonders what to do here, what to say. He decides to say nothing, to lean down and kiss her lips. He unbuttons her blouse and kisses her breasts.

She says, "No, Prosper. Not now."

"Why not?"

"My period."

"The hell with your period. I don't care about your period."

"I do. I don't feel very . . . rapturous."

Murphy sits up, stands up, and sits on the floor next to the bed. Angela moves to a point on the bed just above him. "I'm sorry, Prosper," she says.

Murphy looks at her face, looks at her breasts. "It's all right," he says.

"Would you like a beer?" she asks.

"I'd love one."

She returns with two Genesees. He takes a sip. If she won't sleep with him, maybe she'll talk to him. "What kind of name is Echaverria?" he asks her.

"Basque," she says.

"Were you born there, in Spain?"

"No, in New York."

"And Ray?"

"He was born in Spain."

"When did your family come to America?"

"In 1947. When Ray was eight years old."

"He doesn't have an accent."

"Prosper, do you want the whole story? The family history?"

Herr Schliemann, shall we continue to dig? "Tell me," Murphy says.

# 18

# The War Hero

Her mother, whose name was Fernanda Arrieta, married a man named Esteban Echaverria in 1935. Fernanda was seventeen at the time, Echaverria was thirty, and they lived in San Sebastián. Echaverria was a lawyer and a Basque nationalist.

Does Murphy know about Basques and Spain?

Not much.

Well, there's too much to tell. Suffice it to say that many (if not most) Basques have never considered themselves Spaniards, but have tended to put up with any government that has let them alone, has allowed them a good degree of self-rule, or autonomy—and that was pretty much the way things stood in 1935, under the Spanish Republic.

Does Murphy know about the civil war?

The basics.

The Basques, she tells him, or two of the four Basque provinces anyway, sided with the Republic against the insurgents, who were also known as the Nationalists or the Fascists. The war began in July of 1936, when a general named Francisco Franco engineered a successful mutiny in Morocco and by September the Nationalists controlled most of Spain, including San Sebastián. Fernanda, her mother, and her three younger sisters had fled to Paris.

Echaverria, a colonel in the Republican army, had endured with his regiment the siege of Bilbao, which lasted from April until mid-June of 1937 and was particularly gruesome. Already something of a hero, Echaverria escaped by boat to France. He met Fernanda in Biarritz, whence they traveled overland to Barcelona. By this time the Fascists had taken most of the south, all of the west and north, while the Republicans held Madrid and the southeast. Things didn't look very good for the Republicans.

But Fernanda and Echaverria lived fairly well in Barcelona for a year or so, until Echaverria was sent to the front in September, 1938. Fernanda, pregnant, was dispatched to France. She refused to join her family in Paris, waited instead in Perpignan for the war to end. Her son was born. Barcelona fell in late January, 1939. Fernanda left her infant in Perpignan and virtually camped by the border, waiting for word of her husband. The border was chaotic: what records there were were pathetically incomplete. She had no idea whether Echaverria was dead, imprisoned, or a refugee like herself. After a vigil of several weeks she returned to Perpignan, picked up nine-month-old Ramon Esteban Echaverria Arrieta, and made her way to the French side of Euskadi, the Basque country.

"My mother must have told me this story a hundred times," Angela says. "They rode on the back of a truck, they took a train and they stood up all the way, they walked about twenty miles, and then she'd always say: 'He never cried. He was a baby, Angelita, just nine months old, and he never cried.'"

Fernanda chose to settle in Hendaye, directly across the border from Irún. It was hardly the most comfortable location, but it was where she stood the best chance of hearing about her husband. And, Angela has always supposed, Fernanda's fantasy was that Esteban might some night just slip across the frontier and find her.

But as it was she was caught between wars. Her mother wired a great deal of money to her in Hendaye, begged her to return to Paris, and within days the Nazis were in Paris, the Arrietas en route to Argentina.

Fernanda remained in Hendaye. In October of 1940 she was a mile away when Franco and his erstwhile helpmate, Adolf Hitler, held their only tête-à-tête. In June of 1942 she was speaking to another young woman, another refugee, who asked her if she happened to be related to Esteban Echaverria.

"He is my husband," Fernanda said.

The other woman clucked and looked at her feet, revealed after considerable prodding that her brother had served under Echaverria in Bilbao, and would say no more.

Fernanda shook the woman, screamed at her, "What do you know?"

"Only," the woman said, "that he is dead."

"Was he?" Murphy asks.

"Yes," Angela says.

"Did she ever find out how it happened?"

"Never. She just gradually got used to thinking that he was dead."


As the war continued, more and more of Fernanda's fellow refugees made their way back across the border. She stayed in Hendaye, living on her dwindling cash, raising her son, waiting for the war to end so she might join her family in Buenos Aires, wishing that they might all one day return to San Sebastián.

But instead her fate was to be introduced to Antoine Bordagaray.

"My father," Angela says. "He was the local hero, and he swept her off her feet. She'd been living like a nun for six years, and suddenly this good-looking guy in a British uniform shows up and wants to take *her* out, over all the local girls, despite the fact that she's a widow with a seven-year-old son. And of course Ray loved him, because he was the envy of all the other kids. My mother used to tell me this as if she was apologizing . . ."

"Why did she need to apologize?"

"Because my father wasn't a very nice man."

"Wasn't?"

"Isn't, I guess. I haven't seen him since 1958."

"Have you heard from him?"

"No. He could be dead, for all I know."


Perhaps two months after meeting Fernanda, Bordagaray was off to Paris in search of a job befitting his stature. Although her mother never spoke explicitly about the extent of their relationship, Angela knows when she was born, knows that Fernanda must have been pregnant when Bordagaray took off for Paris. She speculates that on his return he must have given Fernanda an ultimatum: come with me to America or do what you will. She can think of no other reason why her mother should have agreed to emigrate to New York.

Bordagaray's job was with the Bank of Paris. Angela has no idea what he did—only that he'd had no training as a banker in France. But she knows he was paid well, she imagines that with his silk suits and his elegant, British-inflected English he must have cut an impressive figure. They lived in a large apartment in Washington Heights, whence every morning Bordagaray left for Wall Street, leaving Fernanda—who spoke not a word of English, who had to tend an eight-year-old son and an infant daughter—to fend for herself. Perhaps, Angela conjectures, Bordagaray assumed that if Fernanda had managed to survive both wars, had managed to convey one newborn child from Perpignan to Hendaye with no apparent ill effects, she should have been able to cope with a considerably more mundane situation in New York.

But in 1946 Spanish was not spoken at the A & P, nor was Basque at the drugstore. Fernanda, in the face of devastation, had been able to transcend her *haute-bourgeoise* inhibitions to keep herself and her son alive. But in Washington Heights she couldn't bring herself to shop by pointing at things, to pay for them with little green bills that made no sense. Bordagaray would return from work, find the apartment in perfect order, no speck of dust in sight, and no speck of dinner on the table, because the elements necessary for dinner, the food, had not been bought.

"He'd yell at her—he'd call her stupid, and incompetent, and he'd call her a Spanish bitch. She couldn't be Basque, because a Basque would have the sense to learn the language and go out and buy some chicken and some lettuce. And then he'd go out to a restaurant, by himself, have a nice dinner, and the hell with everybody else.

"He put Ray in public school right away, in the second grade, in the middle of the school year, and Ray knew about twelve words of English."

The son was not encumbered with his mother's inhibitions. He had grown up so far bilingually, and the third language came naturally. By the time Angela was two months old, eight-year-old Echaverria was near the top of his class, and was as well his mother's interpreter.

Whatever rancor Fernanda felt for Bordagaray went largely unexpressed. She cooked his dinners, ironed his shirts, and gradually gained the courage necessary to communicate in the New World. She spoke to her children, however, only in Spanish, to her husband only in French. For his part, Bordagaray would speak to Angela and Echaverria only in English.

In the spring of 1950 word came from Buenos Aires that Fernanda's mother had died. Bordagaray would not permit her to fly to Argentina for the funeral, but allowed her one international telephone call. Her sisters wired her plane fare. She wanted desperately to go, but was terrified in anticipation of Bordagaray's fury. Echaverria, now twelve, virtually dragged her to the taxi, assuring her that he could take care of his stepfather.

"I think that's my earliest memory," Angela says. "She couldn't have been gone for more than a week, but it seemed to last forever." Bordagaray, returning from the Bank of Paris the first night, reading Fernanda's note of explanation, confronting Echaverria, who was making dinner, slapping his face, Echaverria refusing to react, refusing in fact to reply at all, Bordagaray stomping out of the apartment, not to return until the weekend, four days later, having caused Echaverria to miss four days of sixth grade. "He took good care of me," Angela says. "He cooked all my meals and he took me to the park every day, and he kept telling me everything was all right, and I guess I believed him."

Fernanda returned with a keepsake, a fat leather album of photographs. One eight-by-ten she furtively gave to her son: a picture of herself and Esteban Echaverria taken in 1936, he in his Republican uniform, she in a blue dress. "Don't let Antoine see this," she told him. He didn't let his stepfather see it until the following winter, by which time he had saved enough money to buy a gilt frame, and hung the photograph above his bed.

"We were eating dinner," Angela says, "and my father was in a very bad mood. He said something to Ray in French, so I wouldn't understand, and Ray said to me in Spanish, 'He wants to know why I have that photograph over my bed.' And my father said, 'There will be no Spanish spoken at this table.' And Ray said something to my father in French, and then my mother said something to Ray in French, and Ray said something like 'It's none of his business' in Spanish, and my father said, 'No Spanish!' And Ray said something to my father in French, and my father's face got completely red, and he stood up and slapped Ray in the face.

"And Ray, who was almost as tall as my father then, and probably a little stronger, stood up and punched him in the stomach. My mother screamed, and my father slapped Ray again, and I got up and ran into the bathroom and hid under the sink. I could hear my mother yelling at Ray to stop, he was going to kill him, and there was all this scrambling and screaming. And then my mother came into the bathroom. She carried me to my bed and she said, 'Don't worry, Angelita, everything's going to be all right.'"

"Was it?"

"No, it got worse. My father got nastier, and more distant . . ."

"Why did your mother stay? Why didn't she take you and Ray to Argentina?"

"Partly, I think, because she was supposed to obey her husband, and partly because there was always an understanding that we were all going to go back to France some day, and maybe when we were back in France my father would start being a nice man again."

"What about your father? He obviously wasn't very happy, unless he had a strong sense of sadism . . ."

"I would guess that he was getting a fair amount of satisfaction elsewhere, Prosper. He probably had quite a few mistresses. He wasn't home very much, and when he was he used to spend most of his time with me."


She was Bordagaray's *petit ange*. On weekend afternoons he took her to the park, to the movies, to the skating rink, to the zoo, spoke to her absentmindedly in French, remembered that she didn't understand, said, "Someday, my little angel, I'll teach you to speak French and we'll go to Paris together." He was so gentle and graceful on their excursions, so kind to her and so at

ease with her that she loved him, but it was an emotion to be
kept to herself, because at home Bordagaray was the outsider.
To Echaverria especially she described her Saturday and Sunday afternoons as exercises in tolerance.

"What did you do today, with him?"

"We went to the zoo."

"Did you have a good time?"

"It was all right."

"What did you talk about?"

"Just about the animals."

In the spring of 1956, when she was nine, Bordagaray took her
to Playland, an amusement park in Rye twenty miles northeast of
Washington Heights. This was the farthest from home they'd
been, quite an adventure for Angela. Bordagaray seemed preoccupied. He'd bought her a book of tickets that entitled her to
every ride in the place, but after only a few he dragged her away
from the roller coaster she wanted to ride to the ferris wheel,
and several hundred feet above the Long Island Sound he asked
her if she wanted to come to France with him.

This seemed different from the fantasy of someday going to
France together. She asked when. He said soon. She asked if her
mother and Ray were part of the bargain. He said no, it would
be just Daddy and his little angel. She decided immediately that
this was not for her, allowed a respectful pause before replying
that she'd rather stay in America. Bordagaray hugged her, said
no more. When the wheel brought them down he took her home,
half her tickets unused. Three weeks later Bordagaray was gone,
for good.


He had left behind most of his clothes, all of his medals, and
two thousand dollars. His absences in the past had never ex-
ceeded three or four days, and when this one reached a week
Fernanda began to talk about contacting the police and a lawyer.
Echaverria, now eighteen and about to graduate from high
school, told his mother that lawyers were not to be trusted, the
police were out of the question, and he would take care of it.
He took the subway down to Wall Street and confronted his
stepfather's astonished superior. Bordagaray had been reassigned

to Paris. Didn't the family know? He had instructed that a third
of his monthly salary, about four hundred and fifty dollars, be
sent directly to his wife. It was the superior's understanding that
this arrangement would last only until the end of the school
year, when Bordagaray's wife and children would join him in
Paris.

Echaverria informed the banker that Bordagaray had deserted
his family, that his family had no desire to join him in Paris, that
it was prepared to make a great deal of trouble were it not
granted *half* his monthly salary. Further, if Bordagaray were
fired as a result of this incident, his family would sue the bank
for support. Negotiations were brief, and Echaverria's terms
were accepted to the letter.

"All of a sudden we were rich, Prosper. We were getting almost seven hundred dollars a month, and that was a lot of money.
My father must have been spending everything on his girlfriends, or maybe he had a secret bank account. But after a
couple of months Ray went out and bought our first television,
and he bought my mother new clothes, and in the summer he
bought us a car, a 1954 Oldsmobile 88, and in August we drove
up to Maine and spent a week at some little place in the woods,
and I was in ecstasy just to get into Connecticut." Conceived in
France, embryonic across the Atlantic, she had spent nine and
a half postnatal years confined in a tiny section of the state of
New York.

"Did you miss him?"

"Yes. Of course. But I wasn't allowed to."

"Did you ever hear from him?"

"On my birthday, every year until I was sixteen or seventeen.
He'd send me a card, some cute little thing in French, and write
something in English about how he hoped to see me again
someday. He always signed them 'I love you very much, Your
Father.'"

"Do you think he did?"

"I think so. In his way, I think he does."

"But the cards stopped coming?"

"Either that or I stopped getting them."

Echaverria went to Columbia on a full scholarship. He played football.

"Football?" When Murphy thinks about it, it doesn't really seem so incongruous.

He was an All-City quarterback in high school, was the starting quarterback for the freshman team at Columbia, the backup quarterback for the varsity his sophomore year, and then lost interest.

"He told the coach he needed to concentrate on his studies," Angela says, "and in a way that was true, but Ray had been selling marijuana at Columbia since his junior year in high school, and I think he decided that was a more valuable extra-curricular activity than football." Echaverria moved off-campus in 1958, into a large Morningside Heights apartment, where he sold dope purchased in Harlem to Columbia's legion of would-be hipsters at a 500 percent markup, studying Romance languages on the side, conceivably the first big-time marijuana dealer in the history of the Ivy League.

Murphy considers 1958: General Eisenhower was President; John Lennon was learning to play the guitar; marijuana was a drug used by jazz musicians, a stepping stone to heroin.

"He graduated _magna cum laude_," Angela says. "He speaks eight languages. Did you know that?"

"I don't know anything," Murphy says.


"What about you?"

She looks at him, then looks away. "It's pretty boring."

"Nothing about you is boring."

"I don't know what to tell you. I went to school. I watched _American Bandstand._ I had some friends. I had a crush on a boy who was in ninth grade when I was in seventh grade. He was Italian and he looked really tough—he wore a leather jacket and had a ridiculous haircut. He took me to the movies once and he turned out to be really shy and a little stupid. He's probably working in a garage now, or running numbers. My girlfriends all thought Ray was the sexiest thing around, and he probably was.

"I got good grades in school, and I had a summer job all

through high school at a luncheonette about three blocks from where we lived. Ray got me that. Every winter my mother went to Buenos Aires for a month, and Ray stayed with me in the apartment, and he'd take me to all sorts of weird places. I mean, we'd go to see Lenny Bruce one night and Thelonius Monk the next, when my level was Bob Newhart and the Everly Brothers. It was . . . exotic, I guess. It was exciting."

"You never went to Buenos Aires with your mother?"

"No."

There is a long pause. Murphy suspects that he has trodden on something. She has been talking effortlessly, as if it had been a question of her not having been asked before. She has been unconcealed. He wishes he might retract the question, wonders if he should instead continue the assault. It becomes academic.

"I was going to," Angela says, "my second year at Barnard. I was going to go during Christmas vacation, but my mother had a stroke December tenth." Another silence.

"She died?"

"She was unconscious for three days, and then she died."

"She was young," Murphy says.

"She was forty-nine," Angela says. "But I wasn't surprised. I don't think she'd been very interested in staying alive. It was as if she'd already been dead for quite a few years."

"Because of your father?"

"Because of everything. I think my father was incidental. I think she almost invited him to be the way he was. I'm not trying to defend him, because I don't think he ever tried to do anything about it, but I think my mother's life ended the day she found out Esteban was dead. But she had Ray to think about, and then along came this guy who superficially resembled Esteban, and it was like injecting adrenaline into someone who's clinically dead. She stayed alive, Prosper, but she found out that my father wasn't Esteban, and she stopped caring. And poor Ray kept trying to pump life back into her, but it just wasn't going to happen."

A short silence. "Does Ray feel the way you do? Now?"

"No. He hates my father. He's convinced he killed her."

A longer silence. "What happened after she died?"

"Ray was teaching at NYU. He spent his Christmas vacation

flying down to Buenos Aires with my mother's body. I didn't want to go. I moved into a dormitory at Barnard, and when Ray came back we sold the furniture and he took everything else down to Jane Street. That's it."

"Six years to go," Murphy says.

"You know the rest. I met David."

"Where was Ray?"

"He got some kind of fellowship. He went to Paris for a year."

"And then?"

"He came back, he resigned from NYU, then he just traveled around for a year, and then he came back again."

"You married David right after you both graduated, and you moved here?"

Angela nods.

"What did Ray think of that?"

"Not much, but he never said anything."

"He didn't need to, though, did he?"

"No, I guess not."

"He just showed up once in a while and made David look like an asshole . . ."

"But David *was* an asshole."

"You couldn't have felt that way at first, could you? And married him?"

"Prosper, don't you suppose that happens fairly often?"

"People get married to people they think are assholes?"

"No . . . you know what I mean. Especially under the circumstances. I was all alone. It didn't occur to me that he might be a pompous, hypocritical bastard."

"You don't feel that Ray might have manipulated things, with you and David?"

"I'm sure he did. And I'm sure it would have ended almost as soon if he hadn't."

"You don't think that he might be manipulating us, now?"

A pause. "All I know is that he sent . . . that he suggested you come here. He didn't cause me to fall in love with you."

"You were all alone again . . ."

"What's that supposed to mean?"

"He knew you were vulnerable."

Her voice rises. "So what, Prosper? He knew you were vulnerable, too, and he introduced us, in his way. Do you question that? Do you think he's got some kind of sinister plot for us?"

"I know he's trying to pull you away."

"That has nothing to do with you . . . with us. That's been arranged for a long time. And it's probably not going to happen."

"What is it, Angela?"

"Prosper, for God's sake, I can't tell you. I don't even really know."

"Does it have to do with your father?"

"No."

"Does it have to do with killing policemen in Spain?"

Her voice rises again, now in puzzled trepidation. "Why do you say that?"

"Something I read today, in the *Times,* some kind of paramilitary policeman got ambushed near San Sebastián."

The word "policeman" sticks in Angela's mind. The connection is irrational but unavoidable. She feels vaguely nauseated, unable to speak.


Thursday morning, her fourth straight without a good night's sleep, Angela finds an envelope on the desk in her classroom. The note inside reads: "Could I see you during your first break? Ralph Janowicz."

She sleepwalks through her nine o'clock class, Advanced Spanish, whose students are primarily Cuban. She knocks on the principal's door at 9:55.

"Angela. How are you?"

"Fine, Mr. Janowicz."

Janowicz is a man in early middle age, gone to seed, tall and pallid, extremely thin but for a fat belly. There is a large, color portrait of Richard Nixon on his wall, a little American flag on his desk.

"Have a seat," he says.

She sits in the uncomfortable chair on the subservient side of the desk. He displays a piece of paper.

"I don't know what to make of this. I thought you should see it." He hands it to her.

She reads: "Do you know your Spanish teacher is shacked

up with a man. Do you know he's a dope dealer." She tries to smile.

"I'm embarrassed to show that to you," Janowicz says, fidgeting a bit, "but I thought I should."

"I have a guest," Angela says. "He's a friend of my brother's from New York. He's a writer."

"It's none of my business," Janowicz says. "But obviously there's somebody who's got something against you, or just being a busybody . . ."

Angela nods. She feels enclosed, menaced.

". . . You're a heck of a good teacher, and when something like this happens I feel it's my duty to give a warning . . ."

# 19

# Echaverria and the Tree

In the house in Hendaye, Echaverria sits with two men younger than he: Iñaki, who appears to be in his early twenties, and Mikel, perhaps thirty. He's met them tonight, Wednesday night, for the first time, and they're important. They don't look particularly important; they look in fact like a couple of graduate students—well-dressed, well-groomed, academic, and innocent.

"You've been told what's happened?" Echaverria says, in Spanish.

"We know," Mikel replies.

"And you know I don't expect just to be a philanthropist here?"

"We know."

"All right. I wanted to be sure we understood each other. I can replace the explosives. I'd rather not do it, but it can be done fairly easily."

"It won't be necessary."

"Tell me why."

"Because we've raided the armory at Hernani. We have three thousand kilos of explosives."

"What kind?"

"Every kind. We have some Goma Two." Mikel smiles.

"Do you know how old it is?"

Mikel shakes his head.

"Do you have it well wrapped?"

Mikel nods.

"Well stored?"

Mikel nods again.

"These things are important," Echaverria says.

Iñaki answers, "You're not talking to idiots."

"I know I'm not talking to idiots, but I also know you people have never done anything like this before."

"Have you?" Mikel asks.

"No, but I've spent the last twenty years looking forward to it."

"And we haven't?"

"Twenty years ago you were learning how to read."

"Twenty years ago you were in America."

"Look—let's not get involved in some petty nonsense about who's got more right to want to kill the old bastard. I think we all want to do that, so let's just concentrate on how we're going to do it."

"We're *not* going to do it," Mikel says.

Echaverria is speechless.

"He's an old man," Mikel says. "He's going to die soon."

"I don't want him to die in his fucking bed," Echaverria says, "I want to blow him into small pieces."

"It's not practical," Iñaki says.

"I didn't think we were preoccupied with being practical," Echaverria replies.

"Think of Fascism in Spain as a tree," Mikel says. "If you kill the old man you're killing a heavy old branch that's going to die soon, anyway. If you want to get rid of the tree for good, what do you do? You kill the roots."

What is this bullshit? "You'd need a time machine to kill the roots," Echaverria says.

"No," Mikel says. "We're not talking about the same thing. There will always be Fascists, but if we kill the roots we take away their power."

"I'm listening."

"There's something we should talk about before we go any further."

"Talk, then."

"Xabier told me your conditions. I'd like to know exactly what you mean when you say you expect to be 'in charge.'"

"I was referring to what I thought I came here to do, and I meant exactly what I said. I wanted to be in charge."

"And now?"

"Now, I'd say everything depends on what your plans are."

"I can't tell you our plans until I know what sort of role you'll accept."

Echaverria stands up abruptly and walks to within three feet of Mikel, who remains seated. "I don't like being deceived," he says. "I came here with an understanding. I took a lot of risks to do something I believe in, and I think you're fucking around with me."

Mikel looks up at Echaverria. "If someone has misled you, I apologize. We're indebted to you for the money."

"You're damned right you are. You guys would have had to rob a hell of a lot of banks . . ."

"We're indebted to you, but it isn't essential."

"What are you saying?"

"You can't be in charge. You're too visible, you're too obvious, and you don't know the way we operate."

Echaverria heads back to his chair, trying to control his anger. This fucking boy scout terrorist may have shot a couple of cops in the back, may have shoved a submachine gun in a bank teller's face . . .

He elects not to sit, turns, and faces Mikel again. "Look, *muchacho,* I haven't spent the last ten years in school. I'm not some rich cocksucker donating a few million pesetas to the cause. I know I need to learn the way you 'operate' but I know damned well I can teach you a few things, too."

"I'm sure you can," Mikel says, as calmly as ever, "and I hope you will. You can be very valuable to us. But you can't be in charge."

Echaverria suddenly realizes the absurdity of his position, or perhaps its impossibility. He had envisioned himself a latter-day Lawrence of Arabia, Ramon de Euskadi. But Lawrence was truly a foreigner, a man from the old world leading an older world with a nasty mixture of sophistication and dedication. Echaverria is just as dedicated, just as sophisticated, thanks to his new-world education. But his Arabs are Basques. His people, his blood, ready to learn from him, but invulnerable to his power. His power is, in fact, their power.

"You can always take your money and leave," Mikel says.

"No, I'm not going to do that," Echaverria says.

"What are you going to do, then?"

*¿Entonces, qué harás?* Mikel has for the first time addressed Echaverria in the familiar form, neither condescendingly nor contemptuously, but in an obvious offer of friendship. Echaverria feels a sudden wave of giddiness, as if he's just been accepted by some elite fraternal organization he'd been petitioning for years. He is not at all comfortable with the feeling. It is completely unprecedented, entirely alien to him. He waits for it to pass.

"Give me a day to think," he says in the formal imperative.

"Tomorrow morning, then? Here?" Mikel asks.

"Fine," Echaverria says.


Half an hour later, Thursday early afternoon, he tries to call Angela. After a five-minute wait he's informed by the overseas operator that no lines are available; should she try again in an hour? In an hour, Angela will have left for school. Echaverria tells the operator he'll try later.

# 20

# Wilson and Raymond

Thursday morning Murphy chances a swim. The forecast is for partly cloudy weather, and under a dark gray sky he wonders where there might be a part unclouded. A mile from shore he is rained upon; he can get no wetter, and is unperturbed until he hears the first distant rumble of thunder, followed minutes later by a cannon shot. He heads for shore.

Indeed, as he sits in Fat Lou's, the forecast proves to have been understated but accurate. The sun comes out. He drives back to Waterway Cove and spends an hour swimming laps in the pool, half an hour in the sauna. He drives to the 7-Eleven and buys some beer, realizes that the police have ignored him all day, drives back to the apartment feeling light and easy. Placing two six-packs of Genesee in the refrigerator, he remembers that he's forgotten yet again to visit First American Savings & Loan. But what of it?

Angela has the note in her purse.

Murphy greets her at the door. She is pleased to see him, nearly overcome by his ebullience. She has cramps. She doesn't know how to deal with Murphy. She wishes he'd go away for a while, she's awfully grateful for his presence. He wants to know how her day has been, how she feels; she shrugs and shrugs. He says she looks tired, suggests she take a nap and they do something later; maybe they could go back to Miami. Does she have any tests to grade? No. Would she then like to go to Miami? They could leave early. We'll see, she says, heading for the bedroom. Murphy tells her he's bought some more beer. Would she like one? No, thanks. He stands by the bed as she undresses. She wants only and desperately to sleep. He kneels by the bed and kisses her, caresses her breasts. She wants to say, "Leave me alone, will you?"

She says, "Prosper, I'm going to sleep."

Murphy wanders into the kitchen, opens a beer, turns on the television. The two sets of network stations duplicate two soap operas and one game show; *Sesame Street* on PBS, a Ronald Reagan western dubbed into Spanish on UHF. It is briefly amusing to watch the governor of California babble in a most inappropriate tongue. He turns off the television, takes the elevator to the ground floor, walks half a mile to the 7-Eleven, and buys a *Miami Herald;* walks back to Waterway Cove, looks in on Angela, still asleep. He sits with the *Herald* sports section and Monday's Miami jai-alai program which together provide him three nights' results and tonight's schedule—not really enough information to work with, but not an unpleasant way to pass some time. His eye is drawn to a large figure at the bottom of last night's results: Big Q—$2,637.50. What the hell is the Big Q? He looks through the program. Big Q . . . played in the first and second games, again in the eleventh and twelfth. It seems that if you hold a winning quiniela ticket in the first game you may, in lieu of cashing it, pay an additional two dollars and turn it in for a Big Q ticket; then should your second straight quiniela come in, you win a large amount of money. It's a stupid bet. The odds against winning the first quiniela are 27 to 1, the odds against winning the second quiniela are 27 to 1. The odds against winning both quinielas, back to back, are 729 to 1. Of course, Murphy reasons, then again . . . once you've *won* the first quiniela, the odds against winning the second are only 27 to 1. But who in his right mind would turn down thirty or forty or sixty dollars in cash for a 27 to 1 shot at the big bucks?

Angela sleeps for a few minutes, is wrung awake by a bad dream she can't remember, thinks of the note, the police, of Murphy, of Echaverria, drifts back to sleep, and repeats the process at least four times, perhaps five or six times. The last dream is set in her parents' apartment, her own childhood apartment. She wakes up, as if from a dream, to find herself under the sink in the bathroom. She hears muffled sounds of violence from outside. She struggles against a great feeling of weariness to stand up. She opens the bathroom door and walks down a short hallway to the living room. She is not a child but her current self. In the living room which perfectly replicates her childhood living room but for sliding glass windows leading to a deck, she sees Ray squatting over her father, who lies on his back, eyes closed, as Ray hits him in the face, right fist alternating with left fist, again and again. Her mother observes tranquilly, from an armchair five feet away. "Stop," Angela says. "Please stop!" She approaches her mother and says, "Make them stop!" Her mother looks straight ahead, unmoving, her face set in a slight smile. Angela now screams, "Make them stop!" Her mother remains as before. Angela turns to find her father prone on the floor, Ray no longer in the room. She moves cautiously toward her father, expecting to find him dead.

She wakes up. And in doing so, in the instant before she reaches consciousness, she thinks: I've had this dream before.

Murphy kneels by the bed. "Are you all right?" he asks, quietly.

"I'm all right," Angela says. She imagines that her eyes are wild and traitorous.

"You kept saying 'stop.' 'Make them stop.'"

"I was dreaming."

"I know you were."

"I'm all right."

"Tell me about the dream." His voice is gentle.

"I don't remember it."

"Nothing?"

She closes her eyes, shakes her head. She wants to remember; she can hear herself screaming; she can imagine herself screaming, "Make them stop!" But what moves back and forth through her mind like a berserk pendulum, a normally precise machine uncontrollably out of kilter, is the strong and frightening sense of the dream's having been dreamed before. It is eventually the only thing she can return to; it is eventually a downdraft, a whirlpool, something lacking traction.


"No, Prosper," Angela says, an hour later, "I feel lousy."

"Then come on," Murphy replies. "That's all the more reason to go. It'll cheer you up. Do you a world of good."

"It's not going to do me a world of good to sit in a car all the way down to Miami."

"Then we'll go to West Palm Beach."

"No. I don't want to see jai alai anywhere."

"We'll go to a movie."

"No. I just want to stay here."

"Okay, I'll go out and get some food . . ."

"I'm not hungry."

Murphy is running out of suggestions, running low on enthusiasm.

"You go," Angela says.

"Where?"

"Go to Miami."

"Not without you."

"Prosper, look . . . you want to go, I don't want to go, so go ahead. I just need to sleep for about ten hours and I'll be all right."

"I don't think I should go," Murphy says.

"You should, Prosper. You're not going to do me any good tonight. You don't have to suffer with me."

Suffer? "Your period?"

She nods.

"What else?"

"I'm just . . . it's nothing different. Nothing new."

"Do you want to talk to me?"

"I don't want to talk to anybody."

"Angela . . . if you'd like to sit around and have a few beers and talk . . . I'd rather do that than go to Miami without you."

She smiles. "No, Prosper. Not tonight."


There is a Madera Beach police car on the shoulder halfway to the turnpike. It doesn't follow.

Nevertheless, Murphy is not at ease. He feels he shouldn't have left. He replays the conversation again and again, he sees Angela's face with each exchange. It was hardly a question of her not really wanting him to go, of her saying, go ahead, but I'd really like you to stay. She wanted him out, or at least wanted to be alone. Was she expecting another call from Echaverria? Has she suddenly grown weary of him? Has he, in his passion to know her, to possess her, overstepped his bounds?

He pulls into a service complex past Fort Lauderdale, intending to fill his three-quarters-empty tank and call Angela. He stops at the premium pump, sees 45.9, and pulls out, stops at a row of pay phones fifty feet away. If she's asleep, perhaps even if she isn't asleep, his call will be a gaffe, an intrusion, a rude act of insecurity. He pulls back out onto the turnpike.

Game Three is in progress as Murphy takes his seat. He watches an artless series of points; Team 1 wins in the second round; the 1-3 perfecta pays $94.60. Without a glance at the program Murphy heads for the nearest betting window and boxes a 1-2-3 perfecta for Game Four. Eighteen dollars. He doesn't come close, as Team 7 runs through the field in the second round. Undaunted, he makes the same eighteen-dollar bet for Game Five, losing in a three-way playoff for place and show. He guesses the 2-3 perfecta might have paid over two hundred dollars, but he doesn't particularly care. At the conclusion of Game Ten he hasn't cashed a single winning ticket. He's lost a hundred and twenty-six dollars. He turns to Game Eleven in the program and is reminded of the Big Q.


Angela is tormented out of a deep sleep by the telephone shortly after nine o'clock. She turns over, sits up, looks at the clock, picks up the phone, knows immediately that it's a local call, not Ray, by the absence of fuzz on the line. She is tempted to hang up immediately and leave the phone off the hook, but relents.

"Mrs. Wilson, this is the gatehouse. I'm real sorry to have to call you, but I couldn't get you on the intercom, and there's a guy here who says he knows you were in . . ."

"What's his name?"

"Name is Gutierrez."

"What does he want?"

"He just says it's real imoprtant."

She looks at the wall and mutters to herself. Shit. Jesus Christ. "Send him up," she tells the gatehouse.

She sits in bed, half asleep, gradually becoming frightened, not only because Gutierrez's unexpected reappearance connotes a change in plans, or something's having gone wrong, but because she's never been alone with him before. And she doesn't trust him. The money, at least, is locked away in a safe-deposit box, as ordered.

The buzzer sounds. Naked, Angela hurries to the front door and presses the button that lets Gutierrez into the building. Then she hurries back into the bedroom, puts on her underpants, her socks, her shoes, and hears the doorbell. She grabs her bathrobe and puts it on as she walks to the door. "Gutierrez?" she says loudly.

"*Sí.*"

She opens the door, but not to Gutierrez. A large, stocky man with a stocking covering his face puts his shoulder against the door, sending Angela tripping backwards. She keeps her balance. The large man is followed by a taller, slender man similarly masked, who shuts the door behind him. Angela stands trembling in the middle of the living room, more now from shock than fear.

"Where is it?" asks the slender man.

The logical conclusion is that Gutierrez has sent some friends to reclaim his money, and she quickly jumps to it, but says, "Where is what?"

"You know fuckin' well what," says the slender man.

Gutierrez would never in a million years doublecross Ray—thus conceivably these are enemies of Gutierrez. Angela tries to keep her voice as level as possible. "I don't know what you want."

The stocky man looks at the slender man, who nods, and the stocky man lumbers toward Angela.

"*¿Qué quieren?*" she says when he's three feet away.

"Talk English, bitch," the slender man shouts. The stocky man turns to him and says, "It's okay, she just asked me what we want."

"I don't give a shit what she said. She ain't gonna talk no language but English while I'm here. Hit her."

The stocky man gives Angela a half-hearted slap on the right cheek; several tears roll down her face. The slender man joins them in the middle of the living room. "Where is it?" he says.

"Where is *what?*" Angela says.

"Hold her there," the slender man says to the stocky man. The stocky man holds Angela by the arms, the slender man heads toward the bedroom.

"You want to sit down?" the stocky man asks. Angela nods, and he leads her to the couch. They sit there, like two uncomfortable guests at a party, as Angela hears things being broken in her bathroom. "*¿Qué quieren?*" she asks again, and the stocky man shrugs.

"Do you know Guiterrez?" she asks, in Spanish. He shrugs again. Drawers are slammed open and shut in the bedroom. The stocky man speaks in Spanish: "Why don't you just tell him where it is? It'll be a lot easier."

"I don't know what you're looking for."

"Look, he's a crazy guy, the one in there . . . I don't want to hurt you, but I don't know what he might do."

By his accent, the stocky man seems to be a Cuban. "If you tell me what you want, maybe I can tell you where it is," Angela says. The slender man has moved to the other bedroom, and is evidently throwing Murphy's belongings against the walls.

"Just tell me. He'll be rough on you. Please."

"I don't know what I'm supposed to tell you."

"You're a very pretty girl. He's going to mess you up."

"Do you want money?"

The stocky man sighs and says, "Come on—you know what we want . . ."

"I don't. Really."

The slender man reappears, looking angry.

"I warned you," the stocky man whispers.

"You wanna try for a while?" the slender man says to the stocky man.

"Sure." The stocky man gets up and goes down the hallway.

The slender man picks her up, hands under her armpits, and transports her across the room, holds her against the wall. "You can cut the shit now," he says.

Angela again feels tears coursing. "I don't know what you *want!*" her voice breaks.

"You know goddamn well what we want." His mouth is less than an inch from her ear.

Eyes closed, she shakes her head. She feels his hand on her chest, opening her robe. "Anybody ever tell you you got nice tits?" The hand pinches at her left breast, roughly but tentatively. "I bet you'd be great in bed." He turns his body and presses against her, pumps against her in an absurd coital imitation. "Oh, yeah," he says to her forehead, "you'd be great." Every muscle in her body is tensed in revulsion.

"What do you *want?*" she shouts.

The slender man doesn't reply. He pushes the robe off her shoulders, moves back half a step, and puts his right hand down her underpants. She tries to move aside, and he slaps her face hard. The hand wanders. "You're on the rag, ain'tcha?" She feels her tampon being removed. "Hate to mess up your carpet." He presses against her again; there's nothing there. "How's your dope dealer boyfriend gonna feel when he comes back and I've fucked your brains out?"

Angela braces and says, "I don't think you could."

The slender man steps back and slaps her twice as hard as before. She feels blood running down her chin. She looks up at him, and suddenly she recognizes him.

"You're in trouble, bitch," he says. "You know that?"

The stocky man appears in the living room; he seems astonished, or embarrassed, by what he sees. "I didn't find nothing," he says.

"Yeah, well I did," the slender man says. "I found enough."

"We didn't check the kitchen," the stocky man says.

"Then check it."

The stocky man opens and shuts a series of cupboards, the refrigerator, then the freezer. "It's clean," he calls.

The slender man spits on Angela's chest. "You ain't seen the last of us," he says.

They depart, the stocky man giving what might be interpreted as an apologetic wave as he closes the door.

Angela leans against the wall, slides down it slowly into a hunkering position, and begins to sob. Her eye is caught by the Tampax, a small, red object on the carpet three feet away; her contractions and tears cease immediately, replaced by a vague sickness and a much stronger sense of anger. She moves toward the tampon on hands and knees, picks it up, gets shakily to her feet, and walks to the bathroom.

Her cheek is swollen, a black eye incipient; her chin, her neck, and the top of her robe are covered with blood. She fights an urge to vomit. She daubs at her face with a washcloth, then takes a hot shower and gets dressed. She calls the gatehouse.

"This is Mrs. Wilson in 914-C."

"Yes, Mrs. Wilson." The voice is brightly enthusiastic, not the same as before.

"Did I talk to you about an hour ago?"

"No, ma'am, you sure didn't."

"How long have you been on duty?"

"Tonight?"

"Yes, tonight."

"Since five this afternoon, ma'am."

"Someone called me from the gatehouse a few minutes after nine o'clock. That wasn't you?"

"No, ma'am, and it couldn't have been nobody else, either, 'cause I'm the only one that's been in the gatehouse for the last two hours."

"Someone let two men in just after nine o'clock."

"Two men?"

"Two men."

"Two police officers, you mean? The ones that just left?"

Her recognition of the slender man is confirmed. "Why do you say they were police officers?"

"Well, they flashed their badges at me, ma'am. I saw 'em plain as day—Madera Beach P.D. They said they were here to investigate a burglary."

"They didn't mention my name?"

"No ma'am, they said they were goin' to 612-C, to Mr. Taylor's apartment. His car did get stolen today . . . not from here, but from in front of where he works."

"Were they wearing their uniforms?"

"No ma'am, they sure weren't. They were in plainclothes."

"Did you get their names?"

"I didn't, ma'am. No. Are you sayin' they went up to your place instead of Mr. Taylor's?"

"That's right."

"You told 'em they had the wrong apartment?"

"I'm afraid they had the right apartment."

"You want me to report this to anybody? I could call the police, or I could leave a note for Sergeant Hruska. He comes on at nine, and he's in charge here . . ."

"No," Angela says. "Just give me your name."

"I'm Officer Mooney, ma'am. Joe Mooney."

Angela puts together what she can. The slender man, she is now sure, is the younger of the two cops who stopped her and Prosper on Monday night. The stocky man, the Cuban, may or may not be a policeman. The unusually short interval between the call from the gatehouse and the sounding of the buzzer is explained—it was the slender man who called, not from the gatehouse but from the pay phone outside the lobby. The question she kept asking remains unanswered: *what did they want?*

Surely the note in her purse was composed by the slender man or one of his associates. Murphy is surely not a dope dealer. The note was obviously part of a plot to undermine her, to frighten her, to discredit her. To what end? The fact that at least one but possibly three policemen are involved . . .

She could call the police now, or better she could call Hugh Whitaker now. With Officer Mooney's testimony she could prove that two policemen, or one policeman and a friend, broke into her apartment and assaulted her. Officer Mooney might be part of it, as sincere and ingenuous as he sounded on the telephone. And the fact that at least one but possibly three policemen . . .

They must know what they're doing. They must have something, some hard evidence, from Gutierrez or from God knows where. Angela has done nothing illegal, during the last several days or during her life. They must, for some reason, be using her to get to Ray.

She calls the number in Hendaye, praying that at three-thirty in the morning Ray will answer.

On the eleventh ring a female voice says, "*Allo, oui?*"

The connection is horrible. Angela says, "*Vous parlez anglais ou espagnol?*"

"*Non, seulement français,*" the voice says.

Angela wants to ask to speak to Ray. She assumes that if

he were there he would have answered the telephone. She wants
to ask where he is, then, and when or where can she reach him,
but she's spent her life treating the French language as if it were
poisonous . . .

"*Allo?*" the voice says. Angela is frozen. "*Madame, vous savez
qu'il est trois heures et demi ici?*"

Angela says, "Ray. Ray Echaverria."

The voice responds: "*Ah, mais il n'est pas ici maintenant. Il va
rentrer demain, je crois . . .*"

Angela hasn't understood a word, has nothing to say in reply.
"*Madame? Allo? Madame?*"

Angela hangs up and begins weeping in earnest. She is unre-
mittingly confused. She has only Murphy's return to anticipate,
and she finds herself dreading that as much as she looks forward to it.


Murphy whirls through the program, collating and cross-
referencing, determined to win the quiniela in Game Eleven.
Arbitrarily, he allows himself nine choices. Arbitrarily and sym-
metrically: nine quinielas will cost the same eighteen dollars he's
been throwing away betting six perfectas. He rules out team
2 because it seems outclassed by 1 and 3, Team 5 because it
seems inferior to 4, Team 6 because it seems sure to be beaten by
7 or 8, either of whom might then run out for the game. This
leaves him with a 1-3-4-7-8 combination, or ten quinielas. Without hesitation he crosses off the 7-8. A lot of strange things would
have to happen for 7 to win and 8 to place, or vice versa.

He makes it to the window a minute before post time, pulls a
twenty-dollar bill from his wallet, and says, "Give me a 1-3-4-7-8
box, without the 7-8."

"What?" the ticket seller says.

Murphy's instructions have been precise but slightly ambiguous. He could run through his entire order now, bet by bet,
but the line is long. He decides to spring for the extra two
dollars. "Just box the 1-3-4-7-8."

The seller punches out ten tickets. Murphy is smitten by a
gambler's feeling, a notion, an intuition, out of the blue. "Do it
twice more," he says.

"The whole thing?"

"Right." He hands over sixty dollars. If 2 or 5 or 6 sneaks into this quiniela he's going to drive back to Madera Beach feeling like an asshole, but for the moment he is a sorcerer, irrationally confident.

He passes the early points, sipping a beer at the bar, listening to thocks and thuds and the crowd's cheers and groans. He moves to his seat in the middle of the second round. The game goes on forever, gets out of hand. In the fourth round Team 5 beats 4 one game point, mercifully loses to 8. 8 wins a crucial point against 6, wins again against 2. Team 7 now has another chance to win the game, but 8 wins the point.

And wonder of wonders, Murphy can't lose. 1, 7, and 8 all have six points. 8 is about to play 1; the point's winner will be the game's winner; the point's loser will play 7 for place. Murphy sees his destiny, his glorious destiny. 8 makes quick work of 1, winning the game. In the place playoff, 7's frontcourt man puts away the serve. The almost mathematically impossible 7-8 quiniela has come in. There are widely spaced shouts and squeals from the crowd as the numbers are posted. The perfecta is enormous. The quiniela is the biggest he's seen—$110.40—and Murphy has it three times over. He may now return to Madera Beach with a profit of $205.20, not a bad figure for someone who's bought fifty-two tickets and cashed three.

But he knows better. He heads for the Big Q window. What could be more obvious, on a night when he's won a bundle on an entirely improbable 7-8, after losing seven straight games on the old reliable 1-2-3, than to expect the 1-2-3 to appear in Game Twelve?

He trades in all three winning quiniela tickets, all three hundred and thirty-one dollars and twenty cents of them, for what amounts to a 1-2-3 quiniela box in Game Twelve. The decision is utterly illogical. His mathematical advantage is minimized in the last game, when all points count as one and the best players are still seeded in the lowest positions. But Murphy knows what's going to happen.

2 beats 1. 3 beats 2. 3 beats everybody else, runs through them like a sharp knife cutting soft cheese. The 2-3 quiniela pays only $37.60, but the Big Q flashes on the scoreboard at $4,416.00.

To the cashier's window in a daze, he is directed to a small office where he fills out a Form 1099 for the Internal Revenue

Service, is handed four thousand-dollar bills, a ten, a five, and a one. There is something ominous about the four thousands. He asks if he might have ten hundreds in place of one of them. Certainly. A security guard ushers him out of the office, changes the bill for him, walks him to his car. Inside, Murphy removes the boot from his left foot and stuffs the remaining three thousand-dollar bills inside it. He thinks better of that, takes off his sock, and folds the bills inside that. He replaces sock and boot, puts $1,116 and a carbon copy of Form 1099 in his wallet, and drives away.

It's been exactly two weeks since the poker game at Bloom's house. Murphy has won . . . his head swims as he tries to calculate .·. . four thousand tonight, sixteen thousand at Ramon's game, a few hundred at Bloom's game, probably close to a thousand at jai alai before tonight. Minus the thousand-dollar finder's fee to Echaverria, it comes to over twenty, close to twenty-one thousand dollars. What does it mean? What's he going to do with it? He knows the answer to neither of those questions, but he feels a glow, a sense of power that was absent after the big win at Ramon's. He's done this one on his own; he hasn't had to work all night for it, hasn't had to match wits with the likes of Curtis. It was Murphy against the house, with the house guaranteed 17 percent of the take, and Murphy kicked the house's ass.

This is a state of controlled euphoria, as he checks the speedometer every few seconds to make sure he isn't going a hundred and ten miles an hour, driving up the dark, moonless turnpike. It will be past two when he gets to the apartment. He'll get into bed, gently wake Angela, tell her what's happened. They'll fly to Europe first class, buy a Citroën in Paris or a BMW in Munich, drive the length and breadth of the continent in grand style, spend the money, sleep together in hotels *de luxe*. . . .

He leaves the turnpike. He's traveled perhaps a third of a mile down Route 1 when the flashing light appears in the rearview mirror.

Where did they come from? No headlights have been following him. He realizes with a sudden flow of adrenaline that they've been waiting for him; he wheels the BMW into a darkened Texaco station, not trying to escape, but to give himself time. As Officer Wilson approaches, Murphy stuffs his wallet under the driver's seat.

"License and registration," Wilson says.

"I think you probably know them by heart," Murphy says.

"Don't get smart with me, cocksucker," Wilson says. Murphy recoils in fear. The blinding bright light suddenly bursts into his rearview mirror. He begins to get a sense of what's happening here, but that doesn't help much.

He grovels in the glove compartment, finds the registration, hands it to Wilson. "I don't have my license," he says. "I left it at home."

"Get out of the car, cocksucker," Wilson says.

Murphy gets out. "Spread 'em," Wilson says.

Spread what? Wilson pushes Murphy against the BMW, slams his arms up on its roof, kicks his legs apart.

"Stay there," he says. Wilson walks away, returns with Officer Raymond. Raymond gives Murphy a series of brusque chops from shoulders to torso to thighs to ankles, as Wilson begins going through the car. Murphy is thoroughly frightened. He watches Officer Wilson's legs, protruding from the car, wonders what he's doing inside it. He feels a kick in his right hamstring.

"You're a clever cocksucker, ain'tcha?" Raymond says in pure nasty cracker. Murphy has no reply. "Think you can get away with your New York bullshit down here." He kicks Murphy again. "Fuckin' . . . smartass . . . cocksucker."

"I got the wallet," Wilson calls, and pushes himself out of the car. "Under the driver's seat," he says to Raymond. "He's thinkin' all the time, ain't he."

"You don't move a goddamn inch," Raymond says to Murphy.

Wilson and Raymond begin taking apart Murphy's wallet and spreading its contents on the BMW's trunk, examining them by flashlight. Murphy sees Raymond counting his money. What else are they going to find? His New York driver's license, his Master Charge, his library card, a couple of press cards, various receipts dating back to the last time he cleaned out the wallet, two or three years ago. An occasional car passes on Route 1; Murphy imagines passersby admiring the efficiency of the Madera Beach police—here it is two in the morning and those guys have caught a criminal, standing there with his arms up on the car. Wonder what he did?

"You got over thirteen hundred dollars here," Wilson says. "How come?"

"You wanna tell me what this is about?" Murphy says.

Raymond kicks him again, just above the left ankle. "Answer the man, asshole."

"I went to Miami Jai-Alai. I won some money."

"You went to Miami all right," Wilson says, "but you didn't get within five miles of Jai-Alai, did you?"

"How's your buddy Gutierrez?" Raymond says, pronouncing the name "Gutty air ez."

"He's not my buddy," Murphy says.

"Sure seems to be in cozy with your girlfriend," Wilson says. Raymond kicks him again, closer to the ankle.

Murphy speaks to Wilson. "You want to tell this guy to stop kicking me? Maybe we could clear a few things up."

Wilson nods at Raymond. "Clear 'em up," he says to Murphy.

"Did you see a press card in the wallet?" Wilson shrugs. "That's what I do. I'm a writer. I'm a reporter. You understand that?"

"Bullshit," Raymond says.

Wilson begins to look worried. "You ain't gonna hustle yourself outa this one, buddy. Anybody with a goddamn printing press can make himself out to be anything he wants to be."

"Throw me them keys, Claude," Raymond says to Wilson, and Wilson tosses him Murphy's car keys.

Raymond opens the trunk. Murphy can hear his tossing aside the tool kit, pulling out the spare tire. Murphy's calves and shoulders have been aching, are starting to hurt. "Would it be all right," he says to Wilson, "if I got out of this position?"

Wilson nods; Murphy slowly lets his hand off the roof, suspicious, half expecting Raymond to reappear and shatter his ankle, but nothing happens. He turns and leans against the car. "You're looking for dope, aren't you? Or for money?"

"You said it, I didn't."

"You're making a big mistake. You know that?"

"Shut the fuck up."

Raymond returns. "Nothin' back there." He's carrying the tool kit; he opens the driver's-side door, removes the Phillips screwdriver from the kit, begins unscrewing the door panel.

Murphy knows he's made a dent in Wilson, who seems vicious but fairly intelligent, as opposed to Raymond, who seems vicious, stupid, and obsessed. Obviously they've decided he's an ideal subject for a rip-off—a person involved in illicit transactions who'd be unable to go to the police having been robbed, especially since he's been robbed by the police. Wilson, Murphy imagines, has begun to suspect a misconception, and is perhaps beginning to deal with the ramifications of Murphy's being a "reporter." But Raymond seems bent on forging ahead no matter what reason might dictate, perhaps because he is incapable of reason. The question is: how is this little drama going to end?

At one extreme, they could realize they've been barking up the wrong tree, give Murphy back his wallet, maybe apologize a bit, and go away. At the other extreme, they could re-examine Murphy's wallet, find the 1099, read the fine print, discover that he really did go to Miami Jai-Alai, he's got three thousand more dollars on him someplace, damn the consequences, take the money, and head for Rio de Janeiro.

Raymond removes the other door panel. He rips up the carpeting, front seat and back, takes everything out of the glove compartment, flings it aside, rips out the glove compartment itself, unscrews the miserable Blaupunkt, throws that out the door, wires dangling.

"There's nothing to find," Murphy reminds Wilson.

"I told you to keep your fuckin' mouth shut," Wilson reminds Murphy.

Raymond walks around the front of the car, ignores Wilson, and says to Murphy, "Where is it?"

"It doesn't exist," Murphy says.

Raymond makes a fist. Murphy doesn't believe he's going to use it. But Raymond punches Murphy in the solar plexus, and Murphy sinks to the ground, to the asphalt, unable to breathe. He closes his eyes for several seconds, gasps in several cubic feet of humid night air. He has quite possibly misjudged the other extreme.

Raymond kneels next to him, his .38 Police Special a centimeter from Murphy's left ear. The other extreme is that these bastards figure they've got nothing to lose no matter what they do.

"We had a little talk with your spic buddy," Raymond says in a stage whisper. "He told us a little story about coke. Lotsa coke. You know what I'm talkin' about?"

Gutierrez. Did they really talk to Gutierrez? Murphy wishes he had a copy of the script. "No," he says; his voice is tiny and faraway.

Raymond slaps Murphy's right cheek with his left hand, causing a collision between Murphy's left ear and the gun. The gun doesn't go off. Murphy hears Wilson say, "Take it easy, for Christ's sake." He assumes Wilson is talking to Raymond.

"Don't you pull no chickenshit number on me," Raymond says, angrily.

"I've had enough of this shit for one night," Wilson says.

"Well then, get your ass the hell outa here. I'm gonna kill this cocksucker if I have to."

Murphy's ears are ringing; he thinks there might be a trickle of blood running from the left one. He feels on the verge of vomiting, of passing out, of shitting in his pants. It occurs to him that the two policemen may be staging a little semi-improvisatory theater for his benefit, trying to break him down, but he's afraid that isn't the case. He's afraid he's at the mercy of a couple of ruthless, obtuse privateers. He's afraid that if he were to call time, to take off his boot and sock and hand over the three thousand-dollar bills, it wouldn't be enough. He's afraid that maybe just Raymond, or maybe both of them, are positive about something; they *know* something, and they've deduced, whether through faulty information or their own stupidity, that he's at the heart of it. Perhaps they *have* talked to Gutierrez, perhaps under some duress similar to this he's given them some grand and totally false details. Murphy watches moisture accumulate on his shirt, just above the left elbow, blood falling from his ear. In stark terror he wonders: could they possibly think that *I'm Echaverria?*

Raymond yanks Murphy upright and slams his back against the BMW.

"What if I said ten pounds of coke? What if I said *twenty?*"

Murphy looks at Raymond's eyes, and sees death.

*"Where the fuck is it?"*

"This is funny," Murphy says. Raymond punches him in the stomach; he sinks a bit, catches his breath. "You guys are so fucking *stupid . . ."* Raymond punches him in the stomach again. Murphy guesses that he may be smiling as he says, "You're so stupid you can't figure out . . ." Raymond knees him in the groin, and Murphy loses consciousness.

He had meant to say: You're so stupid you can't figure out that it couldn't possibly be me.


He awakens in darkness, stands up with some difficulty. His head hurts, his midsection hurts worse, and it takes him a few seconds to remember where he is. When he does, he looks tentatively around and realizes he's alone. He touches his back pocket; the wallet isn't there; he looks around on the asphalt, opens the BMW's door, and there's the wallet, on the driver's seat. He checks through it under the overhead light. Money and cards are all stuffed together. The money comes to slightly more than seven hundred dollars. Wilson and Raymond have evidently decided that their time was worth the other six hundred. Their fingerprints, Wilson's at least, must be on the cards. This is larceny or grand theft, or something like that. Murphy lurches toward the back of the car, checks the trunk. The spare tire, newly repaired, has been slashed open. He closes the trunk, walks back to the front of the car, stopping to pick up the battered Blaupunkt and the glove compartment, tossing them in the back seat next to the ripped-out door panels. He starts the car and drives away. Touching the clutch he feels three crisp thousand-dollar bills in his sock.

He needs to talk to Angela.


The apartment, like the rest of Waterway Cove, like the rest of Madera Beach, is dark and soundless. Murphy finds his way to the kitchen; flips the light switch and looks at the stove's built-in clock: 5:57; takes a beer from the refrigerator. Seldom has any liquid been so welcome. Leaving the kitchen light on, he creeps down the hallway into the bedroom. Again negotiating in the dark, he makes it to the bathroom; Angela hasn't stirred. He closes the bathoom door silently behind him, takes two aspirins from the medicine cabinet and swallows them, looks at himself in the mirror. There is an accumulation of dried blood below his left ear, a slightly black-and-blue area around his right cheek, minimal swelling. He runs the hot-water tap for a few seconds, feels it, turns on the cold water, gets a warm mixture, picks up the washcloth lying on the counter, wonders for an instant if he's already washed the blood away—the washcloth, normally white, is stained brownish red. His head spins. He looks down at the porcelain counter around the sink and sees several splatters of blood, not his. He turns and opens the door. The light from the bathroom is dim but ample: the bed is empty. He lurches into the bedroom, turns on the overhead light. The bed is unmade, Angela's pillow is blood-smeared. He fast-marches into his ex-bedroom, switches on its overhead light, finds chaos—the bed in three pieces, clothing scattered, drawers out of chests. In the bathroom, the shower curtain has been ripped from its moorings, a collection of odd cosmetics and sundries stored under the sink strewn on the floor. He careens into the living room, flips on the lights, having hoped against hope to find Angela stretched out, alive, asleep, on the couch, waiting for him to come home.

There is no Angela. There is instead further evidence of violence: one large bloodstain on the carpet by the bookcase, a bevy of tiny bloodspots around it. Murphy knows who's been here.

He sits down on the couch, picks up the telephone, opens the telephone book to page two, to Emergency Numbers, and begins dialing the police. After the fifth digit he realizes what he's doing, and hangs up.

*I've had enough of this shit for one night, Wilson said, and then Raymond said I'm gonna kill this cocksucker if I have to.*

They were here *before* they stopped me, Murphy realizes, probably a few hours before they stopped me, since the blood on the carpet is dry. They could have taken her then, but it's more likely they took her after they took care of me. She went to the bathroom, she used the washcloth, she lay down and bled on the pillow. They beat the shit out of me, then they came back here and took her.

The man at the gate would have a record of comings and goings, but then the man at the gate is a fellow man in uniform.

Murphy looks up Hugh Whitaker's telephone number, and calls him. Whitaker answers on the seventh ring, sound asleep.

"Hello, Hugh, this is Prosper Murphy. Look, I'm sorry to wake you up, but I think Angela's been kidnapped."

Whitaker says nothing for several seconds.

"Hugh, this is serious," Murphy says.

"Have you called the police?" Whitaker replies, wearily.

Murphy gives as brief as possible a recitation of his experiences with the Madera Beach police, of his theories as to what's happened and what's happening. Whitaker gradually shows concern, asks Murphy the mandatory questions (You're *sure* you haven't done anything to make them suspicious? You're sure you're not . . . you know . . .).

"Hugh, I swear to you that whatever those bastards are after, I don't have it, and I don't know what it is, and I don't think Angela has it . . ."

"Her brother," Whitaker says.

"Yeah, well, that might have something to do with it, but I have reason to believe he's out of the country right now. I think . . . I'm *positive* these guys are on their own."

"Do you want me to call the police?"

"I want you to call the chief of police."

"He's not going to be there at six-thirty in the morning, Prosper."

"Then call him at home, Hugh. For Christ's sake, there's blood all over the fucking apartment!"

Whitaker agrees to call the chief of police, says he'll get back to Murphy immediately.


Murphy waits. The sun comes up. He goes to the kitchen for a beer, remembers he has an open one in the bathroom, gets it, drinks it, goes back to the kitchen for another. He walks angrily, aimlessly around the apartment. The phone rings at quarter after seven.

"Prosper? Hugh Whitaker here. I'm sorry it's so late, but Chief Arnold had to check with the department and then get back to me . . ."

Murphy, having written "Chief Arnold" on a pad of paper, says, "How long between the first and second calls?"

"Oh, twenty-five minutes, maybe half an hour . . ."

"So he had time to make a few calls."

"Sure, but Arnold is an upright guy, Prosper. He's been police chief here since before the flood . . ."

"Okay, Hugh. Tell me what's happening."

"You're not going to like this, Prosper . . ."

Adrenaline flows. "Angela?"

"No, nothing about Angela. Nothing yet. But when I told Arnold it was you . . . when I gave him your name . . . well, we got off on the wrong foot."

"Oh, Jesus Christ," Murphy says.

"I don't know how you've done it, but you've gotten yourself a bad reputation with the local police."

"I don't know how I've done it, either."

"Okay. I told him you're a writer, you went to Princeton, you're down here on vacation, you're an old friend of Angela's family . . . I softened him up. Then I told him some of what you told me, and he was, shall we say, noncommittal. I told him there was blood in the apartment, and he intimated that the blood might have been the result of something between you and Angela. I said I thought he ought to check on Officers Raymond and Wilson, and that was pretty much the end of the first call. Okay?"

"Okay."

"Now, you should probably write the rest of this down."

"I'm already writing."

"Okay. According to Arnold, Officer Wilson wasn't even on patrol with Officer Raymond tonight. Officer Wilson was on patrol with Officer Guillermo Ortega, and it was Officer Raymond's night off. They have some kind of log system—I don't know whether it's written or on tape—but the log shows that at 2:05 A.M. Officers Wilson and Ortega stopped a vehicle, a BMW, driven by you, because you were driving suspiciously. They searched the vehicle, confiscated some drugs in a white envelope, gave you a citation for a misdemeanor drug violation, ordering you to appear in court on March twenty-ninth, and that's it. At 2:34 they stopped a station wagon with Pennsylvania plates and gave someone a speeding ticket."

"At 2:34 they were still beating the shit out of me," Murphy says.

"Did they give you any kind of ticket?" Whitaker asks.

"No. Not unless they wrote it while I was out cold."

"Okay . . . I think we've got them on that. There's no way we can prove it was Raymond and not this other guy—Ortega— but obviously they wrote out the ticket to you and the ticket for the Pennsylvania car to cover them. You say they never wrote you a ticket, that's one thing, but we can check the Pennsylvania thing. They probably just made up the license number and everything else."

Murphy is grateful that Whitaker's on his side, but growing increasingly impatient. "Hugh, look, I'm sure there's a million ways I can beat the ticket, but I think we should try to figure out what's happened to Angela . . ."

"That's what I'm *talking* about. If we can nail them on this later today we can get Arnold to haul Wilson and Raymond in, we can confront them . . ."

"Hugh," Murphy says, "what if Ortega actually gave a ticket to the Pennsylvania car?"

"Arnold said there was only one car on patrol tonight."

"Arnold doesn't know what the fuck is going on, Hugh! Look . . . somebody came over here tonight while I was in Miami. I don't know whether it was Wilson or Raymond or Ortega, but there were two cars out, because somebody was still driving around handing out tickets. I think these guys are crooked as hell, and stupid, but they're not idiots. I think they've got Angela, and I think we've got to do something about it fast!"

"What?" Whitaker asks.

The blind leading the blind. "What time does Arnold go to the office?" Murphy says.

"I wouldn't do that, Prosper. The cards are stacked against you."

"I have fingerprints, Hugh. I have *proof.*"

"I wouldn't go in there without an attorney."

"Then you come with me."

"I couldn't possibly. I have to be in Boca all day."

"What does she mean to you, Hugh?"

A pause. "Prosper, I just can't believe . . ."

"Believe it," Murphy interrupts. "It's happening, for Christ's sake."

# 21

# A Polymorphous Thing

Whitaker has offered to spend his lunch break with Murphy at the Madera Beach police station; Murphy has accepted, reluctantly. He feels there's no time to waste. Whitaker has been willing to make a compromie, but not a sacrifice, has suggested that Murphy could use a few hours to cool off, but Murphy's principal concern is what might be happening to Angela while Whitaker is wheeling and dealing in Boca Raton and he's cooling off.

He doesn't cool off. He keeps looking at the blood on the carpet, thinking about Raymond kneeling next to him with a pistol against his ear, wondering what they did to Angela, wondering what they might now be doing to her.

At nine o'clock he calls the police. He asks for Chief Arnold.

"Chief Arnold." It is a brusque, old man's voice.

"This is Prosper Murphy. I need to talk to you right away."

"I don't think we have an awful lot to talk about, Mr. Murphy, but if you think you need to talk to me, you just come on over here and we'll talk."

"I'll be there in fifteen minutes," Murphy says.

He gets there in twelve minutes.

Chief Arnold appears to be close to seventy. He is dignified, extremely well-groomed, and smoking a Camel. Murphy is dirty, unshaven, bruised, and has an accumulation of dried blood under his left ear. He offers his hand.

Arnold makes no move to accept it. Sitting behind an immense oak desk, he says: "I'm gonna be straight as I can with you, Mr. Murphy. If Hugh Whitaker hadn't of called me, I wouldn't of let you in my office, but it seems that you and Mr. Whitaker went to school together, up north, so this is a courtesy to Mr. Whitaker, who is a good lawyer and a good citizen."

"I should infer," Murphy says, "that I am not a good citizen."

"You are not at *all* a citizen of Madera Beach, you are a visitor to Madera Beach, and from what I can tell, you have not been a welcome visitor to Madera Beach."

"I've had the same impression, but from a different point of view."

"Why don't you tell me your point of view, Mr. Murphy?"

"I've been stopped by your men twice, for no apparent reason. The first time, they searched my car, for no apparent reason. The second time, they searched my car, they stole some money from me, and they beat me up."

"I can see that somebody beat you up, Mr. Murphy."

"You don't think there's a remarkable coincidence in the fact that your men stopped me seven hours ago and the fact that I'm beaten up?"

"I don't at all."

"Do you have any theories as to how I got beaten up?"

"According to Officer Wilson's report, you were in Miami last night. It seems very logical to me that you were beated up by Mr. Gutierrez, or by associates of Mr. Gutierrez."

"I can prove to you that I was at Miami Jai-Alai until 12:35."

"You're wasting my time, Mr. Murphy, unless you can prove to me that you weren't beaten up before you went to Miami Jai-Alai."

"Angela Wilson could tell you exactly when I left for Miami, and she could tell you I hadn't been beaten up at that point."

Chief Arnold leans back in his chair, says nothing.

"You've got a couple of sadistic, corrupt bastards on your police force," Murphy says. "If you'll come with me to Mrs. Wilson's apartment I'll show you the blood."

"I don't doubt that there's blood," Arnold says. "I don't see what it has to do with my men. It seems much more likely to me that your . . . friend . . . may have been involved with your other friend."

"Who the hell is my other friend?"

"Mr. Gutierrez."

"I've seen Gutierrez once in my life—for about half an hour, Sunday."

"I find that hard to believe, Mr. Murphy."

"*Why* do you find that hard to believe?"

"I don't think it's necessary to tell you that."

Murphy explodes. "You pathetic old son of a bitch—don't you realize what's happening here? Two of your . . . policemen are after something. I don't know what the hell it is. I don't think it exists. I don't know how they got it into their minds that it *does* exist, but they pulled me over at two o'clock in the morning, they ripped my car apart, they kicked me in the balls, they threatened to fucking *kill* me . . . I was out cold in a goddamned gas station for a few hours, I drove back to Angela's apartment, and there's blood all over the place, and she isn't there. So don't give me any bullshit about Gutierrez . . ." Murphy stops here only because he's out of breath.

"Gutierrez . . ." Arnold begins.

"And don't give me any shit about not being a citizen of this miserable little hole. I don't need a passport to come here, do I? Shouldn't I be allowed to drive around Madera Beach without a couple of crazy, sadistic bastards beating me up and stealing my money?"

Arnold agitates, doesn't speak.

"There is a woman," Murphy says, somewhat more deliberately, "a teacher in your public school system, who has disappeared. There's blood all over her apartment. Are you going to do anything about that?"

Arnold seems to be trying to pull himeslf together, to figure out what Murphy's up to. "You're on pretty shaky ground, Mr. Murphy, to walk in here and start giving orders."

"Why am I on shaky ground? I didn't beat anybody up. I didn't kidnap anybody."

Arnold reaches into his desk, produces an envelope. "What about this?" he says.

Murphy peers at the envelope and realizes it's his. It's the envelope Ramon put his money in after the poker game. It's been sitting, empty, in his inside jacket pocket, in his closet at Angela's apartment. "Where did you get that?" he asks Arnold.

"According to Officer Ortega's report, he confiscated this from you at 2:05 this morning, at the Texaco station on Federal Highway. At . . . 2275 North Federal Highway."

"I have never set eyes on anyone named Officer Ortega," Murphy says, staring coldly at Arnold. "It was Wilson and Raymond at the gas station last night. The only thing they confiscated from me was six hundred dollars in cash, and that envelope was in my jacket, at Angela Wilson's apartment."

"You admit that it's your envelope?"

"Of course I do, but you know what that means, don't you?"

Arnold ignores Murphy's question; he turns the envelope upside down, turns back the flap, lets a multicolored capsule roll out onto the desk. It is, or could be, Murphy's remaining Dexedrine. "How about that?" Arnold says.

"The envelope was empty," Murphy says, "and it was at the apartment. There's only one way it could be here now, and that's if one of those bastards *took* it from the apartment. Do you understand that?"

Arnold lights another Camel and gives Murphy a stern look. "I could lock you up," he says.

"I don't think that would be a good idea."

"Not for you, it wouldn't be."

Murphy decides to play his trump, on the intuitive assumption that Arnold isn't in on Wilson and Raymond's game. "I have Wilson's and Raymond's fingerprints all over my wallet," he says. "On credit cards. On plastic. I could leave here this minute and go down to the FBI office in Miami and tell them the whole story." Murphy has this minute guessed that there exists an FBI office in Miami.

"That'd be a little bit like the canary flying into the cat's mouth, wouldn't it?" Arnold says, with a little smile.

"No it wouldn't," Murphy replies.

Arnold takes a gargantuan drag of his Camel, holds the smoke in for several seconds, lets it seep slowly out his nostrils. "The last time I looked, Mr. Murphy," he says, playing a trump of his own, "opening an account at a savings and loan under an assumed name was a federal crime."

Murphy is swept over by an enormous wave of mixed emo-
tions—shock, at first, followed by a sort of recognition of his
own stupidity, or hubris, of paying a strange price for a moment's decision to act like someone else, followed by a gentle,
pleasurable, almost narcotic sense of relief, of insight, discovery,
understanding.

"I have a suggestion for you, Mr. Murphy," Arnold continues.
"You take your money, you take your drugs, you get the hell out
of Madera Beach, and you go back to New York, and you stay
there, because if you ever come back here we'll be ready for
you . . ."

Murphy imagines John Trough, a caricature with his leisure suit
and his orange hairdo, sitting behind his molded plastic desk,
calling Wilson or Raymond, or maybe Chief Arnold himself—
listen, boys, I think we got a suspicious character here; comes
in and deposits ten grand in cash, says he won it at a poker
game, gives me the name of that nigger who plays guard for
New York, says he doesn't have a driver's license. Think he's
probably sellin' drugs, movin' his territory down here. And the
police force, given Angela's precise address, calls the sentry post
at Waterway Cove, alerts its cousins to the presence of a potential criminal. Then who should appear a few days later but
Gutierrez, suspicious by the very fact that he's a swarthy Cuban,
perhaps, beyond that, notorious enough to be known as a cocaine
impresario even in Madera Beach. The connection is made, is
final and finite.

"I have no drugs," Murphy says, "Your officers have some
of my money. I think they also have Angela Wilson. You're going to do something about this right now, or I'm going to the
FBI."

Arnold stares at Murphy; Murphy stares back. Arnold picks
up the telephone.


Officer LeRoy Garland, a dull, sluggish young man, surveys
the apartment with Murphy. "Somebody messed this place up,
good," he says. He examines the sink. "That's blood, all right."
he says. "You got any pets?"

"No pets."

"A lot of times," Garland says absently, "people see some

blood and they get all bent out of shape, 'cause they didn't realize it was their dog. You know, or their cat. In this case it'd be a cat, 'cause a dog wouldn't jump up on the sink."

"No pets allowed in the building," Murphy says.

"No pets allowed where I live, either," Garland is scraping the blood into a little plastic bag. "But you'd be surprised what people get away with. There's a guy down the hall from me with a goddamn snake . . . biggest fuckin' thing you ever seen. Feeds mice to it. He says the snake don't shit on the floor, it don't bark all night, so what the hell. I guess he's got a point. You know what type she is?"

"What type she is?"

"You know her blood type, the lady that lives here?"

"No. But they probably have it at the high school."

"She works at the high school?"

"That's her blood," Murphy says.

"Yeah, but they got to check. Everything's gotta be checked. By the book."

In the living room, Garland bends down to look at the carpet. "You mind if I pull some of this up?"

"Go ahead," Murphy says.

Garland rips out a tuft of carpet. "You see a situation like this, and there's always a chance it's one person's blood in there and another person's blood out here."

Murphy nods, by now unwilling to waste words on Garland.

"The way I figure it," Garland says, "somethin' happened out here, and then she went into the bathroom to clean up."

"Sounds right," Murphy says.

"But there ain't any blood between here and the bathroom, so maybe somebody *carried* her from here into the bathroom."

Murphy approaches the end of his tether. "Don't you think, if she'd been hit in the face, for instance, that she'd cover the wound with her arm, or pull her shirt up over it? It seems to me that if she were carried she'd bleed on the floor just as much . . ."

The telephone rings.

"Excuse me," Murphy says. He hustles into the bedroom.

"Prosper? This is Elsie Whitaker. That was you who called really early this morning, wasn't it?"

"Yeah, it was, I . . ."

"I got the impression that you thought Angela might be in some kind of trouble? Hugh didn't want to talk about it."

"Yes, I . . ."

"Well look, she's just called here."

"She has!" Murphy says. "Did she . . ."

"She said she'd just tried to call you but there was no answer. She said to tell you she was all right, she said please not to worry about her, and she said she'd see you in a couple of weeks if you wanted."

"Elsie, look, do you know where . . ."

"It sounded like the airport, and it sounded like a long-distance call, so I'd guess she was calling from Miami, from the airport."

"Did she sound . . . all right? Did she . . ."

"She sounded a little flat, a little depressed, Prosper, that's all. She said she'd written you a letter, and she said that you shouldn't make any decisions . . . no, that isn't right . . . she *asked* you please not to make any decisions until you'd read the letter."

Any decisions? "Did she say anything about what happened last night, Elsie?"

"Prosper, I want you to know that I like Angela very much, but she's always been a very cryptic person, and I accept that from her. But when the phone rings in my house at six in the morning, I want to know what's going on, and when Hugh bustles out of the bedroom and locks himself in his study for an hour, that *bothers* me . . ."

"Elsie, I'd be delighted to tell you what's going on, I'll tell you everything that's going on, but I wish you'd tell me if Angela said anything about last night."

"Not that I recall," Elsie says. "Prosper, I hardly know you, I don't know what's happening between you and Angela, but I feel I'm being *used* here."

"No, you're not, Elsie, some strange things have been happening . . ."

"Prosper, there's someone at the door, and I have a million things to do. Can I call you back?"

Officer Garland is sitting on the couch, holding two little bags containing russet flecks that a few hours ago were liquid, running through Angela's veins. Murphy speaks to Garland as if to a backward child: "I want you to tell Chief Arnold that Mrs. Wilson appears to be all right, that she hasn't been kidnapped. I want you to tell him that nothing else has changed."

John Trough is wearing the same ridiculous costume—red and white checked leisure suit, white belt, white shoes. Perhaps, like little Orphan Annie, he has an entire wardrobe of identical garments. He gives Murphy a shifty smile.

"Mr. Frazier. Did you get that driver's license?"

"You can cut out the bullshit," Murphy says, sitting down.

The smile remains as Trough says, "I think you better watch your step."

"You're a slimy, surreptitious bastard, Trough, aren't you?"

"You keep talkin' like that, and I'm gonna call the police."

"Go right ahead and call the police. I think we might be pretty much even up, you and I. Just give me my money and I'll go back to Madison Square Garden."

Trough speaks a line he's been rehearsing for years, waiting for just this moment. "I'll need to see some identification." John Wayne couldn't have said it better.

"Up your ass," Murphy replies.

"No identification, no money," Trough says, with his silly smile. "I don't know you from Adam."

"You're acting on orders, aren't you?"

"Standard procedure. You prove to me who you are, you get your money."

"It's over, Trough. Your buddies have fucked everything up, and you're gonna lose your job."

"I don't have the slightest idea what you're talkin' about."

"Let's imagine," Murphy says, "that somebody walks into a savings and loan with a lot of cash and no identification. He wants to open an account. He happens to deal with a slimy bastard who takes his money and then calls the police. He doesn't just call anybody on the police, he calls some friend of his. He suggests that this guy might be worth a shaking down. So his friend the cop, and another cop, spend the next few days following this guy around. They stop him, they search his car, then they wait a few days, they break into his girlfriend's apartment, they beat her up, they rip the place apart, they scare the shit out of her, and then they stop the guy again, they rip his car apart, they beat him up, and they leave him lying in a goddamned gas station. The guy gets tremendously pissed off about all this, and he decides he's going to get back at all the fucking swine bastards involved in it. And the first person who comes to mind is the slimy bastard who started it all."

Trough's smile has evaporated. "I called Chief Arnold," he says. "I don't know a damned thing about the rest."


LuAnne brings the money, beaming ingenuously, huge breasts bouncing. "Real nice having you as a customer, Mr. Frazier," she says, and is gone.

"I'd appreciate it," Murphy says to Trough, "if you'd walk me out to my car."

"I've got a lot of work here," Trough says.

"You'd better come with me. I don't want to get arrested for bank robbery."

"Look . . . I'm not going to . . ."

"Just *come* with me, will you?" There is a severe note of command in Murphy's voice. Trough shrugs and stands up. Murphy hands him the money. "I'll feel a lot more secure if you're carrying it," he says.

Trough leads the way, walking like a man with a gun at his back. LuAnne looks up and waves as they pass her desk. Out the door and into the parking lot. They're side by side now, and Murphy says, "It just doesn't make any sense to me, to do what you did." Trough looks at the pavement, makes no reply. "If you had the remotest notion of the trouble you've caused," Murphy says, "the totally unnecessary trouble . . ."

Trough stops and looks piteously at Murphy. "What are you going to do to me?"

"You really think I'm some kind of gangster, don't you?" Murphy is yelling. This is sweet and cheap revenge. "Some kind of terrorist drug smuggler?"

Trough looks away.

"You think I've got my hit squad out here in the shopping

center parking lot? We're going to leave you in a pool of blood a hundred yards from your goddamned savings and loan?"

Trough's entire torso lurches to the right, away from Murphy. "Don't . . ." he gasps, and embarks upon a stumbling flight toward First American.

"Trough," Murphy shouts, "for Christ's sake . . ." This ridiculous instrument of fate, his orange locks bouncing in the breeze, is running away with ten thousand dollars, plus interest. Murphy lopes after him, catches him halfway, and tackles him. Trough's chin hits the pavement with a thud.

"Oh God!" he says. "Please!"

"Just give me my money," Murphy says.

Trough rolls over and sits up, blood slithering from his lower lip. There is great fear in his eyes. "Please," he says, handing Murphy the money.

"Are you okay?" Murphy says. Trough nods. Murphy helps him up, and they go their separate ways.


The sentry has no record of Angela's comings or goings since yesterday afternoon.

Murphy calls the school. Mrs. Wilson phoned in this morning, said there had been a death in her family, back in Europe, and she would require two weeks' leave of absence. What time? About eight. Did it sound like a long-distance call? I couldn't say, sir.

He chooses a travel agent at random from the Yellow Pages, identifies himself as an imminent traveler to San Sebastián, Spain. The most convenient means would be via National to London, then BEA or Iberia to Bilbao, then by bus or rental car to . . . wait a minute, Iberia flies from London to Fuenterrabía, which is much closer to San Sebastián, right on the border with France. And when are National's flights to London? Well, there's one every morning at eleven. Good enough, Murphy says, I'll get back to you when my plans are more concrete. He hangs up. Angela by now is a thousand miles east, over the Atlantic.

The phone rings.

"Prosper? Elsie Whitaker again. Listen, I only have a minute. I forgot to tell you that Angela said there's a key to the mailbox under the clock radio. Okay? I'll call you back."

He slides the clock radio back a few inches, and there's the key. What's this about? He takes the elevator to the ground floor, locates 914-C among the complex of mailboxes, finds an envelope addressed simply to Prosper, without postage. Her letter. Written last night, left here so he mightn't be able to track her down, to dissuade her. He returns to the elevator, waits for its descent in the company of a mailman holding a package.

They enter together. Murphy presses 9 on the left side of the elevator as the mailman presses 9 on the right side. The elevator stops; Murphy exits first, turns right; the mailman pauses, seeking direction. Murphy is two steps inside the door when the bell rings; he turns and reopens the door.

"Special delivery," the mailman says. "Guess I could've saved myself some trouble."

The package is about six inches square, wrapped in brown paper, addressed to Angela Wilson, lacking a return address, postmarked Stamford, Connecticut. Murphy puts it down on the kitchen counter, takes a beer from the refrigerator, drinks half of it before opening Angela's letter.

At first the letter is a blur. He wonders if he has a concussion, guesses that he needs to sleep. He blinks a few times, puts the letter on the counter, shakes his head, finds the range.

Dear Prosper,
Something horrible has just happened here. I don't want to burden you with it, but I do. I want to tell you every detail, but I don't. I love you. I think that you've been drawn into something you couldn't possibly understand. I'm fairly close to it, and I'm afraid even I don't understand it. Please don't think I'm running out on you. I think it would be safer for both of us if I leave now. I don't think I'll be gone long, maybe two weeks at the most. I don't think it would be a good idea for you to stay in Madera Beach. I think you would be wise to get out of here as soon as possible. If you go back to New York, call the Whitakers and give them your address and phone number, and I promise I'll call you soon. I hate Madera Beach as much as I love you.

Angela

Murphy walks to the living room, sits heavily on the couch, and reads the letter again. He closes his eyes, spends a blissful moment thinking only about the "I love you's," two of them. Unfortunately he can't stay there very long.

"I think you've been drawn into something you can't possibly understand." He imagines that "something" as a mathematical problem: $x$ plus $y$ equals $A$. $x$ might stand for Echaverria, both for his relationship to Angela and for the errand he's sent her on; $y$ for last night's vicious madness; $A$ for Angela's departure, her reasons for leaving, her state of mind.

"I'm fairly close to it, and I'm afraid I don't understand it." He imagines "it" first as most relevant to $y$ and $A$, then realizes that "it" could refer to $x$ as well. Certainly she doesn't understand the maraudings of Raymond and Wilson; she couldn't possibly have had any knowledge of their genesis, of public-spirited John Trough. But couldn't she be saying as well that she doesn't understand what Echaverria has sent her to do, or even that she doesn't understand why she's agreed to do it?

Or that she doesn't understand why Echaverria is doing whatever he's doing.

The equation expands: $A = w + x + y + z$.

Or that she doesn't understand why she *has* run out on him, why at a time of great nastiness and uncertainty she's fled. "Something horrible has just happened here." She alludes to the fact that one or two or three Madera Beach policemen broke into her apartment and drew blood. But isn't it possible that after, or perhaps before their entrance, Echaverria called her. She left in a hurry. Only his own belongings were scattered about. Maybe Raymond and Wilson's intrusion was irrelevant, grotesque and irrelevant.

Or maybe Raymond and Wilson really *did* talk to Gutierrez, or vice versa. Maybe John Trough is irrelevant, and Raymond and Wilson actually know what's going on—know what Murphy doesn't know, what Angela doesn't know. Or does she? Maybe the "I love you's," as well, are irrelevant.

The equation ceases to be an equation. It has transcended algebra, leaped into solid geometry, surged past the third dimension, become a polymorphous thing stretching into modes far beyond Murphy's comprehension.

The telephone rings. Elsie again? No, but close enough.

"Prosper? This is Hugh. I thought we had an appointment."

"Oh, Jesus, Hugh, I'm sorry. I meant to call your office . . ."

"I just had a little talk with Chief Arnold. Evidently you didn't need my help . . ."

Are his feelings hurt? "Hugh, it was a spur-of-the-moment thing . . ."

"Don't worry about it, Prosper. You seem to have made your point."

"What did he say?"

"He wouldn't tell me much about your conversation. But it seems that some guy named John Trough called him just before I got there. You familiar with John Trough?"

"I'm familiar with him."

"Well, John Trough wanted you arrested for assault and battery. He told Arnold you removed him bodily from . . . First American Savings and Loan . . . you took him out into the parking lot, you knocked him down, and you kicked him in the jaw."

"This is getting tiresome, Hugh, I . . ."

"You didn't do it. I know. The point is that Arnold apparently told Trough he could take his assault and battery and stick it you-know-where. And the most important thing is that he sat me down and spelled it all out for me. He was making sure I'd tell you, and the impression I got was that he felt he owed you a favor . . ."

"He owes me a hell of a lot more than a favor."

"Well look, you must have convinced him. You must have convinced him and you must have scared him, and Arnold's a tough old bird."

"Did he tell you about Angela?"

"Just that you'd sent word she was all right."

"She's not necessarily all right. She just didn't get kidnapped by two insane policemen. She called Elsie. From the Miami airport, Elsie thinks."

"Going to meet her brother?"

"Why do you say that?"

"You told me this morning he was out of the country."

"Has she talked to you at all, Hugh?"

"No, not since Sunday. At the beach."

"Do you know anything about this?"

"Nothing more than you've told me. And what I've seen before between her and . . . what's his name."

"Ray. Echaverria. What have you seen between them?"

"Prosper, look . . . you're a friend of his, I'm not going to . . ."

"Hugh, for Christ's sake, it's Angela I'm interested in."

"I've got to get back to Boca, Prosper. Why don't you come over for dinner tonight, and we'll talk some more."

"I'd love to, Hugh. I don't know whether I'll be able to. I'll call Elsie later. Just give me about two minutes now."

There is a short silence. "It's nothing very clear. Nothing very profound. I don't know whether I can distill it."

"Try. Please."

"I wasn't disinterested, Prosper. Dave Wilson was my friend, and my partner. And I thought, Elsie and I both thought that Dave and Angie were the perfect example of opposites attracting. Dave was sort of garrulous, a hail-fellow-well-met, and Angie was, well, quiet and mysterious, and . . . I *knew* that Dave was fooling around. That's the kind of guy he is. I assumed Angie just accepted it. Then Ray started showing up. He'd fly down here every few months, stay at their place, drive down to Miami every other day, bring his goddamned Cubans over to the apartment, and it was just hell for Dave, and that's when he really started seeing other women. Her brother was a sort of *threat* to Dave . . . it was as if he came down periodically to test Dave, to see if he was taking good care of Angie, and Dave couldn't stand that. I was convinced that the brother was trying to break up that marriage. Trying to drag Angie back down to his level. And that was a funny thing, you know, because . . . Ray?"

"Ray."

"Ray would sit there talking, and it'd be 'fuck this' and 'shit that,' real gutter talk, and then he'd turn around and tell you something about Descartes . . ."

"He speaks eight languages," Murphy finds himself saying.

"Does he. Anyway, Prosper, it seemed to me that he had some sort of . . . *power* over Angela . . ."

Old news.


Murphy picks up his beer, walks out to the deck, sits down. He is out of synchronization with the day, as in a bad case of jet lag. It feels like midnight, yet the sun is bright and hot. Far below, in a little dock off the lagoon, somebody works on a boat. Between intermittent taps, Murphy hears the water lapping, hears a woodpecker, a mockingbird. The manta ray, he imagines, is a nocturnal creature, and lurks currently in some crevice far below the surface, perhaps dreaming (if fishes dream) of the activity to come.

Murphy closes his eyes and falls asleep in an uncomfortable position.

# 22

# Angela
# Inamorata

Angela had reached a plateau of calm, logical anguish. If there had been any doubt in her mind that the police were interested in her, not Murphy, there was no longer. She imagined that Gutierrez had told them a lie, probably a series of elaborate, convenient lies, perhaps in exchange for his freedom. She had no desire to contact Gutierrez, she supposed that even if she had, she couldn't. Thinking of Murphy, and particularly of Murphy's return, she vacillated. She wanted him to be back, she wished he were there. She knew that when he returned he would be shocked, angry, and more inquisitive than ever. She could clean up the blood, put the apartment back in order, but she couldn't hide her swollen face.

She made her way, still somewhat shakily, to the extra bedroom. God, what a mess. The bed was overturned, Murphy's clothes scattered about the floor. The bathroom was worse. She began picking things up, putting half-empty and nearly empty containers of suntan lotion back in the cabinet under the sink, then decided this would be a perfect time to get rid of all this garbage. She went to the kitchen for a plastic bag, got halfway back to the bathroom, suddenly questioned the importance of what she was doing, and sat down in the hallway.

What was she going to do? What *was* important? She was baffled. Baffled and frightened. In love and guilty. Guilty? This was her fault. How could it possibly be her fault? Because she should immediately have told Murphy everything. But that would have betrayed Ray. Her head swam. Where were her loyalties? Where had her loyalties ever been? In loving her father she had betrayed both her mother and her brother. In marrying David Wilson she had betrayed her brother and her mother's memory, because David was a man very much like her father. *But what now?* What would Ray want her to do? She wasn't supposed to come unless he told her to, but it was important that he know what was happening. Murphy could call Hendaye and speak to the French woman, but she didn't want to drag him any further into this. She sat in the hall, cross-legged, pulling and distending the plastic bag, eventually ripping it into innumerable tiny pieces.

She obviously had to leave.

She called National Airlines in Miami and made a reservation on the morning flight to London. She took the elevator to the basement, to her storage area, retrieved her large suitcase, went back upstairs, threw various articles into the suitcase, fearing that Murphy might have made an early departure from jai alai, might show up any minute. She left the apartment, pushed the elevator button, remembered she'd forgotten the safe-deposit-box key, re-entered the apartment, saw the bloodstain on the carpet. She was tempted for an instant to cover it—with a pillow, a record album—but realized that once Prosper discovered it he would be all the more concerned at its having been hidden. She started a note: "Dear Prosper: Please don't worry. I am all right." She tore it up. She found the key in the bedside cabinet and put it in her purse. She began a second note. "Dear Prosper, Something horrible has just happened here . . ."

The rest of the money—coming by mail within several days. Back to the cabinet. She slid the duplicate mailbox key under the clock radio. It was almost twelve-thirty. Out of the elevator, suitcase in hand, halfway down the garage steps she remembered the note, still attached to the small spiral notebook, in her purse. She retreated. The thought of returning to the apartment was abhorrent. She stopped at her mailbox and stuffed the note inside it.

She drove a mile and a half to the Holiday Inn on Route 1, checked in wearing dark glasses, rented a room for twenty-four dollars.

She couldn't sleep. She turned on the television, watched the last twenty minutes of the CBS late movie and the sermonette, switched around the dial, found nothing, and turned off the television. Still sleepless at 2:15, she called her own number, wondering as it rang what she might say to Murphy. Her wondering was academic. She tried again at 3:30, again at 4:30. Had he unplugged the telephone? Was he out looking for her? Or had the slender man, the policeman, intercepted him on his way back from Miami? She couldn't call the police. She called Madera Beach Hospital, which had no record of a Prosper Murphy or anyone matching his description. By five o'clock, distraught and exhausted, she was asleep. By seven she was awake. She took a shower and called her number again, infinitely relieved to get a busy signal. He was there. Or was someone else calling her? She dialed again, busy again. Again and again, busy and busy. Prosper was there.

She drank some grapefruit juice in the Holiday Inn coffee shop, drove half a mile to the First National Bank of Madera Beach, camped in the parking lot. At 8:25 a man in a suit unlocked the front door. She told him she was aware that it was before banking hours, but she needed desperately to get to her safe-deposit box. He looked at her, carefully.

"Are you all right, miss?"

"I'm quite all right. I had an accident."

He let her in, led her to the box.

She stuffed the money, still in its bulky envelope, into her suitcase, drove to Miami. She bought her ticket, was about to check the bag, remembered the money. She carried the suitcase into the ladies' room and transferred the money to her purse, which barely contained it. She checked the suitcase, asked at the counter where she might find a carry-on bag. Directed to the gift shop, she bought a small vinyl bag, returned to the ladies' room, put the money in the flight bag.

She called her number again. Now there was no answer. She called Elsie Whitaker, asked her if she'd please try to get in touch with Prosper, tell him she was all right, tell him she'd be in touch with him in a couple of weeks.

"Where *are* you, Angie?"

"I'd rather not tell you that, Elsie."

"Well, this is cloak and dagger, isn't it?"

"I feel silly. I just can't tell you."

"How do you think that makes me feel?"

"Elsie, please." Feeling thoroughly compromised, Angela proceeded.

And flew to London.

The plane is almost empty. Angela rejects both cocktails and lunch. Blessed with the ability to sleep on airplanes, she does so, waking up toward the end of the movie. She watches Gene Hackman dismantle an apartment, wonders why, and falls back to sleep. She wakes up again, accepts dinner, asks the stewardess collecting plates if she might talk to someone regarding a connecting flight. Within minutes she is joined by a steward. She explains that she needs to get to northern Spain as quickly as possible.

"Well, I'm afraid you won't be able to get anything tonight . . ."

"Nothing at all?"

"We'll be getting in close to midnight. You might be able to get a flight to Madrid . . ."

"No."

"Well, I'd say tomorrow's your best bet. For sure."

"Is there a place to stay near the airport?"

"Sure. No problem. I could make a reservation for you."

"That would be nice."

"Okay. Now . . . where would you like to go tomorrow morning?"

"San Sebastián."

"San Sebastián," the steward murmurs to himself, looking through a large book. "San Sebastián. There doesn't seem to be an airport in San Sebastián."

"Bilbao, then."

"Bilbao." He flips through a few hundred pages. "Bilbao.

Okay. There's all kinds of stuff to Bilbao. Iberia at eight A.M.,
BEA at eight-thirty . . ."

"Can you get me a reservation on the first one?"

"Sure thing."


A tall, red-faced man asks if her visit to the United Kingdom
is for business or pleasure. Neither, really, she's spending the
night at the airport and flying to Bilbao in the morning. He
stamps her passport, motions that she proceed. She finds herself on a customs inspection line, and recalls that she has many
thousands of dollars in her flight bag, that her face is bruised
and swollen. She has no idea whether it's a crime to carry large
amounts of money into England. She can't imagine why it
would be. The inspectors seem arbitrarily to be passing some
of her fellow travelers through, making cursory checks of others'
luggage, turning others' inside out. Surely her inspector will take
one look at her and rummage through everything she has, find
the money. And then what? Call ahead to Bilbao. There's an
American girl with a swollen lip and a black eye coming in
tomorrow morning, carrying a fortune. Says she doesn't know
why she's brought it. She takes it with her wherever she goes.

Her inspector, a young man with a mustache, asks her a
series of short questions. She listens without hearing, shakes her
head at each pause. She has none of whatever he wants to
know about. She enters the United Kingdom officially, un-
violated.

# 23

# The Love That Loves to Love

Murphy is sprawled on the deck's hard floor, somewhere between waking and sleeping, at twilight. His left arm, twisted under his head, is asleep. A cool breeze rustles the trees across the waterway, gives Murphy a chill. He pushes himself into a sitting position, using his right arm. He shakes the left arm, gets the blood circulating. His head still aches. With a great deal of effort, he stands up. It's difficult to differentiate between sleeping-stiffness pain and getting-beaten-up pain. He walks cautiously into the apartment, to the bathroom, takes off his clothes, looks in the mirror. He has an excellent tan. There is a large, gaudy bruise on his lower abdomen, a matching pair of purple semicircles on his thighs. Both his knees are scraped. Did he fall on them? The backs of both legs are tender and discolored from Raymond's kicks. He is alive. He takes a shower.

The phone rings as he's dressing. He hurries to answer it. Long distance; Angela from London, it must be.

"Murphy?" The connection is much better this time.

"You want to talk to Angela?"

"Right. Can you put her on?"

"She isn't here."

"Where the hell is she?"

"Right now she's a hell of a lot closer to you than she is to me."

"What the fuck are you talking about?"

"She's headed your way."

There is a pause. "Do you *know* that?"

"I'd bet on it."

"She wasn't supposed to."

A good five seconds of dead air. "You could probably pick her up at Fuenterrabía tonight."

Another five seconds. "What's she told you?"

"Nothing. What's she told you?"

"About what?"

"About what's been going on here."

"I don't have time for any guessing games, Murphy."

"You'd better make some time, then. I don't know what you're up to over there, but there've been some repercussions."

"Like what?"

"Like some greedy cops beating the shit out of your sister when I wasn't here."

Seven seconds. "Gutierrez? Is he fucking around?"

"That isn't clear."

"What happened to Angie?"

"I'm not sure. Two cops stopped me last night . . . I was on the way back from Miami. They turned my car inside out and they knocked me out. When I got back here there was a lot of blood and Angela was gone. She called Elsie Whitaker this morning, probably from the airport."

"Jesus Christ," Echaverria says.

"Where are you?" Murphy asks.

"I'll talk to you later," Echaverria says, and the phone goes dead.


Murphy dials Eliot Bloom's number in New York, gets no answer, calls *Newsweek*. Bloom is there.

"You still in Florida?"

"Yeah. Eliot, how long are you going to be there tonight?"

"Tonight? Oh, Jesus, two or three in the morning, at least."

"Could you get me into the library?"

"Tonight?"

"Yes, tonight."

"Sure I could, but couldn't I just send you whatever you need? Probably save you a few bucks."

"I'll see you later, Eliot."

He calls Eastern Airlines; there is a flight to LaGuardia at seven; he makes a reservation. He calls the Whitakers. Elsie answers the phone.

"Oh, hi, Prosper. I'm really sorry I didn't get back to you today, but one thing led to another . . . oh, Hugh's just come in and he's invited you to dinner. Can you make it?"

"No, I don't think I can. I need to speak to Hugh, Elsie."

"He's with the kids. Can he call you back?"

"I'd appreciate it if I could talk to him right away."

"I'm sorry, Prosper, but this is the only time he spends with them . . ."

"Elsie, it's important. I wouldn't be calling if it weren't important."

Murphy hears her shout her husband's voice, hears muffled conversation, Elsie's palm covering the phone. Whitaker eventually gets on.

"Prosper. Elsie tells me you won't be coming to dinner."

"I have to fly to New York, Hugh."

"Business triumphs, eh?"

"Not exactly."

"Have you heard anything from Angie?"

"No, not yet. Hugh, look, I'll be gone for a few days. I'd be grateful if you'd check with Arnold and see if he's done anything about those two cops."

"Prosper, I'd guess that unless you pester him he's just going to let sleeping dogs lie."

"You tell him that I'll be back, and when I get back I'm going to sue his goddamned police department."

"You'll be jousting with windmills, Prosper."

"I don't give a shit, Hugh. I want to *get* those bastards."


It's six o'clock. Murphy gathers various belongings and tosses them into his suitcase. He sets the thermostat at eighty, to save Angela some air-conditioning money, finds the circuit-breaker box in the kitchen, turns off everything but the refrigerator, checks the apartment to see if there's anything he's forgotten to do. This afternoon's little package sits on the dining room table. What to do? Bring it.

He heads west on the two-lane road to the turnpike, hitting eighty-five miles per hour, confident that the Madera Beach police will disregard him, and they do. He reaches the West Palm Beach airport at 6:35, leaves the BMW at a meter, hauls his suitcase and the package into the terminal, pays cash for his ticket, and flies to New York.

He emerges from the terminal into a cold, stale drizzle, feels a sudden wave of distaste for this familiar atmosphere. He takes a cab into Manhattan. Picking up the huge stack of mail on the doormat, he enters his apartment tentatively, as if he's just encountered an old acquaintance and doesn't know quite what to say to him.

He flips on the kitchen light. No roaches; perhaps all dead, perhaps gone to greener pastures. He imagines that if he were to stay a few days they'd be back. They won't be getting that chance.

In the living room he riffles through the mail. Among the scores of promotional announcements, screening notices, concert tickets, there is one letter, from Montreal. His mother has been trying to call him, she says. Where is he, she asks. There is an odd sort of logic here, very characteristic of Anne-Marie, to assume that if he were away by telephone he would be home by postal service.

He calls Montreal, and she answers. She tells him that Labossière is very ill, is scheduled for a coronary bypass operation, and may not live. She suggests that it would be good and kind for Murphy to visit him before he enters the hospital. When is that? In two weeks.

"Okay, mom. I'll be there. I can't say exactly when."

"This is very important to me, Prosper, and to Jean-Claude."

"I know it is, mother."

"You should come right away."

"I can't come right away. There's something I have to do."

"Where have you been, the last two weeks?"

"In Florida."

"You're going back there?"

"No, I'm not going back there."

"You'll be in New York?"

"No, I won't be in New York."

"Prosper, I may have to be getting in touch with you . . ."

"I'll call you next week, mother. I promise."

"You're not going to tell me where you're going?"

"Not right now, mother." It's contagious.


He calls Bloom, tells him he'll be over in a few minutes. He calls TWA, Iberia, BOAC, and Air France, trying to arrange a schedule that would get him to northern Spain by tomorrow afternoon, but it proves impossible. He settles for a nine o'clock reservation, tomorrow morning, to Madrid via TWA.

Shivering, he walks to Broadway and 82nd Street, buys a six-pack of Schaefer at the delicatessen, crosses the street, buys a quart of Glenlivet for Bloom, hails a southbound cab, and heads for *Newsweek*.


Bloom, fortunately, is immersed in his seventh rewrite of someone else's story. He accepts the scotch with great ebullience, tells Murphy if he weren't so goddamned busy they could sit down and drink some of it, and talk about what Murphy's been up to. He lets Murphy into the library.

"See you at the game tomorrow?"

"No, probably not."

"Come on, Murphy—if you're not there I might win some more money. You know what that's gonna do for my ego?"

"I'm afraid you'll just have to deal with it, Eliot."

"Going back to Florida?"

Murphy shrugs.

"Okay, what the hell. Look, if anybody gives you any trouble here just tell 'em to talk to me, okay?"

"All right."

Bloom turns and walks away. Closing the door, he says, "That's a hell of a nice tan."

Murphy whirls into action. The Spain file is massive—thousands of clippings, Xeroxes, photographs. He concentrates first on the civil war, discovering a few brief synopses, setting them aside. Next he removes all documents concerning events of the past three years, puts them on top of the civil war. He moves down the row of cabinets, opens the first "B" drawer, hoping for a Basque file. There it is, and a fairly fat one, too.

Like a thief in the night he turns to the Xerox machine, first copying all one hundred seventy-eight entries in the Basque file, then the civil war material. He realizes after ten minutes on the Spain file that much of it—maybe 30 or 40 percent—duplicates clippings he's already copied from the Basque file. What does this mean? That he's made fifteen or twenty superfluous copies; that Basques make 30 or 40 percent of the Spanish news deemed worthy of salvage by *Newsweek's* librarians. To the tedious process of remove document from folder, place document on glass, press button, remove document from glass, is added a new step: take a careful look at document between removing from folder and placing on glass.

Franco celebrates birthday. Basques kill policeman. Spanish economy up. Running of bulls in Pamplona. Basques kidnap. Basques kill. Spanish tourism booming. Juan Carlos groomed as future king of Spain. Basques perform daring series of bank robberies.

Were one to read only the headlines, it would seem that Spain is a delightful place for tourists, run by a small, elderly dictator soon to be replaced by a tall, handsome king, a paradise marred only by a malevolent northern minority of robbers, kidnappers, and murderers.

The process slows to a crawl as Murphy begins reading entire articles. He glances at the clock directly overhead and sees that it's almost two in the morning; he Xeroxes the rest of the file without regard to content or duplication.


Back in the mausoleum at quarter to three, he opens a can of room-temperature Schaefer, puts *Astral Weeks* on the record player, opens his suitcase, discards everything that's unwashed, replaces it with fresh items from his bedroom. The bedroom evokes memories of sadness and stagnation. He carries a pillow, a blanket, and his alarm clock to the living room, sets the alarm for seven, sets the pillow and the blanket on the couch, lies down with the civil war. Van Morrison sings a line Murphy has heard a hundred thousand times and still doesn't understand: "the love that loves to love, the love that loves to love." Murphy closes his eyes. He opens them to peek at something he hasn't wanted to think about: the package that's traveled from Connecticut to Madera Beach to New York City, nearly a round trip. Shall it now come with him to a foreign country?

He gets up and rips it open. Within, there is a small cardboard box, taped shut. Tape off, cardboard opened, more cardboard, several pieces piled on top of each other. Cardboard pieces discarded, there appears a thousand-dollar bill. A neatly, tightly enclosed little pile of thousand-dollar bills; fifteen or twenty of them, he'd guess. He counts. He hits twenty and isn't halfway through.

Fifty thousand dollars. For Angela to take to Echaverria. For Officers Raymond and Wilson to hijack. As much as the sum astounds him, benumbs him sitting here with it in his hands, as much as it dwarfs what he's accumulated during the past two weeks, he suspects that it isn't enough, by itself, to explain everything that's happened.

"*She wasn't supposed to,*" Echaverria told him. She wasn't supposed to come at all, was what Murphy had assumed he meant. Now he wonders if she wasn't supposed to come until she had the money, *all* the money. But how could Echaverria have known the money would arrive only a few hours after she'd left?

Murphy slides the money under the turntable. But on the odd chance that someone might break into his apartment and steal the turntable . . .

No one would steal his records. Too bulky, not worth anything. He stuffs a thousand-dollar bill into each of the first fifty albums on the upper left shelf. The final thousand dollars is deposited in the Beatles' *Let It Be.*

He lies down anew at 3:15, and falls asleep at four.

# 24

# La Bilbaina

Her room seems at most fifty yards from one of Heathrow's principal runways. Angela cannot sleep, has nothing to read. It is a modern, clean, deodorized, sanitized room, almost indistinguishable from the Holiday Inn cell she left this morning. It has a television, but there's nothing on. She doesn't know the time, she guesses that it's between one or two in the morning, early evening in Madera Beach.

She picks up the telephone and consults a decal stuck to its front; she dials "O" and a male voice says, "Yes, may I help you?"

"Is this the front desk?"

"Yes it is, miss."

"Is there anything to read in the hotel?"

"Well, there is a book shop, miss, but I'm afraid it's closed at the moment. Opens at eight."

"You wouldn't have a newspaper, or a magazine?"

"I'm afraid not, miss."

A pause. "Could I make a transatlantic call?"

"Certainly, miss. I'll give you the overseas operator."

Electronic noises. The operator comes on the line. Angela gives her the Madera Beach number. After a minute or so she hears her telephone ringing. It rings five, ten, fifteen times. "There doesn't seem to be anyone home," the operator says.

"Let it ring a while longer, please."

Twenty times, twenty-five times. "I could try again a bit later," the operator says.

"No, that's all right," Angela says. "Thank you."

She lies down, closes her eyes, wonders whether Prosper has gotten her note, wonders where he is. She sees herself, feels herself sitting on the bench in the sauna, Prosper inside her, exploding inside her, the old man coming in, the sense of having done something wonderful and illicit. The delicious, visceral excitement extending as they rode up to the apartment; he lifted her, put her on the bed, put his head between her legs. She remembers the first hint, the first implication of the first tingling, thinking, God, it's going to happen, then the spreading, the tensing, the pleasure, the paradox of being suddenly involved only with herself, and yet of this involvement having been effected by someone else. By Prosper, who in the space of several encounters during several days had led, or allowed, or enabled her to achieve something unattainable during several years with David.

What's she doing here? She's finishing something. Getting rid of it. Completing a loathsome obligation. She picks up the telephone again, asks the man at the desk to connect her with National Airlines. She makes a reservation on the nine o'clock flight back to Miami.

She undresses and gets into bed. But she's not at ease with her new decision. She thinks of Prosper, she imagines his expression as she returns tomorrow night, she tries to force the invading images from her mind, but they persist. If she doesn't deliver Ray's money to him now, she'll have to do it later. She's so close now, an hour and a half from Bilbao, a bus to Zarauz, drop the money off at the hotel whether Ray's there or not, back to Bilbao, back to London, back to Miami, back to Madera Beach, back to Prosper. Just one day gone by.

She remembers her apprehension at customs a few hours earlier. What's going to happen in Bilbao? They'll certainly check her flight bag. She could hide the money in her clothing, both in what she wears and in what's packed, but there's so much money. . . .

She gets out of bed and empties her suitcase. Its interior has a lining of pleated fabric. She goes to the bathroom and gets her toiletry kit, from which she removes nail scissors, a needle, and thread. She snips open the lining to a width of several inches, slips a few bills inside, presses the lining against the vinyl; she can barely tell the difference. She cuts open the lining all around, arranges the money carefully within, three bills vertically inserted next to three more, the width and length of the bag. As she inserts, she sews. It takes her an hour and a half to resew the lining; when she's finished there remains a small stack of bills. She counts: twenty-six thousand dollars. There must be well over a hundred thousand inside the suitcase. She folds the remaining bills into tiny forms, stuffs them inside pockets within rolled-up socks, finally puts seven thousand dollars in her wallet. She gets back into bed and sleeps perhaps a hundred of the hundred and eighty minutes before it's time to get up and return to the airport.

Surrounded by men smoking foul black-tobacco cigarettes, she endures the flight in a daze, nearly a stupor. The airport comes into view, a series of narrow runways on a plateau above the ocean, enclosed by hills. It is not a place she would wish to fly into often. The landing is rough; the plane comes to a jerking halt, a hundred and twenty Spaniards (could *they* be Basques?) jostle for position toward the exits, fore and aft. Angela is the last person off the plane, the last on line to have her luggage searched.

Here there are two inspectors, checking passports as well as baggage. The line moves ever so slowly; no one is waved through, she notices. Inspections range from brief to careful to fastidious, and seem correlative to the apparent status of the passenger. Here a middle-aged, well-dressed man is done in ten seconds, here a young long-haired man has every article of clothing inspected, here a woman (one of four or five on the flight), apparently British, is asked to open her purse, nothing else. Half an hour passes. The Spanish smokers, so eager to get off the plane, accept the delay without complaint. There is little conversation.

She is dressed respectably; she is a woman; she is an American. She tells herself those three things several hundred times. She puts on her sunglasses.

The inspector is some sort of policeman, dressed in gray, wearing a gun. He is a man approaching middle age, clean-shaven, face pock-marked.

"*Pasaporte*," he says.

Angela hands him her passport.

"*Norteamericana?*" he says. She nods. He looks carefully at the passport, then at her, tells her in Spanish the picture doesn't do her justice, tells her she doesn't look like an American.

"What does an American look like?" she asks.

"Ah, you speak Spanish very well," he says.

"No, only a little," she says.

"You have a good accent. A very good accent." He opens her suitcase. "You sound almost like a *Bilbaina*." He rustles through her clothing. "Where did you learn?"

"In school. In America."

A crumpled piece of green paper slips from somewhere inside the suitcase. He picks it up, begins to unfold it. "What's this?" he says.

"Oh, I must have left it in the pocket," she says. "It's some money. My money."

"It's a lot of money, isn't it? One thousand dollars . . . that's more than fifty thousand pesetas . . ."

"I thought I'd lost that," Angela says. "I'm very glad you found it."

He's reaching into pockets now, coming up with more tiny, folded thousand-dollar bills. "It's silly of me," Angela says, "but when I travel I always put my money inside my clothes, in case I'm robbed . . ."

He's come up with nine or ten thousand dollars so far. "Will you please come with me, señorita," he says. He carries the suit-case, she the flight bag and her purse. His arm urgently around her waist, he leads her to a door at the opposite end of the small terminal. Inside are two other men wearing identical uniforms. "I've found this," he says to an older man, evidently his superior. "There's probably more. She speaks Spanish. She has a local accent."

"Please have a seat," the older man says, pointing to a small, straightbacked wooden chair. Angela sits.

"Why are you in Spain?" he asks.

"It's my vacation. I'm a teacher, in America, in Florida." She tries to make her Spanish as American as possible.

"Do you always travel with this much money?"

"Yes."

He turns her suitcase upside down; eveything falls to the floor. "You," he says to the inspector, "go back to your post." He speaks to the third uniformed man, barely post-adolescent: "You go through the clothing." He examines the suitcase, carries it to the room's single, small window, looks at it under sunlight. He takes a penknife from his pocket, cuts open the lining, turns the suitcase over again. A king's ransom flutters to the floor.

"I've found some money," the boy says, surrounded by Angela's clothes. "Some American money."

"Count it," the older man says. "Count it all, carefully."

"Where are you from?" he says to Angela.

"America. Madera Beach, Florida."

"Why have you come to Spain?"

"On vacation."

"Why have you brought so much money?"

"It's my money. What difference does it make if I take it with me, or how I take it with me?"

He looks at her passport. "What is your real name?"

"Angela Wilson."

"Where were you born?"

"New York. New York City."

"Take off the glasses, please." She does. "Someone has struck you in the face, it seems."

"No, I had an accident. I fell down."

He sighs. "I don't think you're American. I don't think you're a teacher. I think we both know what you're doing, and I think we both know it will be much easier if you tell me now. You know where you'll be going if you don't."

She doesn't know. "I am an American. I've never been to Spain before."

The older man turns to the boy. "Have you counted it?"

"Yes, sir. One hundred thirty-three thousand dollars."

"Was this to buy souvenirs?" he says to Angela.

"It's my money," she replies.

"You're a very pretty girl," he says. "Tell me who you were to meet, we'll hold you for a few hours, and we'll send you back to New York."

"Florida."

"All right, Florida. You must understand that I'm a busy man. I don't want to give you to the Civil Guard. But if you don't talk to me soon, I'll have to. And they won't be kind to you."

"I'm an American citizen. I promise you that I don't know who the Civil Guard are. I promise you that the money belongs to me. You can call the United States. I'll pay for the call."

"You're not going to talk to me, are you?"

"No, I'm not. I have no need to. Is there an American consulate in Bilbao?"

"I have no idea."

"Could you find out?"

"No."

He picks up the telephone and dials. "This is Díaz," he says, "with the *armada* at the airport. We have an ETA courier for you."


She is ignored. The older man goes about his paper work, occasionally speaking gruffly to the boy, who is never anything but servile. After ten or fifteen minutes, the man sends the boy for coffee and a sandwich. "Anything for her?" the boy asks. "Nothing," the man says.

She is frightened, but too tired, too numb to be terrified. She speculates that the money is lost, she has failed. She feels no particular sense of disappointment, nor of danger. She imagines that she will shortly be transferred to a place of higher authority, where she will repeat that the money is hers, she is American. She is blessed with ignorance and, for the most part, truth. She knows almost nothing of Echaverria's plans or associations; she knows the address and telephone number in Hendaye, in France. She could give no information regarding Spain beyond the name of the town, Zarauz, and the name of the hotel where word may be left for Echaverria. She assumes that eventually she will be let go. She has, after all, committed no crime.

The boy returns with coffee and sandwiches. He looks at her and shrugs, apologizing for his superior's cruelty. She watches uninterestedly as the older man eats and sips, having no desire herself to do either. He rips at the thick sandwich, particles of bread spilling on his desk, brushes them away, delicately consumes a quarter-ounce of coffee, puts down the cup, brushes away the crumbs, repeats the process eleven times until the sandwich is consumed. The coffee lasts several minutes longer.

"Are they coming soon?" she asks.

"Soon enough."

"Is there someplace I could lie down?"

"No."

"Could I get up then? This chair is very uncomfortable."

"Stay where you are, please."


Half an hour later the door opens, two mustachioed men in green uniforms and tricornered hats enter. The older man stands up quickly.

One of the new arrivals, a man of thirty, with sallow skin and a long, pointed nose, says: "Is she the one?"

"Yes," the older man says, and turns to the boy. "Her things." The boy gathers Angela's suitcase, flight bag, and purse, hands them to the other green-uniformed man, his counterpart, about twenty, tall and thin. "The money, too," says the older man, and the boy paces to the back of the room, picks up a stack of dollars, returns. "One hundred thirty-three thousand dollars," he says.

"*Bueno*." The long-nosed *guardia civil* speaks to the older man: "What do you know?"

"She says she's American. She has an American passport. I'm not an expert on forgery, so I'll leave that up to you. She speaks Spanish very well. Don't let her fool you there. Ortega brought her in here, he said she sounded like a Basque. She's a very pretty girl, isn't she?"

The *guardia* nods, looking at Angela. "Well done," he says, to the older man. "Get up," he says to Angela. She stands, and is escorted roughly out of the room, out of the airport, to a green Seat with a plastic-encased red bulb on its roof. The younger *guardia* tosses Angela's belongings into the trunk, then opens the driver's door. The older *guardia* nudges her into the back seat, sits down beside her. They drive off, out of the parking lot onto a two-lane road.

"You're not really American, are you?" he says with a grim little smile.

"Yes. I am."

"Then what are you doing in Spain?"

"It's my vacation."

"Do you think I'm stupid? Are you trying to insult me?"

"No."

He touches her face. "You've had a fight with someone, haven't you?"

Angela says nothing.

"Who would want to hit a pretty girl like you?"

She breathes deeply, closes her eyes.

"You're obviously delivering that money to someone."

"It's my money."

"Why did you bring it with you?"

Angela experiences the first traces of panic. "To invest."

"Invest in what?"

"I don't know . . . I thought I might buy some land."

"There are banks in America, aren't there?"

"I don't trust banks."

The *guardia* grimaces and shifts his body toward her, reaches back to slap her; she cringes, closes her eyes, waits for the blow. Instead she feels his moist fingertips caressing her bruised cheek. "You're a very pretty girl," he says. "You'd better talk to me soon or you're not going to be so pretty."

# 25

# An English Lesson: Nothing's Easy

Murphy can sleep no longer than a few minutes in anything that moves, and this Boeing 747 is moving at approximately five hundred miles per hour. He has good reason to be exhausted, having slept less than two hours, taken a cab from his apartment at 6:45 to beat the morning rush, used his hour and a half at Kennedy to confirm both a place on the first flight from Madrid to Fuenterrabía and a Hertz car upon his arrival there.

The two hours' sleep has provided absolutely no therapeutic value. He has trouble thinking, boundless trouble concentrating on his clippings. He removes three armrests from a vacant middle row of seats (the plane being three-quarters empty) and stretches out, falls asleep, wakes up, falls asleep. At this rate he might sleep another three hours by Madrid, but he's hungry. From TWA's choice of entrées he opts for Swill *à la provençale*. It proves no match for Fat Lou's franchised sandwiches. He drinks a glass of Coca-Cola and a cup of coffee, becomes remotely awake, and reads.

The Basques, the oldest indigenous people of the Iberian Peninsula, possibly the oldest indigenous people of Europe, speak a language which resembles none of the Indo-European group. Their heads are shaped differently from those of other Europeans. Their blood types are unusual. This is Angela he's reading about. It is assumed that the Basques migrated to the environs of the Pyrenees many centuries, perhaps several millennia, before Christ. From where? There are different theories, based on the shapes of their heads and the inscrutability of their language. Each theory is as enticing as the next, each has its faults. Probably southwestern Asia, but no southwestern Asian languages bear the slightest resemblance to Basque, which leads to the next puzzle: the Basques have, over the period known as Recorded History, shown a fierce and independent nature, most notably exhibited in their refusal to be conquered. You name the invaders—the Romans, Charlemagne's Franks, the Moors, varieties of Goth, everybody who came west looting and plundering—and you find this relatively tiny sector of Europe unvanquished. It has been surmised that the Basques' invincibility was the result of their location, on the high ground. But is it not possible (since, evidently, they chose that high ground as a good place to stop and stay) that their invincibility is more a reflection of their fierce and independent nature? Their language was not written until the 16th or 17th century (authorities differ). It is unrelated to any other European language, and borrows words for such modernities as *"church,"* or *"bow* and *arrow."*

The sole successful invasion was mounted by an abstraction know as Christianity, and the Basques proceeded to become fiercely and independently religious, refashioning—as did everyone else—their ancient pagan rituals into new Christian rituals.

The Basques were unheralded discoverers of the New World: Aguirre probing deep and evilly into South America, Elcano coming in from the bullpen to relieve the dead Magellan and finish the first circumnavigation of the globe.

As the world became smaller the Basques aided its shrinkage, simultaneously resisting it, remaining autonomous or semi-autonomous through a succession of Spanish governments. And at last they sided, or most of them did, with the Republicans in the civil war. With the Left. Fiercely independent, fiercely Catholic, they were on the same side as the Socialists and the Communists, all eventually to be ground into the dust by the Fascists. The formal and symbolic finish to the supremacy of the high ground was provided by the Luftwaffe's Condor Legion. The little town of Guernica y Luno, surrounded by mountains, impregnable by land, the traditional capital of Basquedom,

was bombed to smithereens by Francisco Franco's friends, the
Nazis.

Some of this is news to Murphy, some not. Certainly he knew
about Guernica. He knew Aguirre and Elcano as Spanish explorers, mislabeled by historians in the same manner that the
television commentator refers to the Ukrainian sprinter and
the Uzbekhi gymnast as "Russians." It is what he didn't know
that mesmerizes him: the notion of a prehistoric race managing
to repel not only an impressive series of invaders, but time itself; probably the Western world's longest successful fight
against assimilation. There are compromises along the way, of
course. The language gradually loses ground to its neighbors,
French and Spanish. And Christianity represents a rather large
concession to the outside world. There is something typically
noble, untypically unpragmatic about the Basques' alliance with
the Republic in the Civil War. Traditionally careful, shrewd,
conservative, they align themselves with a hodgepodge of di-
vergent leftists against a stronger, better disciplined, richer
opponent. Traditionally Catholic, they join with a motley collection of atheists and blasphemers to fight an army of Catholics.
But the Republic, if one could cut through the tangled vines of
Stalinists, Trotskyites, Leninists, pure Marxists, democratic
Socialists, and what-have-you, had promised continued autonomy. Franco's Nationalists, fierce and conservative in their own
right, stood for some synthetic homogeneity called Spain, a
patchwork of principalities put together to drive out the Islamic
carpetbaggers five hundred years ago.

What does it all mean? Why should Murphy find himself in
awe and admiration of this particular brand of nationalism, a
credo he considers abhorrent when espoused by his own country-
men? Perhaps, like his father, who suffered with the Philadelphia
Phillies for fifty years, he is naturally attracted to the underdog—
which the United States, at least in this stage of the game, is
not.

He's falling asleep again, a folder full of Xerox copies slipping
down his thighs. In semiconsciousness he crosses his legs and
the folder sprawls, upside down. He picks it up, puts it on the
seat beside him, closes his eyes, pictures Angela's naked body
next to him in various erotic positions, and suddenly his attention
switches from her sleek nakedness to her face, which bears that

familiar expression of removed concern: I can't tell you, the look says. "I can't tell you," she has said or implied every time he's pushed her to a certain point of revelation, and in frustration he's written it off as another skirmish lost to the infernal brother; in Whitaker's eyes the infernal, mythic brother, the mysterious presence who causes this pretty little girl to disdain what David Wilson stood for, what Hugh and Elsie stand for.

Thousands of feet above the Atlantic, halfway between the New World and the Old, Murphy recognizes that his rival for Angela's attention and his own newfound rooting interest are one and the same. "Her family," Whitaker said at the beach—elliptically—referring to Echaverria. Little did the poor bastard know.

Angela's "family" would seem to stretch far beyond Echaverria, beyond the dead mother, the disappeared father. Murphy, half Irish, half French-Canadian, all American, roots scattered and indecipherable, is nothing but his own man. He loves her, and suddenly he envies her. For an attachment he doesn't have—must never have.


Several catnaps later—now less than an hour from Madrid—Murphy hits a thick vein of ETA clippings. The acronym stands for *Euskadi Ta Askatasuna: Euskadi* is the Basque name for the Basque country, four provinces of Spain, three of France, divided by the Pyrenees; *Ta* evidently means "and"; *Askatasuna* is translated here and there as "freedom," more often as "liberty." The composite is "Basque Land and Liberty."

ETA is formed, it seems, to fill a vacuum. There has been a Basque government-in-exile in Paris since 1939, just as there is a Spanish Socialist government-in-exile, a Spanish Communist government-in-exile, a Spanish would-have-been king in exile. Spain must lead the world in governments-in-exile. The governments-in-exile do nothing. They wait for Franco to die, in part because if they were to return to Spain Franco would put them in jail, in part because they expect that when Franco dies there will be a miracle, and they will march down the streets of Madrid in triumph. In the meantime they grow old and do nothing.

ETA doesn't do much either, in its early years, throughout the fifties and early sixties. But in the mid-sixties it begins a series of apparently symbolic bombings, in which no one is injured and nothing of great import is destroyed. In 1968 the bombings are increased, ETA begins robbing banks and commits its first political execution. Melitón Manzanas Gonzales, chief of the national police in Euskadi, reputed to be well schooled in the art of torture, is killed in front of his house by a man with a pistol. The man escapes.

This is the first big-time assassination in Spain since the civil war, and Franco retaliates with a characteristic lack of subtlety. His police are set loose in Guipuzcoa and Vizcaya, the northern Basque provinces (not coincidentally the Republican Basque provinces) and embark on an orgy of arrests and torture. From the many hundreds of people arrested, the government picks fifteen Basques to stand trial for the killing of Manzanas. It is widely accepted, even among the forces of the government itself, that the fifteen people on trial probably had nothing to do with the actual killing. If the Basques may have their symbolic bombings, Spain must have its symbolic retribution. The trial is held in Burgos, a city midway between Madrid and Bilbao.

Murphy remembers. At the time it meant little to him—another political trial, defendants apparently chosen at random, accused of murder, the dead person being a policeman. The defendants had all been tortured. They included several women, two priests. All were Basque; all were found guilty, all given grotesque sentences, ranging from thirty years in prison to death, and beyond death to two deaths. It occasionally happens that an American, having been convicted say, of the axe-murder of numerous paraplegic children, is sentenced to several concurrent terms of life imprisonment. But in Burgos three people were sentenced to be killed, brought back to life, and killed again.

The Pope sent Generalissimo Franco an angry telegram, as did Teddy Kennedy. Western Europe was outraged. In Spain, a general strike was called. The Basque provinces shut down completely, no region of the country was unaffected, and Franco was forced for the first time in his thirty-one years as boss to make a major compromise: the death sentences and the double-death sentences were commuted to life imprisonment. ETA had made waves, had made the front page, had made the big time, had changed the world. Murphy's primary concern at the time had been the woeful state of rock and roll.


Madrid. He takes leave of the printed word and walks down a ramp into Spain, whence he is immediately scooped up in a little bus and taken to the terminal, there to wander in a vast holding area, waiting for his passport to be properly stamped. He is not at ease here, in this tremendous, dark room, in the company of fifty or sixty other travelers. It is perhaps beneficial that his anxiety over what is to come yields to anxiety over what is at hand: there are forty minutes until the flight to Fuenterrabía, now thirty, now twenty.

A green-uniformed policeman studies his immigration card, studies his passport, looks him over, motions him through the gate, not a word having been exchanged. He finds his suitcase in a matter of minutes, and prays that the customs inspection won't take as long as what's preceded it.

Where is customs? Murphy walks through another gigantic room: policemen all over the place, several booths, most of them unattended, plenty of undecipherable signs. He heads for a series of glass doors and a policeman in a tricornered hat, a submachine gun slung over his shoulder. Is it possible that he can walk right through those doors unsearched? He's not going to chance it.

To the policeman with the gun he says, "Customs?" The policeman shrugs. He tries French: "*La douane?*"

"*¿Aduana?*" The policeman smiles. "*No es necesario. Pase, señor.*" The latter sentence is accompanied by a graceful wave in the direction of the glass doors.

Murphy passes. He could have brought Echaverria's money. He could, apparently, have brought anything at all. Is this the country he's been reading about?

He finds the gate for his flight with five minutes to spare, is sent away by a gray-uniformed policeman who tells him things he can't understand; he finds a woman in Iberia uniform; miraculously she speaks English, and leads him through a very complicated process which allows him to get on the plane to Fuenterrabía. The process includes a thorough search of his suitcase.

He might thus have smuggled contraband from Miami to Madrid, but not to Fuenterrabía.

He is eventually awarded a boarding card and returned to the gate, where the gray policeman allows him to enter the aircraft twenty minutes after it was scheduled to leave, and twenty minutes before it does.

There are fewer than twenty people on the flight to Fuenterrabía; most of them have boarded the plane later than Murphy. He spends the hour between takeoff and landing finishing the ETA file.

What ETA does is repeatedly described as "terrorism," not only by the Spanish government, but by *Newsweek,* the *Times,* the Associated Press, and various other sources in his folder. If it be terrorism it seems to Murphy a very refined, civilized sort of terrorism. No bombs are left in airports or marketplaces, no airplanes are hijacked, no midnight raids are made on housing projects. Policemen, described by ETA as "torturers," are killed. Banks are robbed. Bombings are effected at Civil Guard headquarters, at Fascist monuments within the Basque "nation," at yacht clubs catering to rich Spaniards, at the Ministry of Information and Tourism in Murphy's destination, Zarauz.

Bombs explode when buildings are empty. Industrialists are kidnapped; ETA demands that workers fired for striking be reinstated. The demands are met, and ETA releases well-fed industrialists.

Conversely, every action made by ETA is followed by mass arrests, and with mass arrests comes mass torture. The *Guardia Civil* and the *Policía Armada* are frustrated because ETA members routinely escape to France, to northern Euskadi, after their acts of revolution. The government's policy is thus to arrest anyone who's available, to create such an atmosphere of terror that ETA, in deference to its families and neighbors, will desist—or that the latter will eventually choose comfort and safety over independence, and denounce their revolutionist cousins.

It is quite clear to Murphy that the terrorists in this issue are not ETA. As the landing gear drops with a thump, as the pilot makes a lengthy announcement in rapid, incomprehensible Spanish, as Murphy's belly is suddenly filled with fear at recognition that he's about to be where he's been going, he wonders how he'd feel if Angela's last name were Arafat.


Fuenterrabía. Dressed for New York, Murphy is prepared for the cool, humid night air as he walks some thirty yards into the terminal, which resembles a small truck stop. There is a sleeping man behind the Hertz counter, a push bell on the counter. Murphy rings it, and the young man bursts awake. "Do you speak English?"

"Yes. But very little."

"My name is Murphy. I have reserved a car."

"Yes. I am here for you. Regularly I am finished now."

"Thank you very much for waiting."

"Of course. It is my job." He takes Murphy's driver's license and Master Charge and begins very meticulously to fill out a lengthy form.

"Could you give me some directions?" Murphy asks.

"Yes. But wait, please."

It is fully five minutes before the form is completed. "Please sign here," the young man says.

Murphy signs. The car is costing him thousands of pesetas; he doesn't know the rate of exchange.

"This is an excellent car," the young man says. "The tank is full of petrol."

"I need to go to Zarauz," Murphy says.

"Does a hotel expect you?"

"No."

"Then go tomorrow to Zarauz. Stay tonight in San Sebastián."

"I would prefer to go to Zarauz tonight."

"Zarauz is open in the summer, but not now. The hotels finish at five o'clock or six. There are excellent hotels in San Sebastián. I can telephone for you, and in the morning you are twenty minutes from Zarauz."

"Does the car have a backseat?"

"A backseat? Yes, of course it has a backseat."

"Then I shall sleep tonight in the backseat of the car."

The young man considers this. "There is a button on the front seat. You can push it, and then the seat goes back all the way, and you may lie down and go to sleep."

The car is a luxury Seat sedan, quite spacious and powerful. The young man has taken great pains to give Murphy directions to the newly completed section of *autopista* which will take him directly to Zarauz, avoiding the congestion of San Sebastián. Murphy has imagined the *autopista* to be some sort of two-lane bypass road; in fact, it is a six-lane superhighway, and a toll road. He cruises for a minute or two at a hundred kilometers per hour, is passed by a Citroën going half again as fast. He accelerates quickly to a hundred and fifty, remains steadily three hundred yards behind the Citroën's taillights for a minute, and floors the Seat. He gains on the Citroën, passes it at a hundred seventy-five, leaves it far behind on an upgrade curve, multiplies a hundred seventy-five by five, divides by eight, concludes that he's going just short of a hundred ten miles per hour on this large, deserted road. Zarauz pops up in no time at all.

He hands over his ticket to the toll-booth man, asks him if he speaks English. The man shrugs.

"*No tengo dinero español,*" Murphy says, and hands him a dollar bill.

"*No vale,*" the toll-booth man says.

"*No comprendo,*" Murphy says.

"*Más,*" the toll-booth man says. "*Más dinero.*"

Murphy gives him a five-dollar bill. He returns the dollar and two hundred pesetas. Murphy drives on, in the dark.


Cruising slowly down Main Street at a few minutes past midnight, he hears the ocean. As the Hertz man had predicted, there isn't a lot of action in Zarauz. The two biggest buildings on this half-mile-long wide street, the Gran Hotel and the Hotel Zarauz, are dark and shuttered. At the west end of the strip another hotel, La Perla, shows signs of life; its neon sign is illuminated, there are lights shining in several rooms. He parks the Seat at the curb. It is warmer here than at the airport. He can smell the ocean, can hear the waves lapping. The front door is open, but the lobby dark, no one at the desk, no one at the bar down the hall, no one in the dining room. Back in the lobby he rings the bell on the desk, waits two minutes, and returns to the car.

He continues west; the road narrows to two lanes, takes a sharp right curve, tunnels under a cliff, and Murphy finds himself directly over the Atlantic. There is a small turnout, just big enough to accommodate the Seat. This he decides, will be a good place to spend the night. But first, another shot at Zarauz. He makes a U-turn and heads back into town.

Some fifty yards past La Perla, also on the ocean side of the street, he notices the Hotel Etxeverria—a narrow, four-story building separated from the street by a courtyard. There is a light on the ground floor; he drives into the courtyard.

He finds a large, barrel-chested old man reading a movie magazine, drinking wine, smoking a noxious cigarette.

"*Cerrado,*" the old man says.

Murphy doesn't know the old man has told him the place is closed. He says, "Do you speak English?"

"*No inglés,*" the old man replies.

"*Vous parlez français?*"

The old man shrugs, makes an ambiguous motion with his right hand.

"*Vous avez une chambre?*"

"*Non. Fermé.*"

Now he knows. Maybe he can wheedle a beer or two to take back with him to the ocean. "*Vous avez de la bière? Tiene cerveza?*"

"*Sí, sí. ¿Cuantas? Combien?*"

"*Dos . . . tres . . .*"

The old man disappears behind an alcove, reappears in a few seconds carrying three brown bottles. "*Cuarenta y cinco,*" he says. "*Quarante-cinq.*"

Murphy still doesn't know the rate of exchange, but beer seems more of a bargain than the toll road.

"*Ouvrir?*" the old man asks.

"*Sí,*" Murphy says, and the old man uses a churchkey to open the three bottles, then replaces the bottlecaps carefully. Murphy says, in slow, deliberate French: "I'm looking for a friend of mine. An American. His name is Ramon Echaverria."

The old man looks startled. "*¿Usted es norteamericano?*"

"*Sí,*" Murphy says.

"We are closed," the old man says in broken French, "but there is a room available. The water is off, but you can use the bathroom down the hall."

"That would be fine," Murphy says.

"Very well," the old man says.

"Why did you change your mind? Do you like Americans?"

"Oh, very much. And also because your friend has a name just like the name of the hotel. He is Basque?"

"Basque and American."

"An excellent combination," the old man says.

Murphy retrieves his suitcase from the Seat's trunk. The old man opens the window. "*La mer*," he says, as if Murphy might have thought those oceanic murmurings were a recording.


Murphy sits on the bed, barely halfway through his second bottle of beer, when he hears muffled voices downstairs, then footsteps on the staircase. The door is unlocked. Should he rush across the room and lock it? What for?

The footsteps cease by the door. There is a moment's hesitation, then a knock, after which the door is opened immediately. A young man with a pistol steps in, followed by another, younger man without a pistol. "Hello," says the first young man, in English. The pistol is pointed at the floor.

"Hello," Murphy replies.

"Please stand up," the young man says.

Murphy stands up. The second man walks toward him, smiles reassuringly, takes the beer bottle from Murphy's right hand, raises Murphy's arms, and pats his body from armpits to socks.

"*La maleta*," the first man says to the second man, who turns to Murphy's suitcase and begins going through it.

"*Nada*," he says a few seconds later.

"You are American?" the first man says to Murphy.

"I am," Murphy says.

"May I see your passport, please?"

Murphy removes the passport from his inner jacket pocket and hands it over. The young man looks at the picture, looks at Murphy. "Is that right," he says, "to say 'May I see your passport,' or is it better to say, 'Can I see your passport'?"

"Either will do," Murphy says. "Especially when you have a gun."

"But which is more correct?"

"May I."

"Good. I thought it was, but I wasn't sure."

"You speak English very well," Murphy says.

"Thank you," the young man says. "My name is Iñaki." He walks a step or two toward Murphy and extends his right hand, having switched the pistol to his left. Murphy wipes his own sweaty hand on his pants and shakes Iñaki's.

"This is Kepa," Iñaki says. Murphy shakes Kepa's hand. "He speaks no English."


With Iñaki in the passenger seat, Murphy follows Kepa's tiny and battered Seat 850 up the empty main street some two hundred yards, where they turn left onto a much narrower street, barely wide enough for two small trucks to pass each other. Down this street they go, through what seems to be the heart of non-touristic Zarauz, across some railroad tracks, around a bend, under the *autopista*, up a hill to a complex of modern, nondescript tall buildings. "Stop here," Iñaki says. Murphy stops; Kepa's car continues and disappears.

"This is my sister's apartment," Iñaki says. They enter the building, forgo the staircase, head down a long hallway. "My sister and her husband are on their holiday, in Ibiza. You can stay here if you like, or go back to the hotel." Iñaki unlocks the front door.


Echaverria sits on a couch in the middle of a small living room. He says something harsh and abrupt in Spanish to Iñaki. Iñaki says, "A pleasure to have met you" to Murphy, and leaves.

Echaverria doesn't get up. He looks sullenly at Murphy. "What the fuck are you doing here?"

"Where's Angela?" Murphy says.

"I was about to ask you that," Echaverria says.

"You haven't heard from her?"

"We've had somebody at Fuenterrabía around the clock since I talked to you."

"Then maybe she didn't come into Fuenterrabía."

Echaverria gives Murphy a cold, angry look. "Why did you tell me Fuenterrabía?"

"I told you she hadn't told me anything. All I knew was Zarauz, and Fuenterrabía was the nearest airport."

"Oh, Murphy, goddamnit," Echaverria says. "Nothing's easy. Nothing's fucking easy."

"I think there are some things you should tell me," Murphy says.

"You want a beer?"

Murphy nods; Echaverria points to the kitchen.

"You get it," Murphy says.

"Okay," Echaverria says with a little smile, "I guess we know who's giving the orders, don't we?" He stands up and walks to the kitchen, returns with two bottles of El León. "Why don't you sit?" he says, gesturing toward a wicker chair. Murphy sits. "Do you know for sure she was coming here?" Echaverria says.

"Bilbao," Murphy says. "She must have gone from London to Bilbao." Echaverria has already picked up the phone and begun to dial. "Iñaki," he begins, and the rest is in Spanish. He speaks for about half a minute, listens for a few seconds, speaks again, briefly, and hangs up. "He lives upstairs," Echaverria says to Murphy. "I told him to find out if any American woman, if any foreign woman at all, has been arrested in the last twenty-four hours at the Bilbao airport. We'll know by nine or ten this morning."

"What time is it now?" Murphy says.

Echaverria looks at his watch. "Almost two."

"I'd like to sleep for a while."

"Go ahead. There's a bed in there." Echaverria points to a door off the living room.

"I'd appreciate it if you'd wake me up at eight," Murphy says. "I'd like to talk to you."

"Sure," Echaverria says, "we've got a lot to talk about."


Murphy climbs the stairs to Aurore's apartment in Montreal, discovers she no longer lives on the second floor. Something tells him she still lives in the building, so he continues to climb. The staircase becomes progressively rickety and narrow. Six flights, seven. The stairs sway. He's afraid they'll topple and he'll plunge all the way down the well, splatter on the basement concrete. Eight flights and nine. There are no longer doors on any of the landings, yet something prods him to continue. Eventually he loses count of the flights he's climbed. When the banister ends he sinks to all fours, afraid now to look down. He must be several hundred feet up when he sees Aurore's door, removed from the second floor, brought all the way up here. He crouches in front of it, catching his breath. He knocks. She opens the door.

"Prosper . . . where have you *been?*" she says, excited to see him.

"I don't know," Murphy says. "I've been trying to find you. They've moved you all the way up here."

"Yes, I know . . . it isn't easy."

"Nothing's easy," Murphy says.

"I'm very glad to see you, Prosper."

He leans against her, holds her. She strokes his neck and kisses him on the lips. "Can we go to bed?" Murphy says, "I want to . . ."

"No, not now."

"Do you still have the Otis Redding record?"

"No. All my records are gone."

"Oh, God, that's too bad. I really wanted to hear that record."

"Don't you have it?"

"Yes, but it isn't the same. It's been changed. It's completely different."

There is a growing sense of eroticism, a growing sense of dread. He unbuttons her shirt. She makes no responsive move, but breathes more quickly. He unbuttons her pants, unzips them, pulls them down. She stands still, obviously aroused, completely immobile. He slides her underpants slowly down her legs, brushes his left hand against her outer labia, her pubic hair. Her eyes have closed. "Is there someone here?" he asks. She shakes her head. He hears noises, then dull voices nearby, perhaps from her bedroom. "There's someone back there, isn't there?" She shakes her head again. "I don't care," he says. He can't wait. He presses against her, trying to enter. Her legs are close together. He slips in, slides out. The noises, the voices, grow nearer, louder. "*Aurore!*" he says.

# 26

# The Student Council: Murphy Learns His Lines

Murphy wakes up. People are speaking Spanish outside the bedroom. He knows immediately where he is. The sun has risen. He has an erection. He's been dreaming about Aurore. It's been eight years since he's seen or heard from Aurore. He's never dreamed about her before. The erection subsides. He needs desperately to piss. He gets up and puts on his pants. There is no toilet in here, not even a sink. He opens the door a crack, looks out and sees Echaverria, Iñaki, Kepa, three other men. All things equal, he would go back to bed for a while. His bladder, unfortunately, is not equal.

"*Buenos días,*" he says to the assembly. To Echaverria, "Where's the bathroom?" Echaverria points.

Murphy helps himself to some Spanish corn flakes with Spanish milk in the kitchen. The clock on the stove reads 9:07. Echaverria did not awaken him at eight. The revolution proceeds in the living room. He slurps the last of the milk, washes out the bowl, walks through the living room to the bedroom, puts on his shirt, his socks, his shoes, and returns to the living room. There is a vacant spot next to Echaverria on the couch.

"We know where she is," Echaverria says.

"Where?" Murphy says.

"There's a *guardia civil* station in Odriozola. The *guardia* took her from the airport. They didn't take her to Bilbao, so they must have taken her to Odriozola."

"Where the hell is Odriozola?"

"Just this side of Bilbao. About forty-five miles from here. An hour and a half."

"What do they do?"

"The *guardia?* They probably haven't done anything yet, because she's got an American passport."

"What would they do if she didn't have an American passport?"

"They'd beat the shit out of her, for a start, and if she didn't tell them anything, they'd torture her."

Murphy's stomach contracts. Echaverria says something quick and angry to his associates, who subsequently resume arguing among themselves. "You don't think," Murphy says, "that they've done anything to her."

"No. Probably not so far."

"I could call the American consulate in Bilbao," Murphy says, "and tell them where she is."

"And then what?"

"I assume they'd investigate."

"They'd investigate, all right. Some junior foreign service asshole would call up the *guardia civil* and say, 'Excuse me, but by chance are you holding a Mrs. Angela Wilson?' and the *guardia* would say, 'Sorry, nobody by that name here,' and that's exactly as far as it would go."

"Okay. Then what's going to happen?"

"That's the general topic of discussion here."

"You want to give me an idea of the drift?"

"After I get these guys out of here. This is like a fucking student council meeting."


By 9:40 Murphy and Echaverria are alone in the living room. "You got some good clothes?" Echaverria says.

"Good clothes?"

"Something respectable. Super straight. An earnest young American journalist."

Murphy tries to recall what he packed. "I've got a tweed jacket . . ."

"You got a tie?"

"No."

"Okay. I've got a tie."

"Are we going to church?"

"We're going to Odriozola. You're going to visit Angie."

"They'll let me do that?"

"Yeah, if you play it right."

"How do I play it right?"

"Get dressed, for Christ's sake."


Echaverria drives Murphy's Seat back to the main street; he turns left, winds out to the right, to the point where Murphy almost spent the night, and past it, along the coast. It is a gray Sunday morning, cool and windy; the ocean is whitecapped and ferocious. Echaverria leans into the coast road's curves as if this were a grand prix course, which it might well be.

"She wasn't supposed to come," Echaverria says.

"You've said that. You want me to tell you what happened in Madera Beach? You want the details?"

"You can tell me later. Let's talk about what we're doing."

"She didn't just come here out of the blue, though, did she? There was some contingency, wasn't there?"

"There was."

"You want to tell me about that?"

"I can tell you anything you want to know after we get this over with."

"We've got an hour and a half, right? Could you take five minutes to tell me what the hell is going on?"

There is a long silence. Murphy imagines that Echaverria is deciding what to tell him and what not to tell him.

"I had about a hundred pounds of *plastique*," Echaverria says. "You know what that is?"

"Plastic explosives," Murphy says.

"It was good stuff, brand new. Do you know what you could

do with a hundred pounds of that shit? You could put the Empire State Building into orbit."

"What were you going to do with it?"

"That's beside the point. The point is that your old friend Curtis ripped me off. He caught me at the airport. He thought he was getting a hundred pounds of pure Colombian blow, he was gonna be set up for life, he gets back into the city, he opens up the box, he says what the fuck is this, he figures it out, and he sells it to your old friend Ramon, who goes and peddles it in Puerto Rico for a thousand percent profit. Okay? So I've got a date with the student council here. I'm supposed to show up with a certain amount of money and a certain amount of *plastique*, for something we've got planned, and all of a sudden I don't have the *plastique*. So I called Angie and told her she might have to do an errand for me. I got here and it turned out they didn't *need* the stuff, so I called her again and told her she didn't have to come."

"No, you didn't," Murphy says. "You told her there was a chance she wouldn't have to come."

Another silence. "Okay. I told her there was only a very small chance she *would* have to come."

"Why was that?"

"To bring the rest of the money."

"For what?"

"That's irrelevant."

"I've got the rest of the money," Murphy says.

Echaverria looks at him, surprised. "You've got it with you?"

"No. In my apartment. In New York."

"How much?"

"Fifty thousand dollars."

"You don't have the rest of the money," Echaverria says. "You have less than a third of the rest of the money. The only reason these bastards have Angie locked up is that she was carrying a hundred and thirty-three thousand. That's what the student council meeting was about."

"The money?"

"Priorities. Whether we should forget about the whole thing, whether we should just go for the money, or whether we should go for the money and the American girl."

"You didn't tell them she's your sister?"

"No. I didn't want to cloud the issue."

"Do you tell anybody she's your sister?"

"Look," Echaverria glares briefly at Murphy, "it wouldn't have done her a damn bit of good to tell them. Can you understand that?"

Now the silence is Murphy's. The Seat careens through a series of S-curves. Murphy has far too good a view of the Atlantic, two hundred feet below, crashing against the cliffs.

"What did the student council decide?"

"Nothing," Echaverria says. "We're going to explore. You're gonna find out what's happening."

"I don't speak Spanish."

"That's good."

"How could that possibly be good?"

"It provides authenticity."

"What good is authenticity if they can't understand what I'm saying?"

"You've got a press card, don't you?"

"I've got lots of press cards. I've got backstage passes, too."

"Murphy, for Christ's sake, it doesn't make any difference whether you're from the *Times* or *Good Housekeeping*. You go in there, you look tough, you show some ignorant peasant the card, you tell him you don't speak Spanish but you're a *periodista norteamericano*, and you understand they're holding an American woman: *tiene una mujer norteamericana aquí.* You think you can say that? Okay. He wonders how the hell you know that, he goes and gets his boss, who's also an ignorant peasant, you give him the same line . . ."

"I'm not going to know what he's saying to me."

"You say, '*No comprendo. No hablo español.*' Every time he stops, you tell him, '*Yo quiero ver a la mujer norteamericana.*' You tell him, '*Es muy importante.*'"

"Tell me why this ignorant peasant is going to let me see her when he wouldn't even admit to the junior foreign service asshole that they have her."

"Because the asshole's calling on the telephone, and you're an American journalist standing right in front of him. Because he's an asshole, and you're not."

The road veers away from the ocean. They traverse a little town at sixty miles an hour; Echaverria passes a series of tiny cars, a truck, a tractor, zooms down a straightaway, slows down abruptly for what appears to be more than a little town. They come to a dead halt behind a long line of vehicles. Echaverria seems unperturbed. "There's a traffic light up there," he says.

"I didn't think they had any here," Murphy replies.

They move forward a few yards. "This is Eibar," Echaverria says. "My mother's father was born here."

Murphy is quite aware that this is the first time Echaverria has told him anything about himself. He feels, in some strange way, honored.

"I've probably got a few hundred cousins around here, up in the hills, sodomizing their sheep. Down here, working in the factory, bitching because they've got to pay five more pesetas for a bottle of wine than they did last year. They don't know what the fuck's going on."

"What *is* going on?"

Echaverria looks at Murphy with something slightly less than a smile. "Do *you* know?"

"I asked you first."

"Yeah, sometimes I think I do. Right here, right here in this spot, where I'm driving a car that you're renting for more pesetas per day than most of these people make in a month, one of my cousins probably got killed in 1938, or maybe one of my cousins killed one of Franco's cousins. That means something to me."

They lurch closer to the stoplight.

"What does it mean?" Murphy asks.

"Can't you guess?"

"Of course I can guess. But I don't know it."

"Then I can't tell you anything more about it."

They get past the light; Echaverria jerks the Seat into the left lane and passes the line of traffic in the right, steers back into his lane a second before his place in the opposite lane is occupied by a large truck. The truck's horn blasts, Echaverria heads for the next line of traffic at ninety miles an hour.

"What's the something you've got planned?" Murphy asks.

"You'll know in good time," Echaverria says. Then, quickly, he adds, "It was something I *had* planned."

"It's not going to happen?"

"Probably not."

"Then tell me about it."

"Memorize your lines," Echaverria says.


Odriozola. It is a dark little town, hardly the stuff of picture postcards. Murphy feels himself sweating profusely as Echaverria drives the length of this dismal hamlet, makes a U-turn and drives its length again.

"Do you know where we're going?" Murphy says.

"Yeah, I know where we're going. I'm just doing a little sightseeing."

"More cousins?"

"Cousins all over the place."

Murphy watches an elderly couple, the man in a black suit and a beret, the woman in a flowered print dress and black shoes, walk slowly down the street, probably on their way back from church. It is difficult to imagine them as Echaverria's cousins.

Echaverria turns down a side street near Odriozola's western edge and pulls over to the curb. "You see that red brick building on the right?"

"I see it."

"That's where you're going. You know what you're going to say?"

Murphy runs through his dialogue.

"Okay. Don't forget that the important thing is to *insist*. You don't speak their fucking language, you don't know what the hell they're talking about, and you're gonna stay there until you get your way. All right?"

"I know that part, too."

"It's Sunday morning. There shouldn't be more than three or four of them in the place. If you're enough of a pain in their ass they'll let you see her."

"Okay," Murphy says, "It's the stage fright I'm worried about." A dented Seat 850 passes by, proceeds slowly to the end of the street, turns right. "That's the car I followed last night," Murphy says.

"What car?" Echaverria says.

"That was Kepa's car, that little Seat that just went around the corner."

"Kepa's in San Sebastián. There must be a few thousand Seat eight-fifties within a hundred miles of here."

"This one had the same dents."

"More cousins," Echaverria says.

"I'm sure that was the same car," Murphy says.

"It wasn't. It couldn't have been."

"Did you see him leave?"

"I saw him leave."

"He could have turned around and come this way."

Echaverria sighs. "Murphy—do you think you might be trying to avoid something?"

Murphy considers that. "I might," he says.

"Get out there," Echaverria says.

Murphy opens the Seat's door.

"Break a leg," Echaverria says.

Murphy walks self-consciously down the empty sidewalk. It is forty-eight footsteps to the *guardia civil*'s threshold, over which is inscribed: TODO POR LA PATRIA. He thinks involuntarily of Dorothy's dog. Dorothy's dog, the patriot. No, Dorothy's dog was Toto, not Todo. "All for country" is more or less what the inscription says. But whose country? And what is he doing here?

Murphy opens the heavy door. Five steps to his southeast there is an ancient desk, behind which sits a young man in green uniform and tricornered hat. The young man has a mustache and the remnants of acne; he is smoking a cigarette and reading the Sunday paper, doing just what a small-town cop in America would be doing on Sunday morning. He looks up at Murphy and says one unpleasant word: "*Sí?*"

"*Soy un periodista norteamericano,*" Murphy says, "*de Nueva York.*" He hands the *guardia* a press card. The *guardia* looks it over.

"*¿Qué quiere?*"

"*No hablo español,*" Murphy says. "*Tiene una mujer americana aquí, ¿no?*"

"*No. No tenemos.*"

"*Sí,*" Murphy says. "Angela Wilson."

The *guardia* lets go with several rapid sentences. He does not seem happy.

"*No comprendo,*" Murphy says. "*No hablo español.*"

"*Espere*," the *guardia* says, wiggling his hand as he stands up. He walks away from the desk, through the small front room, down a corridor, disappears. Murphy hears him knock on a door, hears him conferring with another man. They both join him presently in the front room. The second *guardia* is older, has a bigger mustache.

"*¿Inglés?*"

"American."

"You espeak English?"

"Yes." This wasn't in the script.

"There is no American woman here."

"I know there is," Murphy says.

The *guardia* shrugs. "I don' . . . understan' what you say."

"I know," Murphy says, pointing to himself, "that you," pointing to the *guardia*, "have Angela Wilson," pointing to the innards of the station, "here."

The *guardia* gives Murphy a long, puzzled look. He examines the press card. He says, "Please to wait." He picks up the telephone and dials a number. This definitely wasn't in the script.

Murphy feels his knees beginning to tremble, sweat pouring down his sides.

"*Oiga*," the *guardia* says into the telephone, and begins to speak rapidly. In mid-sentence he stops, curses, punches the buttons on the telephone, hangs up, dials again. "*Nada*," he says to the other *guardia*.

Murphy's eyes are fixed on the younger *guardia*'s face, waiting for his response. He sees the young man's eyes widen, and a millisecond later he hears, "Murphy! Hit the floor!"

Dropping, Murphy sees the young man bolt for the corridor; midway into his third step there is a quick series of extremely loud noises. The young *guardia* does an awkward, violent pirouette, slams against the wall, and slides down it.

Echaverria, Kepa, and two young men to whom Murphy has not been introduced enter his field of vision. Each wields what appears to be an automatic rifle. Murphy is squatting on the floor, in or close to a state of shock. The older *guardia* is precisely where he was, standing behind the desk, the telephone in his hand.

"*¿Hay otros?*" Echaverria says to him.

The *guardia* shakes his head.

Echaverria points to the corridor, nods to Kepa. "*Con cuidado*," he says. Kepa and one of the other young men begin to stalk down the hallway.

Echaverria looks at Murphy. "Sorry," he says.

Murphy remains squatted and silent.

Echaverria approaches the *guardia*, removes his pistol and his keys. "*La norteamericana?*" he says. The *guardia* nods toward the corridor. Echaverria hands the pistol to the remaining young Basque, who stuffs it in his belt. Echaverria says something to him and heads down the corridor.

Murphy stands up. The young Basque smiles at him, nods, as if to say, "Well done, brother." Murphy cannot muster a smile in return. He hopes this will be over soon, wonders what's going to happen next. The dead *guardia*'s right hand slides down the wall to the floor with a plop. The surviving *guardia* remains behind the desk, his eyes on the man with the gun.

Down the corridor, doors are opened and shut, words are shouted in Spanish, large pieces of furniture are overturned. Murphy listens for Angela's voice, doesn't hear it. There is a burst of gunfire; Murphy closes his eyes, opens them to notice that the *guardia*'s eyes, too, are shut, all the muscles in his face tensed to keep them so. The young Basque keeps his weapon trained on the *guardia*.

For a moment there is absolute silence. The *guardia* opens his eyes. Murphy hears Angela's voice say: "Ray?" He moves toward the corridor. The Basque gestures that he stay where he is; he does not protest.


All three men in the front room of the station hear a car approaching. Murphy wonders whether it contains reinforcements. And if so, for which side? He prays that it pass by. He hears it stop. The young Basque waves his rifle at the *guardia*, who remains motionless. He backtracks to the front door, eyes still on the *guardia*. At the door, he yells two words at the *guardia*, who sprawls behind the desk. The Basque hurls open the door.

Murphy sees the *guardia* stand up, hears the burst of rifle fire from the door, sees the *guardia* open a desk drawer and remove a pistol. The Basque has taken a tentative step out the door.

Murphy's instinct is to disappear, to crawl under the desk, to be as far away as possible from what's about to happen. He has nothing to do with this. The *guardia* lunges around the desk. The Basque begins to retreat through the door, his back to the man with the pistol.

Murphy lunges for the *guardia*'s knees. The pistol fires. Murphy connects. The *guardia* hits the floor hard, his pistol clattering along the linoleum. The *guardia* is fighting for his life, desperately trying to jerk his body free, tearing at Murphy with his fingernails, kicking, flailing, wrenching toward the door and flight— while Murphy, his eyes closed, his heart pumping, tries simply to hold him down. A random elbow strikes Murphy's chin, stunning him. He punches the *guardia* in the face, weakly, to no effect. The *guardia* rolls out from under him, scrambles for the pistol. Murphy is aware of the Basque crumpled by the door, moaning, still alive. He reaches for the *guardia*'s feet, hears someone running down the corridor. The *guardia* grabs the pistol, holds it with both hands, and points it straight at Murphy, the journalist from North America.

Murphy's life does not begin to pass before his eyes. Nor does he wet his pants, nor does he scream, nor move toward or away from the gun. Some part of him manages to stand apart from the scene, to view it from a respectable distance: a still life, a Spanish policeman, about to die, holding a pistol, about to shoot this young man in the tweed jacket and necktie, this young man who doesn't belong here, who writes about popular music. The *guardia*'s face is full of terror and hatred and determination. He holds the pistol, holds it, pointed straight at Murphy's head.

And then he turns. Murphy sees the *guardia*'s head disintegrate in profile, sees the *guardia*'s face stripped of its features, sees him lean and topple to the floor, blood erupting in every direction. Murphy collapses.

Echaverria hauls him up, drags him out the door. There is a great deal of clamor. On his feet, on automatic pilot, going where he's led, Murphy searches for Angela. He is shoved into the back seat of a car, a comfortable, velour back seat. He closes his eyes, is squeezed against the soft fabric by the car's tremendous acceleration.

The car lurches and weaves through a series of high-speed turns. Murphy struggles to sit up, largely because he suspects that if he doesn't, he'll vomit on this excellent upholstery. The car is a Citroën; there are two men in the front seat. One, the driver, is Iñaki; the other is the young Basque who accompanied Echaverria down the corridor. The car is traveling very fast on a narrow, winding road.

"Iñaki?" Murphy says. His voice seems high-pitched and an alien.

"Yes?" Iñaki shouts, far more loudly than necessary.

Murphy clears his throat. "Where are we going?"

"Just a few kilometers. A few more minutes. To meet the others." There is tremendous enthusiasm and glory in Iñaki's voice—a part-time player who's come off the bench to help win the big one.

"The American girl. Is she all right?"

Iñaki confers with his other passenger. "Yes, she is all right. She is fine."

"We're going to meet her?"

"Yes."

The Citroën takes a fifteen-mile-per-hour curve at forty, spins onto a stretch of straight road. Murphy sees a large Seat, perhaps his, several hundred yards in the distance.

"Your friend, the one who was shot, is he all right?"

Iñaki confers again with the young Basque. "Gorka says that you were very heroic, that you saved his life. If you did not stop the *guardia*, he would kill him. He has a wound in the back, near the shoulder, and now Kepa probably has him to a doctor, a Basque doctor."

Heroic. "How many were killed?" Murphy asks. "Of the *guardia*?"

Another conference. "We're not sure. . . . Four, we think."

"Someone was killed in the back of the station?"

"Yes, it was necessary."

Murphy wonders briefly as to the definition of necessity. The Citroën, now on a slight downgrade, takes a few more sharp curves, hits another straightaway, passes a road sign that reads LEMONA. The Seat is parked where Lemona begins. Iñaki pulls up behind it. Echaverria hurries from the Seat to the Citroën, says something to Iñaki, says, "Get out" to Murphy.

Murphy gets out of the car. His legs are a bit wobbly. "Can you drive?" Echaverria says.

"If I have to."

"Drive your car, then. Follow me. I'm gonna be driving this one. Can you keep up?"

"How would I know?"

"Okay, get going. I'll pass you."

"Where's Angela?"

"She's in your car, for Christ's sake."

New life courses through Murphy's veins. He trots to the car, opens the door. She is deathly pale, she looks at him full of melancholy and apology. He leaps into the car, embraces her awkwardly; she sobs, then weeps. He strokes her hair. "Prosper," she says, "I'm sorry."

"You don't have to be sorry," Murphy says. "You don't need to be sorry."

"Murphy!" Echaverria stands by the car, holding Murphy's suitcase. Murphy opens the rear door; Echaverria throws the suitcase in, slams the door, says, "Get the fuck out of here!"

Murphy starts the car, puts it in gear, drives off. "Where are we going?" he asks Angela.

"You're supposed to follow the signs for Vitoria."

Five seconds later there is a choice between Bilbao and Vitoria; Murphy makes a hard left and leaves Lemona behind. "Where are we going?" he asks Angela.

"I don't know," she says.

"Am I supposed to wait for him?"

"No, he said to drive as fast as you could."

Murphy complies. The road is wider and straighter than its predecessor, and within seconds the speedometer has hit a hundred and twenty.

"How long did they have you in there?"

"Just a day. A day and a night." Her voice is weary.

He touches her cheek. "Did they do that to you?"

"No. That was the police in Florida. They locked me up here, and they ignored me."

"God, Angela, I'm so glad to see you . . ."

She weeps again. Under different circumstances Murphy would pull the car off the road. Here, he can only offer a comforting right arm, a stroke on the shoulder. "What?" he says.

"Prosper, I saw Ray *kill* two men. I knew them . . . I talked to them last night. One of them had his gun out, but the other . . . he might have been asleep. He was lying down."

Murphy is caught between his own revulsion and his relief that they're moving very quickly away from the scene of the crime. He doesn't want to hear about it. "Don't think about it," he says.

"It's *my fault*," Angela says.

"No, Angela," Murphy says, "it sure as hell isn't your fault."

He comes out of a curve to see a huge, lumbering truck on the straight stretch ahead, floors the Seat, realizes within a hundred yards that he's not going to get past the truck before the next sharp curve. He takes his foot off the accelerator, still has to brake sharply to avoid ramming the truck as it reaches the curve and an ensuing upgrade. The truck cannot be moving at more than five miles per hour up the hill. Murphy peers around at each opportunity, but opposing traffic, until now almost non-existent, suddenly streams downhill. The Seat reaches the hill's apex bathed in noxious exhaust; the truck descends, picking up speed, slithering down the hill, and still no opportunity to get by. At last there appears some straight, level roadway. Murphy waits for an oncoming truck to snort by, flicks on the left blinker, checks the rearview mirror, sees the Citroën approaching at the speed of sound, blinking its lights. He pulls over and lets Echaverria pass.


Angela sleeps. Murphy follows the Citroën—the road is a roller coaster of steep climbs and dips, sharp curves in every direction. Occasionally, yawning and swallowing to pop open his eardrums at the top of a pass, Murphy looks down, looks across, and wishes he could stop, or slow down at least. He is surrounded by mountains: lush, green mountains, craggy mountains, mountains with clearings, with tiny areas of population, mountains with sheep grazing, mountains with nothing at all. Then a lake on the right, then an immense lake on the left. The Citroën disappears ahead of him as he enters every curve, descends from view as he approaches every upgrade. Emerging from each curve, descending each hill, it gains implausibly. Angela moves with the car, sliding toward Murphy, sliding toward the window, hitting it on the sharpest curves, remaining asleep.

The Citroën is definitely more powerful than the Seat. Echaverria must wait for him to catch up before passing, wait for situations when they both may pass the rare vehicle in their path.

Vitoria grows near—now twenty kilometers away, now eleven—and Murphy wonders what's going to happen in Vitoria. Another meeting with ETA? Passage to France, to Portugal? The Civil Guards who read his name on the press pass are dead. Presumably no living person of authority has seen his rental car. But Angela has been detained almost twenty-four hours. Surely that information has been transmitted from Odriozola.

Vitoria. The Citroën ignores signs pointing to Burgos, Madrid, and Portugal. Nor does it take the left turn that bypasses the city and goes on to Pamplona, and France. The Citroën, instead, goes straight through the city. Having covered more than forty miles of mountain road in just under an hour, they now stop and start through heavy traffic, traveling six miles in half an hour. Obviously there is to be some sort of encounter in Vitoria.

There isn't. The Citroën barely makes a traffic light; Murphy is prepared to run the red light but the car in front of him stops. He wakes Angela, shaking her arm. "Are we supposed to do something in Vitoria?"

"I don't know, Prosper. I don't know where we're going."

Murphy crosses the intersection. The Citroën waits on the other side. Five minutes later they're out of Vitoria, following signs for Logroño. Murphy has never heard of Logroño. The road narrows, remains flat and straight, and soon the Citroën has surpassed a hundred sixty kilometers per hour. Angela sleeps again. A town, another town, the terrain becomes hilly, the Citroën slows, Murphy slows. Echaverria is much easier to keep up with when the road is straight. Murphy wishes he knew where they were headed.

At the onset of twilight they reach the northern outskirts of Logroño. The Seat's gas gauge reads slightly less than a quarter full. Conceivably, the Citroën is connected to an invisible pipeline. Murphy pulls to twenty yards behind it and runs through the Seat's full repertoire of headlights three times. Echaverria waves, and three minutes later pulls into a gas station.

"Where the hell are we going?" Murphy says. Angela remains sound asleep in the Seat.

Echaverria gives a series of brusque orders to an obedient man in blue coveralls. "We're going to France," he says to Murphy.

"We've been headed almost due south, haven't we?"

"We have."

"Traditionally, isn't France to the east?"

"It is."

"Then where the hell are we going?"

Echaverria removes a map from the Citroën's glove compartment, spreads it out on the trunk, points to Logroño, near the map's upper right corner. "We're here," he says.

"Why didn't we go there?" Murphy asks, pointing to the extreme upper right corner, to the Irún/Hendaye frontier.

"Six cops just got killed in Odriozola," Echaverria says.

"*Six?* I thought it was four . . ."

"Four inside, two outside."

"Oh, Christ," Murphy says.

"We'll be a lot better off if you don't worry about how many of those bastards are dead," Echaverria says.

Murphy says nothing.

"Probably," Echaverria says, "the only thing they have to go on is Angie. I don't think there's anybody alive who's seen you or me, or either of the cars. But I don't know that. We could probably have turned her over to Iñaki and he could've smuggled her across. He's been back and forth over the mountains about three hundred times. And you could probably have driven across at Irún, or dropped the car off at Fuenterrabía and taken a plane wherever you wanted to. But there's always a chance that somebody saw something, or that one of the student council boys got picked up, and they'd torture the shit out of him, and if he gave them any names at all they'd be yours and mine. We're expendable . . . especially you."

"Okay. Where are we going?"

Echaverria traces a line with his finger, southeast to Tudela,

Zaragoza, east to Lérida, Igualada, all this on a thick red line, a major highway. Then northeast on a yellow line, a secondary highway, through Catalonia to Manresa, Vich, Olot, Figueras. Back to a red line for the last few miles, up across the Pyrenees to France at Le Perthus.

"What makes you think they won't be looking for Angela there?" Murphy asks.

"They'll have her name," Echaverria says, "and that's all." He removes an American passport from his jacket pocket and hands it to Murphy. "Open it."

The passport belongs to Elizabeth Murphy, who entered Spain at Fuenterrabía last night. The small photograph is of Angela. Murphy cannot detect any sign of forgery—the seal is on the photograph, naturally, since the photograph was obviously removed from Angela's actual passport, but the blue imprint down the side of the photograph meshes perfectly with the blue imprint on paper to the right of the photograph.

"Congratulations," Echaverria says.

"How far is it?" Murphy asks.

"Three hundred miles, maybe a little more."

"Five hours? Six?"

"No, there's a hell of a lot of mountains. Probably nine or ten hours. Can you make it?"

"If I have to, I guess I could. But I'd be a lot more confident if I could sleep for a while."

"If we show up at two or three in the morning," Echaverria says, "and if I go first, we're gonna run into a couple of stupid fucking sleepy border guards, and I'm gonna ask them a bunch of hard questions—why are the Spanish roads so bad? and where can I get some gas across the border? and how many kilometers is it to Toulouse?—and then they're gonna look at your passports and send you through."

"What about tomorrow night at two or three in the morning?"

"No," Echaverria says. "Tonight."

"You have something planned for tomorrow night?"

"Murphy . . . Jesus *Christ*, the longer we wait . . ."

"What?"

Echaverria folds the map, pays the attendant several thousand pesetas for two tanks of gas. "Let's do it tonight," he says to Murphy.

"The way you set it out," Murphy says, "we could do it tomorrow night or next month."

"Look," Echaverria says, "I could just go back up to Zarauz and leave you here."

"With your sister, the fugitive," Murphy says.

"Let's go, for Christ's sake," Echaverria says.

"We'll go as far as we can go," Murphy says. "If we have to stop, we'll stop."

"Okay. Let's get the hell out of here."

"Before we go, I'd like to get something straight."

Echaverria shrugs, grimaces.

"What happened back there . . . I realize it was a very quick and effective way of getting Angela out and getting your money back, and I realize that if you'd told me what was going to happen, there's no way in hell I would've done it . . ."

"That's the point," Echaverria says.

"Yeah, I *know* that's the point. But from now on there's not going to be any more of that. You've got a hell of an advantage over me—you know where we're going, you speak the language—but from now on I expect you to be absolutely straight with me. Do you understand that?"

"I had never intended anything else," Echaverria says.

"Okay. Why is it so important to cross the border tonight?"

"It's just a question of practicality. If there's one chance in a hundred they might be looking for us tonight at Le Perthus, there could be one chance in fifty tomorrow night."

"There's no ulterior motive?"

Echaverria almost smiles. "Do we have a touch of the boy-who-cried-wolf syndrome here?"

"That's for you to say."

"There's no ulterior motive."


Back in the Seat, Murphy replays the conversation. He suspects that nothing has changed. There are unquestionably many wolves between Logroño and France, wolves with green uniforms and tricornered hats, and guns, wolves that Murphy would just as soon not encounter. Echaverria, it has been proved, can handle the wolves. Murphy knows that, and Echaverria knows that he does.

The Citroën pulls away from the gas station, the Seat follows. Angela stirs.

"Prosper?" There is a hint of terror in her voice, as if he might be someone else.

"It's me." He strokes her leg.

She opens her eyes wide. "Oh, God, I was dreaming that we were in this car together, and then I woke up and I was back in that cell . . ."

"You're here. We're here. It's all right."

She takes his hand and kisses it, holds it against her breast. Murphy wants to enfold her, but can't.

"Where are we?" she asks.

"Just leaving Logroño," Murphy says.

"Where's Logroño?"

He searches for some point of reference. The Citroën whips past a truck; the Seat follows. "In Spain," Murphy says. He switches on the headlights.


Angela sleeps again, her seat in full reclining position. She is silent and motionless except when she dreams, and Murphy needs no sophisticated equipment to tell when she's dreaming. She murmurs at first, then begins to twitch, then to groan quietly. Her hands move, sometimes clutching, sometimes pushing away. On several occasions she wakes herself up; once she jerks upright, looks wildly around in the dark automobile, and reclines, slowly, again. Murphy leans toward her, runs his right hand gently across her stomach. She's already back to sleep, perhaps never having been conscious.

He follows the Citroën. The speedometer nestles consistently between a hundred fifty and a hundred sixty, dropping to eighty in deference to widely separated villages, to sixty for a couple of towns: Calahorra, half an hour out of Logroño, Tudela, twenty minutes later. After Tudela there is virtually nothing for forty-five minutes. The Citroën begins to pull away as the Seat cruises somewhat painfully at a hundred eighty kilometers per hour; Murphy loses sight of it following a curve after a slight upgrade. When the road straightens, the Citroën seems half a mile ahead. Murphy flashes his lights; with the accelerator on the floor he begins to gain, catches up. They continue.

There is a large city ahead. From the top of a rise Murphy looks down on a vast constellation of urban lights. Zaragoza, the sign says. His eyes are beginning to hurt; he doubts his ability to follow the Citroën through city traffic, doubts in fact his ability to maneuver through any traffic at all. The road widens to four lanes. Murphy downshifts as a truck turns onto the road after the Citroën, brakes sharply as the truck doesn't accelerate to his expectations. Angela wakes up. Traffic passes on the left. Murphy waits for an opening, pulls out, passes the truck. Where's the Citroën?

"Where are we, Prosper?"

"Zaragoza."

"Ah." She knows where they are.

"I've lost him," Murphy says.

"Ray?"

"Yeah . . . just now. I hope he realizes we're not behind him."

"Do you know where we're going?"

"Yes and no. I'm afraid we're about to get lost in a huge god-damn Spanish city." Traffic slows and stops. There's a red light a hundred yards in the distance. It becomes green. Large signs indicate Zaragoza straight ahead, Barcelona to the left. Barcelona's on the coast, Murphy knows, not too far from France, and he doesn't have any chance at all of getting back into the right lane. So what the hell. He reaches the light while it's still green; the road separates; the Seat bears left, toward Barcelona.

The Citroën waits, nestled against a traffic island. Echaverria has seen them coming, darts out into traffic, and order is restored. They cross a bridge, bypass most of Zaragoza. The road becomes a veritable freeway for a few miles, then reverts to wide, dark, nearly deserted two-lane highway.

"We're going to France," Murphy says. "The long way around. Can you last another seven hours?"

"Can you?"

"I don't know."

"I could drive."

"You might have to."

The Citroën has resumed its grand-prix pace. Murphy presses on in silence, assuming Angela has gone back to sleep. He is startled when she speaks.

"What are we going to do, Prosper?"

"I guess we'll drive to Paris," Murphy says. "Then we could fly to New York and fly to Miami, or I guess we could go from Paris to London to Miami. I don't know what the hell to do with the car."

"I meant after that, when we get back . . ."

When *we* get back. This is virgin territory. Murphy is at once elated by the "we" and puzzled by the question.

"We have some things to take care of in Madera Beach," he says.

"I don't want to go back there, Prosper."

"We have to, for a while, anyway . . ."

"I want to pack up my things and go."

"Okay. We can go to New York, to my apartment."

"I don't want to stay in New York, either."

"Neither do I," Murphy realizes.

"What are we going to do?"

"We'll think about it," Murphy says. "We'll get out of here, we'll spend a few days on the beach, and we'll figure it out."

Kilometers pass in silence. "I've never seen anyone killed before," Angela says.

"Neither have I."

"I keep thinking about Ray shooting the man who was lying down."

"He had to."

"If I'd stayed in Florida he wouldn't have had to."

"He would have killed someone else, then."


An hour later, the temperature gauge on the Seat's dashboard begins to edge up, finally shooting into the red. Murphy can smell the overheat. He blinks his lights eight times and the Citroën pulls over.

Murphy and Echaverria peer into the Seat's engine, steam soaring out. "We need a flashlight," Echaverria says.

"We don't have a flashlight."

"This is a new car," Echaverria says. "It couldn't be the radiator. It's probably a hose."

"What difference does it make? We're in the middle of nowhere."

"No, we're not. We're about ten minutes from Lérida. Get in and drive the son of a bitch."

They limp into Lérida, pull into an open gas station on the city's western fringe. Echaverria drags a middle-aged attendant out to the Seat's engine. After ten minutes he reports to Murphy: "It's the fucking water pump."

"Can they fix it?"

"If they had the pump, they could. We've got to leave it here. He says they'll get the pump first thing in the morning."

Murphy's suitcase is transferred to the Citroën, in whose trunk Angela's luggage already sits. Echaverria drives into Lérida, stops at the Hotel Palacio, where he commands adjoining rooms for himself, Monsieur Bordagaray, and his American friends, Mr. and Mrs. Murphy.

Murphy has taken a quick shower; Angela is in the midst of a lengthy bath. Swathed in an oversized towel, he stands in front of a pair of seven-foot windows that look onto a narrow protrusion, somewhere between a ledge and a deck. He opens the windows, pulling their handles toward him, and steps out on the ledge, leans on a low railing, looks out at Lérida. The hotel is in a very old section of an ancient city. Murphy guesses that the youngest building in his immediate field of vision is at least ten times as old as he, the oldest dating perhaps to the thirteenth or fourteenth century, when it must have taken several weeks to cover the ground he's covered today in a few hours. When the Spaniards, or the Catalonians, were still worrying about the Moors. When guns had not yet been invented, or at least not yet discovered in this part of the world, and killing people was much more difficult.

A cold breeze nips at his feet, and Murphy, resembling in his attire a Roman conqueror who might have stood here two millennia ago, looking out on his domain, retreats from the ledge to the bedroom, closes the window, and wanders into the bathroom.

Angela is drying herself. She looks very tired and very beautiful. Murphy holds her; she neither ignores him nor shows great interest.

"I'm glad you're safe," he says. "I'm glad you're here." He feels what might be a tear on his shoulder.

"You mean very much to me, Prosper."

He leans down to kiss her breasts, first the left, then the right. Her nipples harden. He kisses her stomach, her navel, runs his nose through her moist pubic hair.

"Not now," she says.

Murphy has an epical erection. "When?" he says.

"When we're out of here. When this is over. I feel horrible."

"Maybe you'd feel better . . ."

"No, Prosper. It wouldn't be right. I'm sorry."

They lie together in the large, soft bed. Angela sleeps yet again, now more tranquilly. Murphy is exhausted and athrob. There remain the aches of Officer Raymond, dissipating, but still to be sensed on the odd twist or turn; there is a new bruise on the lower jaw from the dead *guardia* (has he set a record? Most contusions; three days, two continents?); there is a general stiffness about the upper back, a result of the day's drive. But these pall compared to the throbbing of his groin. He presses against her, runs his hand softly over her stomach. It's going to be a long night.

There is a tapping on the door, so quiet that Murphy isn't positive he's heard it until it's repeated seconds later. He steals out of bed, pulls on his underpants, goes to the door. "Who is it?" he whispers.

"Three guesses," Echaverria says.

Murphy opens the door.

"How about a drink?"

There is a hint of alcohol already on Echaverria's breath. "Where? Is the bar open?"

"It just closed. I got an order to go."

"Wait a minute," Murphy says. He puts on his pants, his shirt, his shoes, and accompanies Echaverria next door. Sitting on the dresser are a liter of Johnnie Walker Black, six bottles of El Aguila beer, and a bucket of ice. "The beer was cheap," Echaverria says. "Twenty cents a bottle. The scotch was twenty bucks. They'd never heard of Chivas Regal."

"Or Wild Turkey?"

"Wild Turkey? They've never heard of bourbon, for Christ's sake."

Echaverria hands Murphy a beer, stuffs the other five in the ice bucket, and pours himself three ounces of scotch. "How's she doing?" he says.

"She's all right," Murphy says. "She keeps thinking about you shooting somebody who was asleep."

"That son of a bitch wasn't sleeping. He was lying there waiting for me to turn my back."

"I'll tell her that. I don't think it'll make any difference."

"She'll get over it, Murphy. She's tough. She's resilient."

"Do you know that?"

"I've known her since the day she was born."

"I think you have a tendency to apply certain qualities . . ." Murphy pauses, aware that he doesn't know exactly what he's trying to say. He opts for a different tactic. "Have you ever talked to her?"

"Of course I've talked to her."

"About her father?"

"Murphy . . . I would suggest to you as politely as I can that if you think you can figure somebody out in two weeks' time, you've got your head up your ass. As for Bordagaray, he was a miserable, sadistic son of a bitch, and I don't think Angie knows how much she hated his guts."

"I think," Murphy says slowly, carefully, "you tend to assume that because you feel some way, or because you *are* some way, that she is, too. And I don't think it's always true."

"I sure as hell don't think we're identical twins," Echaverria says.

"If she's as strong and resilient as you think she is, why did she come to Spain?"

"You don't think that took courage?"

"Courage, okay, but we're not talking about courage. I don't think it was a move made from strength. I think she was running away . . . running to you."

"Running from you?"

*Running from me?* Murphy shakes off Echaverria's most practiced maneuver. "That's possible, but at best I'd say it's secondary. There was a simple explanation for what happened with the cops in Madera Beach. It had almost nothing to do with her. But when things got nasty, she left. She came here, to big brother."

Echaverria stares at Murphy; there seems to be more than a modicum of anger in his eyes. "Murphy . . ." he shakes his head, looks away. Then fixes again on Murphy. "Let's talk about this sometime next year, okay? She's alive. We're all alive. What the hell have we got to argue about?"

Is this retreat? If so, Murphy is unable or unwilling to seize the advantage. His mind cannot evade the image of the *guardia's* gun pointed at his face.

"You saved somebody's life," Echaverria says. "Do you know that?"

"I did?"

"The guy who was shot. Carmelo. One more shot and that *guardia* bastard would have killed him."

Murphy sees the *guardia's* face being removed from his skull. Whose life did he save—Carmelo's or his own? Both, is the answer, but if his own hadn't been at stake how interested would he have been in Carmelo's versus the *guardia's?* And who saved Murphy's life yet again? Time to change the subject.

"What happened with Curtis?" Murphy says.

Echaverria is delighted to present an expansive recounting of the drive to the airport, the incident at the airport, the hunt, the capture first of Archie, then of Curtis, the ride down to Wall Street . . .

An hour passes. Echaverria has consumed a third of a liter of scotch, Murphy two bottles of beer.

"What," Murphy asks, "were you planning to do with the *plastique?*"

"No, motherfucker," Echaverria grins and shakes his head. "Not yet."

"Why not?"

"Because I still might do it."

"Without the student council?"

"With or without. There's a couple of guys . . . Kepa, Carmelo, that might feel the way I do."

"So what if you still might do it? What difference would it make if you tell me?"

"If you fall into the wrong hands."

"The police, here?"

"You got it."

"How close are we to the border?"

"A hundred and eighty miles."

"That's a three-hour drive tomorrow, right?"

"Four hours. Maybe four and a half."

"Okay, we're just about out of the woods," Murphy says. "Tell me."

Echaverria drinks, laughs, and pours some more scotch. "You're on the edge of your seat, aren't you?" he says. He laughs again, stands up, walks around the room, chuckles softly for the better part of a minute, and turns to look at Murphy. "You really want to know, don't you, Murphy? You really want to know everything that's happening, all the time, every minute."

"Don't you?"

"You're stealing my lines, Murphy."

"You don't have exclusive rights."

"Okay." Echaverria sits down. "There's some truth in that." He drinks some more scotch. "And imitation is the sincerest form of flattery."

"Yeah, and the best defense is a good offense."

"I don't think you've got that one right."

"It doesn't matter," Murphy says. "Tell me."

Echaverria leers at him. It is an expression born of drunkenness, to be sure, but of awesome strength and knowledge, of confidence and contempt, as well. Again Murphy senses that he is about to be privileged, to be honored by something from within that leer, something he isn't sure he wishes to hear.

"El Caudillo," Echaverria says, "Generalissimo Francisco Franco Bahamonde, spends a couple of weeks every September in San Sebastián. In the traditional palace of Spanish royalty. That old Fascist cocksucker spits in the face of the Basque people. He pisses on my father's grave. That old son of a bitch has been in power for thirty-five years. He's a legend, Murphy. He's surrounded by a fucking invisible shield. You talk to people in Spain, and you always get the same line—the Spanish police are tough bastards, the security is so efficient, and it's all bullshit. If those college boys can pull off what they've been doing for the last few years. . . . Jesus! Can you *imagine* what I could do?"

"What could you do?" Murphy says.

"I could go right to the fucking top."

"How?"

"They don't know about security here, Murphy. They do it all with mirrors. You'd think they'd fly the old bastard to Fuenterrabía, put him in a helicopter, and drop him right into the palace. But they don't. They do it by motorcade—seven million cops on motorcycles, cops all along the roadway, standing there with fucking machine guns. You get the picture?"

"I've got it."

"All right. What if somebody dug a tunnel—a long motherfucker—maybe from under a barn a hundred yards away from the road, maybe four or five feet underground, and they put a hundred pounds of plastic explosive at the end of the tunnel right under the middle of the highway, and they waited for Franco's limousine to hit the exact spot, and they pushed the button?"

Echaverria's leer anticipates a climax.

Murphy simply smiles.

"*Boom!*" Echaverria stands up and flings his arms into the air. "Can you imagine it? Can you fucking imagine it? Can you see this long, black limousine three hundred feet in the sky, straight up, maybe end over end, and then the son of a bitch comes down, nose first, planted in somebody's pasture. The Francisco Franco Memorial, donated to the Basque nation in this year of our Lord, 1973, by Ramon Echaverria . . ."

"It couldn't be that easy," Murphy says.

Echaverria sits down. "Of course it could." His voice is quiet, without a hint of reproof. "It's perfect. It's flawless. But ETA doesn't want to do it."

"Why not?"

"Because he's old. He's gonna die without my help. They want to kill somebody else, in Madrid."

"Who?"

"I'm sure as hell not gonna tell you *that.*"

"Okay . . . don't tell me who, just tell me why."

"They're looking toward the practical. Their idea of practical, anyway."

"But you still want to blow up Franco?"

Echaverria slops more scotch into his glass. The bottle is slightly more than half empty. "When I'm dead," he says, "you tell my nephews about it." He chuckles. "Even my nieces."

"You planning on dying soon?"

"That depends."

"On what?"

"On whether there's anything around that's worth dying for."

Murphy suspects that Echaverria is being neither ironic nor melodramatic. "Do you actually think there could be something worth dying for?"

"Those guys do," Echaverria says, pointing to the northwest. "Those idealistic little self-possessed cocksuckers are positive there's something worth dying for."

"Worth dying for, or worth killing for?"

"In this case there ain't a hell of a lot of difference. You saw them kill . . . you might just as easily have seen them get killed."

"I mainly saw you kill."

"Yeah, well . . . there you go."

"You're the same as they are?"

"In some ways I am."

"You talk about them . . . about ETA, as if they were a bunch of college kids getting ready for the big game, but you seem to have an awful lot of respect for them . . ."

Echaverria glares at Murphy. "Respect? I fucking *envy* those bastards?"

"Why?"

"Because they've been here all their lives. They've had Franco's assholes looking over their shoulders since they were in first grade. It's occupied territory up there, Murphy, and they really *are* ready to die for it."

"But you're not?"

"I don't know. I don't think so. I think I hate Franco's guts just as much as they do, but I've got a different reason. It didn't bother me to kill those guys today. Do you believe that?"

"It's hard to believe."

"It was like swatting flies, Murphy. Like stepping on cockroaches."

"Why is your reason different from theirs?"

Murphy is surprised when Echaverria answers almost immediately: "Maybe it's a little more personal."

"Theirs isn't personal? They aren't individuals?"

"Of course they are. But they're thinking in terms of their

goddamn fatherland . . . they're thinking about their ancestors who beat Charlemagne, for Christ's sake."

"Your ancestors, too . . ."

"Yeah, but I've been off the farm too long. I'm an American, and they know it. I just want to get even. And they know that, too. And they're stuck here, Murphy. They can kill two cops on a street corner and then get their asses over to France, but they're gonna come back next week, and they know that if they don't get busted somebody else will. I've got six passports. I can be American, French, Portuguese, Argentinian, Italian, or Colombian. I speak all those languages like a goddamned native, or at least well enough to fool anybody over here. I can talk and bluff my ass out of anything, and I can go anywhere I want to."

"Doesn't that give you a certain sense of satisfaction?"

"How do you feel when you win a hundred dollars from those jerk-offs on Jane Street for the eightieth time in a row?"

"I feel all right, glad I didn't lose . . ."

"Was there any question that you *might* lose?"

"There always is."

"Okay," Echaverria says. "Then that's a big difference between you and me."

Murphy opens his third beer. Echaverria says, "Excuse me," and heads for the bathroom. Murphy wonders what time it is. Echaverria returns and pours himself another two ounces of scotch, drinks an ounce off the bat.

"Do *you* think there's anything worth dying for?" he asks Murphy.

"No," Murphy says.

"If you'd been in my position today, and I'd been in yours, would you have done what I did?"

"I think I would have told you the situation."

Echaverria nods, reaches for his glass, almost knocks it over.

"You think Angie didn't hate Bordagaray as much as I did?"

"I think she loves him as much as she hates him."

"You're putting esses where there should be dees."

"What?"

"The past tense, Murphy. Use the past tense."

"He's dead?"

"Yeah, he's dead. I killed him."

"You mean, you . . . indirectly . . ."

"There wasn't anything indirect about it."

"When . . ." Murphy begins a question.

"Five years ago. In Paris. I called him up one night. He said he was really glad to hear from me, he said we should get together for dinner some night. So I said how about tomorrow night. He didn't seem too happy about that, but he said fine, excellent, tomorrow night it is."

"You didn't tell him about your mother?"

"No, I figured I'd save that for later." Echaverria empties his glass, pours some more. "He had a penthouse in one of those new buildings—all glass and concrete, nine hundred stories, ugly as shit—you know what I mean?"

Murphy nods.

"Okay. He shows me around the place, and he's got this tiny Matisse, you know, and he tells me what he paid for it to the fucking centime, and he's got all this fucking velvet furniture. He's made it big. He's the senior vice-president in charge of bullshit. But he's really nervous with me. He must have had three drinks before he asked me what I was doing, and I told him I'd gone to Columbia, I'd been teaching, and I'd decided to take some time off. I said there were some things I had to think about. He let that go, and he had another drink, and he said, 'How's your mother?' And I told him she'd died, and he came apart. He unraveled."

Echaverria speaks with a particular intensity, glaring at Murphy. "He started shaking. Then he started crying. He asked me what I thought of him. I told him I thought he was an evil, selfish bastard. I told him my mother had lived through the civil war on her own strength, she'd gotten kicked all around, she'd married him, she'd depended on him, and he'd taken her to America and set her adrift. I told him that was a hell of a lot worse than the civil war. He said he couldn't compete with my father's memory. Every time he looked at me he saw my father. I told him I never even knew my father. I expected *him* to be my father. He said he was very sorry, about everything, and he'd do anything he could to make it up to me and Angie. I told him there wasn't anything he could do, as far as I was concerned."

Echaverria downs another ounce of scotch. Murphy completes his third bottle of beer.

"He went out on the terrace. He got up from his chair and he walked to this big glass door, and he couldn't get the son of a bitch open. Then it gave, all of a sudden, and he fell out the fucking door, and he got up, and he walked to the edge of the roof, and he stood there, weaving. So I went out, and I said, 'Are you thinking about jumping?' And he said, 'Yes, as a matter of fact, I am.' And I said, 'Do you think you'll do it?' And he said, 'No, I don't think I have the courage.' And I said, 'Would you like some help?' And he said, 'If you'd be so kind.'

"So I gave him a push."

Murphy opens his fourth beer. Echaverria pours another double shot; the Johnnie Walker bottle is two-thirds gone.

"Would you guess," Murphy says, "that if you'd left him there and allowed him to sober up . . ."

"He'd still be around," Echaverria says. "I saved us both a lot of trouble."

A pause. "There weren't any repercussions?"

"I called the police," Echaverria says. "They were there in two minutes. He just missed somebody on the sidewalk, hit about two feet away from some lady walking her dog. Scared the shit out of her. I told them he was my stepfather, he'd just learned that my mother was dead, and he jumped while I was in the bathroom. They checked my papers. They said they were profoundly sorry."

A long pause. "Angela doesn't know anything about this?"

"No," Echaverria says. "Innocence is bliss."

"I don't think you've got that one right."

"Yes, I do."

A longer pause. "I think you should tell her," Murphy says.

"You tell her, then."


Some minutes later Murphy returns to the adjoining room, where Angela is still sound asleep. He gets into bed next to her, kisses her on the cheek, and she stirs, but doesn't awaken.

# 27

# Le Perthus

Murphy awakens to a persistent pounding on the door. He sits up. Where is he? The shower is running. Angela. In Spain, in Lérida. The pounder in all probability is Echaverria. Murphy gets out of bed in his underpants and walks to the door. The floor is ice cold. "Who is it?"

"Spiro Agnew."

Murphy opens the door to Echaverria, whose eyes are a bit red. Otherwise he seems none the worse for wear. He hands Murphy a thick tabloid and says, "Page eighteen."

Murphy flips through the newspaper, whose name is *ABC*. It has a rather eclectic layout: several pages of advertising at the start, followed by what seem to be editorials, followed by the news. The big news is that 6 *guardias* have been *matados* in Odriozola by *asesinos de ETA*. He hands the paper back to Echaverria. "What does it say?"

"A cowardly act of murder," Echaverria summarizes, "six civil guards slain, four in their barracks, two in a car outside the barracks, presumed to be the work of ETA, although no credit has been claimed. No witnesses. The murderers freed the only prisoner, a young woman . . ."

"They don't know her name, then?"

"They know her name. They don't want to complicate things."

The shower stops. "What time is it?" Murphy asks.

"Nine-thirty."

"It's cold," Murphy says.

"It's a shitty day," Echaverria says. "It's been raining."

"How long have you been up?"

"A couple of hours. I walked down to the garage. They don't know what the fuck they're doing. They couldn't find a water pump in town, and the guy told me he'd have to order one from Barcelona. I told him I could build a fucking water pump before he'd get one from Barcelona. I gave him two thousand pesetas and told him to have the car ready by noon or I'd break his jaw."

"How much is two thousand pesetas?"

"Thirty dollars, thirty-five . . ."

"What's he going to do?"

"He's gonna find a water pump. He'll probably pull one out of somebody else's car, and he'll have us ready sometime this afternoon."

Swathed in a towel, Angela emerges from the bathroom. "Hi," she says. "Good morning."

"How do you feel?" Echaverria asks.

"I'm all right," Angela replies.


They eat breakfast alone in the hotel dining room, the Frenchman and the young American couple, touring Spain separately in the off-season, thrown together by fate. They pay their bill, check out of the Palacio, stuff their luggage in the Citroën's trunk, and see the sights. The temperature is just above freezing. They visit a church built in the twelfth century, on the site of a mosque destroyed in 1149, when the Moors were driven from Lérida, according to the tiny handout; the mosque, in turn, had been built on the site of a Roman temple. They visit a castle built by Spaniards eight hundred years ago around the ruins of a castle built a thousand years ago by Arabs. They visit a crumbling cathedral that took seventy-five years to build and stood intact for four hundred twenty-nine years before it was destroyed, along with most of the rest of Lérida, by a Franco-Spanish army during the War of Succession, in 1707. The War of Succession? Who, Murphy wonders, was attempting to succeed whom? It must have been important at the time.

"It's sad," Angela says. She and Murphy stand outside the *catedral vieja* in a cold drizzle. Echaverria is walking rapidly back to the Citroën.

"What's sad?" Murphy asks.

"To be here by accident. Someone designed this eight hundred years ago, and he must have been dead before it was finished. But he knew it *would* be finished. And then somebody else came along and knocked it down four hundred years later, but it's still here, Prosper. It deserves something more than us."

"I'm sure," Murphy says, "that there are people who come here specifically to look at this cathedral."

"That's not the point," Angela says.

Murphy knows it isn't, just as he knows there are myriad points everywhere you look, and a melancholy reverence for the past at this juncture seems irrelevant. He takes her by the waist and they walk rapidly down Lérida's ancient sidewalk, in pursuit of Echaverria.

The Seat is ready at three. Luggage is transferred, Murphy pulls his suitcase from the Citroën's trunk and notices a gray cylinder protruding from the spare tire well. He lifts the partition and finds a sleek automatic rifle; he tucks it back so it's entirely hidden. Does Echaverria intend to go through customs with this monstrous gun in his trunk?


Spain seems to consist of an endless succession of hills progressing to mountains, mountains receding to hills. The road east from Lérida is amply wide and well kept but Monday's traffic is considerably heavier than Sunday's. The two-car convoy, Echaverria again in the lead, spends much of its time trailing a line of fume-belching trucks on winding upgrades, passing furiously on intermittent stretches of straight roadway, only to discover the next cordon of trucks around the following bend.

But it's no longer important to make good time. By Echaverria's calculation, it is 183 miles from Lérida to the frontier. Having left Lérida at three-thirty, they might reach Le Perthus before nine even at their present pace, but nine would be too early, by Echaverria's reasoning, to cross the border.

"Prosper?" Angela says. "I've been thinking—about what we were talking about yesterday. About what we're going to do?"

"And?"

"It's funny. My mother always used to talk to me about Spain . . . about San Sebastián, and Barcelona. She used to tell me bedtime stories about San Sebastián. And then she'd say, 'Some day, Angelita, some day, we'll go back there, when Franco is dead and Spain is free again, and I'll show you everything I've told you about.' I used to dream about coming here. Spain was a sort of gigantic Central Park with beaches and mountains . . ."

"You were right about the mountains," Murphy says.

"Prosper, I keep thinking this is where we should be. It could be so wonderful. . . . Not forever—maybe just for a couple of years. I could teach English somewhere . . ."

"What could I do?"

"You could write a book."

"A book about what?"

"I'm sure you could think of something."

Murphy tries to think of what he might write a book about.

"Prosper, I've dreamed about coming here, living here . . . since I was five years old, and now I'm here, and I can't come back, can I?"

"It might be prudent not to. Not for a couple of years, anyway."

There is a long silence. The Citroën and the Seat creep up a long grade behind a gasoline truck, unable to pass.

"What *are* we going to do?" Angela asks.

"We could go to Montreal for a while."

"To your parents?"

"To my mother and my stepfather."

"Would you want to stay there?"

"I don't think I'd want to stay there."

The Citroën pulls out to pass during a brief break of westbound traffic. The break is much briefer for the Seat; a downhill westbound Mercedes flashes its lights furiously as Murphy pulls back into the eastbound lane.

"Is there anywhere you'd like to stay?"

"Oh, Jesus, I don't know, Angela. I have to think about it." There is no anger in Murphy's voice. "We'll figure something out."

"We're going to Paris, right? After we cross the border?"

"Right."

"Why don't we stay a few days?"

"What for?"

"I've never been there. I'd like to see it."

A pause.

"And I'd like to find my father."

"We won't have time," Murphy says. "We should get back right away."


At nightfall they stop for gas in Igualada. It is a good twenty degrees warmer here than it was in Lérida. Echaverria spreads the map out. "The trucks are all going to Barcelona," he says.

On the map, Barcelona is two inches away from Igualada.

"We're going up here, to Manresa and Vich and up to Figueras. We should get to Figueras by eight. We'll have dinner there, we'll just hang around till midnight, and we'll cross over."

"Why don't we just go through Barcelona?" Angela asks.

"Because it's too complicated. It's at least two hours out of the way. We don't know what the traffic's going to be like, we could get separated, and everything could get fucked up."

"Ray," Angela says, "you just said we had *four* hours to kill, so what difference would it make if we used two of them going to Barcelona? Prosper's perfectly capable of following you."

A sibling quarrel. Angela may speak to Echaverria as Murphy may not, but may have no greater effect. Murphy knows why Angela wants to go via Barcelona (because of her mother, because she may never have another chance); Murphy knows why Echaverria wants to go via Manresa and Vich (because that's the route he's planned, and he's not about to depart from it). Murphy wishes only to get out of Spain as quickly and painlessly as possible.


They go to Figueras on roads now wide, now narrow, now smooth, now ragged, always winding, climbing, descending, meandering. Traffic is light, but the 113-mile trip takes three and a half hours. Angela sleeps. Murphy grows increasingly weary of driving on this road, of following Echaverria, of driving at all. They reach Figueras, reach a magnificent four-lane highway, and Murphy prays that Echaverria will reconsider, will disavow the plan and speed north to France, twenty minutes away.

But he follows the Citroën off the highway into Figueras, stops behind it at the Bar-Restaurant Teixidor. Echaverria has a five-course dinner; Angela nibbles some shrimp; Murphy has a salad and a breaded veal cutlet, a travesty. Echaverria has a lengthy conversation with the waiter.

"We're French," Angela translates. "We're wondering if there's someplace between here and the frontier where we could have a good time, someplace that's open late. He says there's a place about five kilometers from the frontier, the last exit off the highway. It's open all year. It's really a lot of fun in the summer, but there isn't much going on now. But it's the only place between here and the frontier."

It is a bar, essentially, with a dining area, a snack bar, and a huge dance floor whose tables and chairs are stacked up along the walls, waiting for June. Murphy spots a Wurlitzer jukebox just short of antique status, set against the far wall of the dance floor. It is a few minutes after eleven; there are no patrons at the bar, one bartender behind it. Echaverria orders a beer, Angela a glass of water, Murphy a Coke.

"I'm gonna go look at the jukebox," Murphy says.

Echaverria speaks to the bartender, who replies.

"It's turned off," Echaverria says to Murphy. "He says he'll turn it on if you want to play something."

"I'll see," Murphy says to Echaverria. He says to Angela, "You want to come look?"

"I don't feel like standing up," she says.

Murphy walks seventy feet to the jukebox. In dim light he studies its repertoire. Mostly in Spanish. But look, there's "Jumpin' Jack Flash" by Los Rolling Stones. "Nights in White Satin" by Los Moody Blues. "Good Vibrations" by Los Beach Boys. "Suspicious Minds" by Elvis Presley. "Dock of the Bay" by Otis Redding.

"Tell him to turn it on," Murphy shouts. The Wurlitzer flickers to life. Murphy deposits twenty-five pesetas and begins pressing buttons. He plays all five of the above, plus "Hey Jude" by Los Beatles, then discovers another trove as "Jumpin' Jack Flash" strains through the Wurlitzer's aluminum-foil speaker. "Wouldn't

It Be Nice" and "God Only Knows" by Los Beach Boys, one of the great two-sided hits, is here. So is Marvin Gaye's "What's Goin' On?" and so is Bob Dylan's "Lay Lady Lay." He searches his pockets for another twenty-five peseta coin, doesn't have one.

Murphy turns and begins to walk toward the bar, to do a modest little boogaloo toward the bar during the brief but immortal guitar bridge from "Jumpin' Jack Flash." He stops abruptly after his fifth step as two green-uniformed *guardias* walk casually past Echaverria and Angela. They sit at the bar.

There's nothing to be concerned about, Murphy tells himself, what we have here is just two off-duty cops coming in for a drink. He takes a step forward and sees Echaverria turn his head, looking at Murphy. Echaverria's hand, extended below the bar stool, is pointing him back, telling him to stay where he is. Murphy raises his shoulders, asking, why?, and the hand movements accelerate. Murphy retreats to the jukebox. "Jumpin' Jack Flash" fades out. The jukebox whirs and clicks. Paul McCartney says, "Hayee Jude . . ."

There is a side door to the left of the jukebox. Murphy walks cautiously toward it. Standing by the door he can't see the *guardias*, they can't see him. The door is locked from the inside, bolted. He pulls the bolt, opens the door. It creaks ever so slightly. The Beatles are louder. He looks out into the parking lot: the Seat and the Citroën are out there, intact. The *guardias'* car is parked illegally next to the front door. There are no other *guardias* in sight. Murphy closes the door and walks to the other side of the jukebox. From this vantage he may see Echaverria and Angela, but not the *guardias*. He waits, "Hey Jude" lasts over six minutes.

The next record clicks into place. Somewhat anemically, Otis Redding sings about sitting on a dock in San Francisco Bay. Loneliness won't leave him alone. Murphy thinks of Aurore and remembers the dream. A chill slithers down his spine. He has descended to a crouching position, against the wall, watching Echaverria and Angela, who seem to sit rather stiffly at the bar. He wonders what they're talking about, or if they're talking. The bartender, to their left, is methodically rinsing and drying glasses. The *guardias* are not in the picture.

Until now, when one of them, just one of them, enters from stage left. Is he leaving? No, he stops behind Echaverria and

Angela, stations himself behind them. Echaverria's head turns. They speak. A casual conversation? There's Echaverria's hand again, below the stool, now motioning Murphy to the right. Does Echaverria know about the rear door? Does he just want Murphy out of sight? Murphy moves slowly toward the door; in front of the jukebox, he sees the other *guardia* stand and walk, with purpose, it seems, toward the couple at the bar. Murphy freezes. The second *guardia* doesn't look his way. The bartender is still drying glasses, now watching what's transpiring between four of five patrons. Echaverria has handed a document to the first *guardia;* the second is talking to Angela.

Murphy tiptoes to the door, opens it, closes it silently behind him. What now? It is a pleasantly cool night here in Catalonia, five kilometers from the border. There's a gun in the trunk of the Citroën. Murphy doesn't have the key. If he did, he wouldn't know what to do with the gun. In his thirty years he's never touched a gun. What does Echaverria expect him to do? To escape? To go for help? To make a person-to-person call for ETA in Zarauz? He reaches the Citroën: the trunk lock is the European type—a button which may be left locked or unlocked. Could Echaverria conceivably have left it unlocked? Murphy presses the button. The trunk springs open.

Jesus Christ. Murphy pushes Echaverria's suitcase aside, pulls away the trunk partition, and there is this fine gray instrument, this M-16 or AK-47 or something. He picks it up and walks toward the front door of the bar. The upper half of the front door is glass, and Murphy sees Echaverria and Angela spread out in the frisk position against the bar, a *guardia* behind them, his pistol still in holster, the other *guardia* behind the bar, on the telephone. What am I going to say? Murphy wonders.

Hands: *manos*. Up: *arriba*.

Two of the twelve Spanish words he knows.

*Manos arriba* or *arriba manos?*

He pulls the door open and shouts, "¡*Manos arriba!*" The *guardia* behind the bar drops the telephone and puts his hands up; the other *guardia* seems to be going for his pistol, and Murphy thinks for a horrible moment that he's going to have to use this thing he's holding. But Echaverria whirls and punches the *guardia* in the belly, kicks him in the balls, then jumps over the bar and rips the telephone from the wall.

For a full second no one moves. It is a portrait: Murphy standing by the door with a rifle in his hand. Angela standing by the
bar, her eyes wide with fear and surprise. One *guardia* curled
up on the floor. Another *guardia* reaching for the sky. Echaverria
holding the deceased telephone. The bartender (not pictured)
on the floor behind the bar.

"Kill them!" Echaverria shouts at Murphy.

"No!" Murphy shouts back.

"Then give me the fuckin' gun and I'll do it!"

"No!"

Echaverria leaps over the bar. "Give me the gun and close
your fucking eyes! They know us, for Christ's sake!"

Murphy looks at Angela. She shakes her head.

"Tie them up," Murphy says.

"With what?"

Murphy speaks to Angela: "Ask the bartender if he's got some
rope." Angela speaks to the bartender, who answers, stands up,
and scurries away, out a door behind the bar.

"Why the hell do you want to tie them up?" Echaverria says.

"So they don't have to be killed."

"Oh . . . Christ," Echaverria says. He leaps the bar again and
punches the conscious *guardia* in the jaw; the *guardia* collapses.
Echaverria shouts something to the bartender, walks to the end
of the bar, opens a little swinging door, and walks toward
Murphy. "They know us," he says.

"We're leaving." Murphy replies. "They don't know who *you*
are."

"Okay," Echaverria says. "Okay. Let's go." He kicks the prone
*guardia* in the head for good measure.

They leave the bar.


"Give me the gun," Echaverria says.

"What for?"

"I'm not going to kill them."

Murphy hands him the gun.

Echaverria looks it over, scowls, then smiles, as if to himself.
"You were running a hell of a bluff, Murphy . . ."

"I know," Murphy says.

"No, you don't know. The safety was on."

Echaverria directs a fusillade at the *guardia*'s car, flattening all four tires, blowing out the windshield, obliterating the radio and every instrument on the dashboard. The ensuing silence is awesome.

"Are we still going to wait?" Murphy asks.

"No. Of course not. We've got to go now."

Echaverria replaces the rifle under the trunk partition. "You lead now," he says to Murphy.

"Why?"

"Because things have changed."

"What do I do when we get there?"

"Just hand over the passports. Play dumb. Angie . . . for Christ's sake, don't speak any Spanish."


Murphy and Angela pass the first two kilometers in silence. The Citroën's yellow headlights are fixed in the Seat's rearview mirror.

"Angela," Murphy says, "the guy was on the telephone. Did you hear what he said?"

"He was describing me and Ray."

"Any names?"

"I heard Bordagaray."

"But not yours? Or mine?"

"No. My passport's been in the car all along."

"How about the cars? Did he describe the cars?"

"I don't think so, but he might have. I don't know."

"You don't know where he called?"

"No."

The frontier. At twenty minutes to midnight there is one gate in operation, there are three cars in front of the Seat: a Renault, a Peugeot, a Spanish Dodge. The Renault pulls away; the Peugeot follows ten seconds later. The border guards order the Dodge's driver out of his car. He opens the trunk; they perform a brief inspection. He gets back in the car and drives off to France.

Murphy pulls the Seat to the gate. *"Documentos,"* says the guard. Murphy gives him Mr. and Mrs. Murphy's passports, the registration, the green card. The guard enters his booth. Other guards begin to converge. Does this mean anything? The Citroën's headlights flash. Murphy looks in the rearview mirror and sees Echaverria getting out of the car. The guard speaks brusquely to Murphy.

"He wants you to open the trunk," Angela says.

"But I don't understand him," Murphy says.

Murphy looks in the mirror, sees Echaverria opening the Citroën's trunk. The guard gestures to Murphy: pointing to the back of the car, pantomiming the turning of a key. There are now four, no, five guards within several feet of the Seat, one of them holding a submachine gun.

"He wants you to get out," Angela says.

"I don't think I should get out, Angela."

Echaverria stands behind the Citroën, making a throwing motion with his right hand: Go! he's saying. The guard speaks angrily.

Murphy puts the Seat in gear and pops the clutch; the Seat lurches forward, brushing the guard, knocking him aside. There is a gunshot, a thud on the Seat's right side, then a burst of fire from behind.

Angela turns in the passenger seat and screams, "Ray!"

The Seat crosses no man's land at moderate speed, France ahead, tremendous noise behind. The French border guards, two of them, are running toward Spain, running to see what's happening. "Prosper!" Angela screams. "They're going to kill him!"

Murphy knows that. He drives straight ahead, through France's deserted station, up the road toward Perpignan, toward Narbonne, Toulouse.

"If it is possible to accept the premise that dolphins may communicate with human beings," Murphy typed, "and if it is possible to accept the further premise that dolphins may communicate with George C. Scott, then *Day of the Dolphin* is merely a very bad movie." Not a bad lead. An excellent lead, in fact, but for the implication that George C. Scott is not a human being.

*Day of the Dolphin* would be opening in Montreal tonight, and Murphy's copy was due at the *Gazette* by three, giving him less than two hours to finish the review and make it through two miles of snow to the newspaper office. He had seen the movie a week earlier at a screening; he had seen, it seemed, at least fifty movies in the last two weeks. The Christmas season. He worked now from notes, separating *Day of the Dolphin* from the other trash. Trish van Devere, altogether too cute in this role, real-life wife of Scott. Director Mike Nichols apparently attempting to appease the ghost of Walt Disney. Best acting undoubtedly turned in by aquatic mammals.

Finished at ten past two, he phoned for a taxi, shaved, put on his boots and his parka and trotted down two flights of stairs to the ground floor of the apartment building. There was one envelope in the mailbox, addressed to Prosper Murphy & Angela Wilson, return address Sloane & Whitaker, Madera Beach, Fla. "U.S.A." has been fastidiously added in pen below the printed address, as if Hugh Whitaker imagined Canadian postal authorities, unable or unwilling to deliver his letter, capable of returning it to the Madera Beach, Florida, located in Sweden.

The taxi honked. Murphy moved delicately down the icy steps to the sidewalk, slogged to the curb, got into the cab. *"Gazette,"* he told the driver, and off they slid.

He opened the envelope: a letter several pages long, filled most probably with further cautions against selling Angie's apartment at this point in time because of the glut of condominiums on the market, with charming anecdotes concerning Mark's and Jason's precocity. He was in the process of stuffing the letter back in the envelope, to give Angela the privilege of reading it first, when he noticed a newspaper clipping stapled to the first page. It was from the *Fort Lauderdale News*.

## MIAMI MYSTERY KILLING— 2 MADERA EX-COPS SLAIN

Miami (Dec. 10)—The bodies of two former Madera Beach policemen were found early this morning in a warehouse basement. Claude L. Wilson, 26, and Willie E. Raymond, 40, had both been shot once in the back of the head.

The murders, described by Miami police as "gangland-style executions," were committed in the heavily Cuban area of the city known as Little Havana. Both Wilson and Raymond were discovered in the kneeling position, their hands bound behind their backs.

It was estimated that the victims had been dead between three and four days.

According to Madera Beach Chief of Police Bertrand O. Arnold, both Wilson and Raymond resigned from the force "sometime earlier this year." He declined to give a reason for the resignations.

Chief Arnold issued a formal statement, which read in part: "To the best of my knowledge there is no connection between the tragic deaths of these men and our department.

"Claude Wilson and Willie Raymond were excellent police officers and good friends of mine. I extend my heartfelt sorrow to their families and loved ones."

Wilson is survived by his parents, Mr. and Mrs. Claude F. Wilson of Ocala. Raymond's estranged wife and four children are believed to have moved to Alaska.

Miami police have no suspects in the killings.

In the chilly back seat of the taxicab, Murphy felt himself sweating. Sweating and smiling. He read the clipping again, top to bottom, and laughed. It was a sudden, high-pitched chirp of a laugh.

"It's something very funny, eh?" the driver said.

"Very funny," Murphy said. "Very funny."

He pictured Chief Arnold sitting solemnly in his office, surrounded by the press. Maybe even television cameras. Chief Arnold sucking deeply on his Camel, extending his heartfelt sorrow. It was indeed very funny, but not in the same league as Gutierrez standing behind the two excellent police officers, ready to pull the trigger. That was much funnier.

Angela sat in the faculty lounge at the Academie Ste.-Thérèse, chatting uneasily in French. Prosper's stepfather had gotten her, on very short notice, a job teaching Spanish at a private girls' high school in Outremont. He had paid as well for three months of intensive French at Berlitz. He seemed to her a very nice man, not worthy of Prosper's distrust. As for Prosper's mother, Angela guessed that she herself might not have survived her first several weeks in Montreal had it not been for Anne-Marie, who swathed her in comfort and affection. When Prosper spent most of April in Madera Beach and New York, having first her and then his belongings shipped to Montreal, Anne-Marie was Angela's savior and confidante. When Prosper refused Claude's offers of employment and free housing, it was Anne-Marie who helped her search for an apartment while Prosper looked for work.

Angela was above all quite happy—happy with Montreal, happy with Claude and Anne-Marie, happy with the apartment in Maisonneuve, happy with her growing control of French, happiest with Prosper, who himself seemed happy.

The bell rang, signaling the beginning of the day's final class. For Angela, this was Advanced Spanish, five students, all Spanish conversation, a pleasant and easy way to end the day.

Out on the lounge and several steps down the hallway she encountered M. L'Evêque, the history teacher, who stopped her and held before her a newspaper, *Le Devoir*. *"Tiens,"* he said, *"c'est quelque chose, non?"*

Angela looked at the headline:

GRAND ACTE DE TERRORISME EN ESPAGNE:
LE PREMIER EST ASSASSINÉ À MADRID

Murphy dropped off his review, stopping to chat with a few new friends in the *Gazette*'s city room. He felt unusually ebullient, and imagined that he must seem so, but no one appeared to notice.

His daily perquisite, this morning's Late City edition of *The New York Times*, waited for him at the reception desk, enclosed in a manila envelope. The *Times* would be especially delicious this afternoon because he hadn't even looked at the *Gazette* this morning.

In the cab back to Maisonneuve he read Whitaker's letter. The first two pages, single-spaced, laid out an appeal for letting sleeping dogs lie: "We don't *need* a scandal here, Prosper, and as corrupt as these men may have been, as much bodily and psychological harm as they may have inflicted upon you and Angie, I do really think it would be in *all* our best interests. . . ."

By plea's end, Murphy's long-forgotten fantasies of legal action against the Madera Beach police department had been revivified. What a sniveling hypocrite Whitaker was, how unlike Chief Bertrand O. Arnold, who was an imperious, militant hypocrite. Murphy resolved to write Arnold a letter pregnant with apocalyptic insinuations, and to leave it at that—to leave the old bastard hanging, and waiting.

Murphy dreamed now and then of the huge fish with whom he'd had so many one-sided conversations, the manta who lived in the waterway below Angela's old apartment. In his dreams, the location seemed irrelevant, but was generally *his* old apartment, or some other unlikely habitat for a giant fish. Equally unlikely was the manner of the fish's appearance, which never varied: always, toward the end of the dream, the manta would suddenly manifest itself above him, hovering, shuddering like a fish out of water. And Murphy, fearing for his life, fearing that this immense, supernatural creature was about to fall on him and smother him, would try to remove himself from its path, but find himself unable to move at all.

They had driven through the night, the morning, the afternoon, and well into the evening, reaching Orly an hour before the final Air France flight to New York. They exchanged no more than fifty words during the drive. Angela seemed in a state just above catatonia. Murphy dropped his Spanish Hertz car at the French airport. A huge premium was demanded, but no questions were asked. He bought every newspaper available at the airport; each evening paper carried the same brief story in the environs of page 38: a French national, Jean-Pierre Bordagaray, aged thirty-five, was killed last night at the Le Perthus frontier. Evidently a smuggler, Bordagaray had produced an automatic rifle and begun firing at Spanish border guards, wounding four of them before he was killed. One of the guards was in critical condition. That was all.

During the flight Angela slept in Murphy's arms; Murphy stared at the soundless movie, drank some beer, slept a few minutes here and there. An hour from New York she said, "He *had* to die, didn't he?"

Murphy might have considered that question for hours, or days or weeks, but he was no fool. Immediately he said: "Yes, I think he did."

They spent that night in his apartment, a strange, very disoriented night, and the following afternoon they flew to Montreal.

These days, Murphy is content almost to the point of complacency. Angela has left her shell: she likes, maybe even loves what she's doing, and it's because of him, with a little help from his mother and stepfather. Knowing that does Murphy no end of good. As well, he's the hottest English-language movie reviewer in Quebec: a limited field, to be sure, but the sky's the limit.

Bushels of free phonograph records still make their way to his door from New York and southern California, and he keeps his hand in here, too, contributing regularly to the *Voice* and various Canadian periodicals. He's got a new poker game, a dollar-limit game with *Gazette* people, and to this point he's close to a thousand dollars ahead.

He stuffs his poker winnings in record albums, augmenting the fifty thousand dollars already hidden therein. He doesn't know what to do about that money. He hasn't told Angela about it.

Nor has he told her about her father.

At odd moments he sees the *guardia's* face disintegrating.


He takes a bottle of Labatt's from the refrigerator, returns to the living room, switches on the radio, sinks into a lavishly plush easy chair. The chair, like the rest of the furniture in the living room, is a gift from Labossière. Murphy suspects that Angela's presence, more than any surgeon's skill, is responsible for the reconstruction of his stepfather's heart.

He removes the *Times* from its envelope. The newspaper is folded in thirds, and by the luck of the draw the first thing Murphy sees is the bottom third of the front page, whose left corner bears the headline: 2 AT COLUMBIA INDICTED IN SALE OF COCAINE. He reads about two college boys who are members of the same fraternity, members of the wrestling team, who have identical surnames, and who have been gulled into selling two ounces of cocaine to an undercover agent of the New York police department. The students are free on minimal bail. If convicted, they will be sentenced to at least fifteen years in prison. The campus is shocked . . . Continued on Page 12, Column 1.

Murphy considers how stupid these Columbia wrestlers must have been, how stupid the new drug law in New York must be, and he thinks of Echaverria.

His eye wanders rightward two columns. MIDEAST PARLEY BE-GINS TODAY; EARLY ACCORD IS HELD UNLIKELY. Hardly man-bites-dog.

Now one column further. This is not a headline but a guide, in bold print, breaking two paragraphs. It reads: "Assassins Used Tunnel."

Just above that, the top four lines of the bottom third of the front page, right column:

> confirmed, it would be the first
> time that the group had acted
> outside the northern Basque
> country.

Adrenaline surges as he unfolds *The Times* and sees the two-column headline.

### SPAIN'S PREMIER IS KILLED
### AS ASSASSINS BOMB AUTO;
### APPARENT HEIR TO FRANCO

Two photographs: of the street where the explosion took place, now containing an immense hole filled with water and parked cars; and of Premier Luis Carrero Blanco's automobile perched ungraciously on the second-story terrace of a church. A subhead:

HINT BASQUE ROLE

Murphy now must force his normally perfect eyes to focus on the small print. The explosion sent the premier's car five stories into the air. Madrid police said there were some indications the assassination might have been committed by members of the Basque terrorist organization ETA. Reports from Bordeaux, France, said the group was claiming responsibility. The explosion had at first been ascribed to "unknown causes," but officials have since revealed that *a tunnel was dug* from an apartment across the street; they theorize that the charge was set off with split-second timing by remote control. General Franco, who is eighty-one years old, remained in his palace outside Madrid and made no public statements. The appointment of Admiral Carrero Blanco as premier had been seen as a way to ensure against deviation from Francoism by the future king, Juan Carlos.

But with the death of Carrero Blanco, Juan Carlos is now considered to have more room to maneuver Spain into government more acceptable to the rest of Western Europe. Three days of mourning were decreed. President Nixon sent a message: Carrero Blanco's death will cause "deep mourning in Spain as well as the Western world." Secretary of State Kissinger sent word from Paris: "a tragic loss" to Spain and the West.

In this frozen and detached far-northeastern portion of the West, Murphy reads two final addenda, both from the Associated Press. Vice-President Gerald Ford will fly to Madrid and attend Admiral Carrero Blanco's funeral. Basque leaders in exile said they knew of no Basque connection with the assassination, and did not believe the claim.

Murphy, who had what might be called inside information, believed the claim. He might even know who did it, but he was hardly in a position to call a press conference.

As it was, as things were, he had no alternative but to walk aimlessly about the apartment, to look occasionally down at Sherbrooke Street, to open another beer, to look at the little Christmas tree in the living room, to look again down on the street, wishing for Angela's return, wondering just what he'd have to say to her.